A Four
Treasures Novel

The
Spear
OF
Truth

CAROLINE
LOGAN

gob stopper

First published in 2022 by Gob Stopper

Gob Stopper is an imprint of Cranachan Publishing Limited

Copyright © Caroline Logan 2022

The moral right of Caroline Logan to be identified as the author of this work has been asserted by her in accordance with the Copyright, Designs and Patents Act, 1988.

All rights reserved.

No part of this publication may be reproduced, stored in a retrieval system or transmitted in any form or by any means, electronic, mechanical, photocopying, recording or otherwise, without prior permission of the publisher.

ISBN: 978-1-911279-89-1

eISBN: 978-1-911279-90-7

Wildcat Illustration © Shutterstock.com / Michael John Fisher

Floral Illustration © Shutterstock.com / Long Summer

Map Illustration © Caroline Logan

www.cranachanpublishing.co.uk

@cranachanbooks

cranachan

To Vince

You had my
heart a long,
long time ago
In case you
didn't know

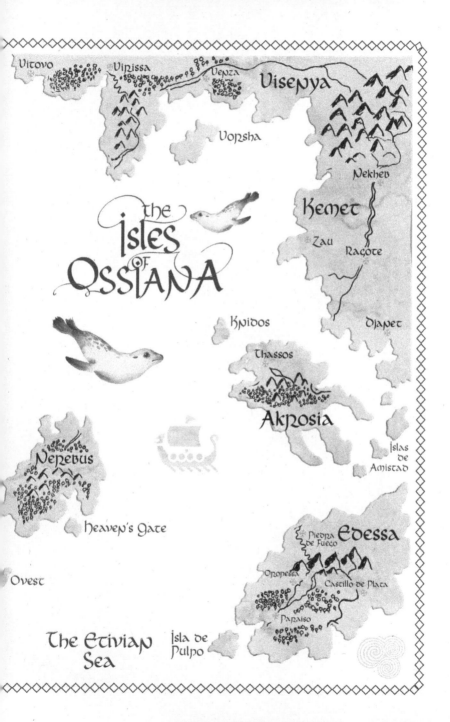

Chapter 1

The King of Eilanmòr dragged himself into his bedroom and gently closed the door behind him, careful not to wake his sleeping queen. It had been a long day, liaising with his advisors, reading letters from outposts, drafting a plan for the oncoming battles.

The country was on a precipice. Everyone knew war was coming, but no one could tell him when or where. Eilanmòr was vast and its armies small after many years of peace. He'd already written to Visenya and Edessa for support, but he'd had nothing back, save vague rumours.

Duncan scrubbed his hand over his face, blinking against the burning behind his eyes. He hadn't heard from his brother in over three weeks. Angus was meant to be helping the Edessan princess reclaim the Four Treasures, but what if that had just been a ploy to lure his younger brother away? Would he receive a letter from their enemies soon, declaring they were holding Angus to ransom?

What would they ask of me? Duncan wondered. *What would I be willing to give?*

These were worries for the morning. They were heavier at night, roosting on his shoulders like overfed crows, but the only way to make them lighter was to close his eyes and try to sleep. *Vashkha is here, Douglas is here,* he reminded himself. At least he had his wife and his son close by, where it was safe.

He crept across the room, removing his clothing as quietly as possible and slipping under the blankets. The mattress

1

beside him held Vashkha's comforting weight, but she didn't move or make a sound as he settled in. *Good, she needs her sleep too.* It had been Vashkha who had been writing the letters to her homeland in the north, and Vashkha who had overseen the fortifications around Dunrigh, just in case they were forced into a siege. Duncan hadn't wanted to tell her that was unlikely. Even during the war his grandfather, King Alasdair, had fought in, no enemy force had made it to Dunrigh.

Think of something nice, he told himself. The smell of his son's hair. The way Vashkha snorted when she laughed. Making dens with Angus when they were young.

He'd almost fallen asleep when he felt the cold steel against his neck.

"Don't move." The voice came from above him, deep and with a strange accent.

Duncan opened his eyes, peering through the dark. There was barely enough moonlight through the curtains to pick out a tall man, dressed in dark clothing. "What do you want?"

"To watch you die," said his assailant. "But we can't always have what we want. I've to take you to our commander. Get up from the bed, slowly."

Duncan tried to calm his breathing, listening intently for any other noises; Vashkha hadn't yet stirred. "I'll come with you peacefully if you leave my wife and son behind."

"My orders are to take you. Up you get, Your Highness," the man sneered.

Duncan pushed himself up carefully. How could Vashkha be sleeping through this? Perhaps she was awake and had the good sense to stay quiet. Maybe if Duncan got the intruder to talk, he could leave her some clues. "You said you had to take me to your commander. Who is that?"

"You'll find out when you meet him."

The dagger moved from Duncan's throat an inch, allowing

him to stand. "Do you mind if I put some trousers and a shirt on before I'm kidnapped?"

The man growled. "Quickly."

Duncan reached for his discarded clothing, careful not to turn his back to the attacker. "Where are you from?" he asked as he dressed.

"The greatest country in Ossiana," said the man. "Mirandelle, of course."

"And are you and your General free agents? Or are you working on the orders of your crown?" *Is this the start of the war?* Duncan sat on the edge of the bed and tugged on his boots.

"King Merlo knows we are here," the man sneered. "He is finally moving against your pathetic country. Eilanmòr is diseased, and we plan to cleanse it."

Duncan paused. "How are we diseased?"

"Your lands are polluted with fae scum. You and your ancestors have let them thrive and infect every corner of this island."

Gods. Duncan knew Mirandelle was superstitious, but this? His attacker was talking about genocide. "What does King Merlo want with me?"

"Oh, King Merlo doesn't want you." The man curled his lip, sneering down at Duncan. "It was the *Edax Animae* who called for your capture."

"The Edaxi?" Duncan felt the cold slide of dread down his spine, remembering all that Irené had told him weeks before. "How can Merlo work with gods who eat the souls of humans?"

The man raised his blade again, clearly at the end of his patience. "The Edaxi will purify the world, feeding only on the fae and their allies. Get up and let's go."

"I'm afraid he's not going anywhere," said a silky voice behind Duncan's kidnapper.

The light from the hallway illuminated the room and

silhouette of his rescuer. Duncan whipped his head round from the doorway to the bed behind him. Now he noticed the covers were too flat to be covering his sleeping wife. Instead, there she stood, thin sword in hand and her lips in a curling smile. She'd thrown a blue brocade coat over her nightgown and her hair was unbound, flowing in black waves over her shoulders. She had been asleep at some point then, or at least she'd been ready for sleep. Duncan stared, trying to get the world to align itself once more. It wasn't until too many seconds had ticked by that he noticed the sudden quiet.

Duncan focussed on his attacker, prepared for his sneer, but the man was gaping down at himself in disbelief. He lifted his hands from his chest, covered in red. He opened his mouth as if to speak but all that came out was a bubble of blood before he collapsed to the floor. The Mirandelli man rolled onto his stomach, revealing a bleeding wound in his back.

Duncan could only blink in disbelief. "How?"

"While you were standing there gawking, I stuck my sword in him," said Vashkha, kicking the man's body as she moved past him.

"I thought you were in bed." He pulled back the covers to find a pile of books.

Vashka pulled a dagger out of her belt and held the handle out to him. "I was clearing the nightstand when I heard a noise and decided to investigate."

"I didn't know you could use a sword," Duncan said, accepting the weapon.

She shrugged. "Well, in two years of marriage I haven't needed to."

Duncan pressed a palm to his chest. "Do you think there were others?" He turned to the door, the horror catching up with him, wrapping a strangling hand around his throat. "Douglas!" If his son was hurt or taken, he'd tear Mirandelle apart.

But his wife held up a hand. "In the next room, with Velora," said Vashkha. She took his hand, lacing their fingers together for comfort. "I went to him first."

"Does your maid also have a sword?" Duncan asked, feeling lightheaded.

Vashkha pulled him towards the door. "He's safe, beloved. We need to find out if everyone else is."

Duncan took a deep breath. "You're right. You should stay here; I'll send some guards up—"

"I am coming with you. Because, right now, there are probably more Mirandelli soldiers storming this castle, and someone let them in. Since I killed one, I think I can be trusted."

"And Velora?"

"I have known her since childhood. I trust her. Who do you trust?"

"You." Duncan gulped. "My brother…" Gods, there weren't many others. His soldiers, his staff, they'd all been hired by his father. Hadn't he been wondering for a while if he should send them all off with a year's pay and start over? He'd grown up in Dunrigh, but not a single one of his personal friends had stayed. They'd all gone off to seek employment, adventure, love—when had this happened?

Vashkha reached up and cupped his jaw. "First, we must notify the guards. Your kidnapper came alone, which makes me think that this wasn't a coup. If he'd had the backing of your soldiers, they would have all stormed in here."

"Right. What else?"

"We'll lock the castle down. No one gets in or out. If we've been betrayed, we'll find out who it was." She turned to the dead man on the floor and wiped the blade on his clothes. "Now, you must push down your fear and leave this room in a cold fury. Show no weakness."

"My only weakness is for you, love."

Vashkha winked. "I'll allow that. Let's go."

They hurried out into the darkened corridor of their private rooms, clutching each other's hands tightly. Duncan repeated Vashkha's words in his head. *Show no weakness, show no weakness.*

Finally, they reached the door and heard distant shouting beyond. Duncan steeled his resolve before kicking it open. A dark mass was sprawled out on the other side, unmoving. His eyes adjusted until he recognised two legs, a torso wearing the uniform of the royal guards, and a face squashed against the flagstones.

Duncan nudged the man with his foot. "Dead," he said. "No doubt the Mirandelli killed him."

But Vashkha didn't answer. Duncan turned to see his wife was already halfway down the hall, which was swathed in faint golden light. For a moment, it seemed like the glow was coming from her, until he looked beyond to the large window. He raced forward, gripping his dagger. As if that would do any good, as if he could stab something and the scene before him would disappear.

"The tree," Vashkha whispered as Duncan made it to her side. Her fingers shook as she raised them to the glass.

And that, that's what did it. Watching his brave, sword-wielding wife shake as she stared out of the window in terror. Watching Dunrigh's Peace Tree—the symbol of Eilanmòr's strength and fortitude—be swallowed in a wreath of flames. That is how Duncan grasped the cold fury Vashkha had spoken of.

He turned from the window, from the horrific scene below. "I will find who did this," he growled, stalking off down the hallway. "And I will make them pay."

Chapter 2

The woman once known as Ailsa MacAra stared out at the setting sun and traced a finger over her left cheek. Just over a week ago, the skin there had been covered by a birthmark. No, not a *birth*mark. The smudge of darkened skin hadn't been there since birth.

"Why didn't you tell me?" she asked into the evening air.

But no one answered.

Her spirit guide, Ishbel, had been noticeably silent since they'd arrived in the witch palace. Ailsa still felt her presence at the back of her mind, but it was as if the spirit guide was avoiding her. *She's not the only one,* Ailsa thought bitterly, scrubbing at her face.

"Hey, Ailsa, there you are," said a voice from behind her.

That's not my name, she wanted to bite out. But she didn't have another, so Ailsa would have to do, for now.

"Were you looking for me?" Ailsa asked, turning from the large window.

A woman hung around the doorway, her dark purple hair swinging over her shoulder. She wore silk pyjamas, slightly too big for her petite frame. Ailsa would have guessed the woman was ready for bed, except she still wore paint across her brow: a silver and pink galaxy today.

"I snuck some cake from the kitchens. Rain, Keyne and I thought you might want to join us?"

But Ailsa saw the gesture for what it was. *They know you're lonely.*

Part of her wanted to continue to sulk in the windowsill of the empty room but she knew that would only make her feel worse.

"Sure," she eventually answered, pushing off the wall. "Lead the way, Vega."

As soon as Ailsa stood up, however, fatigue hit her body, making her stumble. It had been like this since she'd arrived a week ago. She started off alright in the mornings but by the evening she could barely keep her eyes open, her movements sluggish and clumsy. *It's the altitude,* she guessed. They were perched on top of the highest mountain in the continent.

Get it together, she admonished, heading towards the door.

Luckily Vega hadn't noticed; she was waiting for Ailsa to catch up before padding off through the marble halls. Ailsa marvelled at the high ceilings, the crystal chandeliers, just like she had the day she'd arrived in Findias. She'd turned up cold and shivering, with a demon in toe, and Vega had been the one to find them, merely telling Ailsa *"you're late"* before changing her life.

Ailsa touched her cheek again, where her mark had been. The Faerie Queen had once told her that, when a changeling sees their true mother, the spell will be broken, and they will change back into their true form.

Ailsa had hardly dared to hope that she would experience that, but when she'd imagined the scene, it had just been her and a mysterious woman. Ailsa thought she would look into her eyes and instantly know her. Unfortunately, things hadn't quite turned out like that.

She had asked Vega later why she'd chosen to lead her into the hall filled with witches. Why weren't the women brought out one by one so Ailsa could look upon them to see if she would change? She wasn't the first changeling child to find their way back to the witch palace, Vega should have known.

But the small witch just got a far-off look and said, "It was the way it was supposed to happen."

This meant Ailsa was in a palace full of witches, not knowing which ones she was related to. Not knowing who her true mother was. Right now, she could only narrow it down to all the women that had been in the room when she'd begun to change.

"You'll work it out eventually," Vega had told her. And if she wasn't so sweet, Ailsa was sure she would have kicked her by now.

They rounded the corridor and Vega tiptoed up to a wooden door. While the other portals along the hallway were pale, this one was stained a deep red. Vega knocked on it twice then didn't wait for a reply before entering, beckoning Ailsa inside after her.

Immediately, Ailsa was hit by a wall of sweet-smelling incense smoke. She lifted her hand to waft it away, doing her best not to cough as she took in the room. The shell of the space was much like her own bedroom, with a four-poster bed, a wardrobe, and a desk. But here the light gold wallpaper was covered in drawings, stuck up haphazardly. The plush carpet was barely visible underneath the clothes and books strewn around. The space was chaotic but lived in and Ailsa found she liked it more than the rest of the polished palace.

"Good, you're here," said a silver-haired young woman sitting cross-legged on the bedspread. "I was only giving you five more minutes before I ate your slice."

"I'm surprised you even gave us that, Rain," Vega chirped, squeezing onto the bed beside her.

Rain gave her a dark look. "Do not get crumbs on my bed. I know what you're like." Then she raised her gaze to Ailsa. "Well? Are you just going to stand there?"

"Rain!" admonished the person beside her, lifting their head off the pillow long enough to give her a withering glare.

"Be nice."

"I am nice," Rain said, holding a plate out. "I didn't eat her cake."

Ailsa hesitated, before taking it with a *thank you* and retreating to slump on the chair at the desk. The cake was chocolate and she dug into it to give her hands something to do as she watched the three people on the bed bicker.

Ailsa might not have found her birth mother when she'd arrived at the palace, but in a way, she supposed she *had* been adopted. Vega had immediately decided Ailsa was her own pet project, showing her around and helping her settle. And where Vega went, so did Rain and Keyne.

At least Keyne appeared to enjoy Ailsa's company as much as Vega did. The witch always smiled when they saw Ailsa. And Ailsa had to admit that Keyne was the easiest to be around. They always appeared relaxed, lounging around on whatever surface they could find, wearing their signature flowing robes. Like all the witches, Keyne wore their face painted. Tonight, a smattering of stars danced across their pale face like freckles. They ate the cake delicately, seeming to savour each bite.

In contrast, Rain was carving at her slice with her fork, showing the food no mercy as it was mashed into manageable pieces before she shoved them into her mouth and chewed like she was furious with the dessert. Ailsa had come to learn that Rain existed in a constant state of rage. It simmered underneath her skin, snapping out at anyone stupid enough to get in her way. Rain's face paint matched her mood. Ailsa had only ever seen her with blood-red dye across her forehead, the only decoration a single waxing moon in the same light grey as her long hair.

Rain's dark lips curled into a sneer when she noticed Ailsa was watching her. "What?"

Vega sighed around a mouthful of cake. "Don't mind her, Ailsa. She doesn't mean to be so abrasive."

Ailsa ignored the small woman, keeping her eyes on Rain. "Do you want me to leave?"

But Rain just shrugged. "The door's over there."

Ailsa was too tired to mince her words. "You don't like me very much, do you?"

For a split second, Rain's sneer faded. "I like you well enough, when you're not asking me stupid questions."

Keyne clicked their tongue. "I'm so glad we're all getting to know each other. Don't leave, Ailsa; ignore her."

"If only your demon friend could join us too," Vega said.

Ailsa's heart sank at that. "He says he's busy." *He's been busy since we arrived.* In truth, Ailsa had hardly seen Maalik. Except at night, when she was half asleep. When he was more dream than man.

"I've heard he's been in the library with Zephyr," said Keyne.

It would have been nice if he'd told me *that.*

"Never mind, it gives us a chance to keep you to ourselves," chirped Vega. "The ex-changelings."

Ailsa nodded, returning her smile. At least, if anyone knew what she'd been through growing up, it was the people in front of her. Each of them had been part of the same scheme.

Vega had sat her down on her first day in Findias and told Ailsa a story. A story of a mass relocation, of babies displaced in the hope of hiding Nicnevan's stolen daughter. Their features had been changed to resemble the locals; their identities concealed. All to mislead the Faerie Queen's minions, to hide Nicnevan's child in a sea of infants. The Pact they called it. One by one, those children had made their way back to their families again. Some, like Vega, had been young when they returned. Others, like Ailsa and Rain, had been much older, only learning of their heritage by chance.

Her three companions continued their conversations, but Ailsa tuned them out as she turned towards the mirror hanging above the desk. This had been another mystery: what she'd look like once she'd changed back. Since she'd learned she really was a changeling, she'd often stared at her reflection, at her stolen face and wondered. Would her eyes or hair or skin change colour? Would her nose still be upturned, or would it be straight? Would her jaw be as heavy, or would her face become more delicate? Well, now she knew.

Save from the birthmark disappearing, not a single thing had changed about her appearance. Her eyes were still a piercing grey-blue. Her hair was still dark and her skin still pale.

And after all that wondering, Ailsa wasn't sure if she was disappointed or not.

Chapter 3

It was the stuff of faerie tales, Angus supposed. Princes riding unicorns through the forest, off to save the kingdom. Except the unicorns in stories were always white and elegant, not chestnut brown and made of pure muscle. The forests were rarely dark and dense like the one they were riding through. And the prince always had a beautiful maiden by his side.

This is infinitely better, he thought, as strong arms gripped his middle.

"Let's stop here," he shouted, the wind almost snatching his words away.

The beast below him quivered as she fought to obey his command. The unicorn had been travelling so fast that Angus had barely managed to keep an eye on the surroundings. He hoped the spot he'd chosen was a good one.

"We're only a few hours' ride from Dunrigh," Laire said with a snort. Still, she slowed her steps to a canter and then a trot, before halting.

Angus raised his head, finding that she was right. They were still in the forest, but the trees had thinned out, allowing him to see a darkening sky above. From their vantage point up in the hills, they could see the valley that housed Eilanmòr's capital stretching below. Far off, lights were twinkling beside a grey band of river. If Angus squinted, he could just about see Dunrigh Castle perched above the city. "It's almost nightfall," he said. "We can get there in the morning."

The arms around his stomach gave a squeeze before letting

go. Angus immediately missed their warmth.

"Thank the gods," Cameron groaned, shifting backwards. "I didn't think I could hold on much longer."

"Do you need help getting down?" Angus asked, but the other man was already swinging off the unicorn's back to the mossy ground.

Cameron rolled his shoulders, surveying their campground. "Are you sure we can afford to stop? Don't we need to get back to warn your brother?"

"Even Laire has her limits. I don't fancy her smacking into a tree as she runs in the dark." The unicorn stamped her feet, her eyes steely. Angus gave her a wink as he too slid off her back. "Besides, we'll still get back before Iona, Harris and Eilidh."

"I hope they don't run into any more sea monsters." Cameron shivered. "I really was glad when you asked me to come with you and Laire. I don't think I could have done another journey on that boat."

"Neither could Laire, I think."

The unicorn looked a little green around her snout, as if remembering being flung around the last time. She sank down, bringing her legs under her. "No, thank you."

"Well, I'm glad you took me up on the offer. It's nice to have some company."

Cameron shrugged his small pack off, grinning. "Oh, is that all I am? Company?"

"What do you mean?"

He bent over, raking through the bag's contents. "Magical unicorn, handsome prince," he said, echoing Angus's earlier thoughts. "Don't tell me this isn't some sort of date?"

Angus shifted his feet. "That's not why I asked you—"

"Stop staring at my ass then," Cameron laughed.

Angus snapped his gaze from Cameron's backside to his

face, smiling sheepishly. "Sorry. And though I didn't intend this to be a date, I'm glad you're here. One day I'll take you on a real one, if you'd be up for it?"

"I'd like that. Once the world has been saved." He straightened, unrolling a wool blanket. "In the meantime, what are we eating?"

Angus looked around, considering. "I can't be bothered trying to catch something. I've got some stale oatcakes and we could pick some of those blackberries over there?"

Cameron snorted. "You'll have to do better when it's a real date."

Angus felt his cheeks heat. They'd been doing that a lot lately. It wasn't that this gentle teasing was new; they'd joked around a lot when he and Cam were younger. But that was years ago, and adult Cameron had seemed unreachable. Serious. Burdened. *Something changed in that inn.* When Angus had confessed his feelings. When they'd finally shared a kiss again. Since reuniting in Ephraim, Cameron had been more generous with his smiles. He'd been flirting. And Angus couldn't get enough.

"What about Laire?" Cameron tossed the words over his shoulder as he began collecting their dinner.

The unicorn nickered, clearly pleased she'd been remembered. "I'll find something," she said.

Angus suddenly felt sorry for any unsuspecting rabbits in the area. They'd been her favourites when he'd brought her food in the stables. "I wonder how they're doing on the Nymph," he said, pulling a couple of logs close to where he planned on starting a fire. "I don't like how close their route takes them to Mirandelle."

"They'll be fine," assured Cameron. "They can just duck under the water if they need to."

Angus still wasn't sure how the Edessans had managed to

create such a wonder: a boat that could travel underwater. What other inventions did they have on the island across the sea? "I really haven't seen much of the world," he mused out loud.

Cameron dumped a handful of berries on Angus's pack and then sank down so his back rested against a log. He stretched his long legs out in front of him, crossing his arms. "When I was made a cartographer, I thought it was an insult at first. I thought my superiors were implying I wasn't strong enough or good enough to stay as infantry. But regular soldiers don't get to travel like I have. I can't thank them enough."

"I'm jealous," Angus said, piling up some kindling.

Cameron laughed. "The prince is jealous of a common soldier? You could have just booked a ship and left."

"Maybe I'll do that, when it's safe again," Angus ducked his head, "if you'll come with me."

"That's it settled then," said Cameron. "Our first date can be on the beaches of Edessa."

Angus beamed. "Or in the mountains of Visenya."

"In the cold?"

Angus struck his flint together, sparks showering onto the woodpile. "I can keep you warm."

Laire humphed nearby, rising to her hooves. "Get a room," she told Angus, her voice in his head dripping with disdain as she moved off through the trees.

"Is she okay?" asked Cameron.

"She's off to catch a poor, unsuspecting animal to eat," Angus said, sitting back beside Cameron as the flames flickered to life. Night had arrived in the time they'd taken to set up, but he could still see Dunrigh off in the distance. He brought a blackberry to his lips, tasting the sourness on his tongue. "Maybe Ailsa will be waiting for us when we get back," he mused. But when a reply didn't come, he cut his gaze to the man beside him.

Cameron was staring at him openly, fire simmering in his eyes. "Do you really want to talk about my sister right now?"

Angus gulped. "I don't know?"

"It's just that it's our last night on the road. When we're back, everything will be different."

"It doesn't have to be."

Sadness flickered across Cameron's features. Or was that the firelight? The next moment, it was gone. He raised a hand to Angus's collar, toying with the material. "If you kiss well enough, I'll forget about all of that."

"Challenge accepted," Angus murmured, before leaning forward to brush his mouth against Cameron's.

The last time they'd done this, they'd been interrupted by one of Cameron's visions. Angus knew Cameron still suffered every day, despite his bravado. He kept his touches gentle, pressing feather light kisses against Cameron's lips. But then Cameron was grabbing his chin, holding him in place as he opened his mouth, pressing their chests together, and Angus was lost. Soon both of their shirts were open, and Angus had his back pressed against the pine-needles with Cameron half on top of him.

"Are you sure you're okay with this?" Angus asked, as Cameron moved his lips to the hollow of his throat. "Doesn't your head hurt?"

"If you're talking, you're not doing a good job of distracting me." Cameron stroked a hand down Angus's side. "You don't want me to stop, do you?"

"I don't want you to be in pain either."

Cameron raised his head to hover over him. "There's pain in every moment. But I'm getting used to it."

"What do you mean?"

"I can usually feel a vision coming on, but lately I've been able to stop them before they start."

"How?"

Cameron pecked the end of his nose. "I think about you. So shut up and let me kiss you."

Angus grinned as Cameron's lips descended on his again. Well, if this was helping him, so be it. He slid his arms around Cameron's neck, tugging him closer. No matter what awaited them back home, at least they had this. *You don't need to worry*, Angus vowed as he placed a palm over Cameron's heart. *You're mine.*

With every kiss and touch, he repeated the word in his head like a prayer. *Mine, mine, mine.* When Cameron broke from their embrace, both of them breathing in the cold night air heavily, he said it out loud.

"You're mine," Angus said.

But Cameron wasn't looking at him anymore. Instead, he had his gaze raised to the view.

"What is that?" he asked, going pale in the firelight.

Angus wiggled out from underneath him, turning so that he could see what Cameron was looking at. Down in the valley, the lights of Dunrigh still sparkled. Except the orange halo around the city was larger than it'd been before. It flickered, too bright to be mere candlelight.

"I don't know," said Angus. With a boom, the light rose high above the buildings in a blinding flash, before settling down to consume everything in its glow. The wind changed, bringing with it the faint scent of burning wood. The hairs on Angus's arms stood up as he understood what he was seeing. "It's fire. Dunrigh's on fire."

Chapter 4

Angus smelled the smoke before he saw it, pressed to Laire's neck with Cameron holding him from behind. They raced through the woods, despite the darkness.

"I'm going as fast as I can," Laire assured him.

Angus knew that, and yet he urged her on in his mind. Dunrigh was on fire, and he'd stopped to snog a boy. *We could have been there,* he thought. *This is what comes from hiding, from keeping the two parts of myself separate.* If they'd only continued to the city, maybe he could have stopped whatever was happening.

At his back he could feel Cameron's racing heart and Angus wondered if he was thinking the same things. It had taken Cameron so long to let his defences down again. Angus felt a churning in his gut that had nothing to do with his city burning.

They raced down the hillside, flying over shrubs and boulders. Angus heard the babble of running water only a second before Laire called out to him.

"Hold on tight!"

Then they were airborne. Cameron gripped him tighter in surprise but then they hit the ground with barely a thump and off they went again. Laire was giving it all she had, muscles and tendons straining in her neck under Angus's hands. He wanted to mutter encouraging words into her silky fur, to tell her she was doing so well, but he couldn't make a sound. He hoped she could still sense his gratitude.

Eventually, the firelight became so bright behind his eyelids that Angus knew they were close. Laire slowed and he was able to raise his head again. "Take us to the castle walls," he instructed. "We'll get in through the Queen's Gate." He hoped the entrance would be big enough for Laire.

He felt Laire banking to the right instead of left as they skirted along beside the city walls. Few came this way, except to hike through the mountains and they met no one as they thundered up the stone path. Angus spotted the familiar gate, half obscured by vines. And beyond that, the grassy inner grounds of the castle.

"There," he told her, and Laire slowed, heading for the hole in the wall.

Angus thought back to the last time he'd been through here, setting off to find the Stone of Destiny with Ailsa and Harris a few short months ago. Now the foliage was more overgrown, hanging across it like a curtain. Laire came to a stop, allowing Cameron to dismount and then Angus.

"Can you find your own way in?" Angus asked the unicorn. She gave a whinny of affirmation and then he was drawing his sword without a backwards glance.

He expected to see guards, but the heavy portcullis was unmanned. *They're probably dealing with the blaze.* Angus could no longer see the flames, but the smoke was thick and black against the night sky, blotting out the stars. It must be on the other side of the castle.

"What do we do now?" asked Cameron, crowding in beside him.

"We either try to attract attention or we start climbing." Angus looked up at the towering wall. He'd made many attempts to climb the ivy as a child, every time only making it halfway before his weight snapped the vines. There was no way, as an adult, they'd hold his weight now.

He shared a look with Cameron and then opened his mouth wide. "Help! Guards!" Angus raised his sword, clanging it against the metal. "Let us in."

Behind him, Laire joined in, whinnying as loud as she could. She rose on her two back legs, stomping her front feet on the ground.

"Are you sure this is going to work?" Cameron asked. But then he was raising his own sword, joining in with Angus's desperate calls.

They screamed and shouted, their voices loud to their ears, roaring into the night until their voices were hoarse. No one came.

"It's no use," Angus said, falling to the side in hopeless defeat. He felt something wet running down his cheeks and his face crumpled without his permission. "What if they're all dead?" The fire could have ripped through most of the city by now and they were trapped at the gates.

But Cameron raised his face to the sky. "It's raining."

He gave Angus a small smile. "Come here." Cameron tucked himself beside him, wrapping one arm around his shoulders. "You did all you could," he whispered into the prince's hair. "You can't even see the fire from here. It can't be that bad."

Laire breathed heavily, too exhausted to offer up her own comfort. Instead, she trudged forward, dropping down beside them to share her heat. She placed her great head down upon one of Angus's legs and closed her eyes.

Angus sighed shakily. "I probably wouldn't have been able to do much anyway."

"Stop that," said Cameron. "You'll be there when you can."

But a single word was whirling around Angus's brain. *Useless, useless, useless.*

The heavens opened, unleashing sheets of water upon the

city, soaking them to the skin. Only the press of Cameron and Laire's bodies kept Angus from shaking. It wasn't until the sun was rising over the mountains that a single torchlight appeared from the back of the castle. Whoever carried it was limping badly, leaning on a crutch.

"A guard," Angus croaked. He couldn't find it in himself to move, to begin his screaming and shouting again. But the light grew closer anyway, until Angus saw who it was.

"Moira?"

His cousin startled, seeming to have only just noticed them sitting against the wall.

For a moment, she just stared at him, white as a ghost under her thick cloak. But then other torchlights flickered into view behind her. She caught his gaze, turning to see them herself.

"No," she whispered, barely audibly. Then she threw herself at the gate, fumbling to get her torch in a sconce.

"What's going on?" Angus asked, shaking out of Cameron and Laire's embrace. He leapt up, dragging his sword with him. "Are you okay? Is someone after you? How did the fire start?"

Moira bit her lip, looking over her shoulder again. "I need to leave," she said. But her hands were slick with rain and she kept fumbling over the lever, unable to gain enough purchase to raise the portcullis. The torches behind her were drawing closer.

"Who is that?" Cameron asked, his voice urgent. He grabbed the bottom of the gate, trying to help her open it.

Angus too, abandoned his sword, taking his place beside Cameron. "You just need to get it up enough that you can slide under," he told his cousin.

Am I about to watch one of my family die?

"I can't," she sobbed. "It's too heavy." She collapsed back onto her cane.

Then it was too late. The pursuers thundered down the hill from the castle and Angus finally got a glimpse of them. His mind processed everything slowly after that. The green and purple of the Dunrigh guards' uniform. The familiar faces, all with eyes fixed on his cousin. Moira screamed as they surrounded her, pulling her arms behind her back.

"You're under arrest," said the tallest.

I know him, Angus thought, dumbstruck. "Sergeant Lees? Let my cousin go!"

The sergeant looked over, finding Angus and Cameron on the other side of the gate. "My Prince?" He seemed to collect himself. "I cannot, I'm sorry."

Angus wanted to roar in frustration. Something was wrong and he was still trapped outside. "Why? What happened?"

The sergeant squared his shoulders, looking between them and the struggling woman. Her hood had been thrown back, revealing her normally golden hair, now tangled and soot stained. "Lady Moira is charged with treason. We believe she conspired with the Mirandellis who attacked tonight." He raised a hand to his heart. "I'm sorry, sir. She started the fire."

Chapter 5

*A*ilsa had tried to stay awake, she really had. But, just like every other night here, she found keeping her eyes open was a losing battle. Her body sank into the mattress like a stone and she was asleep almost instantly.

In her dreams she was surrounded by a sea of faces and yet she recognised no one. The figures whispered words in a different language and then laughed when she tried to ask them what they were saying.

"Ailsa," someone whispered.

She surfaced from her sleep, only managing to open her eyes a crack as the bed dipped behind her. She moved her mouth, trying to form words. "Maalik?"

"Shh, it's me," he said, stretching out beside her.

Where have you been all day? She wanted to ask. But her tongue was too thick in her mouth.

There was a light touch on her shoulder and she tried to turn, but her body was too heavy. A moment later, she felt a solid chest at her back and an arm draped over her torso.

"I've missed you," he whispered into her hair and then there was a pressure on her head as he dropped a kiss there. "Being away from you is almost unbearable."

Then why are you avoiding me?

As if reading her thoughts, he pulled her tighter to him. "I'm sorry."

His body was warm, and the bed was soft. Soon enough, she'd fallen back asleep.

This time she dreamed of a log cabin in the woods, of whispered promises and stolen kisses.

But when she woke up to the dawn light streaming through the window, she was alone in the bed once again.

***

The days at Findias had developed into a routine. Ailsa would wake up to Vega's knocks on her door, then she was led to breakfast. The rest of the day she'd spend lying down in her room, the most tired she'd ever been, hoping she'd catch Maalik's return at some point. But he only ever crept in late at night when she could no longer resist sleep and the feel of his body wrapping around her own.

It was like he was two different people. During the day he wanted nothing to do with her. At night he couldn't get close enough. Ailsa had often wondered if he didn't like her anymore, but then why would he come back night after night? She wanted to find him, to get her answers, but the doubt was enough to keep her from seeking him out.

"What's wrong?" Keyne asked, their forkful of pineapple halfway to their mouth.

Ailsa pressed her lips together. "Nothing." She didn't know her new friends well enough to bring up her romance issues and she was sick of complaining about how fatigued she was. She went back to her porridge, taking in the room as Vega continued with her idle chatter.

The hall they'd been led into that first night seemed to be the heart of the castle. Not only did the witches have all of their meals here, but Vega had told her this was where they performed their rites and rituals, and where the High Priestesses met to give advice and mete out rules. The trio of witches that made up their council had been in the grand hall the night Ailsa and Maalik had arrived, but she hadn't seen them since. It was obvious where they would sit. The raised dais in front of the massive round window held the only table in the hall currently unoccupied.

"Don't the priestesses ever come to eat?" asked Ailsa, taking a drink of tea.

"They're very busy," said Vega. "But they try to make it down sometimes, to help us in any way they can."

"Help you?"

"Like if there's an argument and we need their judgement, or if someone wants to leave. Or if we need something. The High Priestesses keep everything running in the castle."

"Including the temperature," said Keyne, pointing to the ceiling. High above them, the roof was open in sections, revealing the stormy sky. "That isn't glass up there."

Ailsa stared. "But it's raining."

"Priestess Sefarina keeps a wall of air around the palace, so the rain won't come through unless she wishes. She keeps the place heated and protects us from intruders."

"That must take a lot of work."

"The High Priestesses have been studying magic for a long time," Keyne said in a hushed voice. "They are very strong and very wise."

Rain snorted. "Right."

Ailsa slid her eyes to the silver-haired witch by her side. *What is her problem?* "What about the other two priestesses?" she asked, grabbing a slice of toast.

"Nasima can sense changes in energy from far away," said Vega. "Not like a premonition. More like vibrations in the air."

Ailsa frowned, trying to wrap her head around her words. "Give me an example."

"Say if there was a volcanic eruption across in Akrosia. That has a lot of energy. She'd be able to sense it happening."

"But something small, like a party or an argument?"

"Probably not."

Ailsa nodded, filing the information away. "And the last one?"

Rain swung back in her chair. "Aster has the power of being a supreme pain in the ass."

Keyne rolled their eyes. "She also happens to be Rain's mother."

Her mother? Did that make Rain some sort of priestess in training?

"No one gets to call her that when she abandoned me," Rain growled.

"How did you find out—what she is to you?" Ailsa asked.

A dark look passed over Rain's face. "She was the first person I came across."

Vega drummed her fingers on her arm for a moment before asking, "Aren't you going to tell her the rest?"

Rain narrowed her eyes and then pushed up from the table. "No. You can tell her if you want. I'm done for the day." With that she was gone, striding off through the huge doors and out of sight.

"Sorry about that," Vega sighed. "She's a little dramatic."

"She's angry," Keyne corrected. "Still trying to deal with *everything*."

"What does everything mean?" asked Ailsa.

Vega cast a glance towards the other tables, full of witches, and leaned in. "Rain grew up in Mirandelle. She found out she was a witch early and her powers allowed her to survive until she could get out. She's never told us what happened to her, just that she was almost killed a couple of times. I think she spent a few weeks in jail or a dungeon or something. Rain found out about the The Pact and decided to come to Findias. Not to find family, but to have revenge."

Keyne stabbed another piece of pineapple with their fork. "Aster was the first person she saw because Rain snuck into the priestess's bedroom to kill her."

Having known Rain for a week, Ailsa could believe it. "Did she know Aster was her mother?"

"Not until she began to change," said Keyne around their mouthful of food.

"And that stopped her?"

"I heard she still tried to kill Aster anyway, but the priestess woke up. Aster has a unique power: she can turn her body into air. The blade went right through."

"She tried to kill one of your leaders and she was still allowed to stay?"

"Once she'd calmed down, Rain saw reason. And so few children have come back after The Pact, they didn't want to send her away again." Vega winced. "Don't judge her too harshly. We couldn't possibly begin to understand what she went through. Her back is covered in scars."

Ailsa's mouth twisted. "And I thought I'd had it bad."

"You look like you've fought your own share of battles. How did you get that scar?" Vega said, pointing to Ailsa's face. "If you don't mind me asking."

Ailsa reached her fingers to her cheek. Not to the left, where her birthmark had been but to the right, where her skin had been carved open only a few months earlier. "I got captured by raiders. One of them decided my face needed evening up."

Vega gasped. "That sounds awful."

"I've had worse," said Ailsa, her mind going back to dark woods, glowing crystals, the sound of bones crunching.

Vega reached out a hand to pet the side of Ailsa's arm. "You can—" she began, but then she jumped, looking under the table. "Oh Hoolie!" exclaimed Vega. "You scared me."

Ailsa ducked down, coming face to face with an enormous gold and brown cat. Its amber eyes darted to her before it mewed loudly, clearly impatient.

"Alright, just one second." Vega reached down, extracting a piece of paper from the cat's collar. As soon as she pulled her hands away, the cat was off, skittering under the tables and disappearing almost instantly.

"Was that your pet?" Ailsa asked, dumbfounded.

"Hoolie is a cat-sìth: a faerie cat. I don't think she'd agree with being called a pet. The cat-sìth are wild but it seems they get on well with witches. Maybe we're wild too. Like calls to like."

"They act as messengers here in Findias," Keyne explained. "Hoolie is highly trusted, especially by the priestesses."

"Which means this note is probably from them," Vega said, unfurling it. Her gaze flicked across the page before she held it out to Ailsa. "It's for you."

"Would you read it to me?" she asked. The confession bubbled up, ready to spill out. *I can't read.* But something had her biting it back.

"It says the priestesses will be here for dinner tomorrow and they'd like to meet you," said Vega.

"Oh, that's exciting," Keyne exclaimed. "They must believe you've settled in enough."

So why was Ailsa's stomach already squirming? "Great."

"Don't worry," said Vega. "We'll be right here with you."

Ailsa nodded woodenly. "I think I'm finished with breakfast," she told them. "You said last night that Maalik was in the library. Could you point me in the right direction?" No more hiding in her room.

Keyne glowered. "I've got cleaning duty today."

"I'll take you," Vega volunteered. "It's on my way to the kitchens."

Ailsa thanked the small witch distractedly. Her new friends had jobs here. They had lives. And yet Ailsa hadn't been asked to do anything except eat and sleep. Not that she could manage the labour anyway, not right now. She felt a flickering in the back of her head and waited, hoping to hear a familiar voice. But then the sensation was gone and all she was left with was a headache.

"You ready?" asked Vega, rising from her seat.

Ailsa fought back a yawn. You can have a nap when you've found him, she told herself. Maybe even in the library. And it was that, the thought of seeing Maalik and then curling up in a plush couch, that gave her the energy to follow Vega from the hall.

Chapter 6

A ngus rubbed his pounding temples and settled into the chair in front of the fireplace. It wasn't lit but that was probably for the best. When they'd finally been allowed through the gate, he'd been torn between following the guards with his cousin and helping to put out the fire. In the end, Cameron had grabbed his wrist, pulling him along as he ran to the castle's courtyard.

"You can't do anything about that now," he'd said. "But you can do something about this."

They'd spent hours fighting to snuff out every ember, terrified that it would spread to the building, but as the rays of dawn cracked across the sky, they were done. He'd briefly met Duncan, covered in soot but his brother had taken one look at him and ordered that he go to bed. Cameron had tried to leave Angus at his rooms, but Angus just tugged him inside, ignoring the mutters of reluctance until they both collapsed on top of the sheets.

When Angus woke that morning, Cameron was gone but a note had been shoved under his door.

Went to clean up. A messenger came and told me your brother wants to speak to you at eleven in the library. See you at dinner. Yours, C.

Angus's heartbeat went up a notch as he thought of that little word. *Yours.*

Get your head in the game, he told himself firmly. Someone had tried to burn down the castle last night. Things were a lot closer to home than he'd thought they'd be. *Well, this* is *war.*

A door slamming caught his attention. There was a muffled command and then his brother strode through the door. Angus leapt to his feet, reaching out a hand to shake Duncan's but then he was being pulled into a tight hug.

"Are you alright?" Duncan asked once he'd drawn back.

Angus's throat bobbed. "Yes. Are you?"

"It was a tough night," was all Duncan said before he threw himself down onto the seat across from him. He scrubbed a hand through his hair, the same shade of dark brown as Angus's. But where Angus's hair was longer, brushing the nape of his neck, Duncan had shaved his own down at the sides. It made his face look more angular— gaunt even.

"Have you been eating enough?" Angus asked, taking in the rest of him, where his clothes hung off his towering frame. "You look like you've hardly slept."

"I've been up all night," Duncan admitted. "I had to make sure the castle was secure."

"Are you going to tell me then? What happened?" What caused the fire? How was their cousin involved?

Duncan sat forward, resting his forearms on his knees. "What I'm about to say cannot leave this room. Only two others know about this."

"Duncan—"

"We were betrayed," his brother told him. "A band of Mirandelli soldiers got in. And someone helped them do it."

"Cameron and I came in through the Queen's Gate. Moira was trying to get out..." He trailed off, realising who the *someone* had been.

Duncan nodded. "She tried to run."

"How do you know for sure?" Moira wouldn't do this, would she? She was family. "Maybe one of the Mirandellis snuck in by themselves and helped their comrades?"

"There's something else," said Duncan darkly. "Their person on the inside knew which guards would be on that night and slipped a drug into their food or drink. They all fell asleep at their posts."

"So, whoever it was had been here for a while."

"They'd have needed access to the shift patterns, which are often changed weekly."

Still, anyone with access could have done this. *We'll sort this out.* He knew Duncan wouldn't have punished Moira, not until he was absolutely sure. And even then, even if she *had* betrayed them, she was still their cousin. "You said two others knew?"

"Vashkha and her lady in waiting, Velora." Duncan's face cleared into something like wonder. "They're investigating Moira right now."

"Investigating?" Angus's stomach twisted. "You mean Vashkha and her lady's maid are interrogating our cousin?"

Duncan held his hands up. "Trust me, I couldn't stop them. I've already had an earful about how back in Visenya women are trained, women are useful etc. Apparently, Velora trained as a spy before working for Vashkha."

"That seems... safe?" Angus weighed his next words carefully. "And you're sure they aren't suspicious?"

"I know my wife's heart," said Duncan, "even if I don't know her past. Vashkha saved me from being kidnapped and ransomed."

Icy terror shot through Angus. "Was that the Mirandellis' plan then?"

"I can't work out what their plan was. Taking me was definitely part of it, but it seems they split up." Duncan paused. "I'm afraid I have some more bad news."

Oh no. "What?"

"They raided the burial cairns. We found the stones moved and some of the bodies missing."

Angus blanched. "Our ancestors are out there." Though their father and mother had been cremated, burial had been more popular in the past. Kings, queens, princes and princesses had been entombed on the hill at the back of the castle, their bodies covered in heavy stones. Angus and Duncan had played around the rocky cairns as children, tracing the names of their long dead family members. Their father had said it was good to keep them company, if you were family, but few outside the McFeidhs were permitted to touch them, so as not to disturb the resting spirits. To hear the cairns had not only been touched, but they'd had their stones removed... it was a violation. "Which ones were disturbed?"

"They only managed to get through a quarter before they were found. Twelve cairns in total. One of them was our grandfather's."

King Alasdair. Angus felt sick. Their enemies were robbing graves. His family's graves. "When are we fighting them?"

"We need to work out our weaknesses here first. I can't have everyone marching south to meet Mirandelle head on unless I know Dunrigh will be safe." Duncan breathed in deep, like he was filling up his lungs. "I've put a call out for aid already. Vashkha wrote to Visenya but there hasn't been any word yet. Princess Irené already promised Edessa would help us. I'm hoping she sticks to it."

"That might be difficult," Angus said. "She was captured by one of the Edaxi."

Duncan's expression turned thunderous. "What happened?"

Angus could not refuse his king. The words flowed slowly at first, about the boat and Cameron's vision, about riding to Ephraim and finding Harris bleeding in Irené's arms. His voice became hushed as he recounted the battle, how Irené had given herself up to save them all.

"And the Faerie Queen?" asked Duncan, his gaze focussed.

"Killed." Angus swallowed. "She died protecting me."

"So, we can't rely on her help." Duncan rubbed a hand over his face. "Without a queen, the fae will have no one to rally behind."

We have her daughter, Angus's mind supplied. But he bit his tongue. Eilidh was the heir to Ephraim, but she was also their sister. Their elder sister. He searched his brother's face. Would Duncan care about that? Would he believe her if she said she didn't want his throne?

Succession was complicated in Eilanmòr. Up until a hundred years ago, the crown had always gone to the eldest son. But then their great grandmother Rhona was left the throne by her parents—even though she had a younger brother—and changed the rules. In theory, Eilidh should be queen. But she was illegitimate, even if she was also the daughter of the Faerie Queen. If anyone opposing Duncan found out, they could use her to stage a coup. Angus doubted that Duncan would care about any of that for himself but... he had a son now.

"I had hoped we might be able to settle our differences and unite, since the Edaxi are threatening her subjects," Duncan continued. "Perhaps we'll be able to count on our selkie friends instead."

Angus nodded, relieved they were moving away from the subject of queens. He didn't like keeping secrets and this one was particularly hard to bear. He'd let it all spill out if he wasn't careful. "Harris and Iona are on their way back in Irené's boat. I haven't heard anything from Ailsa since she left, but they did have a long way to go."

"And the Four Treasures?" Duncan asked, his voice dropping lower. "Did you find any of them?"

"The Sword of Light." Angus smiled; glad he was able to

offer a piece of good news. "And Iona still has the cauldron."

"That just leaves the spear. And the stolen stone, of course. I hope your friend, Ailsa, has had some luck." Duncan pushed up off the couch. "Once we've sorted all of this mess with the attack out, we're heading south. We've heard reports that Mirandelle has sent half a dozen ships to our coast, but as of yet they haven't struck. We'll have a meeting about roles. I'm thinking of hiring some new people to the council, people I can trust."

"I hope I can help," said Angus.

Duncan gave him a level stare. "You and my wife are the only people I truly do trust." He sighed. "But I do need to find more. Maybe your friends will be willing to join?"

"I'm sure they would be honoured."

"But first we need to secure the castle and find out how they got in."

"What are we supposed to do in the meantime?" Angus asked, rising from his seat.

"Everyone is confined to their rooms until we know more," said Duncan. "I'll send for you when it's time."

After all the bad news, this sounded positive. *Duncan has a plan.* But, just before Angus opened the door, he looked back at his brother. Duncan was slumped, his head in his hands as if he carried the weight of the entire world there. Lost. That's how his brother looked. Angus couldn't help but wonder how he himself would look if the fate of Eilanmòr depended entirely on him. *Duncan has help,* he thought fiercely. *We'll help him.* His brother was not alone.

Chapter 7

Iona tiptoed through the metal corridors of the huge submersible boat, balancing a tray on her hip every time she had to open a door. The steam wafting from the food and hot tea coated her skin in a thin sheen and curled the red hair surrounding her face. She'd tied it back that morning with a silk scarf, but it was becoming uncontrollable. It always did that when she was away from the sea for such a long time. She knew her face looked wan and there were bags under her eyes but, despite being surrounded by water, she couldn't bring herself to leave everyone behind and swim for a while. Not when so many needed her.

She came upon the door she'd been seeking, the outside unpainted and unadorned. All of the crew had covered their doors in drawings and keepsakes from their adventures, but her brother hadn't joined in. This was not a place he planned on staying.

Iona knocked on the door then let herself in without waiting. The room was dark, save for the light of a single candle upon the bedside table. The two bunk beds took up most of the space and Iona wouldn't have even known there was someone there if she hadn't been visiting every day since they'd set off from the east coast. Before, Harris had favoured the top bunk, while Cameron took the bottom. Now he neither had the energy nor the vision to make it up there. Instead, he was wrapped in blankets, facing the wall so she couldn't see his features. Only his copper hair poked out, frizzy like her own. But Harris hadn't even tried to tame it. Gods knew when he'd even washed it last. All he'd done since getting on this damn boat was sleep and mope.

Iona cleared her throat. "I brought you food."

"I'm not hungry," came a croaky voice from the pile of blankets.

Iona sighed before placing the tray on the table, then pushing the clothes off the one chair so she could sit on it. "We're almost at Arnish," she told him. "It's just a day and a half to Dunrigh from there, but Orenzo reckons we can make it in a day if we push it."

There was a shifting of the bedclothes and then Harris rolled over to face her. "I don't know how I'm supposed to ride with only one eye."

Iona gulped, taking in her brother's features again. While one eye was the same turquoise as her own, the other was milky white. A scar cut through it, healed as if the injury was years old, not weeks. She'd tried to heal him with the cauldron, but it had been no use. The blast from Chao had blinded him and there was nothing either of them could do to stop it.

"You can ride with me," she said. "We need to get to Dunrigh as soon as possible. To warn them."

"They probably already know." Harris scratched his chin, where there was a layer of bristles. "Maybe I should stay here, help the crew?"

"Help them with what?" asked Iona, chewing the inside of her cheek. "You need to get out of this room, Harris. I can't imagine how it feels to have such an awful injury, but you can't just hide from the world."

"You know this isn't about the eye," he croaked. "Irené is gone and it's my fault."

Iona blinked away the tears in her eyes. Seeing Harris, who was usually full of life, consumed by guilt like this was painful.

"Irené went to save you and everyone else in Ephraim."

"She trusted me to get her back and I can't even get out of bed."

"Then get out of bed," she urged him. "Get up and come with me. You can still save her."

"What if there's nothing left to save? She might be dead." Harris's voice cracked on the last word.

"Chao won't kill her, he needs her. She's still alive and waiting for you to fulfil your promise."

"I just… it's so hard."

"I know," she said gently. "It feels like an insurmountable task. But break it down into little steps. The first thing would be to eat this porridge. You'll need your strength to do this." When he nodded slowly, Iona gave him a soft smile. "After that you need a wash."

Harris raised his head from the bed. "I don't even know if I can get in a bathtub," he said in a small voice.

She placed a hand on his covered leg, giving it a squeeze. "I'll get you a cloth and some soap. You can just sit on the edge and clean yourself."

"Thank you, Noana. I don't know what I'd do without you."

Iona's heart clenched at the sound of her nickname. *He hasn't called me that in years.* "Lucky for you, you'll never have to know. Just listen to your big sister and do as you're told."

Chapter 8

It was clear to Eilidh Buchanan that those around her had no idea what they were doing. Iona's brother had confined himself to his room and Iona was trying desperately to coax him out. Meanwhile, the sailors seemed to be going through the motions. Their captain was gone, some of their fellow crew were dead, and there were barely enough left to man the strange ship they were on. Even the cook had been drafted upstairs to help man the bridge. Fortunately, Eilidh knew a thing or two about cooking for hungry crowds.

She turned to the three children at the table, resting her arm on her hip. "Now you're all going to help me knead the dough."

The cabin girl, Paloma, bit her lip. "I don't know how."

"Don't worry, I'll show you." Eilidh upended the bowl onto the counter and easily divided the dough into four parts with her only hand. When she lost the other, she'd had to re-learn basic tasks, but now doing everything one-handed was second nature. "There you are," she said, passing the dough out. "One each. You push it away from you with the heel of your palm. Yes, just like that."

"My arms are starting to hurt," Diego complained. He was the smaller of the two apprentices.

"You can stop if you want," said Eilidh. "But my arms are hurting too. It's how you get big, strong muscles and light, fluffy bread."

Diego nodded, his forehead creasing as he concentrated, continuing to knead.

So young, Eilidh thought, watching them. Still babies, really. Diego and Cesar were twelve while Paloma was only nine. All three of them were orphans who had been given a place on the Edessan boat, ready to learn and become experienced sailors. For anyone to target such innocents was despicable. The Edaxi must truly be monsters.

Angus had told her later how Chao had lured the sailors and the fae out of Ephraim, just so he could threaten the children. All to lure Princess Irené into going with him. Eilidh knew she would have done the same, if she'd had to watch them face down the barrel of a gun. The cabin girl and the apprentices had survived, but there were scars there that only time and comfort could heal.

As they always did, Eilidh's thoughts drifted back to her own little one. This had been the longest she'd ever been away from Maggie. She remembered the birth had been horrific, almost intolerable. She'd cursed and yelled and screamed but the moment she saw her beautiful, sweet baby girl, she knew she would never love anything as much. Her daughter took up every available space inside her heart and she was glad of it. Watching her grow over the last three years had been a balm in a world of anxiety.

What is she doing now? Eilidh wondered. *How big will she be when I see her again? Will she have forgotten me?*

She would have been beside herself with worry, if not for the little soothing touches she sometimes felt over her shoulder. When she'd left the inn, she'd transformed into a flock of magpies and then shifted back, leaving one behind for her daughter. Even over this many miles, she could still feel when her Maggie touched the feathers.

I'll be home soon, my love.

"Is it done yet?"

Eilidh pulled the dough apart, considering. It was sticking

to her fingers but in her experience that was better than it being dry. She scraped it off her hand and arm as best she could and then took a pinch of salt and some dried rosemary, adding it to the children's dough too.

"There. These will have to stay beside the fire for a few hours," she said, depositing them into another bowl. "Go wash your hands and then you can help me with the soup."

Her little helpers scuttled away to the sink and she watched them with a fond smile. Perhaps, in another life, she could have been a teacher. A life where she could learn and care for others without worry. They'd had to be so careful, her and her guardian Agnes, that Eilidh hadn't been allowed to go to school. Agnes had done her best though. Eilidh knew how to tie her shoes by the time she was four, knew how to read fluently by seven. But it was science that had always interested Eilidh. How do caterpillars turn into butterflies? What are stars made of? Why do we dream? She'd hassled Agnes with the big questions when she was little and even if her guardian couldn't answer, she'd always suggest her theories and ask Eilidh to give her own.

There were some things, however, that Agnes was an expert on. She knew the science of nature, of which plants were best to eat and which plants would poison. She knew which clouds heralded a rainstorm. And above all else, she knew the science of cooking.

Eilidh placed a damp towel over the dough. Right now, the yeast she'd added was producing a gas which would make their bread rise. She knew it was the yeast, because her and Agnes had experimented without it and their bread had turned out as flat as a pancake.

"Would you get the powdered milk for me?" Eilidh asked Paloma once they'd returned from the sink.

The cabin girl stretched up on her toes for the canister then handed it over. Meanwhile, Eilidh was already adding butter to the giant pot on the stove. A stove! It was much easier than cooking with a fire. Maybe she should go to Edessa one day and see what other inventions they had.

"What can we do?" asked Cesar.

"Do you think you could chop some onions? And some potatoes?" She pulled out a pan, setting it onto another burner and added the fish, water and the milk powder. Fresh would have been better, but since they were in the middle of the ocean, she supposed they couldn't be fussy. "Look, do you see the fish is already beginning to cook? It'll change its texture and become flaky, then we can add it to the pot."

"I'm hungry already," said Paloma, sniffing the air.

"Well, once you know how to make this, you can cook it for yourselves."

Diego's shoulders sagged. "If we have to leave the Nymph, there's no way we'll be able to afford all these ingredients."

"Who says you'll have to leave?"

Cesar raised glistening eyes to her. Were the tears from the onions or worry? "I overheard Agustin saying they'd have to leave us behind if they join the war."

"Well, if that's the case, I'm sure we need some extra help in the inn. If you don't mind cooking and cleaning?" she asked.

"We don't mind, do we?"

"Will you really let us come with you?"

Eilidh felt herself deflate as she considered the logistics. "You'll have to stay somewhere safe until I can come back for you. We'll see if there's somewhere in Dunrigh, perhaps."

"I'm sure they'll all be welcome," said a voice from the door. Iona looked tired, but she spared the children a warm smile. "Though I think you're getting ahead of yourselves. I don't think the crew could really part with you. Your captain will get mad at us if she finds we've stolen you away when she returns."

"Do you think she will?" Paloma asked in a small voice. "What if Chao killed her like he did with Nadya?"

"Your captain will be fine," Iona soothed, though her eyes were crinkled in worry. "Now, I need a favour. My brother needs a wash, and I was wondering if you could help him with some soap and water?"

Cesar, Diego and Paloma nodded enthusiastically, running from the room when Eilidh gave them a nod of encouragement. "You've robbed me of my helpers."

"I'll take over," said Iona, grabbing the chopped onions and tipping them into the pot. They hissed in the butter. "I wanted to talk to you alone before we get to port."

"Are we almost there?"

Iona nodded. "Tomorrow morning, we ride for Dunrigh. That's what I wanted to speak to you about. When we arrive, people will ask who you are. What should we tell them?"

Eilidh turned her thoughts over in her head. "That I'm an innkeeper's daughter you met on the road? If you want, you can tell them I had the sword."

"We'll only tell Duncan that," said Iona. "Anything else? He is your—"

"My king." Eilidh's voice was firm. "Nothing more, at the moment. Angus isn't sure about him yet. If he'd accept me or if I would be too much of a threat. We agreed it would be better to tell him when the war is over."

And then I'll hopefully be back at the inn with Maggie and Agnes, and we can forget this whole thing ever happened.

"It's up to you." Iona was silent for a moment as she washed the knife. "Are you ready?" she asked eventually. "For all of this?"

"Of course not," said Eilidh. "But we'd better be." Because losing was out of the question. She'd sworn, when Maggie was born, that she would protect her daughter at all costs.

The Edaxi had no idea what they were facing.

Chapter 9

Ailsa hadn't been around many books growing up. Her mother had kept a small shelf of well-thumbed novels beside her bed, and they'd had a few books loaned to them by other families, meant to teach her and Cameron how to read. Unfortunately, while Cameron had picked it up quickly, the letters kept jumping about the page for Ailsa and she quickly dropped her reading for more practical things, like helping her mother with the bees or the chickens.

She'd always imagined she'd learn eventually, but then her mother got sick and died and she was alone. Overall, her illiteracy hadn't affected her too greatly. There wasn't much reading material, anyway, when you were hunting and fishing and just trying to survive. But, walking into the palace library behind Vega, she wondered what was in those books. What exactly had the authors found to write about?

"I promised I'd go help with dessert for tonight," said Vega. "You'll be able to find your own way back to your room?"

"Of course," Ailsa told her. *Maybe it's best she isn't around for this anyway.*

Vega skipped off down the corridor, leaving Ailsa just inside the door. The shelves towered above her as she tiptoed in, and she craned her head back to get a good look. A round window had been cut into the ceiling to let the light in, but the roof was so far away it was dark where she stood. Dozens of lanterns were hung between the bookcases, casting a warm glow, enough that one could read the titles, if one knew how.

Fire and paper? Ailsa wondered with a grimace. And people who read are supposed to be smart.

A jingling caught her attention, and she weaved her way towards the noise, using the shelves to keep herself upright, until she found the source. A man was sitting on an overstuffed leather armchair, rifling through pieces of paper. Not much could be seen of his body, due to the massive orange scarf wrapped around his neck and shoulders. At his feet, a beat-up looking cat-sìth the colour of a stormy sky was pacing back and forth, apparently waiting on orders. A piece of its ear was missing and around its neck someone had tied a bell, so it tinkled as it walked.

"So impatient," the man mumbled, noting something on the paper. "Done. Could you please bring this back to Nasima?"

The cat-sìth looked like it would meow, but instead it made a sound like a collared dove. It accepted the paper in the pouch at its neck and ducked off with it into the shadows.

"Can I help you?" the man asked, and Ailsa turned her gaze back to him.

He was young, probably only a little older than her, she thought. His unruly curls reminded her of Harris's, though they were brown instead of copper. His eyes and skin were almost the same shade, and he might have looked bland if not for his vibrant clothes. Below his enormous scarf, a heavily embroidered jacket peeked out and around his wrists he wore bracelets of turquoise.

"I was looking for someone and heard he's been hanging around the library," Ailsa said, fidgeting with the hem of her top. "He came here with me, but I haven't seen him around in a while…"

"Oh, of course," said the man, straightening. "You're the new girl."

"Ailsa," she told him. "And my friend is called Maalik."

"Yes, he's told me a lot about you." The man rose from his seat but instead of placing his feet on the floor, he floated up, levitating a few inches off the carpet. His legs hung down, but he didn't seem to notice as he drifted towards her, hand out. "I'm Zephyr, the librarian."

Ailsa took his hand and shook it. "The librarian? There's only one of you?"

"If I had another, they'd only do it wrong." He floated back, giving her space. "Though I'll admit having another person around has been nice these last few days. I don't usually trust people with my books, but Maalik takes good care of them."

Great, and now I'm jealous of some books.

"Can you tell me where he is?"

Zephyr bobbed back towards the armchair. "Would you mind if I just put this book away," he said, holding up a thick hardback. "Then I'll take you to him."

Ailsa waved her hand for him to carry on. It wasn't like another few minutes would really matter. Then again, with the size of the library, maybe it would take longer than that. She eyed the floor, wondering if she should settle in.

But instead of replacing the book straight away, Zephyr dropped down onto the cushioned seat and lifted a strange leather belt from the table. Securing it around his waist, he pulled two straps down and then lifted his feet into them. Ailsa couldn't help noticing he used his hands to shift his legs around, as if they couldn't move on their own. She tore her gaze away, suddenly realising she'd been staring. That was rude.

"Don't worry," said Zephyr. "I'm sure you've never seen one of these before. I had the harness specially made for me so my legs wouldn't dangle and smack into things." He slapped his clothed thigh. "I can't feel them, and they were always causing trouble."

"But you can fly—"

"Happily, the talent I have is exactly the one I need. I know witches can learn new magic, but we always start with one type, and it tends to be the one we're best at." He tapped a finger on his chin, considering. "The goddesses are wise; they know what power we require."

What does that say about me then? Ailsa wondered.

Zephyr picked up the book and studied the spine, looking around. Then he seemed to spot its place. Ailsa watched as he floated up the shelves with his legs tucked under him, higher and higher, defying gravity. He levitated almost to the ceiling and then slid the book into the shelf. As he flew back down, he wore a self-satisfied smile, as if pleased everything was back in its place.

"Okay, follow me," he said, winking. "Maalik has been holed up in the history section."

Ailsa's legs were already shaking; she hoped it wasn't far. "Probably reading about the Four Treasures," she guessed.

Zephyr's eyes lit up. "Ah, that's why he keeps reciting the same poem over and over. Have you ever seen one of them?"

"I helped find the Stone of Destiny a couple of months ago," she stifled a yawn. "And I've seen the Cauldron of Life too."

"Wow, I bet you they were cool. I've only ever seen the Spear of Truth—"

Ailsa stopped walking. "You've seen it?"

"Sure," said Zephyr over his shoulder. "It's up in the west tower. We keep some old grimoires up there."

"So, anyone could just go up to look at it?" She tried to swallow; her mouth suddenly dry.

"I mean, if you're with one of the priestesses, yes. Or me, since I look after it. The door is spelled to only open in exchange for our blood." He wiggled his fingers and his voice as he spoke. "All very gothic and spooky."

"Do you have to cut yourself every time?"

Zephyr snorted. "Imagine! No, I keep a vial of pre-drained stuff, just in case."

"Would you take me?" asked Ailsa. The thought of climbing a tower had her sweating but if it was for the spear, she'd drag herself there.

"You'd be better asking the priestesses," said Zephyr. "I'm sure they wouldn't mind."

"I'm supposed to meet them tomorrow night."

"There you go, a perfect opportunity." He winked. "Okay, history section. Here you go."

"Thanks, Zephyr. I can find him from here."

He nodded, already flying back the way they came. "Nice to meet you, Ailsa."

"And you. Thanks."

Ailsa kept her steps slow and deliberate as she searched amongst the bookcases, hoping she wouldn't make too much noise. She spotted a faint light near the far wall and followed it like a beacon. She wiped her sweaty palms on her trousers, running through things to say inside her mind.

Ishbel, she thought. *Now would be a good time to help me.*

Her spirit guide had been an almost constant presence before they'd arrived in Findias, which made it all the more strange that she had disappeared. Ailsa held her breath as she waited for Ishbel's snarky voice to fill her head but was met with silence.

I guess I'm doing this by myself then.

Ailsa wasn't sure why she was so nervous. Hadn't they both admitted their feelings on the mountain side? And even if Maalik felt differently, they were still friends first and foremost.

She crept closer until she was able to see his head behind a pile of books. He was sitting on the floor, bent over something in his lap with a lantern beside him. His black hair fell into his eyes and Ailsa's fingers itched to brush it away. She noted his hunched position and the fort of tomes he'd made around himself. *Perhaps he really is just busy.*

"You can't possibly have read all of those," she said by way of greeting.

Maalik jumped, snapping his eyes from the book up to her face. "Ailsa! I thought—"

"That I'd be too cool to come to a library?" she asked lightly, watching the way his face had drained of colour. "I wanted to see you."

"You have seen me. I share a bed with you."

She leaned her shoulder against the shelf, hoping he didn't notice how exhausted she was already. "You've been arriving late and leaving early." *And I can't seem to stay awake.*

He ducked his head. "I've been trying to find anything that'll help us."

"Right. I'm surprised your eyes haven't fallen out with how much you must have read," she said, her joke sounding weak even to her own ears.

Maalik smiled but it looked strained. "I found all these historic records. They detail everything that has happened in Ossiana since the continent formed, thousands of years of writings. They've got it all. Royal lineages, accounts of wars, the creation of civilisation."

"Is any of it useful?" she asked, perking up a little. "For our current threats I mean."

"Well, first I started looking into witch traditions so we could understand our hosts better. Have you met the priestesses yet?"

She bit her lip. "Tomorrow."

Maalik nodded. "I was reading about common witch powers and traits too. A lot about you makes more sense now."

"Anything else?"

"The Edaxi and the Four Treasures. There isn't much new information about the gods but there are better descriptions of the weapons." He tapped on the book with a pencil. "I keep coming back to the poem though. Something about it doesn't seem right."

Ailsa blinked slowly, fighting to keep her eyelids open. "I don't think I even remember all the words."

"Allow me." He cleared his throat and held the book out in front of him.

"Treasure o' yird, the Destiny Stone,
Transports the bearer tae whaur it is known,
Treasure o' water, Cauldron o' Life,
Reverses conditions o' magik an strife,
Treasure o' fire, the Sword o' Licht,
Cleaves through rivals, bringer o' micht,
Treasure o' air, the Spear o' Truth,
Niver misses, bites lik a tooth,
Handlit apart, fierce i' the hour,
Held close tae hand, maisterfull power,
Exack magik these weapons require,
Else wieldit by man, life they desire.
A warnyn, mortals handle thaim not,
'Cept Sovereign's bluid, whose talent forgot."

Ailsa scrunched up her brow as her brain tried to process his words through her fatigue. "And?"

"It's the bit in the end. '*Mortals handle thaim not.*' But didn't you say Duncan wore the Stone of Destiny around his neck?"

She shrugged. "Maybe it had a coating on it? Maybe the poem got it wrong."

"I hope not." Maalik looked unhappy. "There's a lot riding on that information."

"Are you finished here?" she asked.

"I'll be another hour or so." He squinted up at her, taking in her slumped posture. "You look tired. Why don't you go lie down and I'll come find you."

"Okay," she said, pushing herself off the bookcase. "Don't be too long though. This much work can't be good for you."

"I'll see you in a bit."

She hesitated. "Maalik?"

His attention was already on the page in front of him. "Hmm?"

"I love you."

For a split second, Ailsa watched his eyes widen and his jaw clench. But then he reigned in his expression, flicking her a quick smile before ducking back down behind his book. "I love you too."

Chapter 10

Ailsa staggered halfway back to her room before she stopped, leaning her forehead against a wall. She was exhausted, but the thought of spending the rest of the day alone was too much to bear.

Despite Maalik's words, she knew he wouldn't be returning to their room until she was asleep. He was hiding something, avoiding her.

What if he was lying? What if he doesn't love me anymore?

There was a fluttering in her mind and she screwed up her eyes, willing her spirit guide to speak.

Please, Ishbel. I need someone to talk to.

The seconds ticked by and the fluttering grew stronger but still there was no scathing voice to answer her back.

"Fine," she said out loud. "Be that way, both of you."

She let out a groan of frustration and thrust her hands into the pockets of her tunic, setting off on a blind meander down the corridors. How had she found her true home and yet she was more alone than ever?

Her friends were back in Eilanmòr, probably facing down their enemy and Maalik and Ishbel weren't speaking to her. What was she even doing in Findias anyway? She'd come to retrieve the spear, not to find a family. A week had already gone by, and she still hadn't set eyes on it.

At least I know it's here. Meeting Zephyr had been most fortuitous. He'd been kind and helpful. *Maybe I should go back and ask him to help me work out what's wrong with Maalik.*

But no. She didn't know these people. Having a bunch of strangers learn about her shaky relationship would be too embarrassing. She'd have to confront Maalik about it on her own, and soon. If she could just find out where the spear was, perhaps convince the priestesses to let her have it, she and Maalik could leave and hopefully whatever rift had sprung up between them could be mended.

Ailsa only realised she was almost outside when she felt the cold hair brush her face. Halting her steps, she located the door, slightly ajar.

Some air will do me good.

As she neared the door, she could hear the sound of grunting and dull impacts, like leather hitting leather coming from outside. Peeking through, she first spotted a huge climbing frame surrounded by stone walls—but there was no roof. A courtyard. The ground was covered in sand. Along one end was a rack full of wooden swords and squishy rolled mats were propped up against the side.

Ailsa stepped into the space, hunching her shoulders to combat the cold. It's a training arena, she thought, just as a loud grunt caught her attention. She spun, immediately feeling lightheaded as she looked for the source but could only see a blur of black and silver.

"Oh, sorry. I didn't mean to interrupt you," Ailsa said, blinking away the spots in her vision.

Rain levelled a kick at the leather bag in front of her and then wiped her brow with a bandaged hand. "You can stay," she said, out of breath. "It's a free palace." The witch had braided her hair and donned a pair of tight-fitting trousers and a vest. She'd removed her face paint too, somehow looking much softer, less intimidating.

"I didn't know this was here," Ailsa said, stepping closer. "What do witches need to train for?"

"They used to be fierce warriors. Maybe it's tradition or maybe it's so they don't look like the soft, privileged folk they actually are."

"But that's not why you're doing it," Ailsa guessed.

Rain spat on the sand. "I do it because old habits die hard."

"I had a friend—"

"I didn't think you'd do this much talking." She stripped off her dressings and dropped them carelessly at her feet. "I'm done. You can have it to yourself."

Ailsa bit the inside of her cheek as she watched Rain stalk off to another door. As soon as she was gone, she slumped to the ground. Yet again, she was alone. You should go find Vega and Keyne, she told herself, but she didn't have it in herself to get up. *You'd only be a burden.* Better to sit in the fresh air a bit longer.

She breathed it in, filling up her lungs. In and out. The air ran through her, and it was as if she'd blown the dust off her nerves. It was only now that she could feel it returning, that she realised her magic had been depleted. It zinged beneath her skin again. She looked around, making sure there was no one watching from any of the windows and slowly brought her electricity to life until sparks danced between her fingers.

That's better, she thought. If only the rest of her problems could be fixed just as easily.

What problems? Asked a familiar voice. It was weak, barely a whisper, but it was there.

"Ishbel?" Ailsa gasped. "Where have you been?"

Away. In the quiet.

"Why? What's wrong?"

There are wards around the palace, she croaked. *Very clever. Ever since you neared the mountain's summit, I felt myself fading away.*

"But you're back?"

Ishbel hummed in agreement. *What did you do today that was different?*

"I visited Maalik in the library? Then I came out here and used my magic."

Must have been that then. It was probably enough to allow me to break through the spell.

"Well, I'm glad."

Did you miss me? I know my presence is a gift.

"It was too quiet," was all Ailsa said, fighting back a smile. "Do you think you'll get pushed back again when I go inside?"

I feel that I am here to stay.

"Wait, I should be mad at you! Why didn't you tell me that I'm a witch?"

I enjoy surprises, said the spirit guide. Ailsa knew that if Ishbel had a face, it would be smiling slyly.

"I can't believe you! Are there any other surprises?"

Of course. If there weren't, life would be quite dull.

Ailsa swiped her hand through her hair, scrunching it near the scalp. It hurt and she hoped Ishbel could feel it. "And if you're my ancestor, that would make you a witch too."

I was. Though I've never been to Findias. It was built after my time.

"Honestly, I don't know whether to be furious with you or happy you're back."

You can be both. But can I suggest you go inside before you freeze? Then you should find some food and eat it in your room so that you can tell me all that has happened.

"Oh really?"

I like gossip and chocolate cake, if you are taking requests.

"You're despicable."

Chapter 11

I'm in over my head, the King of Mirandelle thought as his nose was pressed to the floor in his own throne room.

Merlo De Santis was a brave man, once. In the early days of his reign, he'd done everything to prove he was a true warrior to his people and a formidable force to his enemies. He'd fought in battles, conquered new lands, and sailed in the harshest of storms. He'd turned his country from the poor, quiet land his sickly father ruled into the wealthiest and most powerful in Ossiana.

Had he allowed his mother to seize his throne? No, he'd thrown her in the prettiest prison in Storia.

Had he hid inside when hurricanes pummelled their cities? No, he'd stayed and built everything back better the next day.

Had he grieved when his youngest daughter ran away with a northern commoner? No, he'd taken the opportunity, blaming Eilanmòr and declaring war on them instead.

Yes, he'd been brave once. Strong too. But over the years his gut and his fears had expanded. Only a few months ago, he'd caught sight of himself in a mirror, with his sagging skin and receding hairline, and realised he was truly afraid. Afraid of ageing, afraid of appearing weak. His skin had prickled, as if he could feel the greedy eyes of his enemies on him.

He'd prayed to the gods that night, but they hadn't answered until weeks later. He'd been sitting in his reception room, drinking port and listening to his grandson plink away at the harpsichord. The child was dim-witted, he'd often heard, but he played beautifully under the instruction of the tutor Merlo had procured. His eyes were heavy, ready to close on their own when he'd heard a female voice calling his name from outside the open veranda doors. Merlo had heaved himself to his feet and wandered out, as if in a trance. There, leaning against one of the columns, was the most stunning woman he'd ever seen.

"Your grace," she began, stepping forward out of the shadows. "I heard your plea, and I've come to help."

It was then that Merlo had noticed something was wrong. Her skin was ashen grey, her clothing and hair moon-white, as if all colour had leached out of her.

The woman smiled with black lips and ivory teeth. "How would you like to be a champion of the gods?"

"What would I need to do?"

"What you've been doing all your life. You have warred and pillaged your way through Ossiana. Your palace is full of stolen treasure and your countrymen itching to prove their might. But for too long have you all squandered. Mirandelle has grown soft." She raised her chin, exposing the long column of her throat. "But I can make you great again. How would you like to take Eilanmòr for yourself?"

He didn't answer her at first, mesmerised by the undulating curves of her body. It was only when she raised one arched eyebrow that he said, "I tried that once. They couldn't be defeated then."

The woman hummed. "That is because of the fae scum that live within their borders. They fought for your enemy and with their magic they drove you back, even when their king was dead. But what if there were no more fae in Eilanmòr? If you fight for me, I'll give you Eilanmòr. And one other thing. A new body."

Merlo's mouth dropped open. "How?"

She had just smiled. "Join me and you'll have the body of your youth and an empire to rule."

Well, he still didn't have a youthful body all these weeks later. His knees were aching from kneeling on the marble floor, but he didn't dare rise until he was told.

When he'd made his deal, he thought he'd only been speaking to a beautiful, but singular, goddess. Dolor had made him feel comfortable. But then her siblings had arrived, and he felt true fear. Now, shivering in his throne room, King Merlo was in a nightmare of his own making.

"Ah, look," squealed a high, childish voice nearby. "The soldier is back. You'll have to sit up, Merlo, so you can greet him."

Merlo raised his head and slowly sat back on his haunches, pushing his robes out of the way and flicking his gaze over the room.

Dolor sat upon a chair that had been fetched for her, her silk gown spilled out beside her. She eyed her nails with disdain while a number of servants surrounded her, holding various dishes. Each of the poor souls was covered in scars and winced every time she plucked a piece of fruit from their bowls.

Chao, meanwhile, knelt at the massive fireplace, sticking his hands in amongst the flames and snatching them away again. Occasionally he'd let out a laugh, as if getting burnt was the most fun he'd had in years. He'd smudged his face with ashes, reminding Merlo of a skull.

Another squeal came from the window and Merlo turned to face the third deity. This one looked like a little girl with auburn hair twisted into two buns atop her head. Except, Timor, the goddess of fear, was no innocent. Merlo remembered the first time he'd laid eyes upon her and was met with the overwhelming feeling of wrong-ness. There was something in her eyes, something cruel and calculating. As if some dark creature was only wearing the skin of a child and it didn't fit.

The goddess bounced on her toes, excited by something she could see. "He's taking forever. If he takes any longer, I'll pull his legs from his body."

"You mustn't, Timor," drawled Dolor. "Then he won't be able to fight for us."

The door at the end of the hall opened and a man appeared, with a helmet under his arm. Merlo hadn't seen Chester Scarsi since he'd promoted him from Captain to Major, but it appeared Timor had become acquainted with him already. She ran from her window perch, throwing her arms around the soldier, who grimaced before snapping his mask of neutrality back into place.

"Chester," she said with a lisp. "You're with us at last. Pick me up so that I may greet you properly."

Scarsi bent down and allowed the goddess to climb into his arms, though he held her away from his body. She pecked his cheek with a kiss and then his forehead, then she whispered something in his ear. For a moment, the man was stock still, the muscles in his neck tensing, but then he strode forward, depositing the girl at the foot of the throne as quickly as she would allow.

Timor twirled, throwing her arms out. "Sister, brother, my soldier is back." She came to a stop, grinning widely. "What have you to report?"

Scarsi cleared his throat. "We successfully infiltrated Dunrigh, but the king awoke before my man could kill him. We had to make a quick escape."

"That is disappointing," said Timor sweetly. "Would you bring me your man? I would like to speak to him."

"He is dead, I'm afraid."

Timor's shadow grew, crawling across the marble floor, sprouting horns and fangs and claws. "Pity," she said, her voice a few octaves lower than before. "We would have had some fun."

Merlo shivered but the soldier kept his cool. "It was clear that none of the other treasures were at the castle, but we did find something interesting in the library." Scarsi threw a book to the floor. "This says that the spear was hidden in Monadh, at the top of their highest mountain."

"With the witches," said Dolor. "Interesting."

Timor tapped her chin. "Anything else?"

"I found you more soldiers."

"Oh good!" said Timor, clapping her hands. "We'll have to wait for Desper to get back, though."

"He's with my captive," said Chao with a pout. "I should be the one down there; I can make her sing."

"The princess might benefit from a visit from each of us," Dolor mused.

Merlo blanched. He'd been there the day Princess Irené had arrived in Mirandelle but there was no banquet, no warm welcome for foreign royalty. She was spirited away, tears streaking her face. That was the last time he saw her, but he'd heard her screams, even from the throne room.

"She's mine," said Chao. "Get your own toy."

Dolor turned her attention back to Merlo, her gaze as sharp as a hawk's. "Perhaps our king can help with that. How many fae have been found within your borders?"

"Fifty or so," said Merlo eagerly. "But we know there are more, hidden and sheltered by traitors. My men won't stop until they're found."

"And where are your captives?" she asked.

"In the dungeons."

She tapped on the arm of her seat with her long, sharp nails. "Bring me one," Dolor said. "I wish to be entertained."

"I'll have them sent for—"

"No," she snapped. "Bring me one yourself, Merlo. Or I'll have my fun with you instead."

A phantom finger dragged down Merlo's back in warning and he couldn't stop the whimper that burst from his lips. "Yes, my lady," he said when he could speak again. "I'll go now."

"Bring them to my room," she drawled.

He bowed, loathe to turn his back to the gods but without a choice. At least he could escape, even for a little while. Scarsi didn't seem to have the same luck, remaining behind as the little goddess danced around him. *Still, he's braver than you,* Merlo thought. Scarsi was playing the part of a devoted soldier well. Merlo gritted his teeth. *He'd better remember his place.*

Distant screams met his ears as he entered the hallway.

Chapter 12

"Ailsa, wake up!"

Ailsa blinked her eyes open to find herself in bed, one of her arms thrown out across the empty mattress. The last she remembered she'd been curled up on the windowsill, watching the sky darken as she talked nonsense to Ishbel. Which meant someone had picked her up and wrapped the duvet around her while she slept. Maalik must have returned late and left early again.

So much for "another hour or so".

Still, she had no time to dwell on broken promises. She wasn't alone in the room.

"We're going to be late," Vega said, throwing open the wardrobe and disappearing inside.

Ailsa stifled a groan and sat up. "How long do we have?"

"Thirty minutes," came Vega's muffled reply.

"Isn't that plenty of time?" Now that Ailsa was up, she took stock of her body. Her eyelids were lighter, and she didn't have the urge to roll over and go back to sleep. *I feel better than I have in a week.*

Probably because I'm back, said Ishbel.

A scoff drew Ailsa's attention to the door. Rain was leaning against it, dressed all in black, her face paint fresh upon her brow. She ran her tongue over her teeth taking in Ailsa's bare room with apparent disdain. "Not everyone takes as long as you to get ready, Vega."

The petite witch appeared with a bundle of dark green

fabric. "I suppose you won't be painting yourself yet?"

Ailsa swung her legs out of bed and took the proffered clothing. "Is that something I should be doing?"

"Only if you want to," said Vega, hugging her arms to herself. "Only if you feel ready."

"Ready for what?"

"Vega," said Rain, cutting off the smaller woman. "Don't you need to get Keyne up too? Maybe you should meet us both there."

"Oh, great!" said Vega, heading towards the door on light feet. But as she reached Rain, something unspoken went between them. Ailsa watched as Rain's face twisted, her mouth pressing into a hard line before she pushed off the door.

"Be nice," Vega warned, then she slipped out of the doorway, and they were left alone.

Ailsa braced herself. Rain had made it clear she didn't like her, hadn't she? But there was a softness in the witch's eyes when she turned to her.

"So," said Rain, "Do you need help with that, or can you put your clothes on yourself?"

"I think I can manage," Ailsa replied. She waited a moment to see if Rain would give her some privacy, but the woman just sat on the edge of the bed, not taking her eyes from her.

Fine, thought Ailsa, shrugging out of her sleep clothes. "Vega never answered me about the face paint," she said, to fill the silence as she changed. "Why do you all wear it?"

"It's tradition." Rain dropped her attention to her nails as Ailsa took off her underwear. "Once, the witches wore it into battle. These days it's a symbol that they're part of the coven, that they've accepted who they are—once they come of age."

"You speak like you aren't one of them but you're wearing it," Ailsa said as she pulled the soft leggings up to her navel.

"It took me a long time to decide to wear it."

Ailsa pulled the velvet tunic over her head and frowned. "Why?"

Rain fixed her with a hard glare. "You of all people should know why. Aren't you angry? We were given away as babies, sacrificed to save a fae princess in another country. Doesn't that disgust you?"

"I suppose they thought they were doing what was best." Yet, with her head a little clearer, she allowed herself to truly think. She had been so alone for years. An outcast. Worse than that, really. Being a changeling was dangerous. An image came to her unbidden of a white wrapped bundle left in a tree. Of a tiny, freezing, lifeless body. *That could have been me. Or Rain, or Vega or Keyne.* Ailsa clenched and unclenched her fists. "Yes, I am angry."

"Vega was found when she was six, Keyne when they were eight." Rain's jaw tensed. "I was eighteen when I travelled to the witch kingdom. But you were older still. If what you went through is anything like my experiences, I wouldn't blame you if you wanted to burn the whole place down."

"Is that what you want?" Ailsa asked quietly.

"I came here for revenge," said Rain. "But I failed. Aster would have locked me in the dungeons but Vega and Keyne vouched for me. Said they'd watch me." She crossed her arms, curling into herself. "I fought and raged when I first came here, but then those two idiots became like family. I wear the paint for them and only them."

"Was I the last to return?" Ailsa asked. "Or are there more still?"

"More," she said, her face guarded. "Much more. Apparently, I had a sister. I'm still waiting for her, but—"

She didn't need to finish the thought. The world was harsh and cruel. The fact that they were alive was a bit of a miracle. Rain's sister may not have had the same luck. "I'm sorry."

Rain's mouth twisted. "Don't be. You were a victim as much as me." She pushed off from the wall, eyes wild. "I'll meet you in the hall." And then she was gone, like an animal springing from a trap.

"Why?" Ailsa asked the empty air. "How could they do this?"

I have no idea, said Ishbel. *But I suppose we'd better find out.*

Ailsa straightened her clothes and took a deep breath. Answers were important but she couldn't lose sight of why she was here. The spear was somewhere in the palace and time was running out.

Chapter 13

arris could tell the Nymph was nearing the harbour by all the stamping going on outside his door. All hands would be on deck, preparing to dock. He fought the urge to pull his blanket over his head and hide for a bit longer. No, this was a new day, and he would be different. If he had to be upset, let it be anger. Anger got things done. Anger would sustain him until he could get her back.

He pushed his freshly washed curls out of his face and sat up. The small porthole bathed the cabin in a warm light. *It must be a nice day.* Harris wished it was raining.

Step one, get dressed, he told himself. *Step two, eat something.* If he just went with Iona's idea, he could do it, he could get to the final step. *Save Irené.*

***

By the time he arrived in the hold, where the gangplank was kept, Harris felt much more himself. Every step he took was easier than the last, like he'd just had to build up momentum. The handful of crew members were rushing around, readying the boat for arrival. No one seemed to notice him, so he sat down on a wooden crate and crunched into the apple he'd taken, not tasting it.

The problem with plans and steps and routines, he mused, *is that sometimes things are out of your control.* He'd always been good at adapting, at going with the flow, but the very thought at that moment was more than he could bear. He wished he could find the route through the immediate future. Harris was at point A and Irené was at point B. The irony wasn't lost on him: now that he'd been partially blinded, he wanted to see everything. *I'll just have to have multiple plans,* he decided. *Think of every outcome, every eventuality: then I can't be surprised.*

Just as he thought this, he felt the prickling sensation that he was being watched. Turning his head, he saw the ship's doctor, Egeria, was approaching, holding something in her hands.

"It's not nice to sneak up on someone who can't see you," he said, taking another bite of apple.

She grimaced. "Sorry, I didn't think. I brought you something." Holding out her palm, she nodded expectantly. "It's an eyepatch."

"Do you think I need to cover my eye?"

"No, I think it makes you look heroic." She gave him a tight smile. "You sustained the injury trying to save our captain, after all. But I wanted to give you the option. Others I've treated with similar injuries have found bright sunlight to be painful. Plus, not everyone is as open minded as us. You may wish to wear it to avoid excessive questions."

Harris took the material from her and opened it out. Any eyepatches he'd seen were black and plain but this one had been made with the Edessan colours. Three long orange ribbons were attached to a larger, navy and teal panel, obviously meant to cover his eye. It was patterned, like the fabric had been cut out of clothing.

"I know the captain would have wanted you to wear our colours," Egeria said. "It'll make her smile when you see her again."

"What if I can't find her?" he asked in a smaller voice.

"You will." She squeezed his arm. "We're heading back round the coast when we drop you off, but we'll meet you on the battlefield. Or battle water?"

He nodded. "Please be careful."

"Harris?" Iona stormed into the hold, carrying her cloak under her arm. "I went to your room to wake you up and you weren't there."

Egeria slipped away with a final grin. Harris would miss this crew, all of them. Another time, another place and he could easily imagine himself staying with them. They were more than friends now. Grief can push you apart or it can bind you together. They'd all lost someone, but Harris would bring their captain back. "I was waiting," he finally told his sister. "Figured you'd want to get going early."

"You look better."

Harris flashed her a quick smile. "Just taking your advice." Then he turned his gaze to the woman behind his sister. The journey from Ephraim to the coast was a blur of pain. He'd been too miserable to notice who they travelled with. Now he took a long look, and it was like staring into the sun. The daughter of the Faerie Queen glowed, from her golden hair to her rose hued skin. She'd done nothing to hide her delicately pointed ears or the buzz of magic around her. Her only features that looked human were her eyes, one brown and one blue. Everything about her made Harris want to do something stupid, like drop into a bow or grovel at her feet.

"Princess," he said instead. "I'm sorry I didn't speak to you much on our journey so far."

Eilidh rolled her eyes. "I'm not a princess."

Harris frowned in confusion. "Your mother was the queen and I'm assuming you haven't taken her crown yet?"

"Harris," Iona hissed, looking around surreptitiously. "Eilidh doesn't want people to know."

He snorted. "Well, you're going to have to put a damper on yourself." He frowned at Iona and Eilidh's confused looks. "Can't you see this? She's shining like a beacon."

Iona turned to regard the woman beside her. "I suppose—"

"Don't look at her with human eyes. Look at her with *fae* eyes."

It took her a moment of staring but then Iona's expression cleared, and her mouth popped open. "My gods, yes. Why didn't I see it before? I must have been out of the ocean too long."

Eilidh looked between them and then down at herself. "What?"

"The Faerie Queen isn't just royal by title," Iona explained. "All fae are magically bound to recognise and serve her."

Eilidh's nose wrinkled. "I'm not a queen either."

"Tell that to the magic," said Harris.

Eilidh's cheeks had pinked even more. It was ridiculously endearing. "I don't want you to serve me."

"We're not slaves, we still have our free will." Harris grinned, fluttering his one eye. "It's just that you look really nice and are you happy? Because if you're not I can get you something? Do you need food? A chair—"

"Harris!" Iona admonished.

"Kidding," he said with a laugh. "Mostly."

Eilidh huffed. "Can we leave yet?"

"If you don't want other fae knowing, you have to cover up," Harris told her. As if that would make any difference. Even if they couldn't see her, they'd for sure smell her. *This is going to be an interesting journey.*

"Here," said Iona, thrusting out her cloak. "Make sure it stays up over your head. We'll see if we can sort something else out when we're at Dunrigh."

Chapter 14

Angus had been to Moira's rooms many times as a child, but the door had never been triple-locked and guarded like it was now. With a wave of Duncan's hand, it was opened, revealing the sitting room within.

The decor hadn't been changed in years, the walls that same pale lavender from Angus's memories. A striped couch sat before the empty fireplace, holding a myriad of floral cushions and nothing else. His cousin was nowhere to be seen.

When they'd been little, Moira had always known when to speak and when to stay silent, how to appear poised and which forks to use for which course during banquets. A true royal, even if her claim to the throne had been given up before her birth. Her mother, Princess Afric, had chosen to renounce her birthright to become a soldier. Everyone had thought she'd change her mind one day, even, apparently, Angus's own father. But then she'd been killed and never had the chance, which had meant her brother, Conall, became king and Moira was left behind.

Does that still make her a princess? Angus wondered. *A duchess?* To him, she'd always just been his perfectly composed cousin.

But then she had that accident. Angus and Duncan had been climbing trees and had dared her into joining. It had been fun, until she'd fallen, breaking her leg. *A few weeks in bed will set you right*, the doctor had said. But her foot had swollen up and they had to take it to save the rest of her.

Angus had seen a change in his cousin after that. She'd forget details. She slept a lot more. And she never, ever played with them again.

Is this our fault? They'd tried to include her, to make her feel like part of the family, but maybe they hadn't done enough.

"What are you going to do with her?" Angus asked as Duncan made his way over the plush carpet to the bedroom door.

His brother stopped beside the next pair of soldiers, guarding the entry. "I'm going to find out how much she was involved."

"And then?"

Duncan's chin was set. "I will act accordingly."

"She's our cousin," Angus reminded him. Surely that had to mean something.

Duncan stopped, placing a hand on Angus's shoulder. "The Mirandellis tried to kidnap me. They would have managed too, if not for Vashkha. If she helped them, that's treason."

Well, Angus couldn't argue with that. "And then?"

"One step at a time." Duncan reached out for the door handle. "Come on."

Stepping inside the bedroom, ahead of his brother, Angus was greeted by a wall of heat. The heavy curtains had been drawn across the windows and a fire was crackling in the hearth, providing the only light. It was hard to tell in the dark, but Angus knew the walls were adorned by floral paper, the armchair was blush pink and there was an ornate rug at the foot of the canopy bed. He cast his gaze over the side table, with a vase, its roses wilted and dried. A glass of half-drunk water sat beside it along with a well-thumbed book of poetry. And lying on the bed, under the satin coverlet, his cousin was propped up against the pillows. If Angus hadn't known better, he'd think they were merely concerned family visiting a sick relative. But it was not a sickness that kept Moira in this room.

"Duncan. Angus." She said, placing the parchment she'd been reading on the blankets beside her. "Are you here to tell me my punishment?"

"That depends if you are guilty," said Duncan, standing a little away from the bed and crossing his hands behind his back.

Moira smoothed back her golden hair. "What am I charged with, and I'll tell you."

Angus cast around for something to do, grabbing a couple of stools from the dressing table and setting them side by side. He waited until Duncan sat before he did. There, that was more comfortable.

"Aiding the Mirandellis," said Duncan once they were settled. "Selling your king out to them." His tone was still light, as if they were discussing the weather.

Moira sighed. "What if I'm guilty of one but not the other?"

Duncan waved his hand. "Make your case."

She gave a mirthless smile. "Shouldn't I be saying this in front of the court? Do I get a trial?"

"We don't have time for that. Either you stay under lock and key until we're back from war or we settle this now." The edge of Duncan's voice was harder.

Moira fidgeted with her fingers. "Do you know Major Chester Scarsi, of the Mirandelle army?"

Angus gritted his teeth. "We've met, actually. When we were looking for the Stone of Destiny; he wasn't very nice to my friend, Ailsa."

At the mention of Ailsa's name, Moira gave a quiet scoff. "I met Captain Scarsi, as he was then, at your coronation ceilidh," she began. "Do you know that's the first time someone has asked me to dance since I was sixteen? Everyone always thought I couldn't, because of my foot. But he asked and I danced with him all night. After that he kept bringing me flowers and visiting me up here. When his king had him away on errands, he sent me letters." She indicated the papers surrounding her. "The night of the farewell ceilidh, he was supposed to oversee the dismantling of their camp, but he came and found me here instead." She smiled wistfully. "He proposed."

Duncan frowned. "You didn't say anything."

"I was going to but then there was an explosion in the ballroom. Chester went down to investigate and he found this." She pulled a parchment from an envelope and held it up. On it was a twisting symbol, drawn in thick black ink.

"A drawing?" said Angus.

"A ward." Moira held the paper out for Duncan to take. "It was on the wall near the blast and Chester copied it. It's the mark of the Faerie Queen."

"I've never seen it before." *Probably because it's a lie*, thought Angus.

"Chester told me about the secret war Mirandelle has been fighting against the fae," Moira said, wringing her hands. "You think they're our friends but you're wrong. Queen Nicnevan stole the stone so that she could seize the crown."

Angus began to speak but Duncan held up a hand. "What else has he told you?"

"That your judgement was clouded by your fae friends. The selkies, the changeling girl, they're all in league with Nicnevan." Her eyes were shiny and wide and she spoke in earnest. "He told me that's why they really went to Ephraim. Everything they told you about her being imprisoned is a lie."

Angus couldn't believe this. "I was there. I saw her."

Moira gave him a soft, sad smile. "You only think you saw it. I'm very sorry, Angus, but you were deceived."

"*I* was deceived?"

Duncan gave him a look. "What happened when the Mirandellis left?"

"I had to stay here, or you'd suspect they knew. Chester kept writing to me, updating me on what was happening. He told me the Edaxi had offered to help them with the fae threat."

"And then he told you they needed to get into the castle?" Duncan guessed.

"They wanted to rescue you. Since the selkies and changeling were gone, they thought they could convince you of their corruption." She closed her eyes. "I told them about the second river."

Angus blinked in shock. *Of course.* The Snecky, which cut through the west side of Dunrigh, was not the only river. The second, The Killie, ran under the city, collecting waste and sewage before dropping further down into the earth. "They got in through the sewers? Why didn't they just use the Stone of Destiny? They have it, don't they?"

"Apparently Dunrigh is warded, they can't use the stone to get inside the city walls."

Well, that's a small relief.

"They opened a portal in the mountains. The Killie has an entrance there," she said. "If you follow it south, it'll take you straight under Dunrigh. Every building is connected."

How did she even know about that? "I doubt our ancestors meant for the sewage system to be used by an invading army."

"No, but they also didn't mean for fae to rule Eilanmòr."

Duncan wiped a hand down his face. "You'd better tell her."

Angus cleared his throat. "Nicnevan is dead. She was killed by one of the Edaxi at the battle of Ephraim."

Moira's expression cleared. "Good."

"She died saving me," said Angus, fighting to keep the

anger from his voice. "The Edaxi don't just want to kill or enslave all the fae, they want the souls of humans too."

"We've had reports from spies in Nefino," said Duncan. "It seems that Mirandelle made a deal with them. Merlo will get Eilanmòr's throne if he aids them in the war."

Moira shook her head. "King Merlo wants to help Eilanmòr."

Duncan leaned forward. "You like your history books, but it seems you've forgotten, cousin, how your mother died. We were at war with Mirandelle only twenty years ago."

"We have a truce," Moira told him fiercely.

There would be no arguing with her, Angus realised. Moira believed the lie she'd been fed with her whole heart. The worst was that she'd been led to believe she was helping her family.

"Where is your Captain Scarsi now?" asked Duncan.

She slumped back, crossing her arms. "I was supposed to meet him in Stravaig Forest after you were taken. Then we were going back to Mirandelle."

Duncan regarded Moira for a moment before letting out a sigh. "I'll have some food sent up to you."

"You're not letting me leave," Moira guessed.

Duncan rose from the stool. "No." The word rang across the silence: a verdict.

"Please think on everything I've said," Moira said thickly. "I don't want you getting hurt."

He was almost killed or captured by Mirandelli soldiers, Angus wanted to scream, but he bit his tongue. Nothing he could say would make her see sense.

Duncan headed to the door and Angus followed, his eyes on the carpet so he wouldn't have to look back at his cousin. He couldn't stay mad at her; it was clear she was brainwashed. But would Duncan see it that way? He gathered together all of his defences as they passed through the sitting room and into the hallway. The guards stood outside the door, waiting for instructions and Angus held his breath.

"Don't let her leave, she'll be staying for a while," said Duncan.

The guards nodded solemnly, and Duncan set off back in the direction of his own rooms.

"You're not sending her to the dungeons?" asked Angus. Or worse.

"She's unwell or deluded." Duncan scrubbed at his short hair. "Let her be imprisoned in comfort. When we're back from war we'll get her the help she needs."

"That's very generous of you."

"I'm sorry to say I haven't always been... trusting of the fae," said Duncan. "Father gave me lessons when I was young, on how to run the kingdom. The subject of many of these was how to deal with fae threats. He hated Nicnevan but he was also frightened of her. To most he was a compassionate and fair leader, but he had his prejudices."

Angus frowned. "But he welcomed Iona and Harris to court."

"I invited them to court when I thought he was dying. He told me the selkies had hidden the Stone of Destiny and that it would protect me from Nicnevan. He also told me the selkies had helped him in the past."

"So, they were a means to an end?"

Duncan sighed. "Yes. But knowing them and knowing your friend Ailsa made me rethink things. I've come to realise that I have a duty to all Eilanmòrians, even those who are fae. Even more so now that their queen is dead. It all makes me wonder how much Moira picked up from Father. Her mother was killed by a fae, after all."

"I didn't know any of this," Angus said slowly, redrawing the image of his father in his head.

"You made them your friends straight away." Duncan's grin was fond. "And just as well. It seems they are the key to winning this war."

Angus slowed his footsteps. "Sometimes I wish I could fight with them. That I had powers."

Duncan turned back to appraise his brother. "There's power in being human too," he said. "Which brings me to my plan. I need you to train them."

"Me?" Angus's mouth gaped.

Duncan nodded. "If the future of Ossiana is riding on your friends, I want them prepared to fight. As far as I know, none of them are soldiers."

"But I don't know magic," said Angus weakly.

His king looked him up and down. "You know how to handle weapons. How to assess your opponents. How to stay on your feet."

"I'd have no idea how to help them." It had been years, after all, since he'd done his own training. What if he'd forgotten?

"This battle will most likely take place on Eilanmòr soil or water." Duncan reached out to grab the back of Angus's neck, bringing their foreheads together. "You are a prince of the realm and therefore their leader. You don't need to have all the answers or have the same skills as those you lead, you just need to support them."

Angus let out a breath. "I'll try. I suppose I better get training myself."

Duncan gave him a crooked smile. "Maybe I'll meet you in the sparring ring. If I won't cramp your style."

Angus tried to return the grin. "My king might. My brother won't."

Duncan clapped him on the arm and walked off. "Dinner. Tonight," he said, over his shoulder. "I want all my family in one room. At least the ones who didn't sell me out to our enemies. Now I'm going to hire some more people I can trust."

As soon as Angus was alone in the hallway, he dropped his head to the stone wall, letting the cold ground him. With Moira's revelations, the war felt even closer and now Angus knew what role he'd play. Train them? How was he supposed to do that?

Cameron could help. He was a soldier after all. Angus would have to petition Duncan to let Cam stay with him. For now, though, he couldn't think of anything better than heading back to his room and letting Cameron wrap him up in his arms. Well, maybe a few things, but they weren't quite ready for that yet.

"I'm back," Angus called once he'd closed the door behind himself. "I'm not supposed to tell you but—" Angus stopped, noting the silence. "Cameron?"

Angus searched his rooms with mounting panic, his heart thudding in his ears. It didn't take long, so Angus looked again and again, hoping for a different outcome each time. When he finally found the note on his pillow, he knew what it would say.

Cameron was gone.

Chapter 15

Ailsa turned her rehearsed words over and over in her head as she approached the halls' doors. *My name is Ailsa MacAra and I've heard you have the Spear of Truth? I'd like to borrow it.*

You need to be more forceful, said Ishbel. *Demand it.*

Why should they give it to me?

Because you intend to use it to save the world? Which, by the way, is very noble of you. I don't know where you get it from.

Ailsa had to hold in her snort. *Funnily enough, I happen to live in the world I'm trying to save. Not so noble.*

Ishbel snickered. *Such a hard exterior but inside you are as soft as a cloud. I know because I am here in your head. I enjoy lounging on your fluffy little thoughts.*

"Shut up," Ailsa murmured under her breath.

"Sorry?" Vega asked, looking over her shoulder as she reached for the doorknob.

Ailsa pressed her lips into a flat line. "Nothing. I'm just nervous."

"Don't be. We need to have breakfast first anyway. You'll feel better after food."

Vega gave her an encouraging smile and then opened the door. The smell of smoked bacon and frying potatoes wafted from the serving table to the door, prompting Ailsa's stomach to growl. As usual the hall was packed with witches, gossiping over their breakfast, chatting with their friends. But was Ailsa imagining it or was everyone a little more on edge than before? The witches sat up straighter at their tables. Their voices were more hushed. And it seemed like each and every one was throwing darting glances at the far end of the room.

Ailsa didn't bother hiding her stare as she followed Vega inside. A long table had been set out. While the others were round and had witches on all sides, this one only had four people seated. They faced out to the rest of the hall, watching everyone as they ate.

"Four?" Ailsa asked.

Vega tugged at her hand, leading her to the table where Rain and Keyne already sat, tucking into their meals. "The man is Nasima's husband, Orion. He sits with them at meals."

Ailsa sat down at her friend's table, never taking her eyes off the group. *I'm assessing*, she told herself. Her eyes were drawn to the four people. She couldn't look away.

The man, Orion, leaned back in his chair, sipping a dark coloured drink in his hand. He'd painted the tanned skin on his cheeks black, with flecks of copper highlighting his cheekbones. His full lips pulled into a grin as he listened to the woman beside him.

The witch spoke animatedly, her hands almost a whir as she acted out her story. Her hair was hidden under a scarf, decorated with pink flowers and, now and then, she'd touch it, making sure it was still in place. Her face paint was a line of fuchsia, starting under her scarf and cutting down her forehead, nose and chin. Ailsa couldn't quite make out what patterns had been painted in the ink from where she stood.

The next woman was the tallest but only because of her dark hair. It crowned her head like a lion's mane. The front had been pinned back and a tiara of gemstones placed upon her head. Her face was mostly bare, save for the gold circle between her brows.

The final witch narrowed her gaze as she watched the

crowd. This one had ash brown hair, braided away from her face to show off her face where a silver, starry sky was painted like a half-mask. Waxing and waning moons danced a path across her forehead, each the same grey as her eyes. Eyes that found Ailsa and her companions the next moment.

The weight of the witch's stare was heavy as it swept up and down her body, leaving ice in its wake. Her expression was harsh, unforgiving, and it raised the goosebumps on Ailsa's arms. Ailsa had no idea what she'd done to this woman. Kicked her favourite cat perhaps? Whatever it was, this wasn't a good start. Ailsa fought the urge to hide, to flee. She grabbed Keyne's hand on impulse and felt the blood rush to her cheeks. "Sorry."

But Keyne squeezed her fingers when she tried to take them away. "It's okay, you don't have to worry about Aster. I'm sure she's just as curious about you as everyone else."

"Curious? She looks like she hates me already."

"That's just her face," said Rain, earning a weak laugh from Ailsa.

You're one to talk.

The grey-eyed witch's attention returned to her food and Ailsa hung her head, breathing a sigh of relief. "They're the witch council?"

Keyne nodded. "The wisest of us all. They make the decisions for the coven."

"But Orion isn't part of it?"

Vega shook her head. "It is tradition to have three women. They each have their roles: Maiden, Mother and Crone."

Ailsa frowned, trying to work out who was who. "They all look the same age though."

"It's just symbolic. They each play their role during the Rites, but it doesn't need to be literal. Sefarina—the one with the tiara—is the most senior, so she's the crone, even though she isn't the oldest. Nasima is married to Orion, so she's certainly no maiden. And Aster—"

"—*is* a mother," said Vega, cutting in slyly.

She was met with a growl from Rain beside her. "Just because she birthed me doesn't mean she's my mother."

Ah, that makes sense. Like mother, like daughter.

"Are you getting food?" Vega asked, cutting across her thoughts.

"I don't think I'm hungry anymore," said Ailsa.

Vega clicked her tongue. "I'm getting you something." Then she was up, heading towards the buffet with purpose.

"You're looking better," observed Rain, giving her a look that rivalled her mother's. "Aside from how you look like you're about to throw up."

"Rain," Keyne admonished, spearing a piece of egg. "Be nice."

"I'm trying to give her a compliment," she grunted. "Your eyebags are gone."

"Thanks?" said Ailsa, shifting in her seat. "I guess I slept better last night. My eyelid twitch is gone too."

"Huh, that's funny," said Keyne, sipping their orange juice. "Rain gets that when she's tired too."

"Shut up," Rain growled. She flicked her gaze between Ailsa and Keyne and pushed out from the table. "I need to go." Then she was off, disappearing through the tables.

"I really don't understand her," sighed Ailsa.

Keyne shook their head, munching on some toast. "Nobody does. Not even Vega. Maybe that's the appeal?"

"Rain and Vega?" A few things clicked into place. The lingering looks, the silent discussions. "But Vega's so cheerful and Rain is so..." She trailed off, wondering how she could describe the witch without using the word grouchy.

"They're not together," Keyne clarified. "Yet. Mutual pining and all that. Sometimes I wonder what damage Rain would have done to Findias if she hadn't spotted Vega first."

"And you're the third wheel?"

Keyne stretched, giving a devilish look. "I've got my own pining to do, don't worry. It's all very romantic."

Ailsa's answering smile was fleeting. She couldn't agree with that sentiment. *I thought I'd moved past pining.*

"Ailsa," Vega hissed in her ear, startling her from her thoughts. "They're ready for you."

That's right, the priestesses. Ailsa raised her eyes to the group, glad that they weren't looking her way. "Alright, wish me luck."

"You'll be fine," said Vega, placing two heaped plates of food down on the tablecloth. "And breakfast is waiting for you when you're finished."

Ailsa nodded woodenly and got up, approaching the top table. She wiped her hands surreptitiously on her clothing while worries whirled in her head. What did they want to speak to her about? She'd been at the witch palace for more than a week and they hadn't sent for her before.

Perhaps they were giving you time to settle in, soothed Ishbel.

That was new. Her spirit guide had never been *soothing* before. What's got into you?

Never mind, she huffed. *I'll take my sympathy elsewhere.*

Gods, I hope they can't tell I'm talking to you, Ailsa thought.

She stopped a few feet away, unsure of how to greet the council. Should she bow? Or would they think she was mocking them? In the end she settled for a respectful nod of her head.

"You wished to speak with me?" she asked, her voice only shaking a little.

"Ah, Ailsa," said the man. *Orion,* Ailsa reminded herself. She'd better get their names right. Or should she address them

as Lord or Lady? Priest or Priestess? "Is that the name you're going by?"

"At the moment," she admitted, forcing her shoulders back. "It's the only one I've got right now."

The woman with the mane-like hair regarded her, swirling her burgundy wine around in her goblet. "We were all in the hall when Vega showed you in," she said. "It's a pity that your ancestry is not clearer."

"I'm sorry about the way it happened," said the priestess in the headscarf. "Usually, we have rules on how we meet those that have found us again. You'll find out where you belong soon enough." She beamed. "I'm Nasima, by the way. That's my husband Orion and Sefarina." She indicated the first woman who spoke. "And this is Aster."

The witch with the grey, piercing eyes nodded, never taking her attention off of Ailsa.

"It's nice to meet you," said Ailsa, biting her lip. "Were there many of us? The children you…" She paused, thinking how best to word it. "…gave up?"

"Twenty-eight," Sefarina said softly. "We're still waiting for many."

Why? Ailsa wanted to ask. After her conversation with Rain that morning, her rage had been stoked. Why had they given up their daughters? Why had they thought that sacrifice was theirs to make, when it was their children who had suffered. But she bit her tongue. Now was not the time.

Sefarina drummed her nails on the tablecloth. "But you didn't come here looking for your family, did you Ailsa?"

She shook her head as a bead of sweat slid down her back. *Here we go.* "I was sent to look for the Spear of Truth. A friend of mine read that it might be here."

They exchanged looks with each other. "They read correctly."

Ailsa's heart skipped a beat. They weren't going to hide it. That was a good sign. "I'm sure you know better than me how valuable it is."

Nasima looked uncomfortable. "Which is why we're keen not to let it fall into the wrong hands."

Nasima wasn't outright saying Ailsa couldn't take it, but she still felt the rejection anyway. "There is a group of gods— the Edaxi—they're looking for it," she said, her voice cracking. "They already have at least one of the other treasures."

"We've heard," said Aster, speaking for the first time.

"Have you heard what they do to people? What they plan to do to Ossiana if they gain all four?" Ailsa's nails bit into her palm as she spoke. "I need the Spear of Light to stop them."

"I'm sorry, Ailsa," said Sefarina firmly. "We cannot let you have it. The spear is guarded; the gods will not touch it here. Findias is the safest place for it."

"From what I've heard, from what I've seen of them, nowhere is safe."

Aster stood, scraping back her chair. Silence fell upon the hall immediately. "Until Findias falls, the spear will remain."

Ailsa jutted her chin out. "Then I'll have to return empty handed."

"You needn't return," said Nasima. "You could remain here. Oh, Aster, please sit down. You're causing a scene."

The witch remained standing for a moment, eyes boring into Ailsa's, before she heeded her friend's words and sat.

"There." Nasima raised a hand to the crowd behind Ailsa. "All is well."

Ailsa swallowed as the noise returned. "I can't leave my friends to face the Edaxi without me," she said, answering Nasima's offer.

"While I'm sure you can already hold your own," Sefarina said, "I wonder how much stronger you would be with some

training. Our offer is this: stay a while, train with us and then, if you feel you must still join the war to the south, you will have our blessing."

I don't need your blessing. Though, if training would give her an edge, maybe she should take the opportunity. Plus, the longer she stayed, the more time she had to convince them to give her the spear. "I accept."

"Good," said Nasima, smiling brightly. "Let's get you out in the courtyard this afternoon and see what you can do."

What I can do, Ailsa thought as she inclined her head, *is anything it takes.* Because she was getting that spear and leaving Findias—with or without permission.

Chapter 16

Ailsa tried not to look up at the windows surrounding the courtyard, but she could feel the eyes on her, nonetheless. Word had obviously spread that the new girl was showing off her powers and half of the witches in Findias had turned up to watch. Vega and Keyne appeared nonplussed, following Nasima into the training ring without an upwards glance. Rain's face, however, echoed what Ailsa felt inside. The witch's lips were pressed together in a hard line and her jaw was clenched but there was another emotion in her eyes. Rain was nervous and it didn't make Ailsa feel any better to know it.

What have I got myself into?

Nasima took in the crowds pressed to the windows overhead and sighed. "Try not to worry about them. They're just curious. We haven't had anyone new find us since Rain."

"And she refused to come here when she was asked," Vega muttered.

Ailsa raised her eyebrows. "So, they don't know what your powers are?"

"I'm sure they do," said Rain through gritted teeth. "I use them often enough."

"But you're here now?" After avoiding it, why bother?

Rain gave Ailsa a long look. "I'm here now."

Nasima clapped her hands. "Keyne, you can start. Show Ailsa what to do."

Keyne stepped forward first, rolling up their sleeves as

they surveyed the courtyard. Ailsa watched, mesmerised, as they spread out their arms and bit their lip in concentration. Then they opened their mouth and Ailsa thought they were going to speak to her but as soon as Keyne's lips peeled back from their teeth in a lazy grin, grey smoke began billowing out. With a wink, the witch blew the fumes into the air until it spread out like fog all around them. Ailsa held her breath, unwilling to let the smoke into her lungs as it took away her vision. She could no longer see any of her companions, let alone the witch creating the vapour.

"It's okay," said Keyne. "It doesn't hurt."

Ailsa blinked, trying in vain to see her companions. She was running out of air. *Trust them.* She breathed in experimentally, finding that the smoke had no taste and no smell. It wasn't damp or hot, as if it was only an illusion.

"That's enough. Thank you," said Nasima.

The fog stayed for a moment, like it was unwilling to follow the command. Then it evaporated, leaving them all standing in the sunlight once again.

"Now you, Vega," said Nasima.

The small witch wiggled her fingers at Keyne. "I need help. Go get some daggers."

Keyne jogged over to the hut and emerged a moment later with five knives. They looked wickedly sharp, even from where Ailsa was standing. But Vega didn't seem afraid. She stood in the middle of the space and smiled before closing her eyes.

Ailsa's stomach dropped. Was she about to watch Vega get stabbed?

Keyne selected one of the daggers and pulled their arm back before snapping it forward, sending the knife straight for the tiny woman. Ailsa let out a cry, the noise escaping from her lips. What happened next Ailsa couldn't understand. One moment the blade was flying through the air, the next Vega had somehow dodged it and it sailed straight past her, landing with a clatter.

The witch beamed. "I'm fine, see."

"How?" Ailsa asked, stunned.

"The wind whispers to me," she said. "It tells me things that haven't happened yet." Then she nodded to Keyne. "Another."

Again, Keyne lined up the shot and threw the dagger. It seemed to be impossibly fast, but Vega was faster. Now Ailsa knew what to look for, she noticed how Vega moved her body, side-stepping out of the way of the blade just as it was about to hit her. The knife joined its sibling on the stones.

Ailsa massaged her chest, trying to calm her racing heart. "So, you see the future?" she asked weakly.

Vega wrinkled her nose. "I get glimpses. Some things are immediate, and some are a long time from now. I have to really concentrate to focus on the present."

"When you first met me, you said 'you're late.'" Ailsa had thought back then that it was a strange thing to say...

"I knew you were on your way months ago," Vega said gently. "I just didn't know the particulars."

"It's a useful talent," said Nasima. "Vega is getting better at reading her magic by the week."

The small witch ducked her head, blushing.

Nasima smiled kindly then turned to the grey-haired woman at Ailsa's side. "Rain, would you mind—"

"Yeah, fine," she said, stomping to the middle of the courtyard to take Vega's place.

Keyne sidled up to Ailsa and whispered in her ear. "I know this will surprise you, but Rain's power isn't being full of hot air."

The witch in question cut a withering glare at Keyne as if she'd heard them. Keyne just chuckled and took a step back.

As soon as they moved, Rain directed her attention to Ailsa.

Her eyes blazed as they stared into Ailsa's, her face unreadable. Ailsa found she couldn't look away. *Does she hate me?* Ailsa wondered. Somehow, she didn't think that was it.

Rain's hands shook slightly and at first nothing happened. Then there was a whoosh and something shiny streaked past their faces and into Rain's fingers. She held the object up for them all to see.

"That's my hairbrush," Vega laughed.

The brass handle glinted in the sun and when it was turned over Ailsa saw a few purple hairs clinging to the bristles. Rain tossed it to Vega with a barely suppressed smirk.

"Can't you just send it back?" Ailsa asked.

"It doesn't work like that," said Rain. "Would you like something brought to you?"

Ailsa bit her tongue. There was only one object she wanted. She couldn't just ask for it now, could she?

Vega jumped on her toes. "Ooh a treat please."

Rain held her hand out again closing her eyes. Something flew up and over the rooftop and into her waiting palm. Rain opened her eyes and held the biscuit tin out to Vega who squealed and grabbed it.

"Impressive," said Ailsa.

Rain gave a mock bow, but Ailsa didn't miss her shaking hands. She went to stand beside Vega. "Now you, Ailsa. I'd love to see what you can do."

Ailsa swallowed and stepped forward. *You can do this*, she told herself. *Your body knows what to do.* She could feel their eyes on her as she raised her hand to the sky.

Harnessing her power wasn't usually a problem. Ailsa had been practising for weeks. Hadn't she powered the Nymph and fought all the demons in Hell only a few weeks ago? But with the witches' attention, she suddenly felt unsure. Her gaze flicked to Rain again, expecting to see the same disdain. Instead, the silver-haired witch gave an almost imperceptible nod.

Like opening a door, Ailsa let her power fill up her body. It fizzled though every muscle, every nerve, and when she let it out, shooting up to the heavens, it was a heady relief. She moved her fingers and pulled the clouds to her, blotting out the sun and darkening the courtyard.

Vega's voice was hushed. "Ailsa, what—"

Ailsa could feel it building, a crackling pressure. The hairs on her arms stood up and something metallic coated her tongue. She grinned, holding the lightning high above them for a moment, and then she let it go. The bolt cracked down, racing through the air until it met her outstretched hand. It hit her skin with a bang, illuminating the whole training ring. Ailsa took the energy in her arms, bundling it into a ball, thrilling at the way it vibrated and then she tossed it up and away from her, back into the sky where it belonged. It hit the clouds with a distant boom, clearing them and revealing the sun once more.

She waited for a reaction. *Is that enough of a show?* she wondered, dropping her arms and her attention back to the witches in the circle. But instead of applause she was met with blank stares and silence.

No, not blank, she amended. *Horrified.*

"What's wrong?" she asked, her smile falling.

"Ailsa, having control over lightning is a rare gift," breathed Nasima. "There hasn't been a witch in centuries that has had that power."

She winced. "Is that a bad thing?"

Nasima licked her lips. "No, it's just the person who last had it—we don't talk about her."

Ailsa felt something cold slide down her spine. "What was her name?"

But, somehow, Ailsa knew the words Nasima would say before they spilled out of her mouth like a death knell. "High Priestess Ishbel Lauchair."

A chuckle filled Ailsa's ears, though no one around her was laughing. No, only the spirit haunting her mind these last few months seemed to find this remotely funny.

Surprise! trilled Ishbel.

Chapter 17

Ailsa knew the rest of Findias was still watching, with noses pressed against glass and gossiping, but the chatter fell away, replaced by a ringing in her ears.

"Why… Why don't you talk about Ishbel?" she asked, her voice coming out breathier than she'd intended.

"She was the head of the witch council, but she betrayed us." Nasima frowned. "It's why we had to leave our ancestral home."

Ishbel, is this true?

Vega took her hand and Ailsa suddenly registered how cold she'd become. "Are you alright?" said the small witch. "You look like you've seen a ghost."

"More like *heard* her," Ailsa whispered.

Nasima narrowed her eyes. "We need to have this conversation somewhere more private. Follow me."

Ailsa nodded woodenly, looking up at the crowds of witches above. Before she'd shown off her powers, they'd been smiling, huddled at the windows to get a better look. Now she could see their mouths moving, their fingers pointing down at her and her heart sank.

"Come on, Ailsa," said Vega, tugging on her arm.

Ailsa allowed her friends to pull her back inside the doors, down corridors and up winding staircases. She fixed her gaze to the back of Nasima's covered head, memorising a whorl in the pattern.

I'd almost forgotten. Even when Ailsa was young, she'd

had to deal with the stares and whispers. Changelings were bad omens in the rural villages of Eilanmòr. But finding her friends, heading to the capital, being surrounded by other fae, had taken away the sting. She no longer expected to see the fear in strangers' faces. And coming to Findias, and losing her mark, had given her hope. She was supposed to belong. But the fear was back, for different reasons. *I'll always be an outsider. A freak.*

This isn't about you, whispered Ishbel softly.

What did you do? Ailsa hissed in her mind.

"In here," the priestess said, opening a wooden door.

Vega went in first, with Rain and Keyne pressed against Ailsa's back. She couldn't look at their faces, at the fear or pity she'd no doubt find. Instead, she surveyed the gloomy tower room. *More books,* she noted absently. *A colossal library wasn't enough?* "Where are we?"

"This is where we keep our records and artefacts, the ones we don't want on display. Some are too precious, while others are a painful reminder of the past." Nasima led them through the room, where thick dust covered the surfaces. "We didn't always live in Findias. Long ago, the witches had a homeland, the island of Rocbarra. It sat off the coast of Eilanmòr and Mirandelle." She indicated a tapestry hanging on the wall. A map was woven into it, marking a familiar coastline. "Before our island sank, we had some warning. Another priestess, Theoris, moved as much as she could with her magic, and we resettled everything here. Her portrait hangs in the hall downstairs."

"How did it sink?" asked Ailsa.

Nasima bent down, pulling on a cream sheet which revealed a painting, leaning against the wall. Ailsa had to squint to look at it in the dim light. It was old, rendered in an outdated style. Unlike the head-on, posed pictures Ailsa had seen in Dunrigh, this picture was more informal; it seemed like the artist had caught his subject in the middle of a meal. The woman in the portrait was older than her, her age more in line with Aster's or Sefarina's. She sat at a table, covered in fruit and cheese and she held a grape to her lips as if she was about to take a bite. Long black hair streaked with grey cascaded over one shoulder and she wore a circlet between her arched brows. Ailsa couldn't decide if the woman was annoyed or amused with the artist but there was a quiet confidence in her expression. She could just imagine the portrait opening its mouth to tease or admonish her.

It has been a long time since I last saw this, whispered Ishbel.

Nasima stepped back, putting distance between herself and the portrait. "Ishbel Lauchair was a very powerful witch. The greatest of her time, actually. But she had a reputation for being chaotic."

The spirit huffed. *Ailsa—*

I'm not talking to you right now, Ailsa told her, planting her feet firmly.

"Her council were given two prophecies, one of peace and one of destruction." Nasima wrung her hands together. "Theoris and Diana, the priestesses who served with Ishbel, wanted to wait to find out which one was true. But Ishbel assumed the worst. She took the Spear of Truth and went looking for threats. Little is known of what happened next, except Ishbel attacked Salacia, the goddess of the ocean."

That isn't true—

Shhh.

"Word came with the selkies: they had mere hours before Salacia would wreak her revenge on the witches. Our ancestors gathered as much as they could and left, just before the waves devoured our island, sinking it to the bottom of the sea. The refugees came here to the highest mountain in Ossiana because it was the furthest from the ocean and the goddess's wrath."

"That sounds awful," murmured Vega at Ailsa's elbow.

Nasima nodded. "Both Ishbel and the spear were lost for centuries, until a selkie arrived at Findias with the weapon and asked for a favour. They planned to overthrow the Faerie Queen and hide her daughter but needed decoys."

Rain growled low in her throat. "So, you gave us up?"

"We owed the selkies a huge debt for saving us all those years ago," Nasima said with a sigh. "We hoped it wouldn't be for long but there are some still missing."

This meant that, if it were true, Ailsa becoming a changeling with no friends or family, the danger she'd endured, all of that was Ishbel's doing. Directly or indirectly.

Nasima cupped the back of Ailsa's neck, forcing her to look into the priestess's big, brown eyes. "After all of it, losing our home and our children, we just want to put this behind us. Which is why we can't give you the spear. I'm sorry, Ailsa." Nasima gave her a sad smile. "It's also why your powers caused such a reaction. Ishbel's betrayal still runs deep, even hundreds of years later. Your magic, unfairly, is a reminder of her."

"It seemed like you'd heard of her before?" said Keyne.

"We've met," said Ailsa weakly. She turned to look at her friends, noting the range of emotions painted on their faces. Keyne's head was tilted, watching Ailsa curiously while Vega was sucking on her top lip, clutching her arms to herself. But it was Rain that caught her attention. The witch had backed away so that no one but Ailsa could see her, chest heaving as she breathed through her nose as if the air around her was too thick.

"What do you mean?" asked Vega.

Should I tell them this? "I've met her spirit. I didn't know who she was."

Keyne's laugh was short and sharp. "You saw a ghost?"

Ailsa nodded. "Though I'm not sure how—"

"You're most likely related, given that you have the same powers," said Nasima, looking her over with a keen eye. "Sometimes our ancestors can attach themselves to their descendants, to guide them. We know she's tried before, eighty years ago. It's why we placed the wards around the castle walls, to keep unwanted spirits and entities out. You're safe from her here."

Wards? Had that been why Ailsa had felt so tired over the last week? Maybe Ishbel had been trying to push through, the struggle zapping her of energy. Like a parasite. She stored those questions away for later. "Great, my ancestor was evil?"

"Ishbel has a rich bloodline," Nasima said firmly. "Many of us can claim some kinship with her. We've just never met a witch with her magic."

Ailsa sucked on a tooth, considering this. "Wouldn't it be useful to speak to her, to find out what happened?"

"These are old wounds, and it doesn't help to pick at them." Nasima raised her chin. "We should leave you to collect your thoughts before you face the masses again." She beckoned Ailsa's friends back towards the door. "Just don't go into the other rooms up here. Some of the objects we've got squirrelled away can be dangerous."

Ailsa waited for them all to shuffle out, avoiding their stares. Once she was alone, she dropped onto an old box, covered in another dust sheet and put her head in her hands.

Are you ready to hear my side? asked Ishbel.

"I don't know," muttered Ailsa into the empty room. "Do you deserve it?"

Ishbel sighed. *That isn't what happened. I went to Salacia for help.*

"Because of the prophecies?"

Because of how Theoris received them." The spirit guide reached out, running a disembodied finger down Ailsa's mind. She knew the gesture was supposed to be soothing but it made her shiver. *"Theoris could open doors between spaces, but she'd been experimenting for months, creating portals to places further and further away. We thought she was just testing her powers until she told us her ultimate goal: to open a door to the Otherworld. Her mother had passed on the year before, and she hoped to speak to her again. But every time her attempts failed. I tried to convince her to stop but she was so intent, often sneaking off to experiment in secret. She opened doors to worlds that should never have been found. That's how she was given the prophecies. But words were not the only things to come through the doors.*

It was almost as if Ailsa could see it, the images flashing across her vision. "What does that mean?"

Monsters, fiends and banished deities.

Ailsa's heart stopped. "Like the Edaxi?"

Possibly. We didn't have as many gods back then. Salacia said she would help but that there would be a cost. To save the world, the portals and Rocbarra had to be destroyed. Ishbel paused and the memories took on a watery quality as if they were too painful to revisit. *Salacia sent word ahead with the selkies and I helped her destroy the island. Together, with her waves and my lightning, we sent it to the bottom of the sea. But I wasn't a goddess. Using that much power killed me.*

"This is a mess," said Ailsa, throwing her hands up. "I'm supposed to believe you saved the world?"

I may be selfish but I'm not evil.

"You did almost make me kill three boatloads of people," she reminded the spirit. "Back when you first showed up on that Avalognian longboat." She had also saved Ailsa's life, but she wasn't about to say that.

Being dead drove me a little mad. I lusted for violence and destruction. But being with you has given me back some sanity, said Ishbel. *Do you believe me?*

Did she? If what Nasima said was true, Ishbel had betrayed her people. And hadn't Ishbel kept things from her, things like her heritage? Still, Ailsa knew she'd never meant to hurt her. In fact, Ishbel had saved her multiple times. "I think so," she finally relented. "You know this has made everything a lot harder."

Ishbel scoffed. *You shouldn't have told them about me. What are you going to do?*

"I'm going to show everyone in Findias that I can be trusted," she said, pushing to her feet.

And how are you going to do that?

"With help from a demon."

Chapter 18

Maalik wasn't in their room when Ailsa checked but that didn't surprise her. Resigned, she tucked her hands into her pockets and retraced her steps down the corridor. No doubt he'd be in the library again. Had it only been yesterday that she'd last spoken to him there? *It feels like weeks.*

Are you going to ask him why he's avoiding you? Ishbel asked.

"He's busy." But even as she spoke the words, they sounded hollow to her ears. She deflated, rubbing her temple. "Ever since we came to Findias, Maalik has spent his days reading. He doesn't come to bed until I'm already asleep. Yesterday, before you came back, I went to see him."

And?

"He said he'd only be an hour or two but, well, you were there. I only know he must have come to bed because I'd been put in it." She turned down the corridor that led to the library. "Do you remember seeing him?"

When you're asleep, I'm asleep, said Ishbel.

"Right. Well, maybe I can convince him to leave today," she muttered as she opened the door.

Wow, this is—

"A lot, yeah," she muttered. Ailsa tilted her head back, taking in the towering shelves again, and spotted a familiar figure hovering high in the air, books in hand. "Hello, Zephyr."

The witch squeaked in surprise but quickly recovered, floating down to meet her at the entrance. "Ailsa," he said, his face splitting into a grin. "Nice to see you again."

"Is it?" she asked, shoulders curling in. "It seems not everyone agrees with you there."

He gave her a sympathetic smile. "I've heard about what happened. Don't worry, though, it was just a bit of a shock to everyone."

"Nasima told me the story and took me to Ishbel's portrait," Ailsa explained.

Zephyr's eyes lit up. "Ah, you went up the west tower. Pretty cool, huh? You didn't touch anything, did you? It's just, everything is so old and delicate. I have to use special gloves when I'm cleaning. Did she show you the spear then?"

"The spear?" She grimaced. "Do you mean the Spear of Truth was there and I didn't see it?"

"It's in a different room from Ishbel Lauchair's picture but, yeah, it's up there."

I was so close.

"Maybe she'll take you up again," said Zephyr, noticing her disappointment.

Or we could sneak in when everyone is sleeping, suggested Ishbel.

We can't. Zephyr said something about the door being spelled. It'll only open with a drop of blood.

And? Just cut your finger.

It has to be one of the priestesses' blood. Or Zephyr's.

The flying man watched her with concern. "Are you alright? Did you come to see me about something?"

Great, thought Ailsa. *He probably thinks I'm having a seizure because I'm talking to you.* "Actually, I needed to talk to Maalik again."

"Ah." Zephyr rubbed the back of his neck. "He went down into the crypts. Following a lead, I think."

Ailsa shifted impatiently. "Well, where are they? This can't wait."

Zephyr grimaced. "He, um, didn't want to be disturbed."

"Maalik won't have meant me."

"Actually," Zephyr bit his lip. "I'm really sorry, I don't know what's going on between you, but I can't lie. He said I was to turn you away if you came looking for him."

"What?" Ailsa breathed. "Why?"

"I have no idea. I'm sorry. But don't you share a room with him? Maybe you should ask him when you see him tonight?"

Ailsa swallowed, the blood pumping in her ears almost enough to drown out his words. "Yes," she said. "Thank you, Zephyr. That's exactly what I'll do."

The witch's teeth worried at his lip. "Good, because I think he has a bit of a crush on you, you're all he talks about. I get the feeling he's just shy. I know how that is; I like someone but every time I see them, I feel like I need to run away and hide. As if they'll somehow know if I'm around them for even a moment. I bet that's how Maalik feels about you."

"I thought I knew how he felt, but I guess I was wrong." Ailsa's face was suddenly hot. "Thanks for telling me, Zephyr."

"Right. If you don't need me then, I have to put these reference books away." He waved a heavy tome beside his head, the weight of it making him wobble in the air.

Ailsa pursed her lips. "Sure, see you later."

"Bye, Ailsa," he said as he flew off, leaving Ailsa alone at the bottom of the stacks.

What are you going to do? Ishbel asked.

Mope? But, no, the time for feeling sorry for herself was over. She turned, stalking out of the library. "I'm going to get to the bottom of this, once and for all."

Chapter 19

*M*aalik sat against the freezing stone wall, his eyes burning from reading by candlelight. When Zephyr had mentioned there were more books down in the old crypts, he'd been intrigued, imagining all the secrets buried with the ancient witches. But it soon became clear that the tombs weren't that old at all and any books he'd found said the same as those above in the library.

Still, it was a good place to hide. No one had come down to check on him, not even Zephyr. The dead were silent in their graves, leaving him to read in peace. If only the thoughts would do the same.

Just another hour, he thought to himself, glancing at the candle beside him. It had been new when he lit it and only half of it was melted now. Ailsa wouldn't be asleep yet.

But no matter how many times he read the same sentence, he couldn't get the words to sink in. The page was in front of him, but he only saw her face. The wind howled up through the vents, but he only heard her voice.

My heart, my soul, my entire being is yours.

The skin on his shoulders prickled. *No,* he thought at the sensation, gritting his teeth. *You can't, you can't, you can't.* But already he could feel the tell-tale shift of silky feathers. When it got this bad, there was only one way to get his body back under control.

Maalik set his book down and closed his eyes, imagining himself back outside a familiar tent. It was dark, just like the crypt. In the distance there had been screams of pain. Normally he would have followed them, given the poor souls some relief, but he'd believed the word of a goddess when she'd told him the secret to stopping the war. In his mind's eye, he pushed the tent open, revealing the young soldier in her armour and a king who knew he would soon die. He replayed those last moments - the blood, the pain, the regret - let them drown him in misery again. And only when the chorus of self-loathing reached its crescendo, did the feathers fade back into the heavy metal upon his back.

***

The candle was down to a nub when Maalik finally let himself climb out of the crypt. He used the fading light to find his way out of the empty and darkened library and through the hallways. Here and there were remnants of the witches who passed through in the daylight. An abandoned scarf, a dropped pencil, watery footprints; all echoes of life littering the corridors. Not for the first time did Maalik wonder if any of it had been left by Ailsa. Had it been her fingers that knocked that painting askew? Had she left that door ajar? Which of these bedroom doors belonged to her new friends?

I wish I knew. But it was better this way. *She's better off without me.*

Still, he couldn't stay away. Which was why, every night, he put himself through the sweet torture of holding her close while she slept and leaving again before she woke.

Maalik found their room and blew out his candle. Slipping inside, he closed the door behind himself gently so that there was only a faint click. He counted his steps, skipping the third floorboard in, the one that creaked. He'd been doing this for more than a week, enough that he knew all of the little noises that could wake Ailsa from her sleep.

But, gods, he wished he didn't have to sneak around. Everything in him wanted to stay by her side. He wanted to watch her smile, to be the reason she laughed or blushed. *You have to save the world first.*

Being with Ailsa could potentially doom them all.

He watched his feet, careful not to trip on the rug. He'd done that the first few nights, but he'd learned his lesson. He crept to the foot of the bed and raised his eyes to the sleeping figure there.

Except there was no one in the bed.

Where is she? He wondered, his stomach falling. *Ailsa was always exhausted lately. She should be asleep—*

The dry scrape of a match against sandpaper whispered to his left and he whipped his head around to find her sitting at the desk. Ailsa held the tiny fire below her chin, casting her face into strange shadows. Then, never breaking the glare she had levelled at him, she lit a candle in her other hand and placed it on the desktop. The mirror behind her reflected the light throughout the room, but it was harder to see her expression.

"I thought you'd be in bed," he said, his voice cracking. *I'm in trouble.*

"I know," she growled.

I'm in big trouble, he amended mentally. "I was just going to sleep."

"Oh?" she asked, tilting her head like a cat eyeing up a mouse. "Another long day?"

Maalik licked his lips. "I thought there'd be better books down in the crypts. It took a while to go through them all."

Ailsa stood from the chair. "Do you want to know what I've been doing all day?"

"What?" Maalik asked, taking a step back.

"The same thing I've been doing every day since we came

here," she said, stalking forward. "I've been wondering what the hell I've done wrong, why suddenly you've decided you can't stand to see me, unless I'm unconscious."

"Ailsa, I—"

"But no more. If you have a problem with me, you need to tell me, because I'm done waiting around—"

She crowded him against the bedside table, coming chest to chest with him. "I'm done with you avoiding me—" She curled her lip, even as the candlelight reflected on the unshed tears in her eyes. "I'm done with having my heart broken."

"Ailsa." Maalik reached down, trying to touch her arms, but she shrugged him off.

"It's like you're two different people. It's like you love me at night and by the morning you hate me."

You're a fool. You thought you could avoid her, and she wouldn't even notice. Look what you've done. Maalik dropped to his knees in front of her, his heart threatening to burst from his chest. "I could never hate you, Ailsa. I love you."

"Then why?" she asked, her voice wavering. "Why did you tell Zephyr to turn me away? Why won't you just *talk to me?*"

The words burst from him. "Because if I let you love me, I can't save you."

Ailsa blinked, staring down at him. "What—"

"Whenever I'm with you, it feels good. *Too good.*" He closed his eyes, so he didn't have to look at the confusion on her face. "Do you remember what happened in the tent?"

"You grew wings," she said.

Maalik sucked in a breath, trying desperately to fight the panic rising in him. "I'm turning back into an angel."

"And why is that a bad thing?" Ailsa demanded.

"Because you need a demon. Only a fae with fire magic can wield the Sword of Light." His voice sounded bitter, even to his own ears.

"So, you've been avoiding me," she said slowly, "so you won't become an angel?"

"I've been avoiding you so that I can save you. And the rest of the world."

A soft hand on his cheek had him cracking an eye open. "Maalik, we can find another fae with fire powers," she said, sitting down on the bed so she was more level with him.

He gave a dry laugh. "Where? You said yourself, you killed most of the other demons when you went to Hell, not that they would have helped you anyway. And I don't know where Calix is."

"There must be other types of fae."

"Not in Eilanmòr. It would take too long for you to find one. The Edaxi could have won by then." *I'll have lost you.*

"Your happiness is important—"

"—not more important than your life," he said vehemently.

Ailsa glowered. "So, what, are you just going to ignore me until we've killed them? What if we don't survive the battle?"

"I don't—"

"Are you telling me you're happy to die before you hold me again? Because, if we only have a few weeks left, I know that I don't want to waste that time." Her expression brightened. "That's why you've been sneaking into bed when I'm sleeping, isn't it? Because you can't stay away."

Maalik hung his head. "Yes. Because I can love you, but you can't love me. It's your love that's changing me."

"It's my love that's healing you." She said it with such wonder, as if this was more than she could hope for.

Maalik gritted his teeth. "Either way, I can't let it happen."

Ailsa tilted his chin at the same time as she shifted so the light of the candle fully hit her face. So he could finally see the devastation there. "Maalik, you can't keep doing this," she whispered. "You're hurting me."

"No." He shook his head, trying to dispel the heartbreak in her voice. "No, I'm saving you." But her lip quivered, and he was up and pulling her into his arms before he could think.

She gasped when he pressed his body to hers, but she recovered quickly, returning his embrace, fitting her face into his neck. "I just need you to speak to me. You were my friend first. I feel so alone here."

He squeezed her tighter, inhaling the scent of her lavender soap. "You have friends."

"It's not the same."

"I promise I won't leave you again," he said, pressing a kiss into her hair. "But we'll have to be careful. You have no idea how easy it would be for me to toss my morals to the wind."

She gave a weak chuckle. "Are you saying *I'm* tempting the demon?"

"You're always tempting. When I saw you the other day in the library, I was this close to doing something I would have regretted."

"Like what?"

Her fingers stroked his back and he had to hold back a moan. It felt so good. "Like letting myself believe you. Like letting you change me irrevocably." He pulled back, searching her face. "I wanted to hold you and kiss you and never let you go."

Ailsa swallowed, a pretty blush staining her cheeks. "When we've saved the world…"

He smiled. "I will follow you to the ends of the earth. I'll worship at your feet. And, if you let me, I'll spend every last moment trying to please you."

"Deal," she said. "But it'll take a while. Maybe the rest of our lives."

Maalik didn't deserve her. There was a prickling at his back again, though, so he stretched his shoulders, willing the feathers down. "Now," he croaked. "You must be tired."

"I actually haven't felt this awake since we got here." Ailsa reached up to push a strand of hair away from his brow. "But maybe we could lie down, and I'll tell you everything you've missed?" When he nodded, she scooted across the bed, pulling him with her until she could rest her head on his chest.

And as Ailsa began to talk, recounting everything that had happened, Maalik allowed himself one moment to breathe her in and remember how lucky he was to have this woman by his side.

One day, he vowed, *I'll get to have this. One day I'll forgive myself and let her love me.*

Chapter 20

The sun was just rising when Eilidh awoke with a start. She was on her side, underneath her travelling blankets, with Iona and Harris lying next to her. The fire they'd used the night before had burned down to ashes and she could hear the whinny of the horses from where they were tied to a tree. Everything seemed normal but a prickling in her gut told her the truth: there was someone else in their camp.

Stay still or move? she wondered. Perhaps it was merely an animal looking for food or shelter.

A twig snapped on the other side of the firepit, and she strained her hearing towards it. It must have been bigger than a rabbit to break the stick, but it wasn't breathing heavily enough to be a wolf or a bear. A fox then? Or a stray dog?

Footsteps padded closer, almost drowned out by the thudding of her heart. Was it best to pretend to be asleep or to jump up to scare it? Should she wake Iona and Harris before they were all eaten? In the end, that was the thought that decided it. Better to know what you're facing than to imagine some sort of monster. Eilidh raised her head and looked.

It was not a fox or a bear or a wolf. The creature that knelt in front of the fire was unlike anything she'd seen before. It looked like a little old man, but its limbs were stretched oddly—too long for its body. Its nose was short and hooked like an owl's beak and its teeth protruded out of its mouth like those of a rodent. It held a wooden staff in one hand with three skinny fingers and wore a crimson hat on its head. The creature stared down at her, frozen for a lingering moment. Then it took its cap off and tipped its head.

Before it could look at her again, Eilidh nudged Iona's shoulder. "Wake up," she whispered, fighting the rising panic.

Iona rolled towards her and blearily opened her eyes. "It isn't time to get up—"

"Look!" Eilidh hissed but now the creature had seen and heard them. It shoved its hat back on, turned and hobbled off briskly in the other direction. Eilidh stared at it with an open mouth, relieved to see the back of it. "Did you—"

"Yes," Iona breathed. "It was a redcap. They're murderous elves who bathe their hats in their enemies' blood."

Eilidh's stomach churned. So that was why its hat was red? "I woke up and saw it."

"Did it try to attack you?"

"No, it just looked at me and then took its hat off and bowed," said Eilidh.

Iona blinked. "A redcap bowed to you?"

"Unless it was showing me the bald spot on its head."

"They're not usually so polite."

Eilidh ran a hand through her hair to hide her shaking. "We must have got it on a good day."

Iona scrunched up her nose. "Maybe."

"Well, there's no way I can sleep. What if it comes back?"

"We should leave soon then, we're only four hours from Dunrigh. Harris, wake up."

Her brother groaned, rubbing his cheek into the blanket. "I feel like I've only slept a couple of hours." Indeed, his eye was red rimmed and puffy, like he'd been awake all night. Or crying.

"We can sleep when we get to the castle." But Eilidh saw the worry on Iona's face as she looked Harris over, as if she was coming to the same conclusions.

Eilidh kicked off her covers and pulled her leather boots on. "I'm going to get some water from the stream."

Iona stopped her with a hand on her arm. "Be careful," she said, scanning the trees. "I can sense there are other fae around and I don't think it's us or the redcap."

An old terror shot through Eilidh, but she did her best to trample it down. Nicnevan was dead and her minions weren't coming for her anymore. "Let's get back on the road quickly." Before whatever else was around came to investigate.

***

The road was clear all the way to the capital, save for a herd of cows that meandered out of their way as soon as they came riding up. It wasn't long before Eilidh passed through the towering gates of Dunrigh, flanked by massive stone statues of a unicorn and a stag. She thought she'd be relieved to be off the road after their encounter that morning, but her stomach kept swooping uncomfortably as her dappled grey horse trotted up to the city. Somehow, in the years she'd imagined and avoided Ephraim, she'd never spared a thought for the capital. Yet, just like the faerie kingdom, Dunrigh was her ancestral home.

For most of my life, my mother was in Ephraim and my father was here.

Somehow, the city was worse than the faerie court. At least Ephraim was a part of the forest, familiar like her real home. Dunrigh was foreign. She followed Iona and Harris's horse through the streets, taking in the sights and smells of the bustling streets, teaming with people, buildings and noise.

"Straight up this road," Iona called back to her.

Eilidh tightened her hand on the reins while the other made sure her hood was secure. No one would recognise her, she knew, but she didn't need anyone wondering who the mysterious blonde woman was. Unlike the face she'd worn before, this one tended to garner attention.

The more she stared at the people on the streets, the more aware she was that there were no children. She'd expected sounds of laughter; they'd always been familiar when she'd visited the nearest village. But the noise was more of a low humming, like bees in a tree. She concentrated, trying to hear the snippets of conversation.

"hurry up"

"a few hours"

"just leave it"

The locals spoke like they moved, quick and sharp. People darted across the road, carrying heavy loads. Every face she looked upon was drawn and tired.

"Has something happened?" Eilidh asked, but then they crested a hill and she spotted it.

The castle looked over the town like a sentry, but it was clear it had recently seen battle. One of the towers was half standing and blackened and she could swear it still smoked from the fire which must have ravaged it. At the wall, dozens of soldiers stood with swords or bows.

"Stop!" one of them shouted and then all eyes were on Eilidh, Iona and Harris. They raised their weapons, totally uncoordinated. Even from down the path, Eilidh could see some of them were shaking.

They're either inexperienced or badly trained. Eilidh guessed the former. A few of them looked barely big enough to fit their armour. Too young.

Iona brought her horse forward a couple more steps and then stopped. "I am Iona of Struanmuir, and this is my brother Harris. We're the king's emissaries."

"And who is that behind you?"

Iona slid her gaze to Eilidh, trying to gauge her reply. Eilidh bit her lip, shaking her head as subtly as she could. "A friend of ours."

"That's not good enough. She'll have to wait out here while you go in."

No. Who knew how long that would take. "I am the daughter of Agneta Dalgaard," Eilidh said, quickly.

As soon as she said the name, most of the guards visibly relaxed. While some still wore their fear on their faces, it was mixed now with curiosity, awe, reverence.

"*The Reaper*?" one of the younger soldiers asked as if she couldn't believe it.

Eilidh thought of the woman who'd raised her, back in Kilvaig. Agnes had soothed her hurts, read her stories, baked her cinnamon rolls. But she'd also taught Eilidh to fight, inspiring her with tales of brave deeds and close calls. She grinned then, feeling warmth in her chest for the first time since she'd left the boat. "That's her."

There was a murmuring amongst them as they decided what to do. Eventually, a stocky man stepped forward, lowering his sword.

"If you can vouch for her, Lady Iona, you may all come in," said the soldier, stepping aside. "But I must warn you, the king is very busy."

"What happened?" asked Iona.

"We were attacked. That's all I'm permitted to say outside the castle walls."

Harris cleared his throat. "Is Prince Angus here?"

"He arrived a few days ago."

"Okay, let's go. I will keep an eye on our friend, don't worry." Iona turned in her saddle to give Eilidh a wink but with the worry clear on her face, the expression didn't hit the mark.

Eilidh smiled tightly in return and followed the white

horse through the gate. The path led up another hill, but this one was not flanked by buildings. Instead, the ground was covered in soft grass and an abundance of wildflowers.

Eilidh watched as an orange butterfly hovered lazily over the blooms before sweeping up and across their path. Ahead, the castle's grey stone glittered in the sun. Beautiful, she thought. Even if there was a discomforting silence pressing in on the place like a blanket.

The horses led them up until they came across another, smaller gate. This time there was no one to greet them. Eilidh held her breath as they passed under the sharp stakes of the portcullis but as soon as they were inside, the air released from her lungs all at once.

"What is that?" she asked Iona.

The selkie came to an abrupt stop. "The Peace Tree," Iona said. "It's gone."

Only the trunk of a massive tree was left, the rest burned and blackened. The fire which had taken it had also scorched the cobblestones around it, and Eilidh was able to grasp the scale of the disaster. How big had the tree once been to leave such a mark on its way out?

"It was a symbol," said Iona quietly. "Of Eilanmòr's strength. Of friendship."

The redhead swung her leg over the horse, stumbling forward into the ash as she dismounted. Eilidh joined her to survey the damage.

"Who could have done this?" she asked.

A tear trickled down Iona's cheek. "We need to find out."

Eilidh reached for Iona's hand, to give her some comfort but the noise of a door slamming open had her flinching away.

"Harris? Iona? Eilidh?"

Iona gave a wobbly grin as the prince came striding out of the door. "Angus!"

Eilidh hung back, allowing him to greet his friends. She was surprised then when, instead of pulling Iona and Harris into a bone-crushing hug, he pulled Eilidh to him first.

"I was worried," he murmured into her hair.

Eilidh froze from the shock of being held but after a moment she thawed, wrapping her arms around his back to return the embrace. "It looks like you've had a lot to be worried about."

"Yes, well, I was concerned about all of you too." Angus bit his lip. "After we were attacked, I started thinking they might have gone your way—"

"Attacked?" asked Harris.

Her brother pulled away from Eilidh and grabbed hold of the selkie's shoulders instead. Angus's attention lingered on Harris's eyepatch for a moment, as if he'd forgotten about his injury in the days they'd been apart. Harris went still, his lips forming a thin line.

"The Mirandellis," Angus said, clearing his throat. "They tried to take my brother."

"They set fire to the tree?" Iona guessed.

"Among other things. But we can't talk about that here, let's go inside." He held out his arm for Eilidh to take and then led them inside the castle.

Eilidh's gaze was immediately drawn skyward into the vaulted ceiling, where the wood was carved into figures of prancing animals. *I don't think I've ever seen a room this massive.* And this was just the entrance hallway. No one spared them a glance as servants and soldiers hurried through the ornate doors lining the walls, carrying boxes and sacks out into the courtyard they'd just come from.

Angus led them up the grand staircase leading to the floors above and down corridors decorated with portraits and tapestries. The stone walls and the dark rugs could have been oppressive but the sunshine leaking through the stained-glass windows brightened the space, showing off the opulence, the history. Finally, they rounded a corner and Angus strode towards a plain wooden door.

"After you."

Harris pushed through first, as if this was his room, not Angus's. He dropped onto the leather couch with a sigh and looked around. "Where's Cameron?"

"I haven't seen him since yesterday." Angus pressed his lips together and his eyes turned glassy.

Eilidh frowned, moving to perch on the arm of the sofa. "Are you alright?"

"It's just been a lot. Let's have some tea first then I'll fill you all in. I think Duncan wants to meet with all of us later too."

"You just sit down," said Iona. She headed to the door. "Take a moment. We'll have a servant bring us up some treats. Come on, Harris."

Her brother groaned before going after her and then Eilidh and Angus were alone.

Angus sank down onto the couch gratefully, pulling Eilidh down with him so that she was curled up into his side. It was much more familial than Eilidh was expecting but she found she didn't care, leaning into her brother's warmth. After all the travelling, sitting on the plush cushions was like heaven and she found she had been missing the close touch of someone she trusted.

"Angus," Eilidh said quietly as he dropped his head back with a sigh. "You haven't told Duncan about me, have you?"

He squinted up at her. "You told me not to, so I didn't. But I think he should know soon. It might be a bit of good news for him amongst all this."

"You really think having an older sibling will be good news to the king?"

He squeezed her hand. "Eilidh, you're our sister. Family. Of course that's good."

Her lips tugged into a smile. She really didn't deserve him. "Just… not right now."

"Fine. But I'm happy you're here."

She grinned down at her brother. "Me too, I think."

Chapter 21

Ailsa woke slowly, emerging from sleep as if it was a warm bath on a cold day. She couldn't remember the last time she'd slept that well and she was loath to be done with it. Scooting back against the pillows behind her, she let out a soft sigh. There was a weight across her middle, pinning her to the mattress, but she didn't have it in her to care. Maybe if she just kept her eyes closed, she'd drift off again.

"Ailsa?" Warm breath tickled her ear. "Are you awake?"

Her head jerked up from the pillow as her brain fought to catch up. She was in her bedroom, soft sunlight streaming through the windows. The blankets were tucked in around her chin and holding them to her was a dark-skinned arm. She shifted, turning to roll onto her back and rubbed a hand over her face, surreptitiously wiping away the drool.

"You stayed," she said, peeking up at the man beside her.

Maalik was lying on his side, dark hair mussed and falling across his forehead. The skin under his eyes looked bruised and he was chewing on his bottom lip. She could almost hear the swirl of thoughts inside his brain.

Ailsa held up a finger before he could speak. "Stop thinking so hard. We're going to be careful, right?"

"That seems a lot more difficult now that we're in bed together—" He spluttered, realising what he'd just said. "I just mean because being beside you makes me so happy—"

"Maalik, relax! You're allowed to be happy." She pushed down the covers. "See, no feathers yet."

He winced. "Right, but I can already feel—"

"I'll distract you." She propped her head up on her arm. "What are we going to do about our problem?"

"Which one? The fact that they all think Ishbel is evil and that you might be too since you're her descendant and have her magic? Or the fact that the spear is locked away in a tower which can only be opened with a drop of the priestesses' blood?"

"I'd say those are both the same problem," said Ailsa. "I might have been able to convince them to give it to me before but now my chances seem even lower. All because of Ishbel."

"And you're sure," said Maalik, licking his bottom lip, "that she isn't evil?"

Ailsa sniffed. "That's up for debate."

Hey!

"She says she's not evil and I'm choosing to believe her," Ailsa said firmly. "It doesn't change the fact that everyone thinks she betrayed them by destroying their ancestral home."

He tilted his head. "Do they know she's your spirit guide?"

Ailsa sucked on a tooth. "I told them she tried to attach to me. They have these wards up to keep away unwanted entities. They think they stopped her."

"But you can still hear her." She felt his gaze rake over her face. "You get this look on your face when she speaks to you. I used to think you were suddenly annoyed by something."

Ailsa rolled her eyes. "That sounds about right," she muttered. "It's going to take a lot of work to get back in their good graces. To make them trust me enough to give me the spear."

Maalik took her hand, enveloping it in his. "You're not Ishbel."

"I guess I need to show them that," she said, squeezing his palm. "And you're going to help me."

He nodded. "What can I do?"

She took a deep breath. "Come to breakfast and meet my friends. If anyone asks, tell them how trustworthy I am."

"I don't know if that'll help if it comes from a demon." He smiled sadly.

You're not just a demon, she wanted to say, but wasn't that along one of those lines Maalik had warned her about last night? Ailsa bit her tongue and threw the covers off her body instead. "Every little helps," she said tightly, pulling a jumper on. She heard him shuffling around on his side but kept her stare trained on the door.

"In the meantime," he said. "We should learn a bit more about the witch council. See if there's one of them who'd be more likely to champion you."

"Nasima or Sefarina are the best bets in that regard. I didn't think Aster liked me before yesterday so I can't imagine how she feels about me now."

Maalik's hands cupped her shoulders, and he pressed a kiss into the back of her head. "It's impossible that she doesn't like you."

"Not everyone finds my sullenness and bad temper as charming as you do."

"Well, they're wrong," he said fondly. "Come on, let's go to breakfast so I can judge your new friends."

***

The hall was full when they arrived which made it especially eerie when it fell silent as they entered. Ailsa stared out into the crowd for a beat, not quite comprehending what was happening, until the events of the previous day came flooding back. Everyone had seen her conjure her lightning, not just the council. Ailsa tried to swallow but it got stuck in her throat. *I can't do this,* she thought, but then Maalik wrapped his arm around her shoulders, lending her his strength and heat.

"Where should we sit?" he asked.

She nodded to the table where she spotted Vega's purple hair, not trusting herself to speak. Maalik tugged her into the ballroom and the chatter started up again, like a spell had been broken.

"Thank you," she murmured as they weaved their way through the round tables. She kept her eyes fixed ahead, where Vega, Keyne and Rain were already eating, but she felt the surreptitious glances as they passed the other witches.

Vega beamed when they got to their table, using her fork to wave. "Ailsa! We were just about to come look for you. We thought you'd slept in."

"Looks like you were late for other reasons," said Keyne, their gaze sliding to Maalik. "This is the first time your friend has joined us."

"This is Maalik," she said, dropping into a seat and pulling him down into the one beside her. "Maalik, this is Vega, Keyne, and Rain."

"I think we met when we first arrived?" Maalik asked Vega.

Her face lit up. "It's lovely to see you again."

"Where have you been?" asked Rain, raising an eyebrow.

Maalik cleared his throat. "I was in the library, doing some research."

She didn't look impressed. "And you just left Ailsa to fend for herself?"

"It was a bit of a misunderstanding," said Ailsa, hoping her tone brooked no argument. Was Rain defending her? Or was she trying to start a fight, as usual?

"Right." Rain folded her arms across her chest and turned back to Maalik. "And you and Ailsa are together?"

"Rain! Leave him be," Keyne admonished. "You spent time

in the library, so you must know Zephyr?"

"Yes," said Maalik, still frowning at Rain. Ailsa pushed her foot up against his, hoping the contact would soothe whatever hurt Rain had caused with her questioning. "He was very helpful."

"Keyne has a bit of a crush on him," Vega whispered conspiratorially.

Keyne flicked a strawberry at her. "I do not have a crush, it is love, albeit unrequited."

"How do you know that?" asked Ailsa.

"One time I went to the library to borrow a book and he just gave it to me."

She waited for more. "And?"

Keyne dropped their head onto the table and groaned into the wood. "If he loved me, he would have taken the opportunity to kiss me against a bookcase. Or to swear his undying devotion."

"He probably didn't realise that's what you wanted," suggested Ailsa.

Keyne looked affronted. "I was wearing my best robe," they said, as if that settled things.

Rain rolled her eyes and then turned them back on Maalik. "So back to you. How long have you known Ailsa?"

He pressed his lips into a firm line. "A few months."

"But you love her?"

"Rain—" Ailsa started to growl.

"Yes. I do," Maalik said quietly.

Rain narrowed her eyes. "And Ailsa? How about you?"

"Maalik knows how I feel about him," she said through gritted teeth. Already she could feel the tell-tale crackle of electricity in her veins. *Keep it together.*

Rain let out a snort. "What makes you think you're good enough for her—"

"Where is this coming from?" The words burst out of Ailsa, too loud even in the chatter of the hall.

Maalik stood from the table. "Erm, I'm going to get us some food. Shall I just get you a bit of everything?"

"Yeah, thank you," she said, never taking her gaze off Rain. Ailsa waited until Maalik was halfway across the floor before rounding on the silver-haired witch. "What is your problem?" she hissed.

"He abandoned you in a new place for a whole week," Rain hissed back. "And, what, you're just going to buy that he was 'researching'?"

"Not that it's any of your business, but Maalik and I are fine. What has happened between us is private." She sat back, willing herself to calm down. "Why are you so annoyed anyway? I didn't even think you liked me."

"You are such an idiot," Rain growled, pushing out of her chair and stalking out of the hall.

Ailsa groaned. "What was that all about?"

"I think that was Rain's way of trying to be protective," said Keyne quietly.

"Why though?" asked Ailsa, frustrated. "It's not like she knows me."

Vega's mouth twisted to the side. "Maybe you should talk to her alone."

No. Absolutely not. "If she's got something to say, she can come speak to me."

Maalik appeared at her side, placing a plate of food down between them. "Did Rain leave?"

"She likes to storm out," said Ailsa with a huff. Was it her imagination or did Maalik and Vega share a knowing look?

"Never mind that," said Keyne, filling Maalik and Ailsa's glasses from the pitcher of water. "Let's talk about something more fun. What will you be wearing the day after tomorrow?"

125

"What's happening the day after tomorrow?" Ailsa asked absently, still flustered from the argument.

"It's the start of the Moon Rites. Every month, around the full moon, we hold three nights of ceremonies to celebrate the triple-headed goddess who gave us our magic." Keyne grinned. "It's basically just three days of partying. We dance and eat and ask the goddess for a good month."

"It's a time to remember our powers are a gift," added Vega.

Ailsa took a sip of water and considered this. "Even mine?"

"Don't let them get to you, Ailsa." Vega patted her arm. "Loads of people here are descendants of Ishbel Lauchair. It just so happens that you have the same power, but that was always going to happen at some point."

"Besides, the castle is on a mountain," said Keyne, "it's not like you can sink us—"

"Keyne!"

"What? Everyone is so touchy today." They scraped back from the table, flicking their robes out behind them. "Now, if you'll excuse me, I've got cleaning duty and then I'm going to go pine at the library door for a few hours."

"I'd better come too," said Vega, jumping up. "I told my mum I'd help her make butter cake for tonight's dessert."

Ailsa waved them off half-heartedly, then went back to staring dejectedly at the food. Great, so now she'd have to go to a party? And what was going on with Rain? *I really don't need this.*

"You know," said Maalik, chewing on a piece of fried potato. "I think the Rites might be your chance to ingratiate yourself."

"I usually spend parties hiding in the back," she mumbled. "How are the Rites supposed to make me seem more trustworthy?"

"It'll prove you're one of them. Vega said they thank the

goddess for their magic, maybe it'll remind everyone that your powers aren't evil. Plus, parties put people in a good mood."

"They don't put me in a good mood." Ailsa glowered. "The last one I went to ended in an explosion."

Maalik leaned in closer, brushing his shoulder against hers. "It might be fun," he said in a low voice. "We've never danced before."

Ailsa's mind immediately supplied the image. A dark room, dancing with Maalik, their bodies pressed together. "Will you… will we be able to do that?"

"I can still touch you," he said. "We shared a bed, didn't we? It's not that different."

She pursed her lips. "If you're sure…"

"Come on," he said, ducking his head. "Give me a tour of the rest of the castle. And if we just happen to end up in a certain tower—"

"We can't get in without the right blood."

He shrugged. "At least show me where it is."

"Okay." Ailsa drained the rest of her water but left the food. She knew she'd regret it later but maybe they could go past the kitchens and convince Vega to give them cake. For now, she wasn't hungry, especially not when the hall quietened again as they made their way out. Go to the party, have fun, make a good impression, earn their trust. It sounded like an insurmountable task, but it couldn't be that hard, could it?

Chapter 22

The joy from reuniting with Eilidh, Iona and Harris was short-lived, quickly turning back to worry and heartache when Angus told them what they'd missed. He found himself repeating what Moira had told them in disbelief, witnessing the same confusion and horror cross the selkies' faces.

Iona seemed particularly sickened by the news that his ancestor's remains were missing. Once he'd finished recounting the tale, they'd headed off to their own rooms to process and catch up on missed sleep.

Which had left Angus alone again. Duncan was off doing whatever kings did in war times and Cameron still hadn't appeared. It had been almost two days and Angus hadn't seen a trace of him. *Maybe he decided he hates me.* A part of him wanted to mope, to leave it at that, but he knew he'd never be satisfied until he found out why. Until he made sure Cameron was alright. Angus took one look at his empty room and knew he couldn't wait any longer, which was how he wound up in a sea of tents several hours later, his anxiety mounting.

He'd stood at the castle's entrance, making a list of possible hiding places. There was the university with its beautiful buildings or the theatre district, which he was sure would still be hosting plays or comedic acts. Cameron liked to paint; maybe he was in the Old Town, sketching the ramshackle structures or ornate fountains? But why wouldn't he have brought Angus?

Something told him that Cameron was punishing himself.

And where better to do that than in the army barracks?

Angus marched through the crowds of soldiers readying for war. Where should he even start? The camp took up much of the east side of the city and the maze of buildings and canvases would be difficult to navigate on a normal day. Now it was being dismantled, the tents packed up and ready to go. With all the activity, the soil had been churned up, coating everything and everyone in layers of dust and brown mud. Impossible.

A voice called out, halting Angus in his tracks. "Come to join the lowly commoners again, Your Highness?"

Angus turned, lips curling into a grin. "I was starting to miss the hours spent covered in blood and dirt."

The hulking man stepped out from behind a wagon, crossing his arms over his bare chest. Purple paint had been smeared down his face and neck, but it was fading under all the grime. The shorts he wore barely contained his tree trunk thighs and around his waist he'd tied a leather strap, covered in tiny daggers. He appraised Angus, looking down upon him from his significant height, but he gave an answering grin. "As long as the blood isn't yours you should wear it with pride."

"It's been a while, Gaven," Angus said, holding out his hand. The massive man took it immediately, clapping him on the shoulder for good measure. Angus almost stumbled from the force.

"A few years," Gaven agreed, letting go. "We were both scrawnier back then."

Angus snorted. "You were never scrawny."

"I was back at the old training camp recently. It looks a lot smaller. The new recruits look smaller too. Not as small as you did, mind, when you rocked up, pretending you were a couple of years older than you were."

Angus swallowed, imagining the hundreds of teenagers

that must have signed up to fight since Duncan's call went out. "I hope they'll have the chance to get bigger."

Gaven grunted his agreement. "Have you come to practise? Or have you gone soft up in your castle?"

"I can still swing a sword." Angus peered around. "I'm actually looking for someone. Do you remember Cameron?"

"Yeah, I do. He looks pretty scrawny too."

Angus's stomach flipped. "So, you've seen him?"

Gaven nodded. "I thought he'd fallen off the edge of the world until he walked into camp this morning."

"He's a mapmaker," Angus said. "He was off exploring until recently."

"That'll explain why he's so bad," Gaven said with a grunt. "He's been in the training ring, getting beaten up all day. He looked rough when he got here but I'll bet he looks even rougher now."

What the Hell was Cameron doing? "Could you point me in the right direction?"

Gaven's smile turned sly. "Still got a thing for him?"

"I thought we had a thing for each other," Angus sighed. Maybe he'd been wrong.

"That way," said the enormous man, pointing west through the tents. "Good luck."

"Thanks, Gaven," Angus said over his shoulder as he walked away. "See you on the battlefield."

Once Angus knew where to look, he found Cameron quickly. When Gaven had used the phrase *'training ring'* he'd been generous. The square of churned up dirt lay between a handful of tents that hadn't been broken down yet. The only things defining the space were some boulders, placed in the corners.

A few wooden posts had been driven into the ground, serving as training dummies. Some young soldiers milled around, testing their weapons but it was the nearest man who caught his eye.

Angus stalked forward, until he was right behind him. He waited until Cameron swung his sword, embedding it in the wood before demanding, "What are you doing?"

Cameron stiffened but didn't turn around. "I am training, Your Grace. It's what soldiers do."

Ah, that was how he was going to play this. "I thought you were a cartographer now?"

Cam pulled at the sword, ripping it from the post. "An army cartographer. I can still fight."

Angus rounded on him, positioning himself so Cameron would have to look at him. "You're still sick. What if you have a vision when you're on the battlefield?"

His face was mutinous. "Maybe it will give me an advantage over our enemy."

Angus threw his hands up. "Fine, if you're a soldier then so am I." He grabbed one of the wooden training swords from the bucket on the edge of the ring, swiping it back and forth for good measure.

"Don't be ridiculous," said Cameron from behind him.

Angus sniffed. "You shouldn't speak to your prince like that." He knew he was being pissy, but Cameron deserved it after leaving without a word.

Cam threw his sword down onto the soil and followed Angus to a post. "Well, which are you? A soldier or my prince?"

"Both," said Angus, adjusting his feet and his shoulders in a way that had once been familiar. "I trained at the same camp as you. I earned every scar and pain and punishment. So, if you're marching in my brother's army, I am too."

"Your brother needs you, Angus. Your people need you."

"I'm only a second son and my brother already has an

heir." There was a pressure on Angus's chest, and he looked down to see Cameron's hand fisted in his shirt.

"That's not why he needs you and you know it."

Something inside him snapped and the next thing Angus knew he had Cameron pushed against the pole, stunned and flushed. Gods, he was only a few inches taller, why did Angus have to tilt his head back so much? "And do you? Need me? Because I need you. I didn't realise how much I needed you until I saw you in Ephraim. I was like a starving man who suddenly remembered I needed food. And what if something happens to you? What will I do then?"

Cameron licked his lips. "Angus, we can't do this."

"I know, you keep rehashing the same argument." Angus crowded into him, noting how Cam's eyes dilated. "You're a commoner, I'm your prince. But what if I want to be *your* prince, just yours, no one else's?"

"I need to fight for my country," he said weakly. "It's what I was trained for."

Angus tossed the wooden sword to the side, placing his hands on Cameron's hips instead. This close it was easy to track the tiny flutters of Cam's eyelashes. "Fine. But I'll be fighting by your side. And since I am your prince, I outrank you, so you'll do as I say."

A shiver ran through Cameron. "And what's your first order?"

"First, you're going to try your best to knock me on my ass and when you fail, I'm going to take you back up to that castle, run you a bath and you're going to get in it."

Cameron's throat bobbed. "I don't deserve you."

"Does that mean you're not going to leave me again?" asked Angus, searching his face. "Because you can't keep doing that. You're mine and I'm yours, alright?"

But instead of answering, Cameron surged forward to

capture Angus's lips in a scorching but brief kiss. "I probably don't have the strength to stay away," he admitted into Angus's open mouth.

"Good." Angus brushed a kiss to his nose. "Now, come on, let's get this over with. Iona, Harris and Eilidh will want to see you before tonight's meeting too."

Cam's eyes lit up. "They made it back?"

"You'd have known that if you hadn't run away," Angus teased.

Cameron reached up to lace his fingers into Angus's hair. "New plan. We head back now so I can say hello, I'll have a bath and *then* I'll knock you on your ass."

"Deal." Angus pulled away but Cameron held on tight.

"I won't leave again," he promised, solemnly.

Angus took his hand, so they were palm to palm, their heartbeats mingling. "I'm holding you to that."

Chapter 23

Burning. Irené's lungs were burning. But how could that be when there was no fire? Only water pushed at her sealed lips, begging entry as she held onto her last breath. So much had already blown from her nostrils, on a silent scream. She pushed back desperately against the hand holding her, fighting to get her head above water. But she couldn't hold on anymore.

She opened her mouth, unable to stop the inevitable. Her body acted on impulse and the water came rushing in and down her windpipe, freezing her insides.

Suddenly Irené was pulled back by the roots of her hair and she had air once again. Her lungs fought to purge the unwanted liquid and she doubled over, emptying their contents and what little food she'd had in her stomach too.

"How about now?" The voice was full of mirth and hidden knives.

Irené curled inwards, her cheek to the wooden floor. She rubbed her skin against the grains, allowing the feeling to centre her. How many times had they done this? "I can't," she croaked.

"You will eventually," said Chao, leaning his long body over hers like a shadow from her nightmares. "The power is in you somewhere, just waiting to come out. That or you'll die, and I'll have to find someone else. We've already lost one. His wings hadn't yet grown in properly, but I enjoyed plucking them off when he was dead anyway. I'll try his brother next."

"Wouldn't it be easier to find someone who already has magic?" Irené gasped.

"That wouldn't be any fun. This way I get to shape you—make you into the image I desire. We require very specific talents, Princess and—"

"You've been down here an awfully long time, brother," a familiar voice whispered from the doorway.

Irené shivered, unwilling to look at the newcomer. That way, she knew, was madness.

"She's holding out on me," crooned Chao. "But she'll come round."

The other god moved silently—he didn't exactly have a body with which to make noises—yet Irené could feel him moving closer. Desper was a void: a black hole where there was no light, no goodness. She'd once thought demons were the epitome of fear, until she'd watched when Desper had reached inside one and devoured its every happiness. It had happened in a flash, leaving behind nothing but a husk. And then Desper had turned to Chao and offered to do the same to Irené. For a moment Irené thought Chao would take him up on his offer. But thankfully, her captor was greedy. He wished to break Irené himself, the slow, torturous way. And she was grateful because every time she surfaced from drowning, at least she was still herself.

"You should try a new method," Desper said in a whisper-soft voice. "Ice perhaps?"

Irené watched Chao's smirk curl up his cheeks. "Perhaps."

"For now, I have some news. The Eilanmòr army is readying to head south."

"I thought our spy was captured?" said Chao.

Desper laughed and Irené cut her gaze to him, unable to stop herself. The shadow parted, raising his hand and opening it to reveal a tiny bird. It lay still against the writhing mass of darkness that was his palm, its neck bent at an angle and its chest unmoving. But then Desper snapped a finger on his other hand and the bird twitched. Irené watched in revulsion as it flapped its wings and flipped over so it could stand.

"Where there is death, I have spies," said Desper.

Irené closed her eyes, dropping her head down onto the cold floor again. Perhaps if they thought she was sleeping, they'd leave her there for a while. Still, she couldn't let her exhaustion pull her under. If she listened carefully, even if she didn't understand it all, perhaps she could help her friends when she escaped. *And I will escape*, she told herself fiercely.

"Does that mean you'll be sending the next wave?" asked Chao with a chuckle.

What's the next wave?

Desper hummed. "Dolor and Timor are leaving also."

"And is the structure ready?"

"Tomorrow. Merlo has assured me."

"When will I have him?"

"Patience. Focus on your current projects."

"Two out of four. But you won't last much longer, will you, princess?"

"I'll leave you to it then," said Desper, his voice further away now. "Have fun."

Irené tried to relax, breathing slowly in what she hoped was a good impression of sleep. For a long moment, she thought it had worked, that Chao had left too. Then there was a burning pain as the god gripped her hair, pulling her head back so he could leer at her. "Wake up, little princess. Desper had a good idea." His smile curled up his cheeks, splitting the skin. Irené was going to vomit. "I wonder what ice will do to that pretty mind. Let's play."

Chapter 24

Angus sat with his back against the claw-footed tub, absorbing the warmth. Droplets of sweat traced their way under his shirt, but he had no plans to bathe himself. No, the hot, lemon-scented water was for Cameron. Angus had called for it as soon as they got back to his room, and he'd heard Cameron sink into it with a grateful sigh from outside the door. He was about to go lie down on the bed when he heard his name being called softly.

"Angus?"

"Yes?"

"Would you mind sitting with me for a while?"

That was how Angus found himself sitting on the bathing room's floor, tracing patterns into the condensation on the tiles and resolutely refusing to look at the handsome man naked in his bath.

"I can't believe I'm in the prince's tub," said Cameron. "What did I do to deserve this luxury?"

Angus chuckled. "I've got to be honest; your shoulders have a lot to do with it."

"You like my shoulders?"

"Obviously." Angus leaned his head back. "And your chest, your eyes; don't get me started on your hands—"

"They've got nicks and calluses all over them," said Cameron with a laugh.

"They're graceful," argued Angus, picturing Cameron's fine wrist bones, his snaking blue veins and long fingers.

"You've got painter's hands."

"I've been told they give good head massages too." The water sloshed and Angus felt Cameron's palms on the sides of his head. "May I?"

"You should be relaxing," Angus admonished, nevertheless closing his eyes and leaning into the touch. "Are you feeling sick?"

"I've got a bit of a headache, as usual, but let me look after you for once." He threaded his fingers through Angus's hair and began to knead his scalp.

Angus let himself sink into the feeling for a moment. He'd always loved his hair being played with, but it was even better with Cameron doing it. He wanted Cameron, sometimes so much he couldn't breathe until he kissed him, but this felt intimate in a whole new way.

"I'll give you a head rub when you're out of the bath," he promised. "And then we have to go to Duncan's meeting. I heard he's found and promoted some old friends of his so there'll be new blood to combat General Fraser's crankiness. Now that Harris, Iona and Eilidh are here, I think he wants to form a plan, maybe even march south."

"Shouldn't we wait for Ailsa?" asked Cameron, his voice strained.

"That depends on how close Mirandelle is." Angus placed a hand over Cam's. "Ailsa will turn up soon. She's tough."

Cameron sighed. "I know. She always was when we were wee too. But I still worry about her. That's what big brothers do."

"Well, I'm glad I'm not one. I don't think I could deal with all of this half as well as Duncan."

"You would, you know," said Cameron quietly. "I hope it never happens, but you would do a good job as king."

Angus hummed non-committally. "The meeting's in an hour. I'll go get a robe for you and then when you're ready to get out I'll give you that massage."

"Okay." Cameron removed his hands from Angus's head, slipping them back into the water. "But I'll probably fall asleep."

"That's maybe a good idea." He hesitated. "As long as I get to hold you while you do."

"I don't deserve you," Cameron sighed.

I love you. The words were on the tip of Angus's tongue, but he swallowed them down. "Be back in a second." He pushed off the floor hoping Cameron thought his blush was just from the heat.

Good gods, I'm in trouble.

***

Angus laced his fingers with Cameron's, tugging him through the corridors. He smelled of the lemon bath oils and Angus had to fight the urge to pull him into an alcove, just so he could wrap his body around Cameron's.

"Not the library?" Cam asked, halting. "That's where we met before."

"Last time the meeting was unofficial. I think he wants to put on a show since he hired those new advisors."

"Does that mean General Fraser won't be there?"

Angus sighed. "He can't get rid of him, not without losing the support of my father's counsellors. But he'll be outnumbered."

"It's funny, I really would have had Fraser pegged as the traitor. I wouldn't trust him as far as I could throw him." Cameron clicked his tongue. "He doesn't think men should be with other men you know."

Angus shrugged. "A shame his opinion doesn't matter."

"Still," Cameron pulled them up short just outside the door, "maybe we shouldn't go in holding hands—"

"Cam—" Angus started to protest.

"I just don't want anyone disagreeing with you because of it." He brought Angus's hand to his heart. "I'm in this with you, I really am, but we have to be careful."

"Fine, but as soon as this meeting is over, prepare to be held. You won't be able to get me off you."

Cameron grinned, dropping a quick kiss to Angus's temple. "Deal." Then he stepped away, putting a pointed distance between them.

Angus took a deep breath, reaching for the door handle. "Okay, let's do this."

The room was already packed with people, some seated around a long table and others standing against the walls. A fire burned hot in the hearth, making the space stuffy and dim from the smoke. Angus briefly shared a nod of greeting with Harris, Iona and Eilidh. The women sat beside Duncan while Harris stood behind his sister, hands on her shoulders. He recognised General Fraser and some others who had served under his father but there were new faces too, younger men and women.

"Angus, good," said Duncan, waving at the only empty seat. "Sit down."

Already they were being separated. Cameron shrugged, moving to the wall like the other soldiers around the room.

"This is newly promoted General Calum MacKenzie." Duncan indicated the burly man with long dark hair, tied in a knot beside him. "He used to train the new recruits down at the barracks. Including me when I was young. And this," he nodded to a sharp-eyed woman, "is Nessa Milne. We studied together at university before I quit. She's already top of her field in the research of physical science." He waved down the table. "Colonel Kyle Aitken, Major Leslie McPhee and Major Rowan Findlay."

As Angus had heard their names, he thought he

remembered some of them, though perhaps only from Duncan's stories. His brother had filled his table with old friends. Angus approved.

"Now that everyone has been introduced," said the king, "let's get on with it. General MacKenzie?"

The General's voice was gravelly. "Reports have come from the coast of Mirandelle's armada. Merlo has a few dozen ships in the strait between our countries."

"Pillaging?" asked Iona.

He shook his head. "Not a single boat has landed on Eilanmòrian soil. They seem to be waiting for something. Between them they've been building something with timber, in the sea between their ships, but our scouts can't tell what it is."

"What are the chances that it's a distraction?"

"It could be, especially after their failed kidnapping." The General's eyes flicked to his king. "But no one has seen any war ships sailing north. The only way to get from Mirandelle to Eilanmòr is by sea. I doubt Merlo would waste his fleet by using them for a diversion. Heading south to meet them is the best chance we have at stopping their advance."

Duncan tapped on the table. "The plan has three parts: gaining allies, securing Dunrigh, and preparing for battle. Let's start with the first. Harris, you said Irené's crew plan to join us?"

The selkie nodded. "That's what they said. But they need to head back to Edessa first to repair their boat."

"I've written to Edessa for aid and to inform them of what happened to their princess. Next, Vashkha will take Douglas to Visenya on our fastest ship. I want my queen and son as far away from the war as possible. They'll be safe with her father, and he can help her convince Queen Viveca to send Visenya's fleet."

"When do they leave?" asked Angus. He'd need to find them after the meeting to say goodbye.

"Tomorrow morning," said Duncan. "We can't wait."

"I'm leaving tomorrow too," Iona added. "To head back to Struanmuir."

"You're asking the selkies for help?" Angus guessed.

But it was Duncan who answered. "If we're going to win this, we'll need the support of every Eilanmòrian, including those who are fae."

General Fraser made a noise of disbelief. "Are you certain they can be trusted? They no longer have a leader."

"Just because their queen is dead, it doesn't mean they don't have leaders," General MacKenzie fired back. "Though it will be harder to unite them. Any fae who are willing to fight are welcome." He turned to the rest of the room. "We aim to reach Inshmore in a week. Once there we'll set up camp. If Merlo can wait, so can we. We'll meet back in Inshmore and hope our allies find us there too."

"But our armies are merely backup," said Duncan, eyeing the map, where miniature ships sailed the painted waters. "What I'm about to tell you all does not leave this room. The only way to defeat the Edaxi is with the Four Treasures: four magic objects. And only those fae with certain magic can wield them." The soldiers and advisors were quiet, taking this in. "We have to get our fae champions close enough to the gods and then the war will be over. Merlo will run with his tail tucked between his legs." Duncan raised his chin. "Have you had any word from Miss MacAra?"

"Nothing. Have you?" Angus asked the selkies.

Iona shook her head. "She'll find us, though."

"Unless the Edaxi already have the spear and Ailsa is on a fool's errand." Harris grimaced. "If we don't have Ailsa or her demon," whispers went around the room at the word, "we'll need to find some other fae with air and fire magic. We'll need a backup—"

"We don't need a backup because Ailsa will find us," Angus cut in firmly. "The question is: how are we going to get the Stone of Destiny back from the Edaxi?"

"Sneak in?" Harris suggested.

"Too dangerous," Duncan decided. "We'll worry about that when we get to the coast." He leaned back in his chair. "General Fraser and General MacKenzie will lead our armies south in the morning. Colonel Aitken will remain here in Dunrigh with our less experienced soldiers. Barricade the city and wait for our return. Vashkha will head to Visenya and Iona will go to Struanmuir. Angus and Harris, stick with me. You're all dismissed."

The room filled with chatter and the sounds of chairs scraping against the wooden floor. Angus skirted the table, reaching the back wall where Cameron stood. He had just grabbed Cam's arm, turning for the door, when he heard Duncan's voice again.

"And Cameron?"

At the mention of Cam's name, Angus jumped. He met his brother's steely gaze and felt his stomach flutter.

If Cameron was surprised to be suddenly addressed, he hid it well. "Yes, Your Highness?"

"You're to protect my brother. I want you as his personal bodyguard." Duncan gave him a wink. "I know you'll be the best person for the job."

Cameron nodded, murmuring a quiet acknowledgement before dragging Angus out of the room.

"What was that?" asked Angus. "Did my brother really just wink at you?"

"Looks like you're stuck with me." Cam grinned and Angus let that sink in, feeling lighter than he had in days.

New faces, new rules. Things were changing around Dunrigh and Angus liked it.

Chapter 25

Iona remained at the table while the rest of Duncan's inner circle filed out. She caught a quick glance of Angus and Cameron through the open door, wrapped up in each other as if they were the only people in the entire world.

Gods, I've missed that. She was happy for them, she truly was, but it was bittersweet. Every time she saw another couple kiss or stare longingly at each other, she was always reminded of what she'd lost. Iona thought of the portrait, a few levels down from the meeting room and tucked away along a corridor. There, paintings of the McFeidh family hung but it was King Alasdair's picture she returned to, time and time again. She'd need to visit it tonight, to look upon his dear face, before she headed back to Struanmuir.

In the meantime, there were other McFeidhs to offer comfort to. Duncan, Angus and Eilidh were Alasdair's grandchildren. It was her duty to look after them.

She bit her lip, eyes flicking from Eilidh on her right to Duncan seated on her left. Of course, the king had no idea the woman on the other side of Iona was his sister. Still, it wouldn't hurt for them to get to know each other. "Your Majesty, have you met our friend Eilidh?"

Duncan lifted his gaze from the map. "Call me Duncan, Iona. Nice to meet you, Eilidh. Iona told me you found the Sword of Light?"

Eilidh shrugged. "My mother had it. You may have heard of her, Agneta Daalgard?"

"Of course." Duncan's grin was wide. "I heard many stories of her as a child. I didn't realise she had a daughter."

"Adopted," said Eilidh.

"Eilidh is half-fae," explained Harris behind them. "She's going to take the Stone of Destiny, once we get it back."

"Well, thank you." Duncan stood, shuffling his papers. "And welcome to the team. Harris, you'd better make sure you look after our guest."

"I have a daughter," Eilidh blurted out. "She's three. You have a son, don't you?"

Duncan's lips curved into a soft smile. "Douglas. He's just almost three months old." He placed a hand on her shoulder. "We will win this. For them." Then he was gone, following his soldiers through the door.

Eilidh slumped back into her chair. "I didn't realise he was so tall."

"Tempted to tell him?" Iona guessed.

"Not yet." She pushed herself to her feet. "I'm going to pack. Please come find me before you go?"

"Will do," said Iona, patting her hand.

As soon as Eilidh was gone from the room, Harris dropped into her seat and kicked his feet up onto the table. "You're going to miss all the drama."

Iona rolled her eyes. "Are you going to be alright?"

He gave her a tired smile. "You've left me alone before, right?"

"That's not what I meant. You weren't doing great on the boat. Do you think you can keep it together?"

"You need to stop worrying about me, I'll be fine."

"I'm your big sister," she said, poking him in the side. "That's impossible."

"Stop clucking and have a safe trip," Harris said firmly. "Tell Aunt Caitlyn and the cousins I said hello."

Iona stood, leaning down to wrap him in a tight hug. "You'll see them yourself soon, hopefully," she said into his hair.

"Love you, Iona." He squeezed her back even tighter. "Be safe."

***

Iona made it to Eilidh's room, right beside her own, an hour later, after she'd sweet-talked the cooks into giving her some treats. It was going to be a long swim and she was determined not to stop. She'd need the energy or that's what she had told them anyway. Now, full of sugar, she knocked on the princess's door.

"Hey, you heading off?" Eilidh asked when she opened it. She was wearing a long, silk robe, similar to one Iona had in her own rooms. Her golden hair was in a braid, showing off her delicately pointed ears.

Iona hovered outside. "Yes. I just wanted to say thank you again for coming. I know you didn't want to."

"It's not been as bad as I thought it would," said Eilidh. "I probably should have got out of the inn before now."

"Still, you miss Maggie."

Eilidh smiled sadly. "Obviously. But perhaps, when it's safe, we can travel together. I don't want her to be trapped like I was. And I realised tonight, after meeting Duncan, I want her to know her uncles, her aunt and cousin. Eventually."

"I'm sure, when Duncan finds out, he'll be over the moon." She hesitated. "Speaking of family, I hate to ask another favour, but would you look out for Harris for me? He seems like he's back to his old self, but I know better. He blames himself for Irené being taken."

Eilidh nodded. "I'll stick close."

"Thank you, Eilidh." Iona leaned forward to pull the other woman into an embrace. Eilidh returned it fully, her body soft and warm and smelling of cinnamon. It was exactly the sort of hug that would comfort a worried child and Iona allowed herself to melt into it for a moment. "Meet you on the battlefield," she said, letting go.

"Stay safe." Eilidh waited by her door until Iona was at hers, waving as she closed it with a click that echoed in the empty corridor. Then Iona was alone.

Well, there's no point in delaying.

Her movements were quick and precise as she lit some candles and pulled out her backpack, the one she'd packed when she last left Dunrigh. She upended it, spreading the items over the bed covers she wouldn't be sleeping in. The spare clothes and bedroll had already been taken to be washed, leaving behind a small pile. A tin mug with rust speckling the sides, a flint in its sewn leather pouch, a creased map of Eilanmòr. Those were the useful things, but she'd also managed to accumulate some trinkets on her travels. There was a picture Eilidh's daughter had drawn for her; the scribbled figure had long red hair, so Iona had assumed it was meant to be her. Next was an old brass brooch she'd found half buried in the dirt. She'd slipped it into her bag when she'd noticed it was a rendering of a squirrel. Lastly, there was a well-worn book she'd found in her room on the boat. She'd only got a few chapters in, but it looked like the soldier loved the princess after all.

It only took the length of a breath to decide. *Breathe in. Breathe out.* And then she turned from the pile. Where she was going, she didn't need anything except the tiny stone cauldron in her pocket. But then something left inside the bag caught her eye. She plucked it out, holding it out in front of her. The blade was small, meant more for breaking down tinder than for defence. But she slipped it into her dress anyway. *Better safe than sorry.*

Iona blew out the candles again and tied her cloak around her shoulders, slipping out of the room before she could get too sentimental. The hallways were dark, most people tucked up in their beds. Let them sleep. She briefly considered knocking on Angus's door to say goodbye to him and Cameron, but her heart was already heavy from the farewells exchanged with Harris and Eilidh. She'd see them again soon anyway—once she'd convinced the other selkies to join in their fight.

But that was a future problem. Right now, Iona felt a little giddy. She was going home. And she wouldn't be travelling by horse or by foot either. No, now there was nothing to stop her.

The guards at the castle doors let her through with a nod. They didn't care about those leaving, only someone arriving posed a risk. Iona hurried down the hill towards the town and out the gate to the streets of Dunrigh. Though the locals were readying to leave, the lanterns had been lit and music was still floating out of many windows, as if they needed the light and the songs to soothe their worries. Iona's feet danced over the cobblestones, through the Old Town towards the theatre district.

When she'd first come to Dunrigh, she'd been amazed by the plays and concerts she'd seen. She'd taken in a show almost every night, watching the dancers move their bodies with fierce attention. Back then, she had never believed she could move her own human body that way. But then she'd practised at the ceilidhs she'd attended and one night a handsome prince had made dancing seem as easy as breathing.

Eventually, she heard it, the sounds of water flowing and churning. The River Snecky had many bridges crossing it, some leading to the barracks, others leading to the temples and kirks of various religions and deities. But she didn't aim for them. Instead, she strode to the bank and kicked her shoes off, grabbing them from the dusty ground and sticking each one in a pocket in her cloak. Then, with a grin, she padded down to the water's edge and stuck a toe in.

Thank goodness the water is clean, Iona thought as her body changed. Otherwise, this would be very unpleasant. In the blink of an eye her human body was gone, along with anything she had been wearing, and she was a seal once again. She dove into the river, swimming towards the middle where the current was fast. In her new skin, she didn't have to worry about the cold, or drowning. She let the water carry her through the town, towards the gates.

Chapter 26

Harris paced in front of the hearth, only seeing the flames during every other turn when his good eye was turned toward the fireplace. But he tried not to think about that. *Keep busy, keep moving.* That was the only way to keep the darkness away. It was why he hadn't been able to return to his room after the meeting. He couldn't stand the long, stretching emptiness, the silence. At least here there were still echoes of life.

He came to a stop in front of the huge table, scattered with maps and models. These were Duncan's battle plans. The tiny longboats denoted everywhere on the west coast of Eilanmòr that the Avalognian raiders had hit. As yet there were only a few, on and around the Isle of Faodail. His stomach twisted, hoping they were still far away from Iona's path. But it was to the south that most of the enemy waited. Instead of longships, galleons were positioned in the water between Mirandelle and Eilanmòr. Thankfully, though, it wasn't only rival ships on the map. Aside from Eilanmòr's own navy, fleets were on their way from Akrosia and Edessa, and Duncan thought it was only a matter of time until his wife could convince the Visenyans to join them.

Harris snapped his gaze back to the Mirandelli ships. Right in the middle, someone had placed a token etched with a question mark. Duncan had said the Mirandellis were constructing something, and Harris had a feeling that it wasn't just a distraction.

"That's where they'll be," he whispered to himself. He didn't know how, but his gut told him what they were building was integral to whatever grand plan the Edaxi had.

There was a noise from the hall and Harris drew his hand back from the figures just before someone appeared in the doorway. Eilidh wore a pale, cotton nightgown and her golden hair glistened in the candlelight. As before, Harris felt a pull towards her, deep in his bones. *It's because she's your queen.* Even if Eilidh didn't want the crown, there was deep magic in her blood that she'd never be rid of. That would forever have an effect on Harris and every other fae she came across. It should have been invasive, the innate need to serve and protect, but Eilidh was so godsdamned *nice* that Harris couldn't resent her.

"I didn't think anyone else would be up," she said. "Sorry, I didn't mean to disturb you."

"It's okay, I was just pondering the map and what we're about to face. You couldn't sleep?"

"I feel fidgety. My legs want to be up and doing things. Going for a walk was my first plan."

"What's your second?" He dropped into a seat.

She grinned. "Going for a fly."

His lips twitched to return her smile. "My sister said you can turn into a flock of birds?"

"Amongst other things." Eilidh shrugged. "I've tried squirrels and hedgehogs and lizards and beetles. I can't go any bigger than a rabbit, though."

Interesting. "What's your favourite?"

"Magpies. I always used to watch them outside the window when I was wee. They were the first things I turned into, so that I could fly around with them. My guardian thought she'd lost me for a full hour."

It struck Harris how blurred the line between different magic was. As a faerie, Eilidh was an earth fae and selkies had water powers, yet they could both change their bodies, becoming beasts of forest and brine. "I wonder if your shapeshifting is the same as my shapeshifting. Does it feel like you're turning into liquid and back again?"

She pursed her lips, considering this. "No, it feels like I'm being squeezed through a hole that's too small. It only lasts a second though."

"It must be useful, being able to fly," Harris said wistfully. "Or being small enough to listen in on conversations without being caught."

Eilidh nodded. "It's the only reason I'm glad I'm part fae. When one of Nicnevan's cronies came looking for me, it was easy to hide. As I got older, I started fighting back too."

"Do you think you're ready?" asked Harris, indicating the battle map. "It seems everyone in Ossiana is counting on you."

Eilidh sat across from him, pulling her legs into her chest. "I only care about one person: my daughter, Maggie."

"And her father?" asked Harris.

"Someone in the nearby village. I've never really been interested in romance, but I thought I would try a relationship out, see if I just didn't know what I was missing. I worked out pretty quickly that it isn't for me."

"But motherhood?"

"I suppose all my love was meant for her," she said with a smile. "What about you?"

Harris ran a hand through his hair, tugging at the roots. "I don't think I know what love is. I've had many dalliances over the years, but no one held me—" *Except Irené.* "A friend of mine—she's different. But just when I thought I had finally found someone, she was stolen from me. A literal divine intervention," he joked darkly.

"This was the princess," guessed Eilidh, "the one who was taken by Chao?"

An image of Irené's terrified face flashed before him. "She's also a privateer captain," he croaked. "She is truly one of the most fascinating people I have ever met, but she's also funny, kind, intelligent and strong."

Eilidh tilted her head like a bird. "It seems like your heart had no chance."

She was right. "I'm going to get her back," he told her, his voice hard.

"We will," said Eilidh kindly. "Once we've defeated—"

"No, I'm going to get her back." Suddenly it was very important that he said this out loud, that someone knew what he'd do to rescue Irené. "I'm not going to wait for other people to save her. As soon as we get to the coast, I'm going off to find her."

"You can't do that, you'll be captured and killed, either by the Mirandellis or by the Edaxi." Eilidh shivered. "Though I think I can guess which of those would be worse."

He turned to the fireplace, narrowing his eye at the flames. "I don't see any other option."

"Do you even know where they're keeping her?"

"I have my suspicions." Mirandelle for now, most likely. And then there was that mysterious wooden structure.

"Harris." Eilidh sighed. "I barely know you, but I know your friends would be devastated if you were hurt. Irené would be devastated if you were hurt. Maybe there's some other way we can get to her, without you sacrificing yourself. You can't help her if you're dead."

Right again. Harris wanted to be reckless, to storm their stronghold and rescue his princess, even if he had to die to do it. But he had to make sure Irené got out first. "Perhaps I could do some reconnaissance? They're out at sea and I can swim. I could swim to the boats in seal form and then turn human and sneak on."

Eilidh considered this, eyeing him carefully. Then, with deliberate movements, she held out her hand. "Could you use another shapeshifter?"

Harris blinked. "You want to help me?"

"Maybe it's time to start being brave," she said.

So, Harris began to plan, studying the maps and shifting counters. Eilidh offered her ideas until her voice trailed off. The next time Harris looked up, she was asleep with her head cushioned by her arms.

Harris let his gaze trail over her sleeping form, drinking her in. Nicnevan had been a terrifying monarch, inspiring fear rather than respect. But Eilidh—he wondered what the future would be like for fae with her leading them, offering insight and gentle smiles and love.

If there is a life after this war, he decided, *I want to make that happen.*

And so, Harris carried his sleeping queen to her room, the future a little brighter than it had been before.

Chapter 27

Angus should have woken with a million worries on his mind. He should have dreaded leaving his home, the long journey ahead of them, and the looming battle at the end. He shouldn't have got any sleep at all, lying awake all night brooding about his friends and family scattering to the wind. And it wasn't that he didn't care about all those things, but having a warm body pressing into his back and strong arms banding his stomach made them seem a lot more manageable.

I will never get used to this, he thought as he listened to Cameron's light snores. But I want to try. Time was not something he'd considered a luxury before, but suddenly Angus was greedy for it. He wanted thousands of mornings like this, stretched out ahead of them. Time to laugh and cry and smile and kiss. But what if they didn't get it? What if they were hurtling towards a near end?

Angus's chest was tighter than it had been moments ago. He rubbed it with his knuckles, dislodging Cameron's arm in the process.

"I can hear you overthinking," came a murmur behind him.

Angus bit the inside of his cheek. "That's usually your job."

Cameron pulled him closer, until he could tuck his chin onto Angus's shoulder. "What's wrong?" he asked, his breath tickling Angus's ear.

"I don't want this to end. I woke up feeling so happy but what if it doesn't last?"

Cameron dropped a kiss into Angus's hair. "I'm going to keep you safe. Trust your bodyguard."

I do. But... "What if something happens to you?"

"That doesn't sound like trust." Cameron shuffled behind him, extracting his arm so he could lift himself up over Angus. "Here, I'll show you how good I am." Then he flattened himself to Angus like a blanket and snuffled his hair.

Angus was sure Cameron was trying to make him laugh, but instead a squeak burst out of him as soon as Cameron's body covered his own. They'd both removed their shirts the night before and the feel of Cam's bare chest against his own was suddenly much different to the comfort he'd felt with the other man at his back. He tried to turn the noise into a cough, cheeks heating with embarrassment. Cameron lifted his head, eyes questioning, and Angus tried to turn away but a thumb on his chin stopped him, holding him in place.

"You know I'm in this with you, right?" Cam asked.

"I just really like you," said Angus, trailing a hand down his arm. "And we have to leave soon and then we'll be on the road, and something could happen—"

"Listen to me," Cameron cut him off. "We're going to protect each other. Your brother made sure we'd be stuck together over the next couple of weeks; I'm not going anywhere. And when the world is safe again and we're back in this huge comfy bed, I'm going to let you show me how much you like me."

Angus felt a grin tug at his mouth. "Are you sure?"

"Well, you could give me some previews. I'm pretty sure we can find a dark corner of a tent to snog in," Cam said with a wink.

Angus reached up to tuck a piece of hair behind Cameron's ear. It was getting long now, and the pink had faded almost back to a light brown. "Does it have to be a dark corner? I want to kiss you out in the sun."

"Do you think you're allowed?"

"No offence," said Angus, "but do you really think my brother made you my bodyguard because of your fighting prowess?"

Cameron raised an eyebrow. "What are you implying?"

"He was giving us his blessing. And he knows you'll look after me, not just because you're a skilled soldier, but because you care about me." He bit his lip. "Right?"

Cam's face grew serious. "You're everything I've ever wanted."

Wow. "So, you do care—"

"—love you," said Cameron. "I love you."

It took Angus's brain a long moment to absorb the words, to feel them in every nerve ending, but then he was surging up to capture Cameron's lips with his own, the kiss as essential as breathing. He felt the tension leak out of Cam's jaw as he returned it, letting the fear and doubt be replaced with warm adoration.

***

Outside his bedroom walls, the castle was a hive of activity. Shouldering his packed bag, Angus dodged between servants carrying supplies and soldiers collecting weapons. He'd left Cam to get his things together but now he wished for his steady presence again. *This is something you have to do yourself.* He really couldn't be late.

He took the stairs two at a time until he reached the entrance hall where a crowd was already gathered. Angus didn't stop though, pushing through them towards the huge double doors and out into the courtyard. The remains of the Peace Tree seemed to suck in all the light, a massive black stain upon the cobblestones. He spotted Duncan's shaved head through the portcullis.

Angus raced to his side and skidded to a halt. "Thank the gods," he huffed.

Vashkha smiled indulgently down at him. "Which ones?" she asked.

"The good ones. Wherever they are."

Seeing Vashkha in travelling clothes was an odd sight. Gone were her bright tunics and mirrored embellishments, replaced by simple khaki trousers and a black shawl, pulled up over her dark hair. "I hope they can hear us," she said, patting him on the cheek.

"Now," Angus said, rounding on his brother. "No one is going anywhere until I get a hug from my favourite nephew."

Duncan rolled his eyes as he rocked his son in his arms. "He can barely hold his head up let alone hug you."

"I can make up for it then." Angus took Douglas from Duncan, careful to support his neck. In the weeks Angus had been away, his nephew had grown fast, in length and in weight. "You're such a chunker," he cooed. "But that's okay, all the best babies are."

"Will you please stop calling my son fat," grumbled Duncan with a grin.

"I've heard your dad was so chunky when he was a baby that he broke his crib," Angus continued.

Douglas's mouth split into a gummy grin, clearly enjoying the noises Angus was making.

"You'd better look after your mother when you're away." Angus dropped a kiss onto the infant's downy head. "And I'll look after your father."

"You'd better," said Vashkha, taking Douglas from him. "I want my boys back here in one piece. All of them." She rubbed Angus's arm, making sure he knew he was included.

"Okay, I'll let you say goodbye to each other." He patted Vashkha's hand before walking away. "Keep the kissing family friendly, though. Douglas doesn't need to see that."

"Good luck," called Vashkha with a chuckle.

"You too."

Angus was almost back to the Peace Tree when he chanced a look back over his shoulder. Silhouetted in the arch of the gate, Duncan held his wife and son. His and Vashkha's eyes were closed, as if they were committing each other's feel and scent to memory. They were a constant in the chaos, the crowds parting around them like forks in a river.

We'll make it back, Angus vowed, turning back to the castle.

"Angus," Eilidh called, appearing in the doorway. When he waved her over, she started towards him, tugging someone with a shock of red hair behind her.

Angus blinked, watching Eilidh pull a tired looking Harris along, his hand in hers. *That's new,* he thought with a frown. "Are you ready to go?".

Eilidh nodded. "All packed."

"Is there a horse for me?" asked Harris.

"There should be. Hands off the unicorn though. She's mine." His eyes flicked down to where Harris was still holding Eilidh's hand. *Should I tell him the same goes for my sister?*

Harris's nose wrinkled underneath the straps of his eyepatch. "I wouldn't go near your murderous beast if you paid me. Want me to find you one, Eilidh?"

"Yes, thank you," she said, crossing her arms behind her back.

Angus waited until Harris stride off to the stables before he rounded on his sister. "Since when have you two been such good friends?"

"Iona wanted me to keep an eye on him," she said haughtily. "He's a notorious flirt, you know."

"Are you really getting overprotective? He's being helpful.

Besides, he's desperate to find Princess Irené. From what Iona told me, he barely ate on the Nymph."

Angus bit his cheek, shifting his thoughts inside his head. "Really? He looks fine now." Angus had seen him smile numerous times since arriving. And yet, had it ever reached his eyes?

"It's all a façade," Eilidh told him, lowering her voice. "A single crack and it'll all come tumbling down. He lost a woman he cares deeply about—and his eye—in one moment."

He mentally kicked himself. *I've probably been too wrapped up in Cameron to notice.* "Should he be coming with us? Maybe he should stay here."

"He needs to come," she said firmly. "We'll look after him."

"Look after who?" said a voice behind Angus that never failed to send shivers down his spine. "You know I'm Angus's bodyguard, don't go angling for my job." Cameron kept his body at a respectable distance but his hands cupped Angus's shoulders. If anyone were to look at them, would they merely see a prince and his protector? Or would they notice everywhere Angus was leaning into him, like a flower to the sun?

Eilidh made an unladylike noise, pretending to be sick. "I've only known you're my brother for a few days and already I'm getting grossed out by you and your boyfriend."

"Because we're both men?" asked Cameron, sounding wounded.

She threw up her arms. "Because you're sickeningly perfect and need to get a room."

"Riding out in an hour!" called General MacKenzie. "Be ready. It's a day's march to the river and we're only stopping once."

Eilidh sighed. "I'd better go help Harris."

Angus watched her go, taking in the noises and smells of the castle courtyard as Cameron held him. "We'll be back, right?"

"If I do my job right," said Cameron. "Come on, let's get Laire ready to go." He tugged his prince along, weaving through the crowds of soldiers and servants preparing for the trip. Angus didn't miss the odd stares they received as they passed.

One day the world will be different, he promised himself as he rolled his shoulders back. *We'll make it different. We just have to save it first.*

Chapter 28

The sun was rising by the time Iona made it to the coast. It lit the sky above in pinks and golds. But she didn't stop to admire the ball of light as it reared up behind the rolling green hills. No, her black eyes were fixed on the ocean.

She'd slept in the wide, slow-moving estuary. As a seal, she only needed to snatch a couple of minutes here or there, bobbing in the water with her nose in the air. But as soon as she'd spotted the familiar outline of the Isle of Jay, she'd known she couldn't linger any longer. A few hours and she'd be home.

Iona dove under the breakers, the briny taste immediately coating her mouth. They called the water in rivers and lochs fresh, but this was what fresh tasted like—as though the sea was filling you up, stripping away any of the gunk and dust of life on land. Down she swam, propelling herself with her front flippers, using the back ones for direction. Though it was still early morning, her eyes easily adjusted to the half-dark. If she'd been human, she would have smiled or cheered. As a seal, she could only blow out a bubble in celebration.

The world below the waves was magical, much more fantastical than the faerie kingdom. Like Ephraim, there was a forest, but this one was made from towering strands of kelp that descended into the blackness and bathed the water in a green glow. Iona weaved through the fluttering kelp-ribbons, spying schools of silver fish with glittering scales and the hulking shadow of a basking shark, grazing on tiny plankton. Unlike the woodlands of Eilanmòr, few creatures had had the privilege of seeing the sea's splendour. This was the selkie domain, and a guarded secret.

Iona flitted to the surface and back, taking her time to admire the diving seabirds above and the corals below. She passed by Jay, watching a pod of dolphins spin and twist through the water. *Show offs*, she thought fondly. She wouldn't be getting too close, however. She'd had to give a particularly amorous bull a nip the last time she'd encountered them, and it had taken days to get the taste of blubber out of her mouth.

Soon, she was out in the open ocean, and she stopped her meandering. It wouldn't be long until she arrived in Struanmuir. She'd see her aunt Caitlyn and her little cousins. Would they still have their fluffy white fur, or would they be sleek and grey like her? Aside from when she'd run off with Alasdair, these past months were the longest she'd left Struanmuir. She wanted to revel in it, this homecoming. Which was why, instead of heading straight there, she made her way to a tiny island.

When Iona was young, she named the islet *Wanderer's Landing*. It was little more than a collection of boulders covered in barnacles and slippery seaweed but perching on top of it allowed her to take in her favourite view of Struanmuir. She could almost see the way the sun would hit the rocky dome, its top covered in sparse vegetation and hiding the secret inside. Struanmuir might look barren to the average human sailing the ocean but the selkies and the birds knew better. Cracks in the stone revealed the inside of the island was hollow. That was where her people lived, in a collection of caves, illuminated when sunlight reflected on the millions of crystals and jewels which were embedded in the rock. And in the centre of it all was a white sand beach, perfect and unspoiled, the water heated by underground volcanoes.

If Iona had timed her journey right, she might see the

sun's rays catch the gems, sending twinkling reflections all the way to Wanderer's Landing. She hurried through the water, a grin already stuck on her face as she found the islet and pulled herself out. *I want to see this with human eyes first,* she decided. They were better at seeing through air. So, she changed back, holding her dress up as she climbed, ready to greet her home once again.

The strange smell should have told her something was wrong, but she didn't fully register it until she saw the smoke blackening the sky. Until she saw the flames licking across the headland. Until she caught a glimpse of the island's shape. For a moment, she wondered if she was in the wrong place. The familiar dome was cracked open like an egg, leaving jagged pieces of rock behind. *What am I looking at?* And then she saw them. Three longships sailed along the horizon, away from her homeland and Iona understood. Struanmuir had been attacked.

Iona leapt into the sea, uncaring as the water soaked her dress before she could turn into a seal. The faces of her family and friends flashed before her eyes as she fought her rising panic. As a seal, she couldn't sob but she felt her heart thundering, threatening to burst from her chest as she swam.

Please don't be too late. Please.

When she arrived at Struanmuir, the firelight was illuminating the sea, making it easy to find the underwater entrance. She swam up the passage, feeling the temperature change as she emerged into the lagoon. Iona wasted no time, hauling herself up onto the beach. But all that she found there was ash and smog. Not a single selkie came to greet her.

"Aunt Caitlyn!" she screamed as soon as she was human again. "Innes! Sloane!" Iona shouted the names of her family until the smoke choked her, sending her diving into the water.

They're not here. Which could be good or bad. The

selkies may have made it out. Or they'd been captured by the Avalognian raiders. A cursory glance around the beach had shown there was no blood, no bodies. *They're alive somewhere.* She couldn't bring herself to imagine anything else.

Iona swam back under, finding her way out of the island. Struanmuir was her homeland, but her people were more important than a piece of rock. She surfaced, taking a deep breath of fresh air as she narrowed her vision on the longboats, sailing back towards Eilanmòr.

Rescue or revenge, that's all she had left. Whether the selkies had been taken or not, the raiders would feel her wrath.

Iona ducked under the savage waves and went to find her prey, leaving Struanmuir burning behind her.

Chapter 29

The General hadn't been kidding when he said they'd only stop once.

At least you don't need to walk, Eilidh told herself. Yes, they had horses but not enough to transport the whole army. Many of the soldiers had to march down the road, their commanding officers setting a brutal pace.

Eilidh had been given a space in a wagon, between sacks of clothing and piles of armour. She knew she was lucky, but with everything stacked up around her she was starting to feel like she'd been buried alive. The constant rocking was making her stomach roil and she didn't know how much longer she could last.

"Doing alright in there?" asked Harris from the other end of the wagon. He too had been afforded a spot, wedged between boxes of food.

"Fine," said Eilidh because she didn't want to complain.

Harris didn't seem convinced. "I can see that it's getting dark. We'll be stopping soon, before we lose all the light."

Eilidh's chest loosened. She'd be getting out soon. "How far away is the river we're heading for?"

"Maybe another hour in the morning? It'll be an early one."

"What are the chances I'll get to wash when we stop?" The morning's bath seemed like days ago and she could feel a thick layer of sweat and grime coating her skin.

"Depends on whether you're up for washing in a stream beside a bunch of soldiers."

Eilidh grimaced, dropping her head back into the wooden slats. Better to just get it over with. It's not like she'd have much privacy on the boats anyway.

The wagons rolled on for another half hour until there was a shout from ahead and they were finally slowing. All of a sudden, the press of the supplies became too much. Eilidh scrambled to push them away, unable to catch her breath, but everything was too heavy. *I'm stuck.* Panic rose inside her like bile. *Out. I need out.* But there was a gap and Harris's freckled face appeared.

"I've got you," he said quietly, as if he could somehow read her fear. He held a hand out and she took it gratefully, allowing him to pull her through.

"Thanks." Her voice was shaking almost as much as her body.

Harris tugged her off the wagon and into the fresh air. "Don't mention it. We've all got fears."

"Oh yeah?" she asked, taking deep, cleansing breaths. "What's yours?"

"Seagulls," he said matter-of-factly.

Eilidh let out a snort. "Really?"

"I didn't laugh at yours." But he was smiling wickedly, clearly joking. "Besides, have you ever seen a seagull up close? They're massive."

"Right." Eilidh surveyed the army caravan, feeling lighter. The wagons were all stationary, in a long line but ahead the foot soldiers had already broken ranks, setting up basic sleeping arrangements and campfires. At the clop of hooves, Eilidh turned and was greeted by the sight of a massive horse, its horn pointed straight at her as it walked forward. The unicorn truly was a formidable beast, much more terrifying than the faerie stories had led her to believe.

"You made it in one piece," said Angus as the unicorn

came to a stop. He looked windswept but happy atop his steed, hands grasping her dark mane. Behind him, Cameron was pressed into Angus's back, his arms wrapped securely around the prince's waist. When the mapmaker raised his head, Eilidh noticed he looked a little green.

"Just about," she said, wondering how she herself looked. "I'll be glad when this part of the journey is over."

"We're going to set up our bedrolls beside Duncan," Angus told them. "You two should join us."

Eilidh nodded. "I'm going to find somewhere to wash first."

Angus looked skyward. "It's getting dark."

"I feel gross. I won't be long."

"Do you need me to come with you?" Harris asked, moving to her side.

She smiled, heaving her pack onto her shoulder. "I'll be fine. If I see you—either of you—" she glared at Angus, "I'll assume you don't think I can handle myself. I grew up with Agneta Daalgard as my guardian. I can brave a stream in the woods teeming with our own soldiers."

Angus frowned but didn't protest further as she slipped off into the trees. Gods, it was much greener here than at the capital and much more familiar. She'd grown up in an inn in the woods, surrounded by the lush, leafy darkness. Here the trees were different species, towering pines instead of the white striped birch, but the sounds and smells were the same. Eilidh wound her way between the trunks and through the sprouting ferns until the caravan was far behind, muffled by the forest.

She eventually found what she was looking for: a burn, brown with peat but flowing fast enough. Eilidh was sure it would run into the main river eventually, but for now it was the perfect size for a wash. The banks were lined with pebbles, following the stream's curve, and nearby branches overhung the water, useful for gripping so she wouldn't fall in the current.

Eilidh dropped her bag and unhooked her cloak. How naked did she dare to be? There were a lot of people in the woods; it was probably best to keep her shift on. It'll dry, she thought, pulling off her dress and letting her hair down. The last thing to go was her boots, which she left close to the water so she wouldn't hurt her feet on the stones.

The first dip of her toe into the burn was a shock. Eilidh shivered, but pressed on, knowing she'd feel better if she could wash her whole body. *In and out, you'll be quick,* she thought. She gave herself until the count of ten to duck down into the cold water.

One. Two.

She bundled up her skirts so she wouldn't trip.

Three. Four.

Eilidh scooped some water up, rubbing it on the back of her neck.

Five. Six.

She waded in further, until the burn was up to her knees.

Seven. Eight.

Eilidh prepared to sit down, turning to face the current.

Nine—

She let out a squeak of surprise. Two little girls, dressed in rags, sat at the edge of the stream, watching her. Eilidh dropped her dress, raising her wrist to her rapidly beating heart.

"You gave me a fright," she said.

The children tilted their heads in unison, watching her with eyes that seemed too big for their faces. They were scraggly and thin, their limbs all bones.

Have they been abandoned out here by themselves? "Are

you lost?" Eilidh asked. "You look like you haven't seen a meal in days. We've got food back at the camp which I'm sure you can have."

The girls half stood warily, each taking a step towards her.

They're terrified, Eilidh thought. And no wonder. They could have been alone in the woods for days, even weeks, judging by their clothes. She looked them over as they crept closer. The taller of the two had dark hair, pulled into two messy strands that may have once been braids. The smaller looked very young, perhaps around the age of six or seven, and had chin length blonde hair and a scar over her lips. Neither wore any shoes and they had no bags or even cloaks with them, as far as Eilidh could see.

She held her hand out but stayed still, trying not to spook them. They looked wet anyway, it wouldn't hurt them to wade down the river.

"I'm Eilidh," she said softly. "I've got a daughter younger than you and I'm—"

"—the queen," said the eldest in a lisping voice. "We know."

Eilidh pulled her hand back. "How did you know-"

"Eilidh!" someone shouted to her left. She whipped around as Cameron came running through the trees, waving his arms. "Stop, they're—"

She turned back to the children just in time to watch them change. Their noses elongated and they dropped onto all fours, growing taller and taller. The eldest girl's skin shifted into dark grey, dappled with green while the youngest turned pure black. Their hair grew into long strands of weeds to match the tails they'd sprouted. In the time it took Eilidh to huff out a shocked gasp, the little girls were replaced by two horses, dripping with water.

"Kelpies!" Cameron screamed.

Eilidh froze. She'd grown up with stories of kelpies, like

every Eilanmòrian child did. *Don't go near the water or the kelpies will get you.* She should have known better; she'd seen many monsters in recent years.

The kelpies splashed forward, not giving her time to run. *They're going to drown me*, Eilidh realised, closing her eyes. She screamed at her body to move but every muscle was paralysed. Vaguely, she could still hear Cameron running over the pebbles, but her senses were focussed, waiting to be pulled under. Eilidh felt a pressure against her arm and waited for the water horses to bite down, her heartbeat thundering in her ears.

But there were no teeth, no claws. Eilidh cracked an eye open and was met with a strong neck and shoulders. The grey kelpie swayed in front of her, its heavy head nudging into her arm. *It's rubbing itself against me.* The second kelpie trotted forward, rubbing its face against her other arm.

Eilidh waited a moment, tensed for a fight, but when none came, she raised her shaking hand, petting the side of the black kelpie's face. It leaned into her touch and made a high chirping noise.

"You're not going to hurt me, are you?"

In response, the kelpies withdrew, stepping back against the current until they were able to make very deliberate bows, lowering their heads until their muzzles touched the water. Eilidh knew her mouth was hanging open, but she couldn't find it in herself to care. The kelpies tossed their heads and turned, making their way back up the stream. Eilidh watched them retreat, until their bodies turned to liquid, dropping into the water with a final splash, leaving her staring up the burn at the place they'd been.

"Did you see that?" she breathed, looking over at Cameron.

The man stood on the riverbank, pale and wide eyed, as if he'd been stopped in his tracks by the sight of the kelpies' strange behaviour. "How?" he asked.

Eilidh shook her head, wading back out of the water, her bath forgotten. "They called me the queen."

"They knew?" asked Cameron.

"I suppose I'm not hiding myself anymore. It's been impossible to sage myself every day on the road. They weren't the first either. There was a redcap on the way to Dunrigh."

"A redcap?" Cameron looked like he was going to faint.

"It bowed to me too." Eilidh wrung out her dress. "I guess I'm glad I'm not being eaten, but I spent many years trying to hide who I am. I don't think that's possible anymore. The fae can just tell." She scrunched up her nose. "How did you know I was in trouble?"

Cameron grimaced. "Angus asked me to watch out for you. You said you didn't want to see him or Harris, but you didn't mention me."

"I didn't think I had to," she said, pressing her lips together. "I thought you might have gone straight to bed. You don't look very well."

The man swayed on his feet. "Now that you mention it, I am feeling a bit off."

Eilidh slipped on her boots. "Come on, you can walk me back to camp."

All the way through the forest, Eilidh thought over her encounter. Kelpies and redcaps were supposed to be terrifying monsters, but all had been polite to her. What other creatures lurked in the woods and waterways of Eilanmòr? If the faerie folk could finally sense her, she imagined she'd be seeing a lot more in the coming weeks.

Eilidh glanced at Cameron. He really didn't look well. He could barely lift his feet up off the ground and it seemed like he was fighting to keep his eyes open. "Cameron, do you need to stop?" she asked.

He raised his face, his mouth opening as if to speak, but

then he was down, falling to the side into the ferns. Eilidh tried to catch him but only managed to grab his arm, slowing his fall so he didn't hit his head against the tree trunk. "Cameron!"

Cameron's body twitched, his spine curling and uncurling. Eilidh glimpsed flashes of visions but they were too quick, flashing across her eyes and away like leaves in the wind. Unlike the last time he'd pulled her into a prophecy, she could still see her surroundings and was still able to move, looking around in desperation for another soul.

"*Help!*" she shouted, crouching down beside her friend. "*Come quick.*"

They were closer to the camp now and it wasn't long until her shouts were answered, with soldiers thundering through the undergrowth towards them.

"Hold on," she told Cameron, pushing his hair back. "I've got you."

Eilidh thought she caught a flash of a young woman's face, screwed up in agony, before Cameron collapsed and sleep took away his pain.

Chapter 30

S he attacked in the night.

The raiders had landed on Eilanmòrian sand, not far from where Iona had first found Ailsa. Back then she had been running for her life until her new friend landed an axe in her pursuers' skulls. Iona knew then that she couldn't take them all on by herself but now her reason had been left where her homeland burned. In its place, rage and wrath swarmed in her chest until she didn't think she could breathe around them. It was with this fury that she stood on the beach, the waves at her back, and went to hunt down her prey.

Iona slipped across the sand, past an old, half-buried rowboat, and scouted the dunes where they'd set up camp. It was thrown up haphazardly, with scattered bedrolls and instruments, as if they didn't intend to stay for long. A fire was burning down to the embers, the band of Avalognians sprawled around it. Some were already snoring, too drunk to haul themselves to bed. Others were leaning against rocks and driftwood, deep in conversation. The long ships had been dragged ashore and a solitary figure slumped against one, his arms behind his back. From the awkwardness of his posture, Iona guessed his hands were tied. A captive then. Paying him no more mind, she turned her attention to those who were awake.

Not a single soul looked up when she stood in front of the camp. Not a single soul noticed when she flexed her fingers, feeling the push and pull of the sea against her skin. Not a single soul thought it strange when the sound of crashing waves ceased. It wasn't until the moonlight was blotted out, throwing them into darkness, that the raiders raised their heads.

"What the—" A bearded man tried to push himself up, his drink sloshing over his fingers. "Who are you?"

Drunk, Iona realised. They all were. For a moment she regretted it, that their emotions would be dulled in the end.

She raised the wall of water behind her ever higher, controlling every drop with her magic. "You burned Struanmuir."

The bearded man barked out a laugh. "We did. Here for revenge?"

"I'll have answers first. Where are the selkies? Are you working with Mirandelle? Or did you see a weakness and seize the opportunity?"

Another man with a shaved head spat on the sand. "Our mission was ordained by the gods. You selkies pissed them off. As for your brethren, they fled when we arrived. They didn't even try to defend their homeland." Around the camp, the raiders' sleeping comrades were beginning to waken, blinking blearily up at her.

Iona paid them no mind, even as she mentally added them to her list of prey. *At least my family is safe.* "So, you're working on the orders of the Edaxi."

"A hundred longboats are currently sailing around Eilanmòr, ready to attack. But we're not the only ones."

"Who else?" Iona gritted out.

One of the men guffawed, loud and booming in the silence. "She's pretty, isn't she? Come sit with us and we'll let you live. We don't bite."

"No," she said, grinning. "But I do."

The men reached for their weapons, throwing themselves down the beach. Iona watched them advance in slow motion, faces pulled back in battle cries and swords and axes raised. Her eyes cut to their captive; his face shadowed by the longboat but his body tense. *You'll be free soon,* she wanted to yell. But instead, she brought her arms above her head, pulling the water with it.

All that time spent on land or enclosed in metal ships had left Iona weak. Too long she'd been away from the water. But her journey to Struanmuir had invigorated her. She could still taste the salt on her lips; feel the cold under her skin. When she'd fought the Stoor Worm with Ailsa, she had been working with a drying well. Now it was full, and she luxuriated in it.

"It's just a bit of water," shouted someone from the back of the pack.

The leader was nearing, his axe glinting in the firelight. The captive at the longboat let out a muffled scream, shouting something unintelligible around his gag. The rest happened in snapshots.

The blade bore down but she leant her body out of the way. With a cry, she sent the wall of water crashing upon them and the raiders were swept off their feet. But as the water retreated, they raised their heads and laughed in relief.

"Is that all you've got?"

Iona smirked as she pulled the water up again. "Interesting choice of last words." And she sent it crashing down their open throats.

It didn't take long after that, but Iona filed it all in her memories anyway. How they dropped their weapons, clawing at their throats. How some tried to drag themselves away. How they landed face first in the sand, writhing until their bodies gave up and admitted defeat. Sometimes Iona forgot how little time it took humans to drown. When it was all over, the water slipped from their bodies, back towards the sea, leaving behind wet silt and motionless limbs.

Iona closed her eyes and pulled in a deep breath, letting her rage go. *They're gone and they won't hurt anyone else.*

Tears pricked at her eyes as she thought back to her island. She desperately wanted to find her family, but they could be anywhere by now and the raiders had said there were hundreds ready to attack the coast. *Warn Duncan,* she decided. *Help them fight.* With any luck she'd see her people again.

A moan to her right caught her attention and she snapped her eyes open. *The captive.* She bit the inside of her cheek, wondering if she should just leave him here. *My enemy's enemy is surely my friend,* she told herself as she slipped up the beach towards him.

"You're fine," she soothed, coming closer. "I'm going to let you loose." Iona slipped the knife out of her pocket, willing him not to struggle. "This is just to cut your bonds."

But he didn't try to get away. *He must know I mean him no harm.* After her display with the raiders, she was surprised but maybe she just had a friendly voice.

The man wore Avalognian clothes, but they didn't fit him well. The trousers were slightly too short above his bare feet and his tunic swamped him. There was a pile of fur beside him like it had fallen off his shoulders in his struggle. His dark hair curled around his ears and neck, calling forth a memory that Iona couldn't quite catch.

He seemed familiar, somehow. Iona shrugged off the feeling, focussing on the task at hand. "If you lean to the side I can cut the rope at your hands first," she said, bending down.

But when he shifted, his face moved out of the shadow and into the light and Iona swore her heart stopped beating. This had to be a dream. A nightmare. How many times had she seen this face after she'd closed her eyes? It all made sense now. Struanmuir burning, killing the Avalognians. None of it was real. Because if it was then the person in front of her was real too. And that was impossible.

She fell back with a gasp, willing herself to wake up. The

knife sliced her finger as she landed on her hand, but she was still there on the beach across from the windswept man. He mumbled something around the fabric in his mouth and shuffled forward on his knees. The movement sent him off balance and he landed on his chest, the impact knocking the breath from his lungs.

I could leave, Iona thought as her brain scrambled to make sense of who was in front of her. It seemed a better alternative to feeling her heart break again. But if this was a dream it wouldn't matter. In her dreams, she could never leave him until she woke up and that didn't seem to be happening. What was left? Scream? Cry? Throw herself into the waves? None of it made sense. Iona did the only logical thing. She took the blade in her hands and threw herself forward.

The man froze, watching her with his face pressed against the beach. She steeled herself, tearing her gaze away from his face and to the task at hand. Iona slipped the knife between his wrists and began to saw at the ropes. They were both quiet as she worked, though a sob was bubbling up behind her closed lips. The rope was thick, and the work was slow, but soon she was down to the last few cords. Doubling her efforts, she hacked at it until the final strand snapped, then she threw herself back again, putting a safe distance between them before the man could sit up.

But he took his time, as if he knew leaping up straight away would spook her. He circled his wrists and then rolled over, pulling the gag from his mouth. Then he pushed himself to sitting, as slowly as one would when faced with a frightened animal. The man watched her with unblinking eyes, illuminated in the moonlight, one blue and one hazel.

And Iona finally allowed his name to escape from her mouth, fully expecting the spell to be broken when she did.

"Alasdair?"

Chapter 31

Iona stared in disbelief and horror at the man across from her. How had her enemy known exactly who to show her, which face would hurt her the most?

"You're not real," she whispered.

The wind whipped the spray over them, leaving sea-salt tears across her cheeks. To her left a single Avalognian flag lashed back and forth in the wind. *I should take that down*, Iona thought absently. There were no Avalognians left. But she couldn't take her eyes off the man.

He wiped his sodden sleeve across his mouth and pushed his curls from his forehead. "I wish I wasn't."

Even his voice was familiar. How had they got his voice right?

"You're dead," Iona told him, because she couldn't think of anything else to say.

The man rubbed at his wrists; his movements tired. "Yes and no. My body is alive, but my soul isn't. Does that make any sense?"

Iona shook her head, trying desperately to dispel the hope clawing at her heart. "I don't believe it. I can't. I can—"

"Iona," he murmured. "It's me."

It was only when he was within reach that Iona noticed she was moving, crawling across the sand. She crouched in front of the man with the terribly familiar face and took in his rounded nose, his tawny hair and his mismatched eyes. "Tell me something only you would know," she demanded.

"I wrote you letters every week for a year," he said. "Until the day you wrote me back telling me to get on with my life. But I never could. I still wrote you letters after that, but I didn't send them until after Saoirse died. The night I was killed, I should have been thinking of strategies for the next day's battle, but instead I wrote to you again."

"One of your soldiers sent it to me," Iona whispered. "What did it say?"

"That I wouldn't rest until I had you in my arms again." He gave a faint smile. "Seems I made good on my promise."

"What do you mean?"

The man stood, brushing the sand off his clothes. "I'll explain everything, once we get somewhere warm and dry." Then he held out a hand to her.

Iona hesitated. Everything he'd said seemed true, but anyone could have read his letters. "This could still be a trick."

A look of exasperation and amusement crossed his face, so familiar she couldn't breathe for a moment.

"You have a freckle between your toes that looks like a heart," said Alasdair. "When you're bored, you twiddle your hair, and you have a secret fear of toadstools. You can't eat crab anymore after that one time you got food poisoning. When my daughter was born you sent her a pearl necklace and when my son was born you sent him a knitted blanket. Sometimes at night you sneak down to the gallery in Dunrigh Castle and look at our picture."

Iona's hand flew to her neck. "How could you know *that*?"

The look he gave her was devastating. "Because for the last twenty years I've been haunting the halls of Dunrigh Castle waiting for you to come back. Because I have been a ghost with unfinished business. But for some reason I'm alive again and freezing my ass off. Now come on."

Iona hesitated only a moment longer, just enough that she

could commit the image to memory. Alasdair was there and alive and he'd just told her a small number of pretty things he'd only ever said in her dreams. *Well, if I'm dreaming, I may as well enjoy it.* So, Iona slipped her hand into Alasdair's and let him lead her away from the lifeless bodies and crashing waves.

***

It was raining by the time they climbed up the headland and found a cave. Alasdair had collected driftwood on the way, keeping it tucked into his jacket. Iona could only watch as he set the kindling out and tried to get it to light. All the while she watched him, taking in the furrow between his brows, his sure hands as they rubbed the wood together.

"You know, it's funny," she croaked. "I had a flint in my pack and left it back in Dunrigh on purpose. I didn't think I'd need it."

"It's not the best joke you've ever told," Alasdair said with a half-smile.

Soon enough, smoke began to pour out of the tinder ball. Alasdair raised it to his lips, blowing it into life and Iona felt her stomach clench.

Get it together, she admonished herself.

The driftwood fire burned green from the salt, bathing the cave walls in an eerie glow, illuminating the paintings etched onto the walls. In them, seals swam through reefs and under stars, unaware of the dangers they faced.

With a wave of her hand, Iona lifted the moisture from their clothes and deposited it outside. Then, taking a deep breath, she faced the man across the flames.

"The world and I have been under the impression you were dead. As you can imagine, it is surprising, to say the least, to see you very much alive." Her speech started off strong but as those strange eyes stared her down, she lost her nerve, her voice becoming reedier with each word. "Do you know why that is?" she finished, biting her lip.

Alasdair lowered himself to the floor, lifting his hands out for the heat. "Let's start off with what's been happening in Eilanmòr since I've been... gone. My captors said something about a war. And four gods?"

Iona nodded. "The Edaxi. It's why I came back to Struanmuir. Dunrigh was attacked and it became imperative that we find allies."

"I know," he said, darkly. "I was there."

"You said you'd been haunting the castle..." She gulped. "You *were* dead, weren't you?"

"I was killed and buried in a cairn just outside the walls. Imagine my surprise when my body was dug up suddenly."

Oh gods. Something in her had begun to hope Alasdair had merely been missing. That his grave hadn't really been desecrated. "Why? Why would they do that?"

"It seems the gods are building an army and they're looking for more soldiers."

Iona shivered, wrapping her arms around herself. "We've been finding people infected with a mysterious illness; they become rotting monsters, unaware and unfeeling. A week ago, the God of Chaos attacked Ephraim with a legion of them."

"I saw some of them when I was taken to Mirandelle," he said. "They clearly weren't enough though. The gods have started stealing bodies and reanimating them."

"Hold on." She held a hand up. "So how did you end up on an Avalognian longship?"

He brushed a hand through his hair. It was longer than she'd last seen it, back to the way it had been when they'd run off together. "When the Mirandelli soldiers took my body and fled under the castle, I went after them. I'm still attached to these bones. We followed the sewers out to the mountains where a portal to Mirandelle was waiting for them. I found myself in a room with thousands of bodies, in different states of decay. The next thing I knew I was sucked down and then I was blinking up at the ceiling with real, live eyes for the first time in twenty years. As far as I can tell, we—the dead— have all been given new flesh. We breathe, we feel pain, we can see and hear and taste. Except, the others don't have souls. They are husks."

"They aren't like you?" asked Iona, trying to understand.

Alasdair shrugged. "It seems like I'm the only one with thoughts and awareness." He scrunched up his nose. "I told you I was haunting the castle. That's actually fairly rare. Most souls pass on to the other side when they die. But I stuck around; I followed my body back to Dunrigh. That must be why I'm here. They brought my body back, but they didn't mean to bring *me* back. They only wanted an unthinking soldier."

Iona bit her lip. "So, you're, what, possessing your body?"

"I guess so. I haven't tried to leave it again, but I suppose I could—"

"No, don't." She reached out quickly, grabbing his arm, marvelling at how solid it was. "We don't know if you could get back again."

"We were herded onto some longboats, heading for Eilanmòr. When the Avalognians noticed I wasn't doing their bidding like they expected, I think they thought I was defective." He laughed bitterly. "Maybe I am. The raiders mostly just let me sit at the railing, coming to terms with my rebirth but when they attacked Struanmuir I started shouting and they tied me up."

At the mention of the Avalognians, Iona's heart sank. "Struanmuir is gone," she said, clutching at her chest. "I didn't see a single other selkie. One of the raiders said they fled but I don't know…"

"I'm sorry," he said, inching closer. "My boat was the last to arrive. It was already up in flames. But he might have been telling the truth. Maybe they all got away?"

"Maybe," Iona agreed, blinking up at him. "What now?"

"Can I?" He licked his lips. "Can I hold you? I've been wanting to do it for years."

It felt like the most natural thing in the world to press herself into his chest, his arms wrapping around her. Alasdair smelled of brine from his time on the longship but if Iona closed her eyes, she could imagine it was from days at their beach instead.

"You should get somewhere safe," he murmured into her hair. "If what I've heard about the Edaxi is true, you shouldn't be anywhere near them."

She gripped his salt-stiff shirt. "If you've been haunting Dunrigh, you'll know we have a way to stop them."

Iona felt him nod. "The Four Treasures."

"And I'm needed to wield the cauldron." She tucked her hand into her pocket, feeling for the small stone vessel. How close had she been to being captured by the Avalognians today? No doubt they would have found it and taken it. "That's why they were at Struanmuir," she realised, pulling back. "They thought the selkies had the cauldron. I need to get it to the southern coast as soon as possible."

"Is that where the fighting is?"

"That's where King Duncan is heading." When he didn't reply, she raised her eyes to his, searching his face. "Do you know them? Your grandsons?"

"I watched them grow up," he said with a croak. "First

Connall; he was barely a man when I died. Then Duncan, Angus and Moira. I watched them take their first steps, make friends and get in fights. I was there for it all." His expression hardened. "I saw Moira betray Eilanmòr too. Just before I was taken."

"She was caught," Iona told him quickly. "Duncan locked her in her rooms."

Alasdair shook his head. "Silly girl."

"I know they would love to meet you. Duncan and Angus, I mean." Iona lowered her gaze to the fire. "They should have had you, alive and well, teaching them and caring for them." She cleared her throat. "What happened, when you died? I was told only that you were stabbed."

He sighed, stretching his legs out towards the flames. "I was in the war tent, tending to an injury I'd sustained that day. Nothing too serious, just a flesh wound. My daughter, Afric, was cutting some bandages. She hadn't even taken off her armour. It all happened so fast. Someone entered the tent and before I could call out, Afric was up and charging at them. I heard her cry and then she fell to the ground. Behind her was... well, I thought it was an angel at first. It had huge wings, tucked in tight. But then I saw it was holding a spear, covered in my daughter's blood. And the point was aimed at me." Alasdair rubbed a knuckle against his sternum, right where Iona imagined the wound had been. "My sword was too far away; I knew there was nothing I could do. The monster stabbed me in the chest. My death was over in seconds."

"I'm so sorry, Alasdair," she whispered. "Does Afric—"

"Did she remain as I did?" He smiled sadly. "No, her spirit passed on. She had an honourable death, defending me. Her husband, Rian, had died the year before and I like to imagine she's with him now."

"But you stayed. Your wife and your daughter were dead.

Didn't you want to join them in the afterlife?"

The look he gave her was piercing. As if he was looking down into her very soul. "I had some unfinished business."

The moment stretched on, but Iona didn't know what to say. *Am I your unfinished business? Do you still love me?*

"We should go to sleep," Alasdair said finally. "It's a long journey to Inshmore. That's where you said Duncan's army was going, right?"

She blinked up at him. "You're coming with me?"

"No, I thought I'd just haunt this beach for the rest of my days instead," he quipped, rolling onto his side. "Though if we're trekking across the country, we'll need to find some supplies." He yawned. "Maybe I'll pillage the raiders' boats tomorrow before we set off."

Iona lay down next to him, cushioning her head on her arm. The weariness was hitting her after such a long day. Watching Struanmuir burn, following the Avalognians, and finding Alasdair—it had all taken its toll. Still, her family had escaped, and her lost love was alive. "If this is a dream," she breathed, "it turned into a good one." She closed her eyes but startled as she felt an arm wrapping around her, pulling her body into Alasdair's embrace.

"I'll still be here when you wake up," he told her, his lips ghosting over her forehead again.

Iona let herself be pulled into sleep, feeling all at once that she'd lost one home but found another.

Chapter 32

The day of the first Moon Rite dawned and still Ailsa didn't have a clue how to make herself seem more trustworthy to the priestesses. They'd ruled out just taking the spear when she'd shown Maalik the tower; they tested the blood lock together, but the door wouldn't open. Since then, he'd spent time in the library researching the Rites, though thankfully in shorter spells. Ailsa had made herself useful helping Vega in the kitchens and assisting Keyne with decorations.

"It looks beautiful," said Ailsa, surveying their handiwork. Placing hundreds of candles around the ballroom had taken hours but now, imagining how they'd flicker together and send their light around the hall, she thought it was worth it. The early morning sunlight shone through the windows, but she could picture how the room would look when it was night-time, like a sky of twinkling stars.

"It's a lot of work to set these out every month but they're one of my favourite parts." Keyne pushed their hair off their face. "Do you notice the smell? I usually throw in some vanilla-scented candles."

Ailsa sat back on her haunches, breathing in deep. "Yeah, now that you mention it, I can. It smells lovely."

Keyne grinned like a cat-sìth who'd got the cream. "They were something I added when I took over this job. The witch who set up the room before me was an amateur."

"Is there anything else we can do?" Ailsa asked.

"That's it for now. A few lanterns get strung up just before the party but apart from that we keep it simple. The moon is the focus anyway."

"What happens during the Rite?"

Keyne picked up one of the empty candle boxes and began tossing any rubbish inside. "During the first one we make offerings to the triple-headed goddess to thank her for the month that has just been. The second night, when the moon is full, the priestesses will strengthen their protections with rituals. On the last night we make wishes for the month ahead and hold the biggest party of all."

Ailsa shifted to sit with her legs crossed and reached out to help with the cleaning. She took a bunch of twine and rolled it into a ball. "What should I bring for an offering?" What did she even have?

"Witches can bring food or even a display of their power. You know, show the goddess what she gave you." Keyne quirked an eyebrow. "But I'm not sure that would be the best idea in your case."

Ailsa winced. "Maybe. Or maybe it would be a good opportunity to let people see I'm not a threat."

"Sure, if you can manage that."

"I'll have to think about it." Ailsa chewed on her lip. "What will you do?"

"My smoke is pretty fun to dance around in, I've been told," Keyne said slyly. "It lowers people's inhibitions when they think no one can see them. It's also great for finally kissing someone you've been pining after."

"Oh? And will Zephyr be at the Rite?"

Keyne scowled. "I wasn't talking about Zephyr. What about Maalik?"

Ailsa threw the twine ball into the box with a bit more force than necessary. "We've kissed plenty."

"But you are *pining*. Welcome to the club."

"It's complicated," she said, rubbing away a scuff on her boot. "He wasn't always a demon, you know. And recently he's been turning back into an angel."

Keyne's grin was wide. "That's great!"

"Not really." Ailsa pressed the heels of her hands into her eyes. "We need him to have fire magic so he can use one of the Four Treasures."

Keyne's silence stretched until Ailsa took her hands away from her face. "You're still planning to fight?" they asked quietly. "Even if you don't have the spear?"

"I can't just stay here and let the world fall apart." *And I still haven't given up on the spear.*

Keyne frowned. "They'll find someone else to help them. And if the spear is here the Edaxi won't be able to take over."

"Which means they'll continue to terrorise Ossiana until they get all Four Treasures. They'll come here eventually."

"They won't make it up the mountain," said Keyne, returning to their task. "And even if they did, they'd never make it inside. Sefarina's shield is strong and there are wards all around the castle."

And yet Ishbel was able to get in. "I need to help my friends."

Keyne hummed. "What about your family?"

"I don't know who they are." *Thanks to Vega.* Yes, she and Keyne and Rain were her friends here, but they weren't in danger. Besides... "I have a brother."

"An adoptive brother," Keyne guessed.

Ailsa swallowed. Did that mean they weren't family? Did it erase all the time they'd spent together, grown up together? "That means he chose me. They both did, him and my mother."

"We want to choose you too, if you let us. Maybe we could even send for him and your friends. They'll be safe here." Keyne squeezed her hand and stood up. "Come on, we got up so early I think I need a nap."

The world could be burning, and you want to nap? Ailsa wanted to scream. Instead, she shoved down the anger and nodded to the witch. "I'll see you tonight."

"We'll swing by your room to pick you up."

As soon as they were gone, Ailsa dropped her head into her hands. "How am I going to convince them?"

So much hubris. They truly think they're invincible. It was the same when I was alive.

"I'm seeing that now."

You should let me speak to them. To tell them what actually happened when Rocbarra sank. Maybe they'll see they can be their own worst enemies.

Ailsa sighed. "I'm going to try winning them over."

Does that mean you have a plan?

"Show them my powers aren't scary?" She didn't even sound convincing to her own ears.

Right. Good luck with that. I'm afraid I've made quite an impression, even all these centuries later.

"This can't be helping your ego," Ailsa muttered, pushing herself up and heading out of the candle-filled hall.

***

"Find anything useful?" Ailsa asked when she got back to the bedroom.

Maalik looked up from the desk where he was leaning over yet another book. "From what I've read, we're in for a treat with the Rites. Though I'm not sure how traditions have changed over the millennia. I don't imagine anyone will be getting naked."

Ailsa felt her cheeks heat. "Thank the gods. I don't think I could look any of them in the eye if I saw that."

Maalik shrugged. "They're just bodies."

"Really? So, you'd be fine if I just stripped off here and now?"

"What? I don't—" Maalik spluttered. "That's not—"

"Relax," she said, flopping down onto the bed. "I'll be getting changed behind the screen, as usual."

"Fine. Good. Right."

Ailsa grinned at the squeak in his voice. "Vega's coming in a bit to help us get ready."

"Zephyr was actually going to scrounge some party clothes for me." Maalik closed the book he'd been reading. "I should probably go find him."

"So, I'll just meet you there?" Ailsa asked, propping her head up on a hand.

"Will you be okay?"

She nodded, smiling. When they'd first met, Maalik had been a recluse. *A bit like me before I met Iona and Harris.* Well, now look at them. They'd won people over before. She'd have to remember that tonight. "Zephyr seems nice. I'm glad you've made a friend."

"Me too," he said, quietly.

"Ailsa!" came a voice from outside. "You ready?"

Maalik grinned. "I'll leave you to it." He strode across the room and opened the door, revealing a purple-haired witch with some sort of pink clay all over her face. Vega bounced on her toes, almost dislodging the pile of boxes and bottles in her arms. "Have fun," Maalik called, sniggering.

"It's still morning," Ailsa told her.

Vega hopped inside before the door could shut and dropped her things on the desk beside Maalik's book. "We have to start now, there's loads to do." She spread out the containers, finding a round one. "I'm so excited I could burst into a million pieces. Have you ever tried a face mask?"

Ailsa didn't answer her, instead she flopped back onto the mattress with a groan as the small witch advanced. It was going to be a long day.

Chapter 33

Iona wiped her face groggily. She knew she'd slept much longer than she'd planned, the sun was already bright and blinding. The dream she'd been having still clung to her edges, refusing to let go as she sat up from her spot on the floor. She often dreamed of Alasdair, even all these years after his death but this one appeared more tangible than the others. She could almost feel his presence in the light of the late morning. But, then again, hadn't there been other times she'd woken and imagined him nearby, only to be disappointed, over and over again?

Your heart can't take it, she told herself. *Get this nonsense out of your head.*

But then she blinked away the sleep and noticed the body lying beside her.

He was stretched out on his stomach, the way he always used to sleep, but his face was turned towards hers. There was a faint smile on his lips but the flickering under his eyelids told her he was still very much unconscious. Iona stretched a shaking hand out, hovering it over his face. She wanted to touch him, wanted to know if he was real.

But what if he's not?

She drew her hand away, unable to break the spell just yet. If she was still dreaming, she'd squeeze every last drop of it out before she woke up.

***

That was how Alasdair found Iona, leaning over him as if memorising every freckle on his nose. He gave her a sleepy grin and stretched. "Good morning. Or is it already afternoon? I feel like I slept for days."

His voice seemed to startle her from her trance. She took her lip between her teeth and Alasdair tracked the movement.

"I didn't dream yesterday," she said in a hushed whisper.

Alasdair rolled over onto his side so he could see her better. She was curled up, holding her knees to her chest, with her dress tucked in around her feet. Her copper hair had been curled by the salty breeze, crowning her head like a halo. *She looks like an angel*, he thought. Except, hadn't he seen real angels? Some had visited him over the years, asking him if he was lost and if he needed help crossing over. The thing that had killed him had resembled one too. No, Iona was no angel. She was infinitely better.

"No," he confirmed, taking her hand in his. Her skin was cold, so he wrapped her fingers in his palm and willed his heat to warm her. "I'm here."

Her eyes turned glassy. "But that also means Struanmuir is gone."

Alasdair ran a finger over her freckle-dusted cheeks, willing her not to cry. "We'll find your people, wherever they've gone," he told her softly. "You'll rebuild it."

She nodded, blinking back the tears. "Did you mean what you said yesterday? Will you come with me?"

"If you'll have me with you? I might slow you down." He'd seen how fast she could swim as a seal.

Iona bit her lip. "We could go by foot, but I think I know an easier way. Come on."

They made quick work of disassembling their little camp. Iona had just wanted to leave it, but Alasdair wasn't keen on leaving their enemies a trail. She led from the cave and down the headland, stopping at the Avalognians' camp.

"Stay here," Iona told him and before he could argue she was off, leaving him crouching behind the tall marram grass.

Be careful, he wanted to shout. But he knew she didn't need to be told. Iona had always been fiercely independent, very unlike all the ladies in court. He'd known it as soon as he'd spotted her, dancing in the castle ballroom with her shoes kicked off and her hair flying free. Then she looked at him like she already owned his heart, and he couldn't disagree.

Alasdair waited a while for Iona until he heard her shouting his name and he followed her voice dutifully. He picked his way through the remains of the encampment, seeing it with fresh eyes in the daylight. The bodies of the raiders were still sprawled out where they'd fallen. Most of them were face down in the sand but a couple lay staring at the sky with bloated faces and dusty eyes. Iona's attack had been sudden and efficient, leaving behind no survivors. He knew he should be sad for the loss of life, even if they were his enemy, but these people had destroyed Iona's homeland and had possibly injured or killed her family. Honestly, he was impressed she'd shown enough restraint to make their deaths so quick.

He climbed over the dunes until he could see Iona and what she stood beside. "A dinghy?" It was half buried in the sand, sea-battered and coated with barnacles.

"A little help?" she asked, scooping the sand out with her hands. "I spotted it on the way in last night."

Alasdair bent down to assist, and soon enough sediment had been cleared so that he could tip the boat over, emptying the rest. He heaved it back onto its hull, pleased to see there were no obvious holes, even if it was a little battered.

"Do you think it'll float?" he asked, giving it a shove. It

took a bit to get the dinghy moving but once Alasdair had the momentum, he managed to push it down the beach towards the sea.

"There's only one way to find out," she said from behind him. "For a dead man, you're pretty spry."

He huffed out a laugh. "I certainly don't remember having this many muscles before. They built our new bodies strong."

"You were always strong, even if you didn't look it." With a flick of Iona's hand, she pulled the waves up to meet the rowboat, making it easier for him to launch it into the water. "I also found these," she said, skipping back up the beach until she reached a couple of paddles and some rope she'd obviously stashed there before he'd arrived. "I'm sure the raiders won't miss them. I can tow you and when I get tired you can row."

"Sounds like a deal," he said, holding the craft steady. "But let me go first. You can tell me everything I've missed over the years."

She took his hand so she could step inside the boat. "You were around Dunrigh, surely there's nothing I could tell you that you don't already know."

"I don't want to hear about Dunrigh or Eilanmòr or even my family. Not right now," he said, giving the dinghy a final push and jumping inside. "I want to hear about you." He sat down and took the paddles with a grin. "You and I have a lot to catch up on and I'm not wasting anymore time. Let's get to know each other again."

Iona gave him a hesitant smile. "I'd like that a lot."

So, Alasdair rowed through the turquoise waves, skirting the coast, while Iona spoke about her life, filling in the gaps when he hadn't seen her. And while he listened and watched, a thought came unbidden to his mind, repeating over and over until it was a vow. *I will never miss another moment with you again.*

Chapter 34

arris was not in a good place. Mentally, he'd been that way for a while. But physically? He could do with being anywhere else.

"It's not so bad," Angus said, clapping him on the back. "They'll get used to it in a day or so."

Harris eyed the man beside him, currently emptying the contents of his stomach into the river below. "Remind me why I didn't go with Iona again?"

"You could always turn into a seal?" Angus suggested. "Swim away for a bit?"

"No thank you. The whole river is toxic."

The thing no one tells you about war is that you've actually got to get your army there. Hundreds of men and women, suddenly living and eating at close quarters and relentlessly marching for hours. They'd made it to River Glainne in a day and a half, just like General MacKenzie said, but it had been long enough for sickness to spread. Nothing major, just a stomach bug, but it was most unwelcome when they were about to be stuck on a procession of riverboats until they reached the coast. Harris had almost begged off, wondering if he could hitch a ride with the unicorn. She'd taken one look at the boats and refused, planting her hooves on dry land until Angus had told her she could just meet them there. But the prince had grabbed the back of Harris's cloak before he could join her and hauled him onboard without room for an argument.

Harris eyed Angus sceptically. "You're not worried about getting sick?"

"I'm pretty hardy but if I get it, I get it. I've got soldiers to look after."

"One soldier seems to be getting more attention from you than the others," said Harris slyly.

"Maybe so." Angus filled his canteen from the fresh water bucket and glanced over his shoulder. "Ah, Eilidh. Holding out?"

Harris turned and saw the golden-haired woman approaching, an odd tingling pricking his skin. She smiled, her cheeks rosy from the cool air and scrubbed at the back of her neck like it was aching. "The best thing for feeling queasy is food," she said, throwing them an apple each. The rest she had bundled in her skirts, the fabric tucked into her belt, acting as a basket. Harris crunched into the fruit, never taking his eye off Eilidh.

"Won't that make them more sick?" asked Angus, polishing his apple on his sleeve.

She shrugged. "I think if you're going to throw up, it's better to throw up something than nothing."

"I'm sure they'll appreciate it, even if it's to get the bad taste out of their mouths. Can I take another one for Cam?"

Eilidh nodded, passing one over. "I hope he feels better." And then she was gone, offering quiet words and food to those who needed it.

"Do you fancy my sister or something?" Angus asked, his voice making Harris jump.

Harris wrenched his eye away from Eilidh's retreating back and scowled. "It's not like that."

Angus gave him a flat look. "You couldn't look away. It's been the same ever since we left Dunrigh."

Harris avoided his eyes. "You're going to think it sounds stupid."

"It can't be worse than imagining you as a brother-in-law."

"She's my queen," Harris told him. "Whether she accepts it or not. Whenever she's around I feel this tug towards her. It's not attraction; I've felt that for plenty of people, believe me. I haven't had that for anyone else since I met Irené. But, I dunno, it's like I need to be around her, to hear her voice. To protect her."

"Well, that's something at least. I feel that too, though I am her brother." Angus sighed. "We're friends, Harris, but I'm not messing around. Touch my sister and I'll have to challenge you to a duel or something."

"Noted." Harris gave him a tight-lipped smile. "Don't worry, someone else has my heart."

Angus's expression softened. "We'll get her back."

"Come on." He clapped the prince on his back. "I'll help you with your patient. I'm a rubbish nurse but maybe I can make him laugh."

Angus snorted, following him below deck. "I'm sure he'll appreciate it."

***

Cameron sat up when they entered the cabin. "I'm fine," he said, sounding impatient. "I don't need to stay in bed anymore."

He looks pale, Harris thought. Cameron had tanned easily on the march down but now there was a grey undertone to his skin, as if all his blood had been sucked below the surface. Ever since Eilidh had found Cameron unconscious the day before, he looked about ready to faint again. The only thing that had stopped Angus from having him carried onboard the boat that morning was Cameron's pride. As soon as they set sail, Angus had shoved Cameron into the cabin and told him not to come out.

"Drink this," said Angus, thrusting the canteen towards his lips. "Not big gulps, just sips."

"I'm not a child." But Cameron brought the water to his lips anyway.

Harris watched as Angus stared openly at Cameron's throat bobbing. *Perhaps I shouldn't be here.* He cleared his throat. "It looks like you've got this covered," he said, backing towards the door. "If you need me, I'll be avoiding the vomit—"

"Wait," Cameron said, his voice harsher than before. He dropped the canteen, the remaining water spilling onto his shirt. It must have been freezing but he didn't seem to notice. One hand clutched at his blankets while the other fisted against his temple. "Not again," he moaned.

Angus was at his side in an instant. "Cam? What—"

"I can't—" Cameron's eyes rolled back into his head and his body seized up.

Harris could only watch as the man shook, his back arching off the bed. "What's happening?"

"He's having another vision," said Angus, holding Cameron's arm. "We can't do anything until it's over."

"Are you sure? I could get more water?"

"Stay. Please."

Harris stayed, drifting closer until he could fold himself onto the floor beside Angus. They watched together as Cameron worked through it, his breath coming out in sharp pants. At one point, Harris put his arm around Angus's shoulders, feeling him shiver then lean into him.

Slowly, very slowly, Cameron stopped shaking, sinking back into the mattress with a broken sob. He opened his eyes, blinking at the ceiling.

Angus lifted his arm, kissing the freckles there. "Are you alright?" he asked.

"I saw…" Cameron groaned, "…I saw the future."

Harris frowned. "That's how your visions work, isn't it?"

"Not the immediate future. This was years ahead. I saw Dunrigh but the castle was a ruin." Cameron's face crumpled. "The fields around the city were dust. I felt like I was standing there, as if I was myself. Does that mean it's something I'm going to see? Will it happen in my lifetime?"

Harris tilted his head, considering this. "How accurate are your visions? Maybe it won't come true?" Except, hadn't Cameron seen the explosion in Dunrigh before it had happened? And the attack on Ephraim too. If those were the only visions the man had seen, he had a pretty high success rate.

"Gods, there was something else," Cameron said, his voice coming out as a wheeze. "I was standing in front of two burial cairns, side by side."

"Were there names?" Harris asked, dreading the answer.

"There were rocks around my feet, like I was getting ready to place them. There was a name on each." He turned his face into Angus's shoulder. "I can't—"

"You don't have to—" said the prince but Harris cut him off. They didn't have time for this. If their friends were in danger…

"What were the names?"

Cameron pulled back, his gaze flicking between the two men in his cabin. "Harris. Angus." At first, Harris thought he was merely saying their names until the list continued. "Iona. Eilidh. Duncan. Irené. Maalik. Ailsa." Every word rang out in the small room, like a death knell.

Harris shuddered. "But you said there were only two cairns."

"The names kept changing," Cameron said in a whisper.

"Is there any chance it's a metaphor?" suggested Angus,

pushing the hair from Cameron's face. "Maybe we'll be so happy after the battle we'll feel like we've died and gone to heaven?" Except the prince looked seconds away from dissolving into tears.

Harris rolled his eye. *I guess it's up to me to hold them together.* "Let's go with that." He pushed himself up, suddenly desperate to be moving. "I'm going to get you more water and then a bottle of whisky. If it doesn't make us all feel better, at least it'll knock us out."

Cameron gave out a short, wet laugh. "That sounds like a plan."

"Great," said Harris, reaching for the door. "Get your canoodling out of the way now. I'm not leaving either of you alone after this." Because they couldn't give up, not now that Harris was on his way. The image of a cairn flashed before his eyes as he ascended the stairs to the deck, and he had to take a deep breath before pushing himself onwards. There was no way he was going to let Cameron's vision come true, even if he had to drag this whole army south himself. He would get Irené back, safe and in one piece and he would not lose a single one of his friends doing it.

If it had to be his name etched into stone in the end, so be it.

Chapter 35

All day, Ailsa had been primped and scrubbed to within an inch of her life, smothered in sweet smelling clay and rubbed with oils that Vega promised were essential. Now, finally, it was time to get dressed in a jumpsuit of the softest velvet, the trousers gathered at her ankles with strings of pearls. She smoothed down the dusky blue fabric of her clothing and considered herself in the mirror.

"All the parties I've been to I've worn a dress," she said, slipping on the pair of silver shoes that Vega had laid out for her.

"No one wears dresses or skirts here," said Keyne, lounging on Ailsa's bed. "Unless you want to expose yourself when you fly."

Ailsa blinked, turning to her companions. "I can't fly though."

Keyne shrugged, their silk wrap falling off their shoulders. "Neither can I, but we might learn eventually. Though, fewer and fewer witches have managed in recent times."

"It's also why most people wear their hair up. You don't want everything floating around and getting in the way. Even if most people can't fly, I suppose it's become a trend," explained Vega, reaching up to fix the braids at her own scalp.

"Have you ever flown?" Ailsa asked, moving to sit on the edge of the bed before Vega could fuss over her anymore.

The small witch grinned. "I managed for a moment. It's not a natural talent but I'm learning."

"I've heard Zephyr has been experimenting with some old brooms," said Keyne with a sly smile.

Ailsa snorted. "Witches actually flew around on brooms?" What a cliché.

Vega pinned her hair in place, frowning at the mirror. "Only in times of war. And they were special brooms, imbued with magic. There are still some relics up in the tower. Maybe Zephyr will show us if we ask him nicely."

Suddenly the door was thrown open with a bang and something gold and furry streaked across the room like a shooting star. Ailsa felt a scream rising in her throat but then the thing jumped into Vega's waiting arms with an annoyed hiss, and she recognised the feline beast.

"Hoolie," Vega exclaimed, soothing the cat-sìth in her grasp. "What startled you, my love?" The cat-sìth growled, its fur rippling between the gold and black. "I don't know what's got her this worried."

The door was flung open again, this time revealing a figure, silhouetted against the bright lights of the corridor. There was a long pause and then the silver-haired witch stalked inside with a face like thunder.

"That cat stole from me," Rain snarled as she approached Vega who was rocking Hoolie in her arms.

Keyne let out a snicker. "What did she steal?"

Rain came to a stop, chest heaving. "A note. But I wasn't planning on sending it."

"You just have to ask for it nicely." Vega tutted at the cat, rubbing her face against Hoolie's ears. "May we have Rain's note, please?"

The cat-sìth shivered, her fur changing from stripes of gold to star-speckled navy. Hoolie moaned, clearly upset to give up her haul, but then spat something into Vega's waiting hand.

"Thank you," the small witch said. Vega held the paper out

to Rain without releasing the cat-sìth. "Here."

Rain snatched it from her fingers and curled her lip as she looked at the cat. "And if you ever come into my room uninvited again, I swear I'll make a rug out of you." Then she tore the note up and tossed it in the basket beside the desk.

Ailsa watched as the paper floated inside and then turned a questioning look on Rain. She was about to ask her what was in the note when she took in what she was wearing. "Lilac? I don't think I've ever seen you in anything but black."

Rain narrowed her eyes. "Well, I surprised you then, didn't I?"

Always so abrasive. She bit the inside of her cheek. "You look nice."

Rain blinked, her fury cooling. She opened her mouth as if to say something but couldn't seem to get the words out.

"You've left her speechless, Ailsa," said Keyne. They rose from their spot. "Now if you ladies are all ready, we should go. The best food will go soon."

Vega's gaze darted between Ailsa and Rain, and she bit her lip. "Right. You'll probably need to finish doing your face paint, eh, Rain? I've left a palette on the desk." She dropped the cat-sìth and Hoolie streaked ahead after Keyne. "Ailsa, you wouldn't mind walking Rain to the Rite, would you?" Ailsa opened her mouth to say, *'yes, actually'* but Vega was already half out the door. "Great, see you both there."

What was that about? Ailsa turned to the other witch, expecting to see a sneer on Rain's face but she only tilted her chin, eyeing Ailsa warily.

"Are you leaving your hair like that?"

Ailsa's hand flew to her unbound locks, squirming under Rain's stare. "I don't know?"

Rain sighed. "Turn around."

The thought of turning her back to the other witch sent a shiver up Ailsa's spine but she did what she was asked. *Rain is*

Aster's daughter. I need to be nice to her too.

"My hair used to be dark like yours," Rain muttered, combing her fingers through Ailsa's tresses to untangle it. "It started turning grey when I was in my early teens."

"I've heard stress can do that to people?"

Rain hummed, pulling gently at some strands from Ailsa's temple. "I certainly had my fair share of that."

Ailsa pressed her lips into a firm line. "I'm sorry." From what she'd heard of Rain's story, Ailsa had been lucky.

"It's not your fault," Rain said, slotting something into Ailsa's hair.

"Not to ruin this nice moment or anything, but I really don't understand you. One minute you're growling at me and the next…" Ailsa waved at her head. "I honestly can't tell if you like me."

Rain dropped her hands. "If you think I don't like you, you're an idiot." Before Ailsa could turn back to her, she'd swept from the room, following after Vega and Keyne.

Ailsa inspected Rain's handiwork in the mirror as she contemplated her words. The witch had braided one side of her hair away from her face. When Ailsa turned, she spotted a single silver hair clip, shaped like a star and holding the braid in place. *What was that about?*

I have an inkling, said Ishbel.

"And you're not going to tell me," Ailsa guessed.

I'm so glad we understand each other.

Ailsa's attention fell to the waste basket, where the pieces of Rain's note had landed. Casting a surreptitious glance at the door, she reached in and pulled out a scrap of the paper. She couldn't tell what it said, but she recognised that the writing spelled out a single word, over and over again.

Shaking her head, she dropped the piece of paper onto the desk so she could read it later.

Hurry up, hissed Ishbel.

Ailsa took one last glance at her reflection and frowned. Something was missing—and had been missing since she arrived—but she couldn't put her finger on what it was.

Chapter 36

Ailsa found Vega and Keyne waiting for them when they reached the grand ballroom. Vega's hand was tight on Ailsa's wrist as the small witch led her through the ornate double doors. Ailsa tipped her head back in wonder as she gazed at the hundreds of lanterns that had been strung between the massive chandeliers. They cast the whole ceiling in light, drowning out the stars above. The skylights held only inky blackness, except for the one right above the top table. Perfectly positioned above the glass, the not-quite-full moon hung as if it had been placed there. Ailsa could barely tell there was a sliver missing.

"Let's split up to find a table," Vega said, bouncing on her tiptoes. "Keyne, you're with me. First to find one gets ice cream." And then the two were off, leaving Ailsa and Rain at the door.

Ailsa eyed the crowds of witches packed into the ballroom. Some were huddled in groups, pushed close together by the bodies on every side. Others had taken to the dancefloor, where there was barely enough room to spin to the fluted music. The long tables had been set up on the far end and even from where Ailsa stood, she could see they were piled with food. Smaller, round tables dotted the edges of the room, but many were already full.

She took a few more steps into the hall, marvelling at the room, but this caught the attention of the nearest witches. A willowy woman with pale pink hair like a halo around her head jumped when she saw Ailsa, quickly turning to her companions to whisper something. As a group, they edged away, exchanging worried glances. Ailsa could imagine what they were saying. *There she is, the descendant of a traitor.* She shrank back, her stomach turning over. This was going to be harder than she thought.

A huff snapped Ailsa out of her worries, and she tore her eyes from the crowds to look at her companion. Rain appeared frozen beside her, her face stormy and her fists clenched at her sides.

"Are you okay?" asked Ailsa.

"It comes in waves, the hate," the silver-haired witch said quietly. "I know I shouldn't despise them all for having their fun and eating their food and feeling safe, but sometimes I can't help it. And seeing the way they're treating you—it's bringing back memories from when I first arrived. It took a long time for them to accept me."

Ailsa bit the inside of her cheek, hesitating, before she reached down. She took one of Rain's hands in her own, half expecting the other witch to flinch away. But Rain allowed her fingers to unclench and then she fit her palm against Ailsa's, never taking her eyes off the dancing people ahead.

"Come on," Ailsa said, pulling gently. "You can use some of that anger helping me shove through the crowd."

Rain's mouth flickered into a smile before she followed Ailsa, her arms tensed to elbow others out of the way.

Ailsa spotted Maalik's golden antlers and manoeuvred them towards the table where he sat with Zephyr. The curly-haired witch was speaking animatedly, waving his hands around as he told his tale. His shirt was a mass of filmy froth, the white fabric sheer enough to see his skin through. An earring dangled from one ear, and he had painted a single black moon on his cheek. Ailsa thought she heard Keyne let out a small whine but if she was honest, she wasn't faring much better. As soon as Maalik raised his head to look at her, her heart stuttered.

In the time she'd known the demon, he'd always been dressed practically. When she'd first come to his cabin, he had been working as a healer and then when she'd found him again, they'd spent their days hiking, looking for Findias. Even in the castle he spent his days studying in the library. Throughout it all, he had dressed appropriately. But now it occurred to Ailsa that she'd never been somewhere with Maalik that required him to simply have fun. Gone were his simple shirts, trousers, and cloaks. Zephyr truly had worked magic.

The deep red tunic hugged his chest but cut off at the shoulders to bare his arms. Around his neck he wore a broad collar made of patterned gold that matched his antlers perfectly. It all seemed so right, like Ailsa was finally getting a glimpse of the way Maalik had been before.

"You look—" she started to say, before cutting herself off. *You're not supposed to compliment him or make him feel good.* But it was hard. He reminded her of an ancient deity or a hero in an old story; all he needed was a sword and a monster to slay.

"Zephyr found me some Kemetian clothes," he said, touching the collar. "It's been a while since I wore stuff like this."

Ailsa nodded, hoping that he understood she was trying to stick to his rules. *As soon as he turns into an angel, I'm going to tell him how good he looks in anything he's in.* Ailsa cleared her throat. "It's nice to see this part of you."

He smiled, looking her up and down. "You look beautiful."

"That's not fair," she muttered, sliding into the seat beside him.

"Are you two are done ogling each other?" said Rain, rolling her eyes.

Vega and Keyne appeared out of the crowd. "Looks like you won the ice cream," said Vega. "Though maybe that should go to Maalik and Zephyr since they had the table first."

"Next port of call is drinks," said Keyne as Vega took a chair. "Anyone want anything?"

"I'll take a wine," said Zephyr.

Keyne swallowed, their eyebrows shooting into their hair. "No problem," they squeaked. "Come on Rain, you can help." And the witch was off again.

"I'll just get everyone the same then, shall I?" Rain asked, before rising to follow.

After they'd gone, Ailsa's eyes drifted back to Zephyr and his gauzy shirt, where she noted his necklace underneath the fabric. *He's even wearing the vial of blood to the party.*

That means he doesn't leave it lying around, whispered Ishbel.

Vega interrupted her staring with a nudge. "Will you dance with me later?" she asked.

"I'm not much of a dancer," said Ailsa. "I've only been to three ceilidhs in Eilanmòr and the most I could manage was a bit of spinning."

"That sounds fun. I'll confess, I haven't been to Eilanmòr since I must have passed through as a baby." When the small witch noticed Ailsa's curious look, she hurried to explain. "All us children were taken to Eilanmòr first, to camouflage Nicnevan's daughter. Then we were spread out. I ended up in Visenya, with my mother's cousin. I'm glad I experienced my family's culture even when I was away from here."

Ailsa swallowed a lump in her throat. *Yes, that would have been nice.* "So, you knew who you were when you were wee?"

"I was lucky," said Vega, ducking her head.

Ailsa nodded. *You were.* But then, listening to Rain's story it seemed so was she. "I… I wasn't expecting to find family when I came here."

"You didn't have an inkling?" asked Zephyr. "About what you were?"

It was Ishbel that pushed me to come. But she couldn't admit that. "I felt a tug," Ailsa said instead. "But I thought it was because of the spear." Her gaze went around the room, brushing over the women and men in all their finery. "I wish I knew who I'm related to. I mean, I know I'm descended from Ishbel, but didn't you say a lot of witches are?" She had a sudden thought. If there were witches missing, maybe some of her family hadn't made it back to Findias yet. "I must be related to someone here, but what about those still missing?"

"Are there many still to return?" asked Maalik.

Vega bit her lip. "Yes, a few. Twenty-eight were sent away and less than half have found their way back."

Maalik frowned. "Has no one thought to go looking?"

"Sometimes we head down the mountain and into New Hope to ask around," the small witch explained. "If we hear of anyone looking for The Mother, we try to find them. But it doesn't always work. The villagers are superstitious, and people have disappeared."

"There were monsters out there," said Ailsa. "We were attacked on the way up."

Zephyr hummed, leaning forward onto the table. "The yetis are just part of our defences. The whole route is spelled with wards to keep people away."

"That's why I couldn't use my fire magic anymore," Maalik realised. "Why I almost froze."

Ailsa thought back to the days on the mountain side, watching the demon get sicker and sicker, sure he was going to die from the frost. She didn't seem to be similarly affected.

"Probably," said Zephyr. "It selects for air magic so that witches can find their way safely to us. The yetis also tend to leave us alone."

Maalik shook his head. "I knew you should have left me at the bathhouse."

"Never," she told him before turning to Zephyr again. "Whenever you leave, do you have to hike back the same way or is there a shorter path?"

It was Vega who answered. "There's a tunnel that goes from the crypts all the way through the mountain. It's a lot of stairs and you have to take breaks, but it beats being out in the cold."

Zephyr gave her a grin. "Of course, you could always fly."

Sure, it's easy for you to say. "I don't know if I want to learn by jumping off the mountain," Ailsa said, wrinkling her nose.

"You won't have to if you had a broom." His eyes twinkled. "I've secretly managed to get a small batch working." Zephyr ducked his head. "Keyne keeps telling me how much they'd love to fly so when I spotted the brooms abandoned in the tower, I thought I'd surprise them. We can all fly together. That is, if no one is afraid of heights." He looked over Maalik's shoulder. "Shh, they're coming back."

Ailsa raised her eyes to find her friends, but her attention caught on something behind them instead. The priestesses were filing into the hall, taking their seats on the dais. Each wore similar clothes to the rest of the crowd with trousers instead of skirts, though each outfit was subtly different. The fabric Aster wore was heavier and a navy and green tartan sash went from her shoulder to the opposite hip. A spiked silver diadem sat atop her brow, matching the stars littering her forehead. Nasima's hair was tucked under a headscarf, this one a pale lilac to go with her flowing tunic. A copper circlet held the scarf in place and two white clouds dusted the apples of her cheeks. Sefarina perched on the seat between wearing a crown like a golden sunburst, its rays extending across her face and down her clothing.

A couple of witches approached them with ornate goblets before heading back into the crowd again. Nasima appeared eager, scanning the crowd until her husband materialised at her side, bending down to speak with her. Sefarina watched the dancers in front of them, but Aster's stare flicked across the crowd like she was looking for something.

Without warning, the priestess's eyes found Ailsa's, locking there, just like they'd done the first day Aster saw her. Ailsa squirmed in her seat, unable to look away from the intensity of the other witch's stare.

"Ailsa? Are you alright?" Maalik asked, squeezing her arm.

"I think I need some air," she said, just as Keyne and Rain returned to their table. As soon as Rain sat down, Aster snapped her attention to the silver-haired witch.

Rain followed Ailsa's pointed look, taking in her mother's glare. "Don't let her intimidate you," she said, looking away.

"Right." Ailsa swallowed. "I'm feeling hot."

"We'll be back in a second," Maalik said, taking Ailsa's hand and leading her away. She pressed in close to his back, his body too warm to be a respite, but a comfort, nonetheless. Witches cast fearful glances at them as they passed, and Ailsa felt their stares like a heavy weight. When they made it into the hall, she leaned against the cold marble wall.

"What now?" she asked. "I thought I'd just come along to the party, and I'd have an idea."

"You will."

"At least *one* of the priestesses openly hates me."

"So, we go back in and show them you're just like anyone else." He fixed her with his liquid black eyes. "Dance with me?"

Ailsa made a noise that was meant to be a scoff, but it came out broken and weak. "I meant it when I said I wasn't much of a dancer." But the thought of pressing up against Maalik on the dancefloor, of finally getting to hold him, was tempting.

"I think it will help." Maalik brushed a strand of hair behind her ear, and she shivered. "You'll look like you're one of them."

"Maybe I should have put on some face paint too."

He blinked. "Why didn't you?"

Ailsa looked away. "I don't feel like I'm part of this. These people aren't my friends, not really. I hardly know them."

"You hardly knew me when you ran into Hell to get my soul back." He touched her chin, tilting her face back gently so she'd meet his eyes. "You have such a big heart, Ailsa. Let them in."

"They don't want me."

"Prove them wrong. Come on, dance with me," he said with a winning grin.

And with that, Ailsa lost her grip on her last thread of resistance. *Let Maalik think this is part of the plan,* she thought as he led her back inside. *Let him think I'm not just agreeing so I can touch him.*

Chapter 37

There had been a time, when Ailsa had been safe and loved, that she considered herself a hopeless romantic. Cameron had teased her for always including a handsome prince or knight in her make-believe games, though sometimes he'd fight her on who got to save him. The local children would join in with their adventures, but she never gave anyone the role. Not until Nico.

Ailsa was nine when he moved to her village from across the sea to live with his aunt and uncle. The black-haired boy was closer in age to Cameron but as soon as Ailsa saw him, she stuck to him like pollen to a bee. Nico put up with her for a couple of weeks, playing her games and smiling indulgently, until one day he threw down his makeshift crown and quit.

Keep your creepy sister away from me, he'd said. *My aunt says she's cursed.* The next time Ailsa saw him, he had a black eye, Cameron had a bandaged hand, and her heart was broken.

Ailsa's mother died three years later, and she gave up on romantic notions. Until she was saved by an Edessan soldier and taught to fight. Gris had been much older than her, but it hadn't stopped her developing a crush. He was, after all, the first person to be nice to her in years. Still, he left, and Ailsa's heart hardened again.

It took Harris's persistence to draw any feelings from her after that. When he'd danced with her around a bonfire on Beltane, she allowed herself to believe she might be worthy of attention. Even though things hadn't worked out between them, she'd always be grateful he'd taken a broken girl and made her feel special.

Dancing with Maalik wasn't the same. This wasn't a pivotal moment in their relationship; there were no confessions of devotion. No, they'd already done that, in a wind-battered tent on a mountain side. When Maalik took her hand and pressed their bodies together, Ailsa didn't wonder what it meant. She could feel his reverence in every place of contact, in the way he couldn't take his eyes from her. The words were unspoken, but Ailsa knew he wanted her there, in his arms. That she was safe and loved once again.

Ailsa followed his lead, letting him pull her into the swaying crowds, moving to the pounding beat. There wasn't much room to spin like the dancers in Eilanmòr, but they tried their best. Maalik twirled her against him, protecting her from the pressing bodies with his outstretched arm.

"See, you are a good dancer," he murmured in her ear when they were chest to chest again.

Ailsa was already breathless, though it had little to do with her movements. "Do you think it's working?"

"No one is avoiding us." His hands slid down to her hips and Ailsa's brain went blank. "Hold on to my shoulders," he said, and then she was lifted above the throng as he turned.

The room flashed by, and her feet were back on the floor before Ailsa could focus on anything. She let out a shaky laugh. "What was that?"

"Maybe I wanted everyone to see how much fun we're having," he said, cupping the back of her neck with a grin. "Or maybe I wanted an excuse to get closer."

Ailsa's gaze went to Maalik's curving mouth, remembering how his lips felt under hers. Gods, she wanted to drag him somewhere private, to kiss him. "You're—"

But the words were drowned out by a clanging bell, ringing out across the hall. The music stopped abruptly, and all the dancers stilled.

"It's time," called Sefarina from the dais.

The crowds parted, forming a semi-circle around the priestesses' platform. Ailsa gripped Maalik's hand tighter to avoid being swept away or crushed, but she needn't have worried. The other witches shuffled away from them now that they were no longer dancing. *So much for Maalik's plan,* Ailsa thought, deflating.

Aster and Nasima joined the other priestess in standing and a hush fell across the room. Ailsa held her breath.

"Here we are safely at the end of another month," said Sefarina. "Tonight is a time to remember we haven't always been at peace, that this is a blessing from Our Lady. It was she who gave us our gifts and who found us our home. Let us come together to thank her with our words and our offerings."

This must be the start of the Rite. Ailsa pressed in closer to Maalik, standing on her toes to see above the other witches' heads.

Sefarina swept from one side of the room to the other. "We present to you, Our Lady, this food and wine to show our appreciation."

"We present to you, Our Lady, these kisses to show our affection." Nasima reached up to take Sefarina's face in her hands, pecking her once on each cheek. Sefarina, in turn, did the same to Aster who seemed to accept it without a flicker of emotion. The witches in the crowd did the same to their neighbours until the room was filled with people kissing foreheads and hands and even mouths. Without thinking too hard, Ailsa turned hers and Maalik's clasped hands and lifted them to her lips to press a kiss against his wrist. He tensed as her mouth touched his skin but didn't pull away.

Finally, it was Aster's turn. She raised her head and her

hands to the sky. "We present to you, Our Lady, the air from our lungs to show our devotion." Everyone followed her movements turning to look at the moon as one.

Ailsa lifted her gaze, expecting to see the silver orb hanging above them. But when she looked, the moon was gone, obscured by clouds.

The witches around her started murmuring.

"That's never happened before..."

"Usually Luna watches the whole ceremony..."

"Should we wait?"

She cast a glance back to the priestesses. They still had their hands up, but uncertainty clouded their expressions. Aster shifted uncomfortably as the room held their collective breath.

This is your chance, whispered Ishbel but Ailsa was already a step ahead.

"I think I can help," she said, raising her arms above her head. She reached out for the familiar power, grabbing hold as easily as breathing.

"What are you doing?" Aster asked.

Showing you my magic isn't just thunder and lightning. Ailsa moved her fingers, locking onto the clouds. How many times had she practised this before? Even before she knew she had powers, her mood had controlled the weather. Now that she could control it, now that she knew who she was, it felt like nothing to drag the vapour across the sky. She scrunched them up like paper, tossing them away into the night. And when the moon was revealed, glowing brightly against the dark, the whole crowd gasped.

Ailsa lowered her arms and stepped back, smiling. *There, that'll show them.* But the silence stretched out, sending goosebumps along her arms.

She looked at the priestesses, her grin dropping from her

lips when she saw them exchanging uneasy glances.

Sefarina was the first to recover, repeating Aster's words from before. "We present to you, Our Lady, the air from our lungs to show our devotion," she said in a shaky voice. After a second, everyone turned back to the sky, blowing a breath to the moon.

Ailsa was too shocked to follow suit, the panic rising from her toes in waves. How had she managed to understand the situation so badly? If anything, the witches around her were drifting further away. Somehow, she'd amplified their fear.

What did I do? She asked Ishbel.

She sensed the spirit's confusion. *I have no idea.*

Sefarina cleared her throat again. "Tomorrow, the moon will be full, and we will strengthen our connection. It appears that Our Lady is displeased but we must be patient and let her show us the light. In the meantime, let us dance into the night, to celebrate the month that has been."

Nasima stepped forward to say something, but Ailsa didn't hear her. She was already pushing her way through the crowd, desperate to leave. Every face she looked into held nothing but naked fear as soon as they spotted her. She vaguely sensed Maalik following her as she ran from the room, but it wasn't until she was back in the empty hallway again that she stopped, sinking down onto the marble floor.

"I messed up," she said.

"You tried to help."

"What if they blame me for the clouds being there in the first place? What if they think their goddess didn't want to see them because of me?"

Maalik sat down beside her. "That's ridiculous. The moon gets covered by clouds all the time."

"You heard them. They said it's never happened before."

"See, this is why I can't get behind religion," grumbled

Maalik. "Come on, let's go back to the room. We'll work out what we're going to do in the morning."

Ailsa let him pick her up, turning her face into his neck as he walked. All of a sudden, she was too tired to protest, too tired to walk.

She looked over his shoulder at the heavy wooden doors as they got further and further away and felt the same was happening with the spear and any hope she had of claiming it.

Chapter 38

harris woke to an elbow shoved into his ribs and the cabin in total darkness. The whole room stank of sweat and alcohol and, while he'd been the one to demand they drink the whole bottle of whisky he'd procured, he certainly regretted his choice now.

"Move over," he grumbled, pushing at the body beside him.

Angus grunted, rolling over to wrap around Cameron, one leg slung over the other man's hip.

"And no getting handsy over there," Harris added, settling in again. *It was this or leave to find a hammock in the communal hold,* he reminded himself. Not that Angus or Cameron had really offered to share their bed. Harris had considered moving to the hold, full of still-nauseous soldiers, and decided he'd rather sleep beside his friends.

"You could just leave," Cameron said over his shoulder.

"I'm helping you cheer up after your vision. Don't worry, I'm here for you." Harris tugged at the blanket, pulling more of it over himself.

"Thanks, but I'm over it. Don't you have your own bed?"

"This is what happens when you give away the only other private cabin," Harris grumbled.

"Eilidh needed a place to sleep," said Angus. "And since she's: one, my sister and two: not a soldier, she gets a cabin."

"I feel like you're playing favourites and I'm at the bottom of the list. I should have gone on Duncan's boat."

Angus mashed his face into the pillow. "Feel free to head on over."

"Urgh, I need some fresh air," Harris said, sitting up. "Now's your chance to get all the kissing out of the way before I get back."

"Harris, we just want to sleep," groaned Cameron.

Harris tugged his boots on and stood. "Sure, sure. Have fun."

The boat was quiet, save for the occasional snore. Harris picked his way through the hold and up the stairs to the deck. Some soldiers were still up, watching the trees and the water with their heads on their hands and sipping from their hip flasks. The ship's captain had retired to bed with the people below but his son, a lanky boy with flame red hair like Harris's, was at the helm so they could sail through the night. The boy's features were sharp, and Harris thought he'd spotted pointed ears before he tugged on a woollen cap.

He made his way up to the quarter deck, raising his hand in greeting. "You're Captain Bain's kid, right? Thought you might want some company."

"I'm not supposed to talk to strangers," the boy said, his shoulders tensing.

"That's good advice. I'll just sit over here then," said Harris, lifting himself onto a barrel and leaning against the railing. He tilted his head back, watching the clouds roll across the sky until they parted. *Huh, full moon.*

"You're fae."

Harris looked back to find the boy watching him curiously. "Sure am. What about you?"

"Half," he said, blinking his big eyes. "My papa said mum was a faerie."

"I know a few of those. Have you met my friend Eilidh?"

The boy's eyes lit up. "Yes, she's the Faerie Queen's dau—"

Harris leapt from the barrel, clamping a hand over the boy's mouth and looking around surreptitiously. "How do you know that?"

The boy's eyes were wide and frightened. "Are you going to hurt me?" he asked.

"Not if you keep quiet." Harris dropped his hand but didn't back away. "What's your name?"

The boy took a moment to answer, as if he was afraid Harris was going to cover his mouth again. "Euan."

"I'm Harris." He gave the boy what he hoped was a reassuring smile. "Eilidh is my friend, and she really doesn't want anyone to know who she is. Tell me how you found out so I can stop it happening again."

"I'm sorry. I could just tell?" He bit his lip. "When I looked at her, I felt it in my blood. Can't you?"

I should have just let him finish his sentence so I could laugh it off. Throwing himself across the deck had confirmed everything. He'd have to be more careful in the future if other fae came looking.

"She doesn't want the crown," Harris told him. "Do you have any idea what all this means?"

Euan shrunk away. "You're not going to chuck me into the river, are you?"

Harris very deliberately looked from the boy to the boat's railing. "It depends on how you answer this question: who do you think Eilidh's father is?"

"My papa told me the story." Euan licked his lips nervously. "The… the hero who chained Nicnevan to the tree was her lover and the princess's dad."

Harris hummed. "That's it? Just a nameless hero?" Not the late King of Eilanmòr?

"I never asked," said Euan.

"Good," Harris said, relieved. "At least the boy didn't know

Eilidh was related to Angus and Duncan. "You get to stay for now. Get back to steering."

The boy was silent for a long moment, doing as he was told while Harris watched him out of the corner of his eye. If even Euan, who was half-fae, could sense Eilidh, surely there would be many others. And even if Eilidh didn't want to be queen, there had to be a way to use her position to their advantage.

"Harris?" Euan eventually said, breaking him from his thoughts.

"Yeah?"

The boy spoke quietly, still staring ahead. "I won't tell anyone else."

Harris chuckled. "I know because otherwise I'd have to eat you."

"I'm not human," said Euan with a frown. "I know selkies don't eat people."

"I'll throw you in the water then." But Harris's tone was light and teasing.

"Harris?" Euan straightened.

Harris sighed. "What, kid? You know I was only joking, right?"

"Yeah, it's not that." Euan's eyes were fixed to the left of the ship. When Harris looked at him more closely, he saw the boy was gripping the ship's wheel tight, his knuckles paling. "There are people on the riverbank."

Harris raised his eye to the treeline and his blood ran cold. Dozens of figures stood between the trees, each holding a lantern and staring at the boats as they passed.

"Go and wake everyone," Harris breathed.

Chapter 39

arris folded his arms to give them something to do. He couldn't stand it, the waiting. *We never should have woken everyone up.* If it were up to him, their floating procession would still be sailing down the river but as soon as Angus and Captain Bain saw the figures, they raised the red flag, stopping the other boats. Their vessel pulled up alongside the lead ship, where a rumpled Duncan leant against the railing, speaking to General MacKenzie and his boat's captain in a low voice.

"What do you make of it, Captain?" Angus asked the man beside him while they waited for their king's decision.

Captain Bain crossed his arms and stared out into the gloom. "They're just standing there."

That was the problem. If the people would just move, they'd know they were alright, but they just stood between the trees with an eerie stillness, clutching their barely glowing lanterns.

"Are they fae?" asked Angus.

"I don't think so," said Harris. "I can't sense any magic around them." At least he hoped not. His first worry when he'd seen them was that they were here for Eilidh. Hadn't he just been wondering how many other faerie folk would find her?

Angus frowned. "So, they're human then. Are they under a spell?"

"Like I said, no magic."

"We should assemble our soldiers," Angus called out to the other boat. "Perhaps they need aid."

225

Harris didn't like this. "Would you tell Eilidh to stay in her cabin and lock her door?" he said as an aside to their captain.

The man nodded and headed below to give his orders. Their deck quickly filled with half-asleep soldiers, all leaning over the side to get a look at the people. Harris glanced over his shoulder where the rest of the boats were queued behind them. If their own soldiers were being woken up, shouldn't the word be given to them too? But before he could voice the question, Duncan was climbing up to the quarter deck and raising his hands to amplify his voice.

"We mean you no harm," he shouted into the night. "If you need help, come closer."

The silence that followed his announcement was deafening, until Angus broke it. "We're with the Eilanmòrian army. You don't need to be afraid."

Unless they're not Eilanmòrian, Harris thought. But Angus's words seemed to have done the trick. One figure shuffled closer to the river, and another followed. Even with the full moon and the lantern light, it was still too dark to really make out their faces, but they moved assuredly.

"How much room do you have on your boat?" Duncan called over when he was beside the railing again.

"Well Cameron, Harris and I were sharing a bed," said Angus. "But we can probably squeeze a few more on."

More figures were moving now, lining up along the riverbank. Captain Bain was back first, letting out a low whistle when he saw the throng.

"There has to be a hundred at least," he said.

"Could you pull your anchors?" asked Duncan. "Sail closer?"

Captain Bain nodded, immediately climbing to the wheel, shouting orders on the way. Euan leapt into action, cranking a lever on the port side as fast as his scrawny arms could manage. Harris and Angus jumped to the edge of the deck as soldiers and sailors prepared, some going to lend a hand with the ropes and pulleys, while the others strapped on weapons. Many of them hadn't bothered to put on armour. Together, they managed to raise the twin anchors while Captain Bain spun the wheel. He used the flowing water to pull them downstream at an angle, sailing closer and closer to the river's edge. The people followed their progress, moving in line with the boat, but something about the way they walked didn't seem right to Harris.

"They're not speaking to each other," Harris realised. Yet they moved together, as if they all had the same thoughts.

Cameron appeared beside Angus, rubbing at his face sleepily. "What's going on?"

"Harris spotted them," said Angus, indicating the people on the shore. "I think they need help."

"We're not letting them on our boat, are we?" Cameron said with a frown. "They're creepy."

"Finally, someone who talks sense," muttered Harris.

Now they were less than a boat's length away; close enough to make out the features of the strange people in the moonlight. Harris scanned their blank stares with confusion. They just look like people. He'd half expected the feral and rotting features of those the Edaxi had infected, but their faces were unblemished, and they didn't appear threatening. They stood as a group, swaying slightly as the boat floated closer and closer to the shore.

"They look like they're in shock," Harris said. He turned to Angus but as he did, the prince took in a shuddering breath.

"That's impossible," he croaked.

"What?"

A woman stepped forward until the river lapped against her feet. Her dress was bright white, but she didn't raise it as it trailed over the soil, staining the hem. She held her lantern higher, casting odd shadows over her face. *She's beautiful,* Harris thought vaguely. The woman looked to be in her late thirties with strawberry blonde hair falling in ringlets around her heart shaped face. There was something familiar about her though. Something Harris couldn't place.

"What is it?" Harris asked again. He grabbed Angus's shoulder to find the prince was shaking.

"She looks like—" Angus shook his head. "—but that can't be—"

"Who?" Cameron took Angus's chin, turning his face so the prince would look at him.

Angus opened and closed his mouth, but the words took a while to come out. "She looks like my mother."

"Your *dead* mother?" Harris said. How old would Angus have been when Queen Mairi died? Five? Six?

Cameron's face softened. "I'm sorry, Angus—"

"No, you don't understand." Angus backed away. "She doesn't just have a passing resemblance. She looks just like her."

There was a shout further down the boat as a soldier threw himself at the railing. "My son!" he shouted. "He's alive!"

Then it was the captain's turn. He wandered down from the quarter deck, half in a trance. "That's my wife."

"Ma?" shouted Euan as another woman approached. She didn't flinch as her feet sunk into the freezing river water.

As one, the group waded in further and further, getting closer to the boat. Harris watched in horror as the water came up to their necks, yet still they didn't stop. Those who recognised loved ones clambered to throw ropes overboard while the people began to swim, their lanterns floating off down the river.

"I don't like this," said Harris. "We should keep sailing."

But Euan had already dropped the anchors again. He pushed a ladder overboard, shouting, "Ma!"

Beside them, Captain Bain shook his head as he watched his wife swim closer. "But she's dead," he whispered.

And Harris understood. "They're all dead," he snapped, giving the captain a shake. "We need to go. Now!"

But it was too late. The first person reached the boat, but instead of hauling themselves up the rope, they pulled, causing the soldier holding it to lose balance and plummet into the water with a splash. Immediately, the swimming figures swarmed on him, pulling him under the icy water as he fought to keep his head up.

"Move!" shouted Harris.

They flew to the anchor levers, pulling them up once more but already the dead were clambering over the railings.

Harris grabbed Angus's wrist, dragging him and Cameron along behind as he raced up the stairs to the quarterdeck.

"They *look* alive," Cameron protested.

"It's a trick," said Harris over his shoulder. "No doubt the Edaxi's latest."

"That was my mother." Angus's voice was thin.

If that really was the late queen, how had her body ended up in Eilanmòr's forest? Her body should have been buried in Dunrigh... "Oh gods," Harris said slowly, realisation dawning on him. "Remember you told me the remains of your ancestors were stolen during Mirandelle's attack. Was your mother buried or cremated?"

"Buried." Angus blanched. "Oh no."

"We need to leave," Harris said darkly. "We all do." He reached for a dangling rope attached to a bell, hanging from the rigging. Harris pulled the rope hard, forcing the clapper inside to hit off the metal with a high-pitched ding. It rang out over the river, catching the attention of the soldiers below and hopefully those in the other boats. Unfortunately, they were not the only ones to hear it. The dead that had pulled themselves onto the boat turned together as Harris continued ringing the bell.

"Harris?" Cameron backed up, away from the stairs where a man in a simple tunic was already ascending. "I left my sword downstairs."

"Here," shouted Angus, throwing him a hammer from a bucket of tools discarded on the floor.

Cameron caught it with ease and faced the dead man. "You need to turn the ship." The dead man launched himself at Cameron who ducked out of the way at the last second.

"Right," croaked Angus, scrambling for the wheel.

Harris continued to ring the bell, eyeing the chaos below. Both the anchors were up now, but the people who'd pulled them were grappled to the ground by the walking dead. Three of the dead pulled a soldier towards the edge as he struggled to free himself. Another man lay on the floor of the boat, fighting off a living corpse with a knee in its chest. Their boat was moving now, carried away from their comrades floating in the water.

"We can't leave the other ships," cried Angus.

Cameron landed the hammer into the back of his opponent's skull. The man fell to the floor. *Thank the gods,* Harris thought. *At least they can die, same as anyone.*

"They'll follow us," he said, tugging on the rope again. "We need to get ourselves to safety."

There was a splash on the port side as a soldier or one of the undead fell overboard. "Hit them in the head," shouted Cameron as another walking corpse, this time an elderly woman, came hobbling onto the quarterdeck. He leapt into action, his hammer coming down upon her skull before she could reach the wheel.

Below them, their soldiers had heeded Cameron's instruction. Fighting through the panic, they aided each other, pulling bodies off of comrades and dispatching their enemies with efficiency, until all that survived stood on deck, chests heaving and covered in gore.

Cameron wiped the blood spray from his face and straightened. "I think that's all—"

But a woman wearing a white dress appeared, shuffling up the stairs slowly. Her face and her hands were empty of weapons, yet Harris could sense the fear radiating off Angus.

"Mother." He choked on the word, shrinking back into Harris.

"Look at me," he said, grabbing Angus's shoulder. "That isn't your mother."

The prince whimpered. "It's her body."

"We need to lay her to rest again."

Angus closed his eyes. "Do it."

Harris nodded to Cameron, skirting around the deck as the woman walked forward. She didn't react when he sidled up behind her, only scrambling when Harris got his arms under hers to hold her in place. It was almost too easy for Cameron to reach out, taking her head in his hands like a caress.

"I'm sorry," he whispered. Then he twisted. Harris felt the crunch of bone against bone and her body stilled.

He gently lowered Angus's mother to the ground and cast around for something to cover her, finding an old piece of sail. "I hope she can stay at peace," he said as he tucked it around her. On the main deck below, a group of soldiers let out shouts as they pushed the last of their attackers overboard. They clutched the railing in exhaustion as they sailed away from the threat.

"Is it over?" asked Angus. He still had his eyes closed and

his knuckles were white against the wood.

Cameron was with him in two strides, pulling the prince into his body. "We're safe."

That was all it took for Angus to dissolve into great hiccupping sobs, pressing his face into Cameron's neck.

Harris knew he should leave them alone but there were too many questions to answer first. "That was too easy." He paced to the aft of the ship, peering through the darkness at the other boats, which, thankfully, were still following them. "If the Edaxi's plan was to create a new, undead army, they didn't do a good job, did they?"

Cameron looked over Angus's shaking shoulder and shook his head sadly. "I don't think that's it. The corpses aren't meant to fight us," he said. "They're meant to torment us."

And, as Harris surveyed the soldiers and crew below, he saw that the mapmaker was right. Many of the men and women were leaning over the fallen bodies, pressing their foreheads into their chests and sobbing. These were people that they'd known in life, resurrected just to fill them with despair and fear.

Chapter 40

Seven soldiers were missing at the last count.

Were they pulled overboard and drowned? Still alive, waiting to be rescued? They had no idea. It didn't matter anyway; those poor people were long gone. Guilt gnawed at Angus's stomach. They'd been travelling for hours in the dark, desperate to put as much distance between their boats and the dead as possible.

It wasn't until the horizon was dusted with the faintest pink that Captain Bain signalled they could slow down. He wiped the sweat from his top lip and waved a hand. "I believe we're safe for now. If you were on the night shift, go to bed."

Not that anyone got much sleep, Angus thought, the weariness heavy in his bones. He eyed the stairs leading down from the quarter deck to the cabin doors, thinking they might as well have been a mountain. He used his last reserves of energy to take a couple of steps back, enough that he was out of the way, and crumpled to the ground, drawing his legs into his chest and letting his head lean against the railing behind.

Angus had described many things as *'life changing'* in his time. The first bite of their cook's famous cheese pie. The first time a boy pushed him to the ground in the training ring. The first night he met Ailsa, Harris and Iona. All memories he cherished. All moments that had changed who he was at his core. But seeing the face of his long dead mother, that was a different sort of life changing. He knew that blank expression would haunt him for the rest of his days.

He barely registered that someone was there until Cameron lowered himself to the floor beside Angus, wrapping an arm around his shoulders. "I sent Harris to look after Eilidh. Are you all right?"

"No." The word cracked out of Angus. "I keep expecting to wake up from a nightmare. I don't think my imagination could come up with something this bad though."

"I'm sorry." Cameron pressed a kiss to his temple. "This should never have happened to you."

"There were others," Angus said, heart sinking. "They took more of my ancestors from their graves. But I didn't recognise anyone else." He clutched at Cam's hand. "I don't want to see that again."

"Your mother's body is at rest. Who else?"

"Not my father. He was cremated." *Thank the gods.*

"There isn't anyone else you'd recognise," said Cameron, "is there?"

Angus thought through the list of long dead family members. "I suppose not. What about you? Do you have anyone?"

"My mother. But they'd have to really look hard to find her grave. Her name was Heather and we buried her out on the moors, with her namesake, so she could watch the bees go about their business." He gave Angus a sad smile. "She always said bees were better than people. She doesn't have a cairn or anything; nobody but her family would know she was there."

Angus took his hand. "And the rest of your family?"

"I have no idea if my grandmother is still alive," he said. "I hope that, if she's dead, I don't see her again, but I don't think I'd be too upset if I had to push her off the boat." Cameron gasped. "Wait, what if they bring fae back to fight for them? Nicnevan—"

"Eilidh and I burned her body," said Angus quickly. The

Faerie Queen would not be coming back.

"Well, at least there's that." Cameron blew out a breath. "You'd do the same for me, right? If I—"

"No." Angus squeezed his fingers around the fine bones of Cameron's wrist. "We're not talking about that right now. When the time comes, far off in the future, when we've had a full life together, I'll do whatever you wish. I need you—"

Angus was cut off with a shout from the main deck. Whipping his head up from where he'd been leaning into Cam, he realised with a jolt that another ship had pulled in beside their own and already ropes were being tied to keep their hulls together.

"Where is he?" came the shout again and then Duncan was striding up the stairs and kneeling down beside Angus, eyes wild and searching. "Thank the gods."

Angus swallowed, seeing a flash of their mother's face again. "I… I'm glad you're safe."

"I'm safe?" Duncan said incredulously. "Yours was the only boat that was attacked. What happened?"

Captain Bain leaned against the ship's wheel like it was the only thing holding him up. "They were dead."

General MacKenzie appeared behind Duncan, taking in the scene. "Who?"

"The people who attacked us," said Cameron.

Duncan frowned. "How could they be dead?"

"Magic, most likely." Captain Bain rubbed a hand over his mouth. "My wife was there. She died three years ago and was buried in Inshmore. Yet, there she stood, as if no time had passed. They were blank. Like echoes of who they were."

"I don't understand the logic," said Duncan, leaning back. "Why go to all the trouble of digging up dead people."

General MacKenzie raised an eyebrow. "Perhaps they've realised the Mirandelli army needs bolstering."

"Duncan," Angus said quietly. He'd better tell him, even if the words tasted like acid on his tongue. "I saw our mother."

"That's not possible. Her burial cairn is in Dunrigh…" His brother trailed off, paling. "The Mirandelli soldiers took their bodies."

Angus nodded, still not quite believing it. "Now we know why."

"They hardly caused much damage," said the General, surveying the lower deck. "What was the point?"

"If you'd seen your loved one, you'd know." His mother's face flashed before his eyes once again. Angus had been so young when she'd died, he hardly remembered her, but his brother had been older. Angus was grateful Duncan hadn't seen her, but if he had, perhaps they could share the horror between them. "They wanted to frighten us. To break us."

"You aren't broken," Duncan told him, his voice turning stern.

You don't understand, Angus wanted to say. But there was no use in arguing. "I think I need to lie down."

"Yes, good." The king stood, placing his hands on his hips. "We'll be at the coast by tomorrow, I'm told. Cameron, please make sure Angus gets some food and water." Then Duncan was gone, back to his boat with his General in tow.

Angus leaned into Cameron's shoulder again, breathing in his familiar smell. "Stay with me," he whispered. "Please."

Cameron dragged him to his feet and wrapped an arm around him, keeping him safe. "Always."

Chapter 41

Ailsa stared at her reflection in the mirror as she twisted her face. First, she pulled her lips into a smile. *Too much teeth.* Then she widened her eyes and blinked rapidly. *I look deranged.*

"What are you doing?" asked Maalik from the door.

"Trying to make my face look more trustworthy." She threw the comb down in disgust. "Turns out I only have three looks: tired, furious, and unhinged."

"Maybe you could change your hair?" Maalik offered. "Vega always wears those little bunches on top of her head. They look sweet."

Ailsa twisted the top strands around her fingers, holding them in two buns so they could see the effect in the mirror. "I look like a rabbit," she said, letting them drop.

"A very cute rabbit." He sighed, coming to stand behind her. "I'm sorry, I don't feel like having me around is much help."

Ailsa quirked her eyebrow. "You were a literal angel—"

"And now I'm a demon—"

"Who still manages to look more honest than me." She leaned back, tapping her fingers against her knee. "All that matters is that I get through the next two nights without causing a fuss. After the Rites are done, maybe I can try appealing to them again."

"Sounds like a good plan. Blend in, bide your time." He dropped a kiss to the crown of her head.

There was a tinkle of a bell and they both turned to see

a nose and whiskers appear through the wall. The cat-sìth sniffed, smelling the room it was about to enter and then pushed its way through. Its fur rippled in green and blue until it solidified, revealing a stormy grey cat with bright yellow eyes and ears that looked like they'd been bitten.

"I've seen that cat before," Ailsa realised. "In the library."

"She works for Zephyr." Maalik hurried across the room, bending down to remove the parchment from the cat-sìth's collar. "Her name is Smirr." The cat in question yowled, growing impatient.

"She's a bit scruffier than the other cat-sìths," Ailsa muttered. Smirr hissed, arching her back as Maalik stood and Ailsa hurried to amend her statement. "But I like scruffy."

Smirr's fur stood on end for a moment, before rippling into the greens and blues again, so she could leave the way she'd come, jumping through the wall like it was water.

Maalik read the note and sighed. "Zephyr wants to dress me up again before the Rite."

"He did a good job last night," Ailsa said lightly. Maalik pressed his lips together, his shoulders tensing. *Right, too much like a compliment.* "I just mean the clothes were cool."

"It's been a long time since I last wore Kemetian clothes. I'd better go find him then," he said, tossing the note onto the desk.

"Wait," said Ailsa, remembering the other piece of paper she kept there. She pulled out Rain's parchment and held it out to him. "Before you go, could you tell me what this says?"

Maalik took it from her, his eyebrows pinching together. "It's just the same word, over and over again."

"Read it to me?"

"Skye." He shrugged. "But not like the sky up above us. It has an e at the end, like the name. I think I've heard of both men and women having it."

"Why would she write a name that many times?" Maybe Keyne had been wrong about Rain and Vega and it was someone else who Rain was in love with. She hadn't heard of anyone called Skye here, but she also hadn't met every single witch. "Thanks," she said after a moment. "I'll see you at the Rite."

"Blend in, bide your time," Maalik repeated as he left.

Ailsa looked back at her reflection. Blend in, right. But how?

But then her eyes trailed down to the bottom of the mirror, where Vega had left her pots and brushes in a neat pile the day before. Perhaps she had an idea after all.

***

Ailsa paused outside the ballroom's doors later that night, fixing her clothing. Vega had left her a pale gold top with sparkling embellishments and billowing trousers to match but she'd dashed off before Ailsa could get ready. *Gods, I hope I look all right.*

Vain, aren't we? whispered Ishbel.

"You know that's not it," Ailsa said, rolling her eyes. "I just hope I've done a good job."

I would have gone for something a little more you. Something darker. But you'll certainly fit in.

"Good." She straightened up, throwing her shoulders back. "Okay, here goes nothing." Then she opened the doors to the packed hall.

The first few witches she passed paid her no mind, which was fine in Ailsa's book. But soon heads were turning. She refused to shrink back, throwing them what she hoped was a warm smile instead. A few returned the gesture, but others stared in confusion, whispering to their neighbour. Ailsa hurried her way through the crowds, finding the table where her companions had sat the night before. Maalik, Zephyr and Keyne were already seated but it was Vega who shrieked, jumping from her chair when she saw Ailsa.

"Your face!" The small witch threw herself forward, grabbing Ailsa's hands.

"I didn't really know what I was doing," Ailsa admitted. "But I wanted to give it a try."

"You look stunning," said Vega, throwing her arms around Ailsa.

She certainly hoped so, it had taken her an hour to get the face paint right. She'd blended the shimmery lilac with blue and blotted it across her cheeks, dotting it with white to make little stars. Ailsa had seen many variations of the same thing on other witches' faces, and she hoped she had emulated it well.

"This means you're officially one of us," said Vega, pulling Ailsa to the table. "I'll have to show you the best way to remove it all for bed though."

Ailsa sank down next to Maalik. "Good, I'd rather not stain the pillow."

"Rosewater," said Keyne conspiratorially.

Ailsa smiled. "Noted."

"You look lovely," Maalik murmured into her ear.

She turned to look at him fully; he wore the same collar as the day before but this time with a jade tunic. Gods, it was hard not to tell him how good he looked. Ailsa grabbed his hand under the table and gave it a squeeze, hoping to communicate the compliment she couldn't give.

"What's the plan for tonight?" she asked.

Zephyr brushed a ring-covered hand through his curls. "We drink and eat and dance and then the priestesses strengthen their wards. We reach out to the triple-headed goddess for guidance for the coming month. Sometimes she sends us messages but other times she's silent."

"She's always silent," corrected Vega. "But if you look closely, you'll know what she means."

"That sounds cryptic."

"You'll just have to hang around until the time comes then."

Ailsa nodded. She could feel the face paint on her cheeks, a film over her skin. The urge to brush it away was there but she resisted. "Do you think," she said, weighing her words, "that you could introduce me to some people?"

Vega let out an excited peep. "Of course! Come with me."

That was how Ailsa found herself being paraded around the ballroom; Vega's arm linked tightly with hers. Every witch Vega introduced her to was friendly and welcoming— whether it was because of Vega's charm or Ailsa's new appearance she wasn't sure. At one point she looked back over at Maalik to find him drinking a cup of tea, of all things, and speaking animatedly with both Keyne and Zephyr. Feeling her eyes on him, his gaze flicked up and he gave her a nod of encouragement.

I think I'm doing well, she thought as she shook hands with a very tall, blond man with a galaxy painted across his jaw.

Making friends, snorted Ishbel. *I'm so proud.*

Shut it you.

"You've been to Dunrigh?" the man asked. "I've always wanted to go. I've heard Eilanmòr's prince is handsome."

"Angus? I suppose he is," said Ailsa, returning his grin. "That's a bit weird for me to say, though. I'm pretty sure he fancies my brother."

Vega grabbed her arm. "Wait, you have a brother?" she asked, just as the blonde witch said, "You actually know Prince Angus?"

Ailsa held her hands up in the air. "Yes, to both. I met Angus in the spring when I helped find the Stone of Destiny. And I hadn't seen my brother Cameron for years, until a month later when we found him in Ephraim—"

"You've been to Ephraim?"

A crowd gathered around her while she tried to answer their questions about Nicnevan and how she'd met Maalik and the explosion in Dunrigh. She gave the barest details of her fight out of Hell, leaving out how Ishbel had taken over for her.

"You managed that so far underground?" asked a young witch with peach clouds across her cheeks and nose. "Your magic must be really powerful."

Ailsa bit her lip. "I probably wouldn't manage something like that again. Though I suppose there wasn't air under the sea when we were fighting the Stoor Worm."

"Under the sea?"

"Stoor Worm?"

And so it went on. Ailsa watched the faces of those surrounding her carefully, waiting for their derision or terror as she recounted her battle in the Nymph. But the only expressions they wore were those of wonder. Soon she found she was enjoying trading stories. A drink was pressed into her hand as another witch told her how he'd snuck into the yeti's den just to draw them asleep. It wasn't until a palm grasped around her shoulder that she realised they'd been talking for such a long time.

"Ailsa," hissed a voice at her ear. She turned to find Rain regarding the other witches with a scowl. "I need to talk to—"

But a bell rang out across the ballroom, drowning out Rain's words. "Later then," she said as the crowd shuffled closer to the dais.

Ailsa allowed herself to be dragged along, sensing Vega's

presence on her left and Rain's on her right. She felt lighter than she had done when she first entered the hall.

That went well, she whispered to Ishbel.

See, you're irresistible.

Ailsa grinned and shifted her attention to the front of the room. The High Priestesses stood together, as they'd done the night before, but this time each of them held a single candle. Even from where Ailsa stood, she could see the wax was melting onto their palms and wrists but not a single one of them flinched.

Sefarina nodded and the crowd grew silent. "You all know this is a magical night. The moon is full once again." She tipped her head back and they all followed her stare. High up above the moon was bright and unobscured by clouds. Ailsa sent up her own thanks for that. "We gather under the sky to show our devotion."

"We pledge ourselves to Our Lady and ask for her protection," said Nasima, dropping into a graceful curtsy.

"We look to her for guidance and vow to heed her warnings," said Aster.

"We have to be quiet now," murmured Vega. "Sometimes the goddess sends us messages."

Ailsa pressed her lips together to show her friend she understood. The room hushed as they looked upwards. *What kind of message?* Ailsa wondered.

Watch the light, was all Ishbel said.

Ailsa counted to one hundred in her head, waiting for something to happen. Her fingers were getting fidgety, and she wanted to shift her feet, but it was so quiet she worried she'd make a noise. She scanned the witches ahead of her and then the priestesses. Each had their eyes on the ceiling, still as statues, until Aster broke her stare and turned her attention to Ailsa instead.

Don't look away. But the weight of her focus was almost too much. Ailsa took in Aster's blank face and grey eyes as her heart thumped in her chest. *What does she want?*

Sefarina cleared her throat as Aster looked away, releasing Ailsa. But before Sefarina could speak, something flashed out of the corner of Ailsa's vision and the witches gasped as one.

"She's here," Vega said.

Ailsa looked up and there it was. Ishbel had told her to look at the light and now she knew what the spirit guide had meant. The moonbeams flickered and moved, images beginning to form.

"What is it?"

"I think that's a boat—"

"Looks more like a castle to me."

Ailsa focussed, trying to discern what she was seeing. But then the light got even brighter, flooding the air above their heads. Shadows crept in from the sides, taking clear shapes, and Ailsa's stomach leapt. She recognised the castle, portrayed in shades of grey and white. It was Dunrigh. She opened her mouth to tell Vega and Rain that but then the picture changed. The castle crumbled, consumed by blinding flashes that had them all raising their arms to cover their eyes. When the light dimmed, the castle was rubble.

"What is this?" asked Ailsa.

No one answered her.

The light changed and they were looking down upon a beach. An army stood in neat lines upon the sand but then a massive wave swept in from the sea, drowning them all. The scene shifted again, and they saw the outline of a person. They lay on their side at first but soon their body was contorting in pain. Ailsa could almost hear their scream. Finally, an island rose from a black sea as lightning crackled overhead. The land buckled and monsters spilled forth from under the soil, spreading over the image until all of the light was extinguished.

Ailsa came back to herself and realised she was breathing heavily. While she'd watched, she'd somehow grabbed both Vega's and Rain's wrists. Unshed tears blurred her vision, but she pushed them back. She did *not* cry.

"What did we just see?" Nasima blinked up at the ceiling.

"War," said Sefarina, lowering her candle to the floor and shaking out her hands. "We knew it was coming; it shouldn't be a surprise."

Whispers were traded by the witches around Ailsa but all she could hear was a low buzzing. Had they seen this before? From everyone's reaction, she thought not. Yet they'd still known what was happening further south. It was why she was here. Suddenly, it was all too much.

"I told you," she shouted over the murmuring. She let go of Rain and Vega, pushing her way through the crowd until she was at the bottom of the dais. "Now do you believe me?"

Sefarina sank down into her chair, rubbing a thumb over her lips. "I'm sorry, Ailsa."

"So, you'll help?"

"We can't," said Nasima. "The Edaxi are too strong."

"And the spear?" she asked through gritted teeth.

"This is the best place for it." Sefarina raised her chin, as if making her decision, though Ailsa was sure it had already been made when they'd seen her lightning. "We'll protect it, I promise."

"Innocent people—innocent fae—are going to die," Ailsa snarled.

An unknown emotion flickered over Aster's face. She almost looked disappointed. "Sef—"

"No." Sefarina pushed her shoulders back, looking every inch a queen in her crown. "We should take the goddess's warning and thank our stars we're safe here. In the morning, we'll look at expanding our shield and send a message to New Hope. For now, let us honour Our Lady."

Nasima and Aster took their places, the former wearing a look of sympathy, the latter staring Ailsa down like before, except this time something akin to anger gleamed in the grey of her eyes.

And Ailsa knew. Knew that her efforts at diplomacy had been for nothing. She turned from the platform and stalked through the throng, who parted before her. Witches she'd just been laughing with gave her a wide berth. Even Vega and Rain kept their distance. It didn't matter anymore. She was done trying to impress them all.

What now? Ishbel asked when they were in the hallway.

The music had started up again, drifting through the partially opened doors. Ailsa knew Maalik would find her soon to try to comfort her.

"I don't want comforting. I don't want to ask. I want to *demand*." But she had spent the last few days showing them she wasn't a threat. They'd never take her seriously.

I could do it. Ishbel ran phantom fingers down the back of her mind. Ailsa was sure it was meant to be comforting, but it only made her shiver. *Let me take over for a while, show them who they're really dealing with.*

"Is that wise?" But asking hadn't worked and neither had winning their favour. Maybe all there was left to do was unleash the monster they feared. "I'm out of options," she said. "Do it."

Ailsa whimpered as she felt the spirit pushing through her mind, towards her lips. Ishbel had done this before, only a handful of times, but it was always when Ailsa had been incapacitated in some way. Maalik had told her how she'd returned to him a few weeks ago, after destroying Hell with

Ishbel, but she didn't remember. Ailsa had been unconscious and Ishbel hadn't disturbed her as she'd piloted her body to the demon. This time she was fully alert. It was uncomfortable, having another entity elbow you out of the way. Ailsa had the sense that she could stop her, send her back to the corner of her head. But without her, wouldn't they just turn Ailsa away again? It was worth a shot. So, Ailsa let Ishbel through, side-stepping out of the way to crouch behind her ancestor.

Chapter 42

Ishbel pushed off the wall and stalked towards the ballroom. She walked more fluidly than Ailsa usually did, swinging her hips and raising her chin to stare down any eyes that fell upon her.

Ailsa cringed. *Show off.*

"They should know who they're dealing with," Ishbel said under her breath. A smug smile curled her lips as she saw first confusion on the faces of the other witches and then fear. Yes, she wore the body of her descendant, but they could sense that she was far more ancient.

Ishbel caught a glimpse of the gaggle of witchlings Ailsa called friends, watching her progress from a round table.

Vega, Keyne and Rain, Ailsa supplied for her.

Ishbel rolled her eyes. "I don't care who they are." But then she spotted the demon, watching her open mouthed, and grinned. "Him on the other hand… it's nice to see him with my own eyes again." She winked at Maalik which snapped him out of his shock. He placed his drink down and followed behind, keeping a safe distance.

One by one the dancers stopped twirling, parting to let Ishbel through, until the crowd's awareness spread, reaching the musicians who ceased their playing abruptly. Silence fell in the hall, all except Ishbel's footsteps as she crossed the floor to where the council sat, watching her warily. Nasima had grabbed her husband's hand, while Sefarina was halfway out of her seat. Only Aster remained still, her nose flaring as she watched Ishbel's approach.

Because, though Ishbel wore her body, they knew she wasn't Ailsa. No doubt they could feel the shift in energy, like an approaching storm. She'd always had that effect on people.

Ishbel licked her lips, revelling in the discomfort. "I assume you know of me?" She spoke to the council, but her voice rang out clear to the rest of the room.

She saw the moment the youngest priestess, Nasima, put it together. "Ishbel Lauchair," the woman breathed as her face clouded in terror.

"*Priestess* Ishbel Lauchair," she said, fluttering her eyelashes. "If it's all the same."

"Of course," said Sefarina, bowing her head slightly. "Ailsa told us she met you. We didn't realise the extent of your... *friendship*."

Ishbel rolled her shoulders and placed her hands on her hips. "I must admit it feels good to have a body again, to feel my magic flowing through her veins. But you've seen that too, haven't you?"

"But it isn't your body, is it?" snapped Aster. "Bring the girl back."

"She's here, aren't you, Ailsa dear?"

Stop messing around, whispered Ailsa. *You're terrifying them.*

Ishbel cocked her head to the side. "Sometimes you must be terrifying to get what you want," she murmured. "Ailsa and I have a special relationship. I would not harm a single hair on her head."

Aster's knuckles were white where she gripped her chair. "But would you overpower her consciousness, in order to live again?"

I didn't realise she cared that much, muttered Ailsa.

Ishbel snorted. "Rich words from those who abandoned her. I have protected her, watched her grow, taught her to control her powers. And you? You sacrificed her to protect one who wasn't even your own."

Sefarina clasped her hands in front of her. "We did what we had to do."

"It is easy to justify these things when you believe the sacrifice was only your own."

"Sacrifice?" Aster snarled. "Don't speak to me of sacrifice. We gave up our children and spent the last twenty years wondering if we'd ever see them again."

"While you sat in your marble palace—"

"Enough." Aster looked ready to throw herself across the dancefloor. "Let her free."

Ishbel grinned. "Why not admit it? Why do you care?"

"Because she could very well be my daughter," Aster thundered, "and I will not have you use her this way."

What?

"You gave up the right to her long ago." Ishbel narrowed her eyes. "She is mine now. And if you don't give her what she wants, I'll make you pay." The air hummed with electricity, raising the hairs on her arms.

Ishbel, what did Aster mean? Did you know?

"The spear?" Nasima said with a gasp. "So that's it? *You* want the weapon. Was it not enough for you to destroy Rocbarra? You want to wreak your havoc across the rest of the world too?"

"*She* wants the weapon," said Ishbel with a snort. Lightning danced across her fingertips. "And I want for her to have all her heart's desires."

Sefarina shook her head in horror. "Ailsa could die if she takes the spear into battle. Don't you want to protect her?"

"I will protect her," said Ishbel, spreading her arms and luxuriating in her magic once more. "But I will also help her unleash her fury on the world."

Chapter 43

Maalik watched in horror as Ishbel curled Ailsa's hand, wreathing it in sparks as she grinned. Her eyes had rolled back in her head, just like they had done the night she'd killed every demon in Hell and brought Ailsa back to him.

"I won't ask again," said Ishbel. "Give the girl the spear."

The look on Ailsa's face was enough to strike terror into his heart but the witch council was made of stronger stuff. Aster stood from her seat, her chin tilting up.

"You have no power here. If you do not leave, we will make you."

"I'd like to see you try, witchling," drawled Ishbel. She extended her arms, building up the charge as lightning crackled over her skin.

This is going to end with someone getting hurt.

The crowd of witches around him were frozen in place, penning him in, but he could see others scrambling for the exit. Sefarina and Nasima joined Aster, rising from their seats in unison. A fight was brewing, and Maalik didn't know who would win.

"As long as I breathe, the spear will not leave this palace," said Aster. She raised her hands, splaying her fingers out and closed her eyes.

"Wait!" he shouted, running towards Ailsa. But it was too late. As one, the priestesses began chanting words, ancient and unsettling. Over their heads, the moon glowed brighter through the windows, casting the hall in blue-grey light.

Ishbel snarled through Ailsa's lips and threw sparks out, scorching the floor around her. Her body curled into the light, as if bowing against a strong wind and Maalik watched as the muscles in her neck strained. Ishbel held her hands to her chest, gritting her teeth as she conjured a ball of crackling energy between them. But she was no match for the moonlight hitting her. Every time she tried to send the lightning across the hall, it fizzled out. She fell to one knee as her hair streamed behind her, letting out a groan.

The riestesses' chanting got even louder and Ishbel dropped her arms, like they were too heavy under the crushing light. With nowhere to go, the sparks danced over her skin, tearing at her clothes. A drop of blood slid from her nostril down into her mouth.

Ailsa's body can't take this. "Stop!" Maalik barrelled forward, pushing onlookers out of the way to reach her, right where the powers were colliding.

Ishbel spared him one sideways glance and an emotion flitted across her face. Then, just as he was about to throw himself in front of her, she collapsed to the ground, sending a final zap of electricity up to the ceiling. Immediately, the moonlight dissipated, as if it had been sucked back up to the sky. Maalik barely had time to catch Ailsa's head before it cracked against the marble floor.

Ailsa's eyes were closed as he stared down at her, finding her pulse. *Still alive, thank the gods.* "What did you do?" he asked the priestesses.

Their chanting had stopped, each of them breathing hard. "We asked the goddess to remove the spirit from Ailsa's body."

"You could have killed her!"

Nasima doubled over, panting. "She could have killed all of us."

He checked Ailsa's body for injuries, finding dark marks

criss-crossing her veins like they'd been burned from the inside. Around him, voices were rising, like an angry hive of bees. *I need to get her out of here,* he thought, looking around for Ailsa's friends. Surely they'd help?

"Maalik?" Ailsa's voice was weak as she blinked her eyes open. "What happened?" She looked dazed and weakened, worse than he'd ever seen before.

"Ishbel took over," he said, gripping her tighter. "The priestesses fought her." *I thought you were dead.*

"I can't hear her," Ailsa said with a sob.

Nasima straightened, eyeing the mass of onlookers. "I think everyone should go to bed. It's been a long night. The danger has passed."

Ailsa leaned into Maalik as the crowd dispersed, throwing them both fearful and curious glances. Maalik hunched over her, trying to shield her from the worst of it. She'd been so worried about tonight, about making them like her, and Ishbel had ruined it all.

"She was too dangerous," Sefarina said, once most of the witches were gone. She lowered herself to sit on the steps of the dais and leaned her arms on her knees. "We had to banish her. I'm sorry she possessed you."

"No, I'm sorry." Ailsa seemed to collect herself, pushing up. "I had no idea she would do something like that."

"Of course not," soothed Nasima. "Ishbel Lauchair was a powerful witch when she was alive, but she was also completely immoral. She would stop at nothing to have her way and it appears she is the same, even in death."

"She wanted the spear," said Aster, narrowing her eyes. She had not relaxed like the other two, her stance still ready for a fight. "We explained that we would not give it up."

Maalik opened his mouth at that. They still needed the spear. But Ailsa pinched his arm, and he snapped his eyes to her. The shake of her head was almost imperceptible, but it stalled the words in his mouth. *What's going on?*

"I understand," she said. "You need to keep it safe."

Sefarina let out a long breath. "I'm glad to hear *you* agree at least."

"I'm so sorry again." Ailsa's lip quivered. If he didn't know how absurd that was, coming from her, he might have believed her contrite. "Ishbel knew we'd come here for the spear, but I know why you need to keep it."

Nasima nodded. "You should rest. Having a spirit guide expelled from you will have left you exhausted. If she's been attached to you for a long time, it may take a few days to get used to being alone inside your head. We will understand if you cannot attend the last Rite tomorrow."

Maalik held in his snort. *Translation: don't bother attending.*

"I think I need to sleep for a week," Ailsa agreed. "Maalik, I don't know if I can stand. Maybe someone could help you carry me?"

He frowned. Just last night he'd lifted her all the way back to their room without a problem. She looked over his shoulder and he followed her gaze. A witch hesitated by the door, floating off the ground. "Zephyr? Would you help?" she asked.

He sprung forward, coming to Maalik's aid. "I didn't want to just leave her," said Zephyr, wringing his hands.

Ailsa bit her lip. "What about the others?"

Zephyr winced. "Rain ran off and Vega and Keyne went after her."

Ailsa took that in for a moment. "Okay," she said in a small voice, "would you help me up?"

They manoeuvred her until she was sitting, an arm over each of their shoulders. Between them, they scooped Ailsa off the ground, carrying her in a seated position.

"This would be much easier if you could fly." Maalik heard Zephyr mutter into her ear.

Ailsa let out a broken laugh that hurt Maalik's heart.

"Let's get you to bed," he said, loudly. He nodded curtly to the priestesses and then they turned. It took everything in him to keep his steps steady.

Outside the ballroom, onlookers had gathered, their whispering intensifying when Ailsa appeared.

"Actually, I think Maalik should just take me," Ailsa told Zephyr quietly. Her next words went unspoken, but Maalik knew what she was thinking. *You shouldn't be seen with me.*

Zephyr let go of her hesitantly, passing her body over to Maalik until she was fully in his arms once again. She turned her face into his neck like she'd done the night before and he gave the librarian a sad smile. Then Zephyr disappeared through the crowds. Maalik's chest ached. He understood, of course, but seeing Ailsa so abandoned filled him with despair. At least he stayed to help. Unlike the rest of her friends.

Still, Ailsa wasn't telling him something. Maybe this was part of her plan.

"Well, are you going to tell me what really happened?" Maalik murmured as he pushed through the crowds towards their room.

"Not here," she said, and he knew his instincts were correct.

***

Maalik made his way down the corridor, his footsteps echoing in the half-dark. As he walked, he felt Ailsa's body grow more and more tense, until she was almost vibrating. One look at her face told him she was completely livid. Finally, they made it to their room. Maalik kicked the door open and was across the room in a few strides, settling her down on the bed.

"Go on then," he said.

"I can't believe them," she said quietly, curling in on herself.

Maalik raised a hand to her cheek. "Did they really do it? Did they take Ishbel away?"

Ailsa's face changed, donning that smirk, though her eyes didn't roll back again. "*They couldn't get rid of me that easily,*" said Ishbel.

"But you made them think they had."

Ailsa shook her head, her face relaxing into a frown once again. "We had to. It was clear they weren't giving up the spear. Let them think the threat is gone."

"So, what was your plan? To bully them into giving it up?"

Ailsa sighed. "Call it a last-ditch attempt. I tried asking for it, I tried proving I could be trusted. But they never had any intention of giving it away. It's clear now; they don't care about anyone but themselves. And I don't belong here."

"Are you kidding me?" Maalik tilted her chin, so she'd look at him. "You're surrounded by your family. Didn't you hear what Aster said?"

Ailsa pressed her lips into a hard line. "She said I might be her missing daughter."

She's so stubborn. "Have you even looked at Aster? You have the same eyes, the same nose. And what about Rain? If you're not sisters, you're cousins at the very least."

"It doesn't matter," Ailsa growled. "They're not my family; I hardly know them. And Rain showed me tonight that she'd abandon me at the drop of a hat. Cameron is my family. Iona and Angus and Harris are my family. *You* are my family."

Though a part of him revelled in her words, he knew she'd regret them. Maalik sat back on his haunches, trying to find the right words. "You haven't known any of us for that long either. Just, think on it. I'd hate for you to alienate them before you can even get to know them."

"They already did that to me when they shipped me off. I don't owe them anything," she said with an air of finality. "If they don't want to give us the spear, I'm going to take it myself."

Maalik blinked. "You're going to steal it?"

"If that's what it takes. I can't just sit up here in the clouds as the world below burns."

But it wasn't that simple, was it? They'd visited the tower, tried the door, to find it spelled shut. "How do you plan—" he started to ask but then she opened her hands to reveal a tiny glass vial. "Is that?"

"Zephyr's blood," Ailsa confirmed. "I saw an opportunity and I took it."

"This is why you let them think Ishbel is gone."

Ailsa nodded. "Can't have them suspecting us. Better to let them think I'm recovering from a nasty possession."

Maalik had underestimated her. "When?" he asked.

"Tomorrow night, at the next Rite." She cleared her throat, suddenly vulnerable. "Are you going to help me?"

He hated that she'd even ask that. *I'll never make her unsure of me again.* "Of course. I just wish you'd tell me these things before I have a heart attack."

She grinned. "Just keeping you on your toes."

"You're a devil," he said, taking one of her hands and kissing it.

Ailsa snorted. "One of us has to be."

Chapter 44

There is something about Alasdair, Iona thought as she watched him speak to the farmer. Something trustworthy. Something that would make even the poorest man give up his last piece of gold. Harris could charm a castle out from underneath a king, but Alasdair's little smiles and soft words weren't calculated or cunning. He genuinely meant every single one of them.

The farmer and his wife didn't know who they were, and it would have taken too long to explain. Still, in a matter of minutes Alasdair had secured them a place to sleep for the night and a warm meal.

"It's just a barn," he said apologetically. "But it'll keep us out of any bad weather. They said they'll bring us some dinner too."

Iona took his arm as he led her round the back of the house. "It's better than we had last night or the one before. Sleeping on cave floors isn't exactly the height of luxury." Still, it meant they hadn't lingered, making good time on their journey along Eilanmòr's south coast. That morning they decided they'd have to travel the rest by land. After a long day of hiking, it had been pure luck to stumble across the farm. "What did you say to them anyway?"

Alasdair elbowed her gently. "That my companion would pay them for their trouble."

"Oh really?" she asked with a grin. "What makes you think I have any money?"

He was silent for a beat too long.

"Alasdair?"

"I may have looked through your things while you were asleep," he admitted.

Iona pursed her lips. "Why?"

"To see if you had a weapon." He pushed the barn door open, releasing a smell of fresh hay. "And to see if you still had *it*."

Alasdair ducked inside and Iona followed, peering into the dark. "Had what?"

"The ring."

"Oof." Iona tripped over a hay bale, landing with a bump on top of it. She blinked, adjusting to her new position and then turned her gaze back to Alasdair. "You were looking for the ring?"

He strode over to the far wall where Iona could just about see some shelves in the late evening light. With a scrape of a match, Alasdair lit a couple of lanterns and brought one over to where she sat. The flames flickered against the angles of his face, turning his expression from annoyed to sorrowful in the blink of an eye. "The one I gave you," he said. "I haven't seen it on your finger for a long time."

So, we're finally going to have this conversation. The journey had been filled with talks of the Edaxi and the Four Treasures and strategy. Of Iona's life since he'd died. Not once had Alasdair brought up what he'd hinted at before: that he might still have feelings for her. Iona fidgeted with her hands, trying to keep her voice light. "I didn't think I should keep it."

He pursed his lips. "I gave it to you."

"You had a wife," said Iona, quietly. "If I were her, I would have felt sick knowing some other woman had your ring."

Alasdair hesitated for a moment before coming to sit down beside her with a sigh. "It was a marriage of convenience.

Saoirse didn't love me. She wouldn't have cared."

She looked down at her feet. "I cared. I cared too much. I've tried to shrug it off a million times. You had to do your duty. I wanted to stay near the sea. No one wants a selkie for a queen. Leaving was smart, Alasdair, but that doesn't mean it didn't hurt."

She felt a finger beneath her chin and then he was tilting her face up, so she'd look at him. "I can't regret how things worked out," Alasdair said. "I had two beautiful children, three beautiful grandchildren—"

"…four." Iona's lips twitched. "Four grandchildren. Connell and Nicnevan had a baby. Her name is Eilidh." She gulped, but the sound was more like a sob. "She has your eyes. You also have two great-grandchildren, you know. And none of them would be here if it wasn't for you."

Alasdair nodded, stunned. "Like I said, I can't regret the end result. But I do have my regrets. One of them has been rectified." He turned his palms out, examining them. "I wish I wasn't the only one to come back, but I also know my daughter and my soldiers are at rest." He closed his eyes. "I spent my first life following the rules, doing what is best for the kingdom. But there's a new king now, it's in safe hands. Maybe in this life I get to follow my heart."

"Where would that lead you?"

His grin was crooked. "A cottage on the beach."

"Is there room for two?" she asked.

"Only if it's you." Alasdair leaned in.

A thrill of panic shot through her and the next second Iona was on her feet. "I don't know," she said, pacing away from him towards the door. "I don't know if I'm allowed to hope for this. We've still got a war to win. What if whatever spell brought you back breaks if we win?"

"Sometimes you have to have a little faith. And live in

the moment. If you're right and I only have until we kick Mirandelle's ass, I'm going to enjoy every minute of being alive again." He pushed off the hay bale, drifting closer. "I'm going to do everything I wished I could do when I was a ghost."

Iona's heart beat faster and she took a step back. "What would that be?"

"That depends on you. Whenever I saw you in Dunrigh, my hands ached to touch you. But if you don't feel the same, I understand. I will take whatever you will give me."

She bit her lip. "Why don't you start, and I'll tell you if it's too much?"

Alasdair considered this for a moment, and then reached a shaking hand out for her own, where it was tangled in her skirts. At the first contact, there was a spark of feeling, like a static shock. He brushed his thumb over her palm, looking into her eyes.

"Is this okay?"

Iona nodded. "You can keep going."

His fingers moved up from her hand, ghosting around her wrist until he had it encircled. Then he did the same with the other. "I used to go down to the portrait gallery to see our picture, you know. I'd stand there, wishing it was really you and then one day it was."

"Then you must know I used to look at it too."

He hummed and then pulled her arms up gently to rest her hands on his shoulders. "I think seeing you there was almost worse," he said, sliding his palms over her sleeves. "Knowing that you were in my home, and I couldn't speak to you. It was torture."

"What would you have said?" her voice came out in a whisper.

"That though my soul was in Dunrigh, my heart was with you." He touched his fingertips to her collarbone. "That a part of me had already died when I left you."

"I would have told you that I missed you. That every day since you left was hard, but it was nothing compared to when you were killed. I could have been happy if you'd been out there, living. But being in a world without you was excruciating."

His hands were surer as they cupped her face. "I'm so sorry, Iona. I wish I could make it all up to you."

She tangled her fingers in his hair. It was just as soft as she remembered it. Suddenly, she was aware of how close he was, his body pressing hers lightly into the barn's wall. "Well, what's holding you back?" she asked. "I've been waiting to kiss you for a lifetime."

He let out a breath against her lips and leaned in. Iona reached up onto her tiptoes to meet him halfway but just before they finally, finally, touched there was a knock at the barn door.

Alasdair groaned, resting his forehead against hers for a moment as she fought back her disappointment.

"That must be the food," she said, her voice coming out strained.

Then his body was gone from hers, the cold a sudden shock as he turned to open the door. Iona stayed with her back pressed against the wall, sure that her heart was loud enough for the farmer to hear. She listened as the man murmured some pleasantries. Alasdair's voice was a little too harsh to her ears, but she hoped the farmer wouldn't notice. Eventually, he accepted a tray and shut the door with a "*thanks*".

"Do you want to eat?" she started to ask, but the look on his face had the words dying in her mouth.

The next happened in a blur. Alasdair pivoted, almost throwing the food down onto the nearest hay bail and then he rounded on her, cupping her elbow with one hand and her neck with another. Iona could only gasp in a breath before his lips crashed down on her own, like a wave upon a shore.

Iona poured everything into the kiss, all the longing and the heartache and the sweet joy of having him there with her, alive once more. *Never again*, she vowed. Even if she had to fight and claw and beg, nothing was going to take him from her. Iona had waited a lifetime; she wasn't going to waste another.

Chapter 45

Angus wished he could scrub the inside of his brain, erase the memories of the last few days. It had all blurred together into a long waking nightmare and, even though he was exhausted, he dreaded what he'd see if he closed his eyes. Images of his mother's blank face, no doubt.

"I think I'm going to be sick," he realised, covering his mouth.

Immediately, Cam was at his elbow. "But we're off the boat."

"I can still feel the rocking."

"Say the word and I'll find you a bush to throw up in. Here, drink some water." Angus reached for the canteen, but a sudden bout of dizziness had him swaying. Cameron surged forward, grabbing Angus around the waist to steady him. "Here, I'm supposed to be the one who's always fainting. You're taking a break."

"We're almost at camp," said Angus through gritted teeth.

"You're not going to get there if you keel over first. Listen to your bodyguard." Then Cameron did something wholly unexpected. He reached down behind Angus's knees and pulled him into his arms.

Angus fisted Cameron's shirt, yelping as he was picked up. "What are you doing?"

Cameron cut out of the marching line and headed towards a tree off the road. "Finding a spot for you to sit."

Angus peered up at Cam, noting the way his skin had paled. "You're not well either. I can walk, you know."

Cameron's footsteps stumbled as he adjusted his hold on Angus's body. "Could have fooled me," he said as they found the shade under the branches. Angus expected Cameron to place him down but instead he slid down the trunk with Angus still in his arms, landing with a bump against the grass.

Angus's breath hitched as he felt Cameron's warmth all around him. "Everyone's going to see us together," he protested as the caravan of soldiers continued past.

Cameron cocked his head. "And that's bad because?"

"Guards don't usually sweep their charges off their feet." Angus could feel his cheeks growing hotter. "Unless they're in a romance book." In truth, he may have had fantasies just like this.

"Do you read stuff like that often?" asked Cameron with a chuckle.

"Perhaps. It's usually a princess getting saved by the knight, though."

Cameron grew serious, dropping his head back against the trunk and looking at Angus through his bottom lashes. "After we win the war, you can write a different story. I think everyone has noticed we're together. We did share a bed on the ship after all."

Angus scowled. "With Harris too."

"Yes, but we'll have the tent to ourselves when we get to the coast. Not as romantic as a river cruise, but I'm sure we'll make do."

Angus had a reply formulating in his mind—a play on the words tent and intense—when a concerned looking Duncan appeared atop his horse, which stamped its feet impatiently. The horse's gesture was familiar, reminding him that Laire was, hopefully, waiting for them at their intended campsite.

"Are you alright?" Duncan asked, looking bewildered.

Angus was suddenly aware that Cameron hadn't yet

dropped him. It must have looked like they were snuggling under the tree. "I was a bit lightheaded. Cameron is looking after me."

Duncan frowned. "Do you need me to get you a horse?"

"I'll be fine." Angus could feel his blush growing deeper as he felt Cam sweep his thumb over his waist. "We don't have far, do we?" he asked, his voice strained.

Duncan flicked his gaze between Angus and Cameron. "When we get to the top of that hill, we'll be able to see the sea. It'll be another couple of hours at most."

Angus nodded. "I think I can manage that."

"Right, well I'll leave you to it." Then Duncan was urging his horse back to the army procession, leaving Angus and Cameron alone.

Angus felt Cam's laughter before he heard it, the movement shaking his chest where they were pressed together. Then the sound burst from him, and Angus was helpless to resist joining him. They dropped their foreheads together, as they giggled, leaving Angus feeling lightheaded in a completely different way.

"I can't believe we get to do this," he said once their laughter had subsided. Only a couple of months ago, Angus would never have dared. His father had made his thoughts clear; Angus had responsibilities. Namely, producing backup heirs.

Cameron scanned Angus's face. "What do you reckon we really give them something to talk about?"

"Are you sure?" Angus's smile was hesitant but then Cameron's lips were on his and their mouths curled together in a sweet kiss.

We'll be alright, Angus realised, *if we have this.* Even if more horrors waited ahead, if he was with Cameron, they would handle them together.

Chapter 46

"Stop," Eilidh said in a strained voice. After hours back in the wagon, she'd reached her breaking point. The walls were closing in, and she desperately needed the fresh air.

"We've not got far to go—" Harris started to say but she held her hand up in warning.

"Get them to stop the wagon. Now." *Or I'm going to lose my lunch.*

She heard him scrabbling about for the door so he could relay her words to the soldiers surrounding the wagon. They came to a halt, the boxes were moved and Eilidh was free to crawl out of her hiding place. She swayed when her feet hit the dirt road.

A hand cupped her elbow. "Are you alright?" asked Harris.

"I need space." Immediately he removed his fingers. "Not from you. From all these people. Come on." Then she was running, her skirts bunched up in her hand as she weaved out of the crowd and into the trees. Footsteps pounded behind her. *It's just Harris.*

"Shouldn't you stay close?" he asked once they were off the path.

Eilidh rounded on him, breathing hard. "I have been stuck inside for days. First in my cabin when we were attacked—"

"—for your safety—"

"—and then in that wagon." She ran a hand through her hair. "I had more freedom when I was a waitress. At least Aggie knew I could look after myself."

"What if a random fae happens to wander past?" Harris crossed his arms. "Like the redcap or the kelpies? They'll know who you are."

"And so what?" Eilidh asked. "Any fae I've met since Nicnevan died has been nothing but nice." She sat down on an old tree stump and sighed. "I used to be afraid of the fae folk. Monsters and beasts would turn up at our inn, ready to run off with me. And throughout it all was the thought that Nicnevan had sent them. I would dream of a faceless woman, wrapping me in vines and thorns, squeezing me until I choked. But she's gone, isn't she? Maybe I don't need to hide myself anymore."

"I can't say I'm not glad she's dead," said Harris, crouching down in front of her. "Angus formed a strange friendship with her towards the end, but I could never forgive her for all of the horrors. Did you know she held Cameron and me captive for weeks? She tortured us. I wonder if that's why he has his visions, because he was so changed by what happened."

Eilidh thought of the look on Cam's face, right before he'd collapsed. "I'm sorry. For both of you."

"Worse things have happened." Harris's face was tight.

"Did you feel the same about Nicnevan as you do me? You know, you've said you can feel a pull. Like your body knows I'm the—" She swallowed. "Queen."

"It wasn't the same." He patted her knee. "You don't know what it's been like for us fae all these years. In the past, Seelie and Unseelie coexisted, two sides of the same coin. But with Nicnevan, things became unbalanced. Chaining her to the tree helped, but we were forever separated. Now the land feels lighter. Nicnevan was prickling thorns and cloying flowers. You're sunshine, Eilidh."

"I'm not doing anything," she said, her voice hushed.

"You could, though. If you wanted. Would it really be

so bad? The Seelie haven't had a benevolent ruler in a long time. They would serve you, defend you. And eventually the unseelie would follow you too. You could unite both courts. Think about it, thousands of fae, all looking out for you and your daughter." He stood up. "Come on, we'd better go back."

Eilidh set her mouth in a firm line. "I'm not getting back in that wagon. I'm sick of being locked away."

"Fair enough. So, let's go on foot. I bet we could be faster anyway." Harris held out his hand, waiting.

She took a deep breath, calming her racing heart before accepting his help up.

"I think I know a shortcut." Harris tapped his nose as they walked through the trees. "I can smell the sea." He veered to the right, away from the procession of people, leading them through the undergrowth.

They walked in silence for a while, allowing Eilidh to breathe in the smells of the forest. *So full of life.* Every now and then, Harris would help her over a fallen tree, lending her his arm like a knight in a story. "I'm glad I met you," she told him quietly. "All of you. I've never really had friends before. The villagers always thought I was a bit weird."

"The best people are," he said with a chuckle. "I'm glad I met you too. I'll be honest, I didn't think I'd ever be able to get out of bed again, after Irené was taken. Iona helped me a bit, but you gave me hope." He bit his lip. "You're still up for helping me, right?"

Eilidh squeezed his arm. "Of course. We'll get her back, Harris."

They continued hiking, breathing hard at a sudden incline. The sun shone through the leaves, dappling the forest floor and heating the air until sweat was sliding between Eilidh's shoulders.

"Are we camping on the sand?" asked Eilidh to fill the silence as they walked.

"Duncan will probably pick somewhere more tactical. There's an old, abandoned castle. It's uphill from the beach and there's plenty of room for the whole camp. That's where we'll wait." He pushed a branch out of the way. "We still need to wait for our allies before we can pick a fight."

"Perhaps they're already there, waiting for us."

"Maybe. I reckon we'll see the coast, just over this hill," said Harris.

Sure enough, when they reached the crest, there it was. Blue, sparkling water surrounded the bay below, the white caps breaking on the sandy beach. It should have been a beautiful sight. Except...

"That's a lot of ships," panted Harris.

This must be the whole Mirandelli navy, Eilidh thought as she surveyed the water below. Around half a mile from the beach, there had to be hundreds of vessels, all floating in one mass, like flies on sugar. And in the middle, mostly obscured by white sails, was a strange tangle of wood and metal.

"What are we looking at?" Eilidh asked, staring at the jumbled mess.

"Our target," said Harris. "That's where we're heading. In the morning, once we've made camp."

Eilidh nodded, speechless, as they sat down to wait. Behind, the noise of the caravan grew louder. Soon, they'd all witness the size of their enemy's fleet. And they'd realise the same thing: not a single allied ship had turned up.

Chapter 47

Ailsa peered down the darkened hallway, clutching her blanket around her shoulders. The music from the ballroom thumped dully from somewhere below, but beyond that there was nothing. No shouting, no doors opening, no visitors. Everyone was celebrating the third night of the Moon Rite.

To her surprise, Vega, Keyne and Rain had tried to stop by earlier, but Maalik had shooed them away, telling them Ailsa needed to rest. At least they hadn't needed to lie to the priestesses. Not one of *them* had come to see how she was.

Good, thought Ailsa. *I don't know if I could have controlled myself.*

I always appreciate a bit of blood lust, said Ishbel.

They tried to get rid of you. Without even asking me first.

And you wouldn't want that?

Of course not. Ailsa frowned. *You're a cantankerous, conniving, contrary old bat, but you're my cantankerous, conniving, contrary old bat.*

Careful. You'll give me a big head. And when my head is inside your head, that can be pretty dangerous. Ishbel paused. *What are you waiting for?*

"Nothing," Ailsa whispered. "It looks like the coast is clear. Let's go get Maalik." Then she turned, sliding on her socks over the polished marble floors back to the room, before she threw herself in the door and closed it behind her. "It's now or never."

Maalik kneeled over their bags, newly packed and waiting on the carpet. "I can't help but feel we've forgotten something."

Ailsa took one, hefting it onto her back. "This is already heavy enough; we don't need more. Don't you remember how hard the journey here was?"

Maalik's mouth twisted. "Hopefully, it'll be easier going downhill."

"We'll go as quick as we can but if you need to stop, just say. Your note will buy us time."

Maalik waved the piece of paper in his hand. "As long as your friends believe you're sick."

"As long as the priestesses do." Ailsa breathed deeply, reining in her worries. "We have to try. What's the worst that could happen if they find us out?"

"I imagine we'll be imprisoned. Possibly banished. Maybe killed?"

Ailsa huffed out a dark laugh. "Same old, same old. Come on."

Maalik snuffed out the candles and then they pulled their cloaks around their shoulders, hiding their bags underneath. The material was dark, enough that they might not be spotted straight away as they moved through the hallways. Their only pause was outside the door, where Maalik attached his note, and then they were off.

Turning right would take them too close to the ballroom, so they turned left instead, taking the long way. Ailsa hadn't taken the alternative route herself, but Maalik seemed to know where he was going. Their walk led them past more bedrooms and then eventually to a non-descript door in the wall. Ailsa nearly walked by until Maalik grabbed her pack. Inside was the narrow, spiralled staircase which led to the west towers.

"Up we go," he said.

It was dim in the stairwell, the only light coming from

slitted windows. Ailsa felt her way up using the stone walls, with Maalik a comforting presence behind.

"I think these were servant stairs, until the witches used enchantments to clean. They should lead us almost to the roof."

Sure enough, just as Ailsa was about to ask if they could take a break, the stairs ascended onto a landing with a door the twin of the one below. Ailsa breathed heavily, filling her lungs with the dusty air and muffling a cough. She reached for a handle, easing the door open quietly and peering into the corridor.

"I think it's—"

Something darted across the portal and Ailsa fell back into Maalik's chest with a gasp. He wrapped an arm around her middle and tried to shove her behind him, but the landing was too narrow. Placing a finger over his lips, he opened the door again and stuck his head out. Ailsa held her breath, pressing into the wall as best she could.

If there's someone there, how are we going to explain ourselves?

But then Maalik let her go and leaned into the hallway. "It was just a cat-sìth," he said.

Ailsa peered through the dark, trying to work out which cat it was, but only its eyes were visible, luminescent and judging.

"Come on," Maalik said, taking her hand. His warmth sunk into her skin, giving her the strength she needed to follow him.

Ailsa recognised the next room as soon as they were inside. It was covered in dust, just like it had been the day Nasima had led her there. Ishbel's portrait still sat in the corner, a white sheet covering her face, but that was not why they'd come. At the other end of the tower, was the wooden door they'd been looking for. Ailsa reached inside her clothes, finding the vial of blood. Unscrewing the lid and placing her finger over the opening, she upended the bottle, forming a perfect circle of red on her skin. "Here goes nothing." She placed the pad of her finger against the door and waited.

They waited a long moment. What if Zephyr's blood didn't work? What if the door is broken? But then there was a soft click and a creak and the door drifted open, leaving a gap.

"I'll wait out here," said Maalik. "You have to be quick."

Inside, the room was bathed in a pale blue moonlight, like water rippling around a cave. Ailsa padded forward, noting the boxes piled around the room with disinterest. Nothing could hold her attention, save for the object in the middle of space.

On its own marble stand, the Spear of Truth glinted in the soft glow. A short silver shaft, around the length of her arm, ended in a sapphire spearhead, roughly cut into sharp angles. Ailsa approached the treasure, decorated with whorls and runes. It looked more like jewellery than a weapon. *It had better work. Soon I'll be using it in battle.* She reached out with trembling fingers, feeling as though the spear was calling to her. *I'm yours,* it seemed to say. This was it, what she'd been searching for—

A movement to her left had her yelping, snatching her hand away from the treasure. "What are you doing here?"

The door opened behind her, and Maalik burst in. "What's going on?" But as soon as he saw them, he froze.

Framed in the window, stood Vega, Keyne, and Rain. Ailsa fought to calm her raging heart, taking them in. No wonder she hadn't seen them as she entered; they were all dressed, head to toe, in black.

"We thought you might come," said Vega.

Keyne nodded, taking a step forward. "You're a terrible actress, Ailsa."

"You need to get out of our way," she grunted. "Now." Her eyes darted from the spear to the door. Perhaps if she could grab it, they could make a run for it.

But they were already edging closer. "We can't just let you take it," said Vega, holding her hands up. "You'll never be allowed to return."

Ailsa rounded on Rain, who hadn't left the back wall. "And what have you got to say about this?"

She folded her arms and looked away. "Leave me out of it," she grumbled.

Vega and Keyne turned back to their friend. "Rain!"

"I say, if she wants it, she can have it. It's not like we'll miss it."

"Good, I'm glad one of you agrees." Ailsa reached for the spear again. "Stand aside."

"No," said Keyne. "You need to turn around and go back to your room. Before—"

"Before what?"

Vega winced. "Before Nasima comes."

"You told her?" Maalik spluttered.

"She gave us the blood to get in. Nasima knows Ailsa only has good intentions; she won't tell Sefarina or Aster—"

But Ailsa's hand was already curling around the spear, lifting it from its perch. "We need to go," she told the demon, turning for the door. "Stay out of our way. I don't want to hurt any of you but the whole of Ossiana depends on this."

But it was already too late. Nasima stood in the portal; a shawl pulled tight across her shoulders against the chill. "So, Vega, you were right." She nodded in greeting. "Ailsa. Maalik."

"We need the spear," Ailsa snarled, readying to fight. Could she use her lightning to scare them without hitting anyone?

"And how were you planning on leaving with it?" she asked. "I thought you'd be too weak after what happened last night. Unless that was an act too?"

Ailsa's lip curled back. "Ishbel is still with me, no thanks to you. And royally pissed off too, just so you know."

Nasima clicked her tongue and turned to the demon beside Ailsa. "Maalik, the spear could fall into the wrong hands. I thought *you'd* see some reason."

Ailsa knew he wanted to fight just as much as she did. Maalik was a gentle soul, more comfortable healing than hurting. But he drew himself up, his hands curling into fists as his skin cracked. The fissures revealed the molten core beneath his skin, glowing red hot in the dim light. "Like Ailsa says: step aside or we'll have to make you."

Nasima took a step forward and Ailsa reached out for her magic, feeling the tell-tale crackle in the air. She knew the others could already see the sparks in her hands. I really don't want to do this.

Suddenly, there was a flash, followed by a deafening boom. The whole tower quaked, the walls rattling and floor shaking. Ailsa's legs nearly gave out from the force of it, and she was thrown sideways, into Maalik's scolding body. She hissed in pain as her knuckle brushed a burning crack on his arm.

"Ailsa?" asked Vega, her voice high with fright.

"It wasn't me," Ailsa gritted out, looking up at the priestess.

But Nasima hadn't moved. Her eyes were fixed on the window behind Rain. "It came from outside."

"Can we pause the stand-off until we see what's going on?" asked Keyne.

This better not be a trick. But from the look on the other witches' faces, they were just as shocked as she was. Ailsa huffed out a breath. "Fine." Then, as one, they moved to the window and squinted through the glass.

Chapter 48

*F*ar below their tower, five figures stood upon the snowy mountain top. Three had their arms behind their backs, like they were tied. The fourth was small. *A child*, Ailsa thought. And then she caught sight of the last and her blood froze.

"Maalik—"

"I see her."

"Who?" asked Vega.

The last time Ailsa met the Goddess of Pain, she'd been tortured until her back was broken. But then Dolor hadn't been present physically in the forest with her. Only her image had appeared inside a crystal circle, but it had been enough to inflict intolerable agony. The only thing that had saved her was Maalik destroying the crystals. She would have been left paralysed, if not for the angel Maalik had called and the deal he'd made. His soul to heal her. That had been the price when she'd first met Dolor. What would be the price now?

"One of the Edaxi," Ailsa said, throwing her a meaningful look.

The goddess was grey against the bright white ice, too far away to see her features. Still, from her body language, Ailsa could tell she looked bored. Her arms were crossed as she looked up at the palace.

The little girl beside her, however, was practically jumping with glee. Her hair was crimson, reminding Ailsa of fresh blood. Ailsa reached up slowly to undo the latch, pushing the window open slightly so they could hear what they were saying.

"Come out, little witches," the girl crooned in a high voice. "We have a present for you."

There was a beat of silence and then the main door opened. From their vantage point, they could just make out the entryway, crowded with people. And at the front, Sefarina and Aster stood their ground.

"I should be down there," murmured Nasima. But the priestess didn't move, as the little girl stepped forward.

"The Crone and The Mother," she said, the wind carrying her voice over the mountain. "But no Maiden? Never mind, there seems to be a lot of you already, and I like making new friends."

"Who are you?" called Aster, clasping her arms in front of her. "How did you get up the mountain?"

"We need to warn them," whispered Ailsa. "They don't stand a chance."

Nasima stopped her from turning with a hand on Ailsa's shoulder. "The priestesses know exactly who they are. Don't you see Sefarina's hands?"

Ailsa tore her gaze from Aster to look at the woman beside her. Sefarina had her hands up in front of her, as if she was holding some invisible orb. Ailsa could tell her lips were moving, even if she couldn't hear what she was saying.

"She's strengthening her forcefield," Nasima told her. "They cannot get in."

Finally, the girl replied. "The Stone of Destiny has been very useful these last weeks. Not only can we step upon Eilanmòrian soil now, but we need only think of a place, and we're taken there. I am Timor, goddess of fear. This is my sister, Dolor, Goddess of Pain. And you may know our guests."

The three figures between the goddesses dropped to their

knees, letting out almighty screeches, as if their skin was pressed against hot coals.

"The witches gave up so many of their young. And for what? To hide the Faerie Queen's daughter? How many are still to return?" Dolor waved her hand and the screaming stopped, leaving the captives panting out clouds of breath. "But look, we found some for you. They didn't even know they were witches until we told them."

"Let them go," Aster demanded.

"I have seen the horrors they have faced, alone in the world, each with a changeling mark. Did you know changelings are killed in Mirandelle?" Dolor kicked the blonde woman in the back, sending her sprawling face first into the snow. "We found this one in King Merlo's dungeons, eating rats to stay alive."

Timor ran her fingers through the hair of another woman, pushing it off her face. "And this one had made it all the way to Akrosia. Do you see her ears? They were cut off when she was found spying on a noble woman."

"This one we found in New Hope, practically a slave to her adoptive parents. So close and yet no one came to find her, all those years." Dolor grabbed the back of the witch's neck, forcing her to tilt her head back. "Look up, girls. The people in this palace were your family once, but they abandoned you, used you as pawns in a secret war that was not your own." As Dolor held the woman there, the witch's skin shuddered. It glimmered golden, moving and shifting, until her features rearranged themselves into a new face. Another changeling, finally home. "Oh look," said Dolor. "Doesn't that mean she has looked upon her birth mother? How lovely."

"What do you want?" Aster's voice rang out with barely controlled rage.

"You know what we want," said Timor. "You've been

guarding the Spear of Truth all the way up here for decades. And we're also on the hunt for a witch."

Sefarina stopped her chanting. "You already have three witches," she bit out.

Timor cackled. "Yes, but the one we want is special. She would have arrived with a demon. My dear sister met her in the woods, only recently."

Ailsa's stomach bottomed out. Gods, they were looking for her.

"There are no demons here," said Sefarina. "I'm afraid you're mistaken."

"Perhaps another lost daughter then, dead or worse." Timor smiled sweetly. "No matter, just the spear then."

Ailsa held her breath, waiting to hear the priestesses reply.

Sefarina licked her lips, eyeing the captives. "And if we give it to you? You'll let them go?"

"Oh no, these are ours." Timor touched the cheek of the witch closest to her and the woman let out a whimper. "I do love having friends to play with. No, if you give us the spear, we'll let the rest of you live. And we won't make you listen to their deaths. Well, not all of them." The witches' screams pierced the night again, ringing in Ailsa's ears.

"They can't let them have it, Nasima." Ailsa grabbed the priestess's arm. "If the Edaxi get all Four Treasures, they could do this to everyone in Ossiana."

But Sefarina had already turned to address the waiting crowds. "We do not surrender," she shouted out, sealing their fate.

Ailsa clutched at her heart. Okay, at least the priestesses weren't going to just give up the spear. "How long can Aster keep the Edaxi out for?"

"Long enough," said Nasima. "And then we fight."

Maalik nodded. "Let us help you."

"No!" Vega turned from the window. "You heard Timor. They want you and the spear."

They'll have to kill me first, Ailsa vowed. There was no way she was going with those monsters willingly.

"What if," Rain said, closing the window and blocking out most of the screams, "we could send the spear and Ailsa away from here?"

Keyne bit their lip. "You could run through the tunnels?"

"That had been our original plan," said Maalik. "But I know Dolor. She'll have her minions patrolling the whole mountain. And if she catches us, we're worse than dead."

"What if there was another way," asked Rain, quietly.

Ailsa's laugh was dark. "Please tell me you have secret teleportation magic."

"No, but I am good at stealing things." Then Rain held out her hand, revealing a familiar amethyst stone.

Ailsa blinked down at the gem, hoping this wasn't a trick. It had been weeks since she'd last seen the Stone of Destiny up close, hanging around Duncan's neck before it was stolen. "How did you—"

"I watched Timor put it back in her pocket." Rain jutted her chin out and turned to Nasima. "As far as I can see it, you have two options. Keep the spear and hope Aster's magic holds. Or send it away with Ailsa."

"Or we could all use the stone," Ailsa said desperately. "Everyone could come."

Nasima shook her head. "This is our home. There are children here, old people too, some too weak or helpless to leave. I am not abandoning a single one."

"They'll kill you all," Maalik told her.

"Perhaps not if they know the spear isn't here anymore." Nasima clasped her hands together. "You may borrow it. We'll need it back, once you've saved the world." She looked over Ailsa's shoulder. "It seems like you're packed, so there is no reason to delay. If any of you are staying, I'll see you downstairs." Then she swept from the room, leaving Ailsa and Maalik staring after her.

"You could all come with us?" Ailsa said, turning to her friends.

Vega smiled sadly. "I need to stay and help."

"Me too," said Keyne.

"Rain?" Ailsa asked, her mouth dry.

The silver-haired witch crossed her arms and shrugged one shoulder. "Well, this lot will probably die without me."

I can't believe this is happening. "I need you all to stay alive. Please."

Rain held the stone out again, dropping it into Ailsa's outstretched hand. "We've lived this long. Be safe."

"And you." Ailsa held the Stone of Destiny to her chest, picturing a familiar place as she felt its magic take over, turning the door into a shimmering portal. Maalik went first, stepping into the portal but she hesitated, taking a moment to look back at her friends, huddled together against the wall, until her eyes locked on Rain's.

You can tell who your descendants are, can't you? She asked Ishbel. *Is Maalik right? Is she my sister?*

I wouldn't know. Not until I'm no longer fixed to you. Ishbel ran a hand across her mind. *They'll be alright, Ailsa.*

She nodded around the lump in her throat and jumped forward, into the opening and out of Findias.

Chapter 49

As soon as Ailsa stepped out of the portal, it shut behind her, blinking out of existence. She wanted to slump to the cobblestones but there wasn't even time to breathe before she was pushed sideways, her shoulder bumping into a barrier.

"Shh," whispered Maalik, holding her tight. "Something's wrong."

Ailsa took in her surroundings. "The portal was supposed to take us to the castle." That's where she'd imagined anyway. Instead, they'd found themselves underneath a huge stone wall. Ahead of them, a forest and mountains were silhouetted against the night sky, but it was hard to see much else in the dark.

Ailsa stepped back, craning her neck at the ivy-covered wall. "I think this is Dunrigh," she said. "But we're outside the gates." *We made it*, she thought. But why was Maalik on edge?

"Do you hear it?"

The place was quiet, but it *was* the middle of the night. "I don't hear anything." But she listened again, straining to hear even the faintest noise. There, far in the distance, was a crack of thunder. Yet the sky was clear. *Not thunder,* she realised. "Canons."

He nodded. "Sounds far away, like it's on the other side of the city."

"We have to get to the castle."

"Will your friends be there?" he asked.

"I hope so." Ailsa pulled him into a run, keeping to the shadows as they skirted the wall. "I think I have an idea of where we are," she said over her shoulder. "There should be a gate around here somewhere."

When Ailsa first set off for the Stone of Destiny, there had been little fanfare. She, Harris and Angus had been shoved out of the secret back gate. It led from the castle to the mountains of the north.

Sure enough, a portcullis covered in ivy came into view. Ailsa rushed towards it through the dark. Something about the shape of the castle beyond was strange but it took Ailsa until they were almost at the gate to realise why. Bits of one of the towers were missing. *What happened here?*

The last time Ailsa had left through the Queen's secret gate, it hadn't been manned, so she didn't expect to see anyone. Which was why she jumped when two guards stood from their posts. In a flash, they had their bows loaded and aimed through the portcullis while Ailsa and Maalik skidded to a stop.

"Halt," said the man on the left. "Tell us who you are." He spoke with authority, but Ailsa could see his hand shaking as he kept the bowstring taught.

"We're here to see the prince," Ailsa panted. "It's urgent." Beside her, Maalik kept his eyes down, so as not to draw attention to their strange blackness.

"Mirandelli spies," the second man spat, raising his bow higher. "They must be, if they don't know—"

"—we're not Mirandelli!" Ailsa held her hands up and elbowed Maalik to do the same. "We're friends of Prince Angus. I'm Ailsa MacAra and this is my friend Maalik."

"If that were true, you'd know he left a few days ago, with the army."

Hag's teeth. Ailsa felt a bead of sweat slide down her back. One wrong move and she'd have an arrow to the heart. "We were away on a mission to retrieve the Stone of Destiny." Not quite true, but she doubted the soldiers would have heard of any of the other treasures. "We've been in Monadh for weeks with no way to communicate with him."

"She does have an Eilanmòrian accent," muttered the man on the right.

The first soldier jerked his chin. "Go on then, show us the stone, if that's what you were doing."

I hope this works, Ailsa thought, holding the Stone of Destiny between her fingers. The problem was, the soldiers had no way of verifying it really was the magical stone and not some rock she'd picked up off the ground. But their eyes widened as if they recognised it.

"Fine," said the first man. "If you really are allies, you'd better get inside. It's not safe." The other soldier lowered his weapon and stalked away, presumably to raise the gate.

"Why?" Ailsa asked. "What's happened?"

"We're under siege." The man unstrung his bow, placing the unused arrow back in his quiver. "A battalion of Mirandellis showed up yesterday."

She frowned as the portcullis moved upwards. "Just the one battalion? Shouldn't they be easy to fight?"

The soldier snorted. "First, there were only a few of us soldiers left behind. Second, it's not just the Mirandellis. The dead are with them."

Ailsa exchanged a look with Maalik. "The dead?"

"Somehow back to life. Except they're not the same. They're blank." Now the gate was raised, Ailsa could fully appreciate the man's sunken eyes, his gaunt cheeks. He looked like he hadn't eaten properly for days. "It's a miracle you weren't attacked on the way here. Luckily, they don't seem to know about this entrance."

Ailsa and Maalik stepped through and immediately the portcullis rolled closed again, as if the soldier had dropped whatever weight had opened it. Now inside the castle walls,

Ailsa breathed a sigh of relief. They were safe, at least for tonight. "Are we allowed inside?" she asked. "I know where to go."

"You can see yourself up then," said the man, moving back towards his post. "We're running out of food but I'm sure you'll be given something if you head to the kitchens."

"We don't plan on staying long," Ailsa told him, eyeing the dark building ahead. "We really need to find Prince Angus."

The other man rounded the corner and crouched down on his side of the gate. "The army should be at least halfway to the coast by now. They followed the River Glainne south."

Ailsa bit her lip as she and Maalik turned away. "We could leave tonight?" For all they knew, the battle could have already begun. Though, if Dolor and Timor were still trapped on the mountain, perhaps they would wait. Her stomach twisted. In their haste, she'd almost forgotten the goddesses' attack on Findias. *Please let them escape.*

Maalik took her hand as they walked. "We don't know how far they've got. If we just head straight for the coast, we might get there before the army and we could be attacked. We need to rest and then find a map."

Ailsa stifled a yawn. After the night they'd had, perhaps he was right.

They marched up the rest of the hill in silence. When they reached the top, they had to skirt around the outside. Most of the lower windows were boarded up so she couldn't look inside for life, but the castle appeared deserted, an empty shell. From the front, Ailsa caught a glimpse of the city below. This high up, there was an unmistakable glow of fire burning just outside the town walls, to the southeast.

"We'll leave first thing in the morning," Ailsa told him when they found an unlocked door. "I just hope we're not too late."

Chapter 50

Harris's stomach was churning like the sea below. *This will work*, he told himself firmly. Still, he froze for a moment as he watched the rising sun's coral-pink light wash over the enemy ships.

They'd spent the previous evening helping to set up camp in the grounds of the ruined castle. Tents were erected and fires started until the place resembled a small village. Harris had been to a fair once, in his youth, where crowds had watched brawny men toss cabers and sampled the wares of traders passing through. With the Eilanmòr flag flying from the canvases, their camp looked just as jovial, except for the dour mood that had descended on the army as soon as they crested the hill. No one had wanted to look too long towards the Mirandelli fleet on the horizon or the beach below, where they'd no doubt stage their attack.

This is where some of us will die, Harris had thought as he and Eilidh snuck over the dunes in the early hours of the morning. In a number of days, a week, blood would mix with the saltwater ahead, staining it pink like the dawn sky.

Though, perhaps they'd never get to that point. Their enemy looked quite content to stay floating off the coast. *How long have they been here?* Long enough to tie what looked like rope bridges between the ships. The Mirandellis had settled in. Waiting. But for what?

"What if we get caught?" Eilidh asked, her voice a whisper.

"We managed to sneak past Angus and Cameron, didn't

we?" It hadn't been hard. They'd sequestered themselves in their tent early in the evening, with their unicorn sleeping at the door, leaving Eilidh and Harris to hash out their plan. "Having second thoughts?"

Eilidh snorted. "No, are you?"

"We'll be fine as long as you can keep up, my lady." He tried to wink but the effect was hard to achieve with only one working eye; the gesture was too slow with his damaged one and closing his good eye left him blind for a second. In the end, he settled for a kind of twitch that he was sure made him look deranged. Eilidh was kind enough not to comment.

They pressed themselves down flat against the dune so they could peer over the top. "Do you see the wooden structure?" asked Eilidh.

The mass of ships looked bigger now they were up close, like an impenetrable wall out to sea. "It's in the middle of all the ships. Whatever it is, they want to keep it hidden."

"Which means we'll have to sneak past a whole load of boats."

"No one will notice us," said Harris. "I'll just be a wee seal and you'll be—what were you going to be?"

"Something that can swim with you until we get there," Eilidh decided. "Then I'll change again."

"A jellyfish?" he guessed.

Eilidh clicked her tongue. "I don't think they have brains? Probably not the best option."

"Well, better now than never." Harris raised himself up and rolled over the top of the dune. "Let's go," he said over his shoulder.

But before he could crawl his way down the sand, Eilidh grabbed him. "Hold on. What is that?"

A flash of blue appeared further down the beach before vanishing, like a candle being blown out. Harris held his breath, watching, until another light winked into existence, a tiny body just visible from where they crouched.

"Wisps," Harris told her. "Mischievous little spirits who like to trick travellers."

"They're trying to trick us?"

Another blue light flashed, closer this time. The wisp's eyes were wide, and its mouth arranged in a perfect circle as it stared at them. It blinked out, only to appear again right in front of them. There was a noise like the chirping of a bird and then an answering cheep from further away.

"They're talking," Harris realised in amazement. "I don't think I've ever heard that before."

Eilidh clutched her cloak tighter. "Why?"

The wisp faded but then it was replaced by two new lights. Then three. Then four. Soon a little group of wisps were hanging in the air in front of them, each with their eyes trained on Eilidh.

Harris cleared his throat. "They're here for you."

She shifted, uneasy. "Can you tell them to go away?"

"I have a feeling they won't listen to me," he said pointedly.

Eilidh sighed. "Fine. Please leave us."

The chirping kicked up a notch, until Harris was sure the Mirandellis would hear all the way down in the bay. "Quiet. Do you want us to get caught?"

The twittering stopped and they retreated a few feet, still watching Eilidh as they went.

"You might as well put them to use," said Harris. "Have them light our way down to the water."

"Will you?" she asked. "Safely?"

The wisps flared brighter for a moment, as if pleased to help, then scattered like shooting stars. Each wisp found a place down the path until they had the whole way down lit by the cyan glow.

"Won't the Mirandellis see?" asked Eilidh as she began picking her way down.

"I have a feeling the wisps won't show themselves to the sailors. They want to keep their queen safe, after all."

"I'm not their queen." But she looked a lot less sure than she had previously.

"We should get you a crown," Harris teased as they followed the wisps down the beach. "I'll make it out of flowers, if you'd like."

Eilidh gave him a light shove. "You're insufferable."

"I think you suffer me better than most." Harris grinned as his feet found the lapping waves. "Okay, ready?"

Eilidh nodded, rolling her shoulders. "Shift and I'll follow you."

Pulling on his seal skin was as simple as breathing. One moment he was standing in the shallows and the next he was allowing the retreating waves to pull his body out to sea. He luxuriated in the feel of the cool surf and the taste of salt. The dawn light was still dim to his human eye, but as a seal it was just enough for him to navigate his way towards the group of ships.

But first, where's Eilidh? He hadn't seen her change and he had no idea what he was looking for, so when he caught a glimpse of silver, he hesitated. *Is that her?* His suspicions were confirmed when the shoal raced towards him; usually wild fish avoided seals at all costs. He only hoped there were no whales or other seals around who fancied a snack.

He blew out a bubble in greeting, before heading off through the water. The school of salmon moved as one, keeping close to his tail. *Fast,* he thought, doubling his efforts. The sooner they were in and out, the better.

In no time at all, they reached the line of ships, their hulls creaking as they moved with the undulating ocean. He skirted along beside the vessels, turning keen eyes upwards to catch any small details that could one day become helpful. Did he recognise the flags flying from the masts or the people leaning against the railings? It was the figureheads which he found most peculiar. Here was a nation who apparently hated the fae, yet they decorated their ships with mermaids, angels, unicorns and gorgons. Perhaps, in the past, Mirandelle had not been so prejudiced, enough that the fae were seen as good luck once.

Eventually, Harris found an opening. He followed it inside the floating island, the gaps between ships a great maze. He spotted Eilidh's school of fish down below him. She didn't need to come up for air like he did.

The next time he surfaced, shouts drifted down to him. *They're awake.* He ducked under again, hoping to avoid any enemy sailors.

The voices grew quiet, until they were drowned out by the echoes of the deep. Then, when he thought it was safe enough, he swam back up to get a breath. This time there were no shouts, no movement, no noise. The ships around him were deathly silent as he bobbed there. *Where is everyone?* Harris wondered. But then a distant scream rent the air.

I'm close.

He weaved between the barnacle covered hulls, until he'd lost track of how many turns he'd made. All the while, the screaming continued, getting louder and louder. Harris's stomach churned but he pushed himself on, until the boats were too close together, suddenly impenetrable.

He stuck his head out once more, looking for a way to get through. There was something strange about the stillness, but he couldn't put his finger on it. When he put his ears under again, he realised what it was. The screaming he'd heard earlier was louder under the water, not above. *It's coming from the ocean.* He angled his head down and peered through the murk.

There was something massive below him, sitting on the seafloor. It must have been the size of the whole group of ships, with dark masses reaching out through the gloom. For a moment, Harris thought it was moving like some sort of monster but when he focussed, he saw the shapes were made of stone. It looked like buildings. But what were they doing under the water? The screams had grown louder again, bubbling up from the depths. *They're coming from down there.* Whatever the thing was, Harris felt his body shying away from it. *Wrong, wrong, wrong,* his mind supplied.

Eilidh's fish circled around him, breaking him from his thoughts. They had a job to do, and Harris was very glad it was above the waves, not below. He followed the shoal until she found a space for them to slip through, squeezing between the wood until they neared the floating platform.

The fish merged together at Harris's side, their bodies breaking and reforming into tiny brittle starfish. Their long limbs stuck to Harris's fur, until he was covered in them. *Hitching a ride,* Harris guessed. Suddenly, he wished Eilidh could speak to him.

He raised his grey head out of the water, coming face to face with the wooden island. What he saw made his blood turn to ice.

Hundreds of figures, of every age, gender, and skin colour, sat huddled together, their hands tied behind their backs. Though some were openly weeping, no one made a sound as they watched the other side of the platform. Harris's stare locked onto a teenage girl wearing a dress that resembled a sack. She shivered and pressed into the legs of the old woman behind her as the platform tilted back and forward.

What's going on? The floating island was flat and held in

place by ropes tied to the surrounding ships, whose masts towered over the area. Harris lifted himself out of the water some more, but no one paid him any attention. They were all staring intently at something. He took a risk, hoisting himself up onto the wood and peered over the shoulders of the figures.

Now he was closer to them, he caught the scent of faerie folk through the brine. With the smell so strong, most of them had to have some fae blood in them.

"When should we start?" a voice rang out.

Harris saw what they were staring at. There in their rich uniforms with their swords stood a dozen men and women from the Mirandelli army. "We need to make room," said one woman, eyeing the crowds. "There'll be a fresh shipment coming in soon."

A barrel-chested soldier kicked at something by his feet. The bundle of fabric gave out a low groan and Harris realised it was a man. "Can we just toss them in?"

"Scarsi was clear; if we need to thin them out, we need to do it properly. Their throats must be slit for the Edaxi's plan to work. Once they have all Four Treasures, the sea must be filled with blood, or the island will stay below the waves."

The other soldier nodded, grabbing the captive by his hair. "Who knows how long before the gods are ready. Just use the ones who look like they're about to die, so no one is wasted. We'll get new fae in soon to replace them anyway." Then he drew his dagger from his belt and hauled the man towards the edge without a fight.

I can't watch this, Harris thought. The arms of the starfish dug into his skin as if Eilidh was echoing his horror.

A gasp rippled through the crowd of captives and Harris knew the man's throat had been slit. He hesitated, looking at the figures around him, wondering if he could drag any over the platform to spirit them away. *They'll never make it. The* sea was too cold, and they'd have to hold their breaths too long to get out of the mass of ships.

"Wait, is that a seal?" the female soldier's voice rang out.

The barrel-chested Mirandelli straightened, blood still dripping from his dagger. "It's a selkie. One of Eilanmòr's."

The teenage girl raised her eyes to Harris's, pure panic on her face. "Run!" she shouted.

Harris didn't need to be told twice. The soldiers started towards him, but he was already diving into the sea. He felt the water ripple around him as arrows or spears narrowly missed his body, but he didn't stop.

Hold on Eilidh, he thought, swimming down and under the wall of boats. The last thing he saw before racing back to shore, was a green, glowing light illuminating the sea floor. Whatever was at the bottom of the ocean, was now awake.

Chapter 51

The scene behind Iona's eyes was peaceful. Turquoise waves crashed against golden sand, the air tasting of salt spray. The gorse bushes growing against the dunes gave off their sweet vanilla and coconut scents and the sun kissed her skin, leaving freckles behind. Iona knew that if she looked behind her, she'd see a little whitewashed cottage, its door wide open to let the ocean breeze inside. This was their beach; hers and Alasdair's. She had dreamed of it many times, only to wake up to an empty bed.

I'd rather stay here. But try as she might, she couldn't remain asleep forever. Not when a rooster crowed nearby, signalling the start of the day. Not when there was so much to do. Her friends needed her.

Iona slid an eye open, trying to make sense of her surroundings. She was in a wooden room, the smell of hay filling her nostrils. Shafts of light found their way between the cracks in the walls, highlighting the dust motes that fell from the ceiling. *It's peaceful here too,* she thought. It took a few seconds for her to piece it all together. The barn. Her half-clothed body. The arm flung over her waist.

Iona snapped her attention to the side, following the arm to wide shoulders and a face pressed into a makeshift pillow.

Oh yes, she thought breathlessly. *I remember now.*

Alasdair always looked so young in sleep. The lines around between his eyebrows were smoothed, his lips parted as he inhaled slowly. A lock of hair hung over his forehead and Iona couldn't resist reaching out to smooth it back. Then she trailed her fingers further, down his neck and over the smooth expanse of his back.

"I wish I could wake up like this every morning," he said, his voice muffled. He didn't open his eyes.

She grinned. "That could be arranged."

Alasdair rolled over, stretching his legs out. "Did you sleep alright?"

"I think I have hay in my hair."

"Probably not from sleeping." He looked way too smug. "When all this is over, prepare to be romanced properly."

Iona felt the blush heating her cheeks. "You were always good at that."

Alasdair pulled her closer, nuzzling into her hair. "I can't believe I get to keep you. When I—" he swallowed, "When I died, you were my last thought. The spear pierced my heart, and I didn't see the face of my murderer. I saw you. You kept me tied here. And now, if you'll have me, I want to spend the rest of this second life with you by my side."

Iona licked her lips. "But you still have duties—"

"—everyone thinks I'm dead. Eilanmòr has a new king. Yes, it would be nice to see my grandchildren, to impart some wisdom, but they don't need me. We could go back to our cottage." He leaned away, scrutinizing her face. "We could get married."

"Are you proposing to me?" she asked, biting her lip.

"Why not? My first marriage was of convenience and, while I came to love Saoirse as a friend, I wanted you. I want you. I don't want to waste this second chance of happiness," he said firmly.

She placed a hand over his heart. "When we've saved Eilanmòr, ask me again. Preferably not when we're in a barn, surrounded by hay."

"What if I made you dinner?" he asked, kissing the tip of her nose. "What if I spun you around a dancefloor? What would my chances be then?"

She giggled. "High. It's *almost* a sure thing."

"Almost?"

"I need to keep you guessing." Iona pulled away, climbing out of their makeshift bed with a yawn. "We should get up. I reckon we can get to Inshmore by early afternoon. Do you think you're ready? To see your family?"

He watched her lazily with one hand propping up his head. "Only if I don't have to share you." But with a huff, he sat up and started packing up their belongings.

Iona watched, mouth dry, as he looked for his shirt, the muscles in his tanned back working as he searched. *This battle better be sorted by teatime tomorrow,* she thought. Then she was going to whisk Alasdair off, just like all the fae in the stories.

Chapter 52

Since Iona and Alasdair had abandoned their little rowboat, they had to rely on walking from the farm to Inshmore; but that wasn't why their journey was slower than planned. No, that was because Alasdair had insisted on holding Iona's hand for much of it, pulling her in to kiss her whenever he had the urge. Their hike soon became a leisurely amble, until it was already early afternoon.

We'll still get there today, Iona reasoned. They'd be another couple of hours at most. It was hard to work up any urgency, not when the sun was shining merrily overhead, and they were being serenaded with bird song. They passed patches of lavender, their scent released by the warm air, and butterflies flitted across their path. The sea sparkled off to their right, guiding their way to the coast.

Everything was serene and peaceful, until they rounded the headland and caught a glimpse of ships on the horizon.

"That's not the Mirandellis, is it?" asked Iona as they stared out over the ocean. There were hundreds of boats, all floating together like an island made of wood.

Alasdair whistled. "I didn't realise they had such a massive navy."

"But they're just sitting there," said Iona with a frown.

"Come on." He pulled her along. "We'd better hurry."

They marched over the hills and through the forest, the terrain eventually dipping down towards a ruined castle, where they spotted canvas. "We made it," Alasdair said, letting go of her hands and quickening his steps.

Iona went to follow him, but movement caught her eye, further back between the trees. She hesitated, straining her eyes to see the source. *Must have been a bird,* she eventually decided. And then off she went, following Alasdair towards the tents.

The camp was packed with soldiers but not a single person stopped them as Iona and Alasdair strolled in. *We're not coming in from the direction of the enemy,* Iona supposed. Still, she'd have to tell Duncan about the lax security.

There was a tension in the air as people darted around, like bees in a hive. Iona thought she recognised a handful of faces, but she didn't stop, not as they weaved nearer to the tents in the middle flying the Eilanmòr flag.

"It's like an echo," said Alasdair, squeezing her hand. "This camp could easily be mine from twenty years ago."

"Except this time, you'll be around when it gets packed up."

"Hopefully," he chuckled.

"I swear it. No one is taking you from me a second time."

Iona spotted her brother's bright hair first, in a clearing between the canvas. He sat at a table, staring at something intently. She pulled Alasdair behind her as she revelled in the opportunity to look Harris over before he saw her, noting his slight tan, his clean clothes. Yes, he seemed much better than he had when she left.

"You ready?" she murmured to Alasdair, her mouth suddenly dry.

He pulled her closer in response, his eyes fixed on Harris.

Iona took a deep breath and called out, "You look like you're concentrating. I don't think I've ever seen you so absorbed in something that isn't a pretty girl or boy."

Harris's head snapped up, a grin already spreading across his face. "Iona, thank the gods—" He stopped, gaze shifting to Alasdair. For a moment, his expression was blank, but Iona watched it shift to curious, then to realisation and finally to wonder. "King Alasdair?" His face had paled, the freckles stark on his nose.

Alasdair gave him a small, closed mouth smile as they drifted closer. "Harris. I haven't seen you since you were wee—"

"No," said her brother, shaking his head and holding his hand out. Was that a hint of fear Iona detected? "We're not doing this. We're not glossing over the fact that I'm seeing a ghost. Or did you fake your death? Maybe I'm hallucinating."

"Harris," said Iona, dropping Alasdair's hand so she could touch Harris's shoulder. *He's trembling.* "Alasdair was dead, but he was brought back to life."

He kept his wide eyes on Alasdair, shrinking away. "Not like the others."

This wasn't going how she'd expected. "Others?"

"We were attacked on the way here." He ran a hand through his hair, making it stick up at odd angles. "There were people on the river, and we just thought they were villagers but then everyone started recognising them. The captain's wife, Angus's mother—they were all dead."

"Did they say anything?" asked Alasdair, exchanging a look with Iona.

The question seemed to calm her brother. "No, they just tried to drown everyone," said Harris. "They were... hollow."

Alasdair nodded. "It's like I said," he murmured to Iona. "Their souls had already passed on. Empty shells."

She rubbed Harris's arm up and down. "Alasdair isn't like them," she said, her voice soothing. "He's been haunting Dunrigh for years so when they reanimated his body, he moved back in."

"Haunting—" Harris's voice cracked on the word. "Right.

This is a lot. Why don't we find your grandsons while I process it all? I think they were meeting in Duncan's tent."

Iona and Alasdair trailed behind Harris as he led them to the right pavilion, right in the middle of the other tents. The flags on the lines flapped in a gentle breeze but there were storm clouds on the horizon, darkening the scene. Harris parted the fabric without hesitation, slipping inside, but Alasdair pulled on Iona's hand, planting his feet in the dirt.

"This is so strange," he said, flicking his gaze between her face and the tent. "What am I going to say to them?"

She brushed her fingers against his cheek, trying to smooth out the worry. "What did you wish you could say?"

Alasdair blew out a breath. "That I love them. I was there when they were born, I watched their first steps. But they don't even know me."

All those years, haunting the castle, watching but never able to join in. Iona didn't know how he could stand it. Was it better to stay around or to pass on and only see your family in the next life? *It doesn't matter, I'm glad he stayed.* "They'll get to know you."

Alasdair gave her a crooked smile. "Alright," he said after a long moment, and Iona parted the tent's canvas.

It was dark inside and it took a while for even Iona's keen eyes to adjust. She'd barely taken in the floor cushions, the low table, the neatly made bed, when someone said her name.

"Iona, you made it," said Eilidh quietly, as if she was trying not to attract attention. She straightened from her seat in the corner; her long, blonde hair tumbling over her shoulder, glowing in the candlelight. Eilidh bit her lip, her attention going back to the scene in front of her.

Iona followed her stare. Angus faced his brother, who stood with his arms folded over his chest. Angus's shoulders were tense, and his feet planted as if he was ready for a fight, while Duncan looked distinctly unimpressed. Right at the back of the small space, Harris had pressed himself up against the canvas, grimacing sheepishly.

"What's going on?" Iona asked, stepping further into the room.

Angus whipped around and behind him Duncan nodded in greeting. "Lady Iona," said the king. "Good. Someone else is here to tell my brother he's being an eejit."

"Hello, Iona," Angus said quickly, before turning back to Duncan. "I just think, if we can sneak in like Harris and Eilidh did, we could end the war before it's even begun."

Duncan barked out a laugh. "And assassinating the king of Mirandelle is going to be that easy? You'll get captured and where will that leave us?"

"Sorry," interrupted Iona, wondering if she'd heard right, "sneak in like Harris and Eilidh? Sneak in where?" Why did she get the feeling she didn't want to know?

Harris licked his lips. "Last night we went to have a look behind enemy lines."

Iona's mouth hung open. "Harris—"

"We were careful," he said, holding up his hands. "We both shifted."

"Do you think it would have been any better if you'd been taken?" Duncan admonished, shaking his head. "You shouldn't have risked it either, Eilidh is too important—"

"Oh good," said Iona, relaxing. "You've told him then."

Eilidh froze.

"Told me what?" asked Duncan.

"That—" Iona bit her lip. *Oh no.* "That—"

"That I'm your sister," said Eilidh, dropping back down into her seat and pulling her knees to her chest. "Surprise."

Iona cringed. She hadn't even been in the camp for half an hour, and she'd already outed Eilidh. She felt Alasdair at her back, as he watched all this in silence. No one appeared to have noticed him, but Iona was extremely glad for his soothing presence. *What have I done?*

Duncan pinched the bridge of his nose. "Would someone please explain?"

"Eilidh is Nicnevan's lost daughter," said Angus, angling his body a little so it was between her and his brother. "That's why she has earth magic, she's half faerie. And she's half human because our father had an affair with the Faerie Queen before you were born."

"You knew all this, and you didn't tell me?" Duncan said sharply.

"I asked him not to." Eilidh's mouth twisted. "I thought you might get worried I'd come for your crown or something. But I hope you know that would never happen." She said the final part in a hurry, her voice going quieter with each word.

Duncan stared Eilidh down, his face unreadable. Everyone in the room seemed to hold their breath, waiting for his verdict. *What if he sends her away?* Iona thought. Then Duncan was across the room, crouching down in front of Eilidh and taking her face in his hands.

"I have a sister," he said with a laugh.

Eilidh's smile was watery. "I'm sorry I didn't tell you. I just want to help win this fight and then I'll head back to my inn."

"But you'll come back to Dunrigh first?" Duncan was staring at her in wonder, like she was something precious. "I want you to meet my son. I can't believe you were with us all this time." He pushed a lock of hair away from her face. "One blue eye and one brown. The same as our grandfather's. I just assumed it was a coincidence."

Angus beamed down at them. "See, I told you he'd take it well."

"You and I will be having words later." He turned back to Eilidh, giving her a wink. "You're already my favourite sibling."

Iona watched them; her heart warmed. Finally, after so many years, Eilidh was reunited with her family. When Iona had found her at the inn, she was unsure if this day would ever come. But seeing them together now was a glimpse of happiness amongst all the worry.

But there was still the matter of Alasdair...

Iona cleared her throat. "So, you've just had a lot of new information thrown at you, but do you think you'd all be up for some more?"

"What is it?" asked Angus, not taking his eyes off his siblings. "Have you heard from Ailsa?"

"No, but I did find someone else we, well I, know." She stepped to the side so she could take Alasdair's hand, encouraging him further into the room. "What's the best way to explain this? Harris told us about what happened with the boats."

Angus paled. "With the dead."

"When I got to Struanmuir, it had been attacked." Harris opened his mouth to speak but she held up her hand. "It looks like everyone got out. I followed the raiders who had done it, finding them on the Eilanmòrian coast." She raised her chin. "I had my revenge. But, afterwards, I found an old friend." Now everyone had noticed the man beside her, giving him curious looks. "Your ancestors' cairns were raided, and their bodies were stolen. The Edaxi can reanimate the dead, creating a mindless, soulless second army. But what if I told you that not all of them came back as empty shells?"

"What do you mean?" Angus breathed. His gaze locked on Alasdair's as if he was noticing those same mismatched eyes that Eilidh had.

Then Iona said the words she'd been practising for days, ever since she'd found her long, lost love tied up on that beach. "Angus, Duncan, Eilidh, meet King Alasdair. Alasdair, meet your grandchildren."

Chapter 53

Ailsa spread the map out in front of Maalik and watched him examine it. The mountains and forests were easy to see but to Ailsa each place name was an indecipherable scrawl. Only Dunrigh, with its castle clearly marked, was familiar. Her eyes followed the first letter, a D. The next was a U. But the longer she looked at the word, the more it appeared to shake on the page.

She scrunched her nose in frustration. How anyone managed to concentrate on reading whole sentences, let alone a book, was beyond her.

"Can you tell where we are?" she asked.

"I think that peak is Ben Bowdie," said Maalik, tapping the paper. "Which means we're almost there."

I'd hope so. Ailsa had been sure they'd have found the army by now. *They must have made good time on their march south.* "Where next?"

"We could go higher?" Maalik suggested. "Maybe we'll see further."

Ailsa picked a spot on the slope, hoping it wasn't too steep. Then she took the stone in her palm, repeating the mountain's name over and over. The light ahead shimmered like air rising from the ground on a hot day and Ailsa nodded to Maalik.

"After you."

It was quite astounding; one moment they were on the banks of a winding river, the next they were transported to exactly where Ailsa had imagined, the wind whipping round them as their feet slid over scree.

The day had been slower than she'd hoped. Every time they stumbled from one spot to another, the stone seemed to use up its store of magic and they had to wait to use it again. There was no rhyme or reason for how long it took, and Ailsa got the feeling it was just being stubborn. They'd been travelling for hours, and the air was starting to cool with the early evening. *We're making good time,* she reminded herself. If they didn't have the stone, they'd be hopelessly behind.

If we didn't have the stone, we'd still be in Findias, Ishbel whispered.

Ailsa cringed. *Or dead.*

Don't say that, said Ishbel firmly. *They'll be okay.*

"Not far to the coast." Maalik raised a hand to shield his eyes. There, on the horizon, Ailsa swore she saw blue that wasn't the sky. "Do you want to pick the next spot so we're ready when the stone recharges?"

Ailsa sat down on a lichen covered boulder and chose a grassy hillock, further down the glen. "What good is a magical weapon if you can only use it every fifteen minutes," she grumbled.

He came to join her, pulling a package of beeswax covered cheese from his pocket. "Maybe your magic isn't compatible."

Ailsa hummed. That could be right. The stone didn't call to her, not like the spear, currently hidden carefully inside her pack. "I hope it hurries up," she grumbled. "We've still got so far to go."

"We'll get there," said Maalik. "You'll see your friends by the day's end."

As long as they really were waiting for her there. As long as nothing bad had happened. *We're on our way,* she told the air. *Hold on.*

Chapter 54

*C*hester Scarsi fought the shiver creeping up his spine as he stood before the God of Chaos and the God of Despair. Chao lounged on the throne, a dead bird in his hands with half its feathers already plucked. The shadow that was Desper hovered nearby, emitting a faint buzzing. Any light that touched him seemed to be sucked away, like he was feeding on it.

By some stroke of luck, neither had turned their powers on him. King Merlo, however, was not as fortunate.

Merlo was slumped in a seat by the window, eyes trained on the square below, though Scarsi was sure he didn't see the figures marching from one end to the other. The procession had been Merlo's plan, made before he truly realised which entities he'd let into his palace. It was simple: round up all the fae across Mirandelle and have them parade themselves before the normal citizens, before they were bundled into carts and taken to their deaths. *Look how many fae scum there are*, the Mirandellis were meant to say. *Look how the Edaxi and our king are ridding us of these pests.*

Except they hadn't found that many fae, perhaps a couple of hundred. Merlo had planned for that too. All were beaten and dirty, so indistinguishable from each other that if the group were taken through the square, then looped back through the streets to the beginning again, no one would know they were seeing the same people over and over again. For the regular Mirandelli, it appeared like there were thousands of fae on parade.

Until the one with the scarf. It was the red and gold of the Mirandelli flag. Scarsi guessed the fae man had grabbed a banner or something to tie around his neck. The man crossed from one end of the square to the other, sporting the bright fabric. And then, exactly nine minutes later, he crossed the square again. And again. The illusion was broken—and Chao and Desper had noticed.

"Stop the parade," Desper seethed. "Lock the fae in the carts and throw them in the sea."

"Not that one, though." Chao dropped the bird's corpse on his bony knee and twisted his long fingers together in glee. "I want to open him up and see if he's as brave on the inside."

Scarsi cringed internally. There were certainly fates worse than death. "I'll see to it myself." He made to bow but then a distant boom resonated and Scarsi's head snapped up as his hands flew to his weapon.

The gods, however, did not seem perturbed. Chao merely continued plucking feathers while Desper drifted over to the window, speaking in a low voice to the king. Merlo jerked as if burned then continued staring out at the crowds.

There was another boom, closer this time; Scarsi sprang into action, heading for the door. If one of his men was responsible, he'd run them through. But, before he could get to the end of the hall, the door was thrown open violently, the bang echoing throughout the room.

"Ah, sisters," said Chao. "You've returned."

Scarsi shrank back, watching as the two goddesses entered. Both looked murderous as they stalked in; even Timor who normally hid her wrath under faux innocence.

The grey Goddess of Pain dragged something behind her and as she passed Scarsi, he realised it was a woman, moaning brokenly.

Dolor threw the woman at Chao's feet when she reached

him and spat on her tattered dress. "Don't even try to claim this one. She's mine."

Chao's grin split up his cheeks. "So, it all went well?"

Dolor let out a blood curdling shriek and Scarsi had to cover his ears.

"Not only did the spear get away," said Timor with a pout, "but they stole the stone too."

Desper moved forward to hover beside the woman. She curled in on herself, clutching at her head and moaning. "It does not matter for our plan," he said. "All will work in our favour, in the end."

"Yes, but we were stranded on that mountain top." Dolor lifted her foot, pressing the pointed heel of her shoe into the woman's leg, eliciting another cry. "My only consolation is that their palace was destroyed."

"So, they're all dead?" asked Desper.

"The witches were sneaky." Timor shifted her hands and a dark, wriggling shadow appeared between them. "They built tunnels deep into the mountain. Many of them escaped."

Chao was practically bouncing on his seat. "How wonderful. And the rest?"

"I took great pleasure in carving them up," Dolor gritted out. "But this one I saved. A priestess deserves special treatment."

The woman's back bowed off the floor and Scarsi finally got a good look at her. Her black hair was matted and tangled, and gold paint was smeared across her forehead. Her eyes were screwed up in pain as she writhed.

"You can't keep her forever," Desper admonished in his rasping voice. "The structure is almost complete, and we'll soon have enough fae to sacrifice."

Dolor waved a hand and the woman slumped back again, her head lolling to the side. *Unconscious*, Scarsi realised. *A lucky respite.*

"What about the Eilanmòrians?" Timor asked. She held out her palms, revealing a black scorpion with a wicked looking stinger. It crawled down her body, dropping to the floor and scuttling over to the woman's inert body. "Are they in position?"

Chao held up a feather. "A little bird told me they have assembled. Still, it doesn't stop me from having my fun. They are so easy to manipulate."

Desper made a clicking sound. "Merlo!" he called, addressing the king at the window. "We had better get you scrubbed up." Then the dark mass turned to Scarsi, and his stomach bottomed out. "Major," he said. "I want the fae taken to the platform and then you must ready your troops to sail out. It will soon be time."

Scarsi bowed again. "Right away," he said. Then he was striding for the door, intent on leaving the room as soon as possible. He almost made it through the portal before the woman's screams started up again. Scarsi didn't look back; he knew he could never unsee the horror being inflicted on her. *You have their favour,* he told himself to calm his racing heart. *And once the battle is over, you'll be rewarded.* So, he left the four gods to their fun and ran to do their bidding, even as the wails echoed all the way through the castle.

Chapter 55

"It's getting dark," said Ailsa, looking up at the sky. The waning moon was already out, staring down at her and she wondered if the witch's goddess was watching her or whatever was happening in Findias. Please let them be alright, she thought silently at the silver disk.

Maalik pulled on the straps of his pack. "We could walk for a bit. Then we'll use the stone when it's recharged."

Ailsa nodded, following him in a steady trudge up the hill. The trees were closing in on them now as they followed the worn path into the forest. Others had come through here and recently too, judging by the flattened grass and the odd pieces of thread snatched by the branches. Ailsa saw apple cores tossed to the side of the road, turned brown but not yet shrunken and decomposed. Occasionally, she thought she saw movement up ahead, sending a thrill through her. What if they were right behind the army? But every time she squinted through the trees, she found she was mistaken. *Must have been the wind.*

"I can't wait to see them all," she said. "And show them we found the spear and the stone." She thought of the weapon resting in her bag then, without really thinking about it, she was shrugging out of a strap and reaching inside.

As soon as her hand closed around the shaft of the spear, a faint buzzing filled her veins, just like it did when she used her lightning. Ailsa pulled out the weapon, taking it in both palms.

"What are you doing?" asked Maalik. He didn't sound angry, just confused.

She eyed the cut sapphire point. "You know, after all of these weeks trying to get it, I still don't know what it does. The stone allows you to transport and the cauldron stores magic. What does the spear do?"

"Try it then," said Maalik. "There's no one else around."

Ailsa came to a stop, holding the silver hilt gingerly. Testing it out was all well and good, but she didn't even have a clue where to begin.

You could ask me, muttered Ishbel.

Ailsa cut her eyes to Maalik, wondering if she could reply to her spirit guide out loud like she did when she was alone.

He'll know you're speaking to me.

"So, you're actually going to help me this time?" Ailsa asked. Maalik, to his credit, only had a moment of bewilderment before he seemed to catch on. "You've never exactly been forthcoming."

Well now I'm concerned you're going to hurt yourself. Or the demon.

Ailsa grinned. "You care about us."

She could feel Ishbel glowering. *Do you want help or not?*

"What do I do?"

Ishbel snorted. *What do you think you do with a spear? You throw it. But the demon may want to duck.*

"She says to get down," Ailsa told him. Immediately he obeyed and Ailsa took a step forward. "Alright, here goes."

She pulled it back, staring straight ahead, before snapping her arm forward and letting go. The spear sailed through the air, shining impossibly in the low light, and headed straight for the trunk of a towering tree. Ailsa winced, not looking forward to climbing up and pulling it out. But just as she had the thought, the spear arced, avoiding it entirely. *I can control it?* Quickly, she tested out the theory, willing it to slow down. The spear obeyed and then followed her imagined trajectory, weaving through the trees with ease. But when the point turned towards them, Ailsa's confidence faltered. It hurtled through the air, heading straight for Ailsa's heart. *It's going to hit me*, she realised. At the very last minute, she threw herself to the side as the spear whooshed past, landing with a thunk point down in the dirt.

"Are you alright?" Maalik asked, looking her over.

Ailsa sat up shakily. "I think I need to practise," she said.

"Can you do that with more armour on, please?" His voice came out strained and she sent him a shaky nod.

Ailsa retrieved the spear, slipping it back inside her pack again. "That's enough for one day, let's keep going."

But as they trudged up the tree covered hill, Ailsa swore she heard music floating on the wind. *Perhaps we're closer than I thought.* She rushed ahead, finding a new burst of energy. The camp could be right over the crest. But when she reached it, her steps faltered. "Maalik, you need to come see this."

Ailsa gaped open mouthed at the scene ahead. Below, the sea crashed against the shore and further out, a whole fleet of ships floated on the horizon. There must be hundreds of ships, Ailsa thought absently. Further inland, on a grassy hill, a village of tents was set up beside a ruined castle. She should be elated to have made it, or terrified by the sight of the enemy. But neither of those sights held her attention. Because, much closer, standing stock still just beyond the forest, were dozens of people.

The frozen figures stared down at the encampment below. Ailsa sensed Maalik stop beside her, but she didn't need to see him to know his expression would be a mirror of her own. "What are they doing?" she asked, watching the people.

"I have no idea," said Maalik.

The crowd was so big, she knew they'd have to double back to avoid them. *They may not be hostile. Maybe they are sick or lost.* "Do you think we should ask? They might need help."

Maalik hesitated, like his need to heal and offer aid was warring with his instincts to turn and run, just like Ailsa's were. "Be careful," he told her.

Ailsa approached cautiously; the soles of her boots muffled against the soft grass. A fresh breeze ruffled the daisies growing there, but none of the figures moved, save from the hair on their heads. *Not statues then.* These were real, living people. From their clothing, Ailsa could tell most were Eilanmòrian, though some were dressed in old styles and fabrics.

She tiptoed up to a short woman wearing a pretty cornflower dress. Ailsa waved her hand in front of the woman's face, but her expression didn't change. "Nothing."

"They don't seem ill," she called back. "Maybe it's magic?"

Maalik crept closer, examining another person, this time a young boy. But then he looked back over his shoulder and gasped. "Wait, there are more coming," he said, softly. "Ailsa, I don't like this."

Just as the words left Maalik's mouth, the woman in front of Ailsa blinked her eyes. Then, as if waking from a deep sleep, her gaze flicked around, settling on Ailsa.

"Can you hear me?" Ailsa asked.

The woman tilted her head and Ailsa's stomach clenched. There was something wrong with the woman's movements, like she was powered by an outside, unknown force. Ailsa had once seen a puppet show in her village and the woman's motions reminded her of the marionettes, controlled by strings from the puppeteer above.

Ailsa backed up, bumping into the figure behind. With horror, she realised the others were waking up too, moving jerkily towards them.

"We need to go," said Maalik. "Use the stone."

The figures were moving faster, raising their arms as if to grab them. Ailsa and Maalik darted through the bodies, looking for a suitable clearing.

"Ailsa!" Maalik's hand was wrenched from her grasp. A couple of people had grips on his shoulders and were trying to pull him into the crowd. Ailsa threw herself back, feet slipping over the slick grass.

Seeing Maalik between these strangers with their blank faces, Ailsa found she had no qualms with kicking one of the men square in the chest, sending him falling into the people behind him. "Come on," she shouted as Maalik broke free. She twisted the stone, thinking of the sea of tents below and saw the familiar shimmer ahead. Dodging and diving between the outstretched hands, she skidded to a halt just before the portal, grabbing Maalik's arm again and pushing him through.

Just before she launched herself after him, she scanned the pressing crowd, trying to make sense of it all. And that's when she saw him. Through the mass, one man stood taller than the rest. He no longer had thick grey fur covering his body, but his eyes were still red when they met hers.

"Gris?" she breathed, but then Maalik's hand grabbed her, yanking her through the portal and she lost sight of her former friend and mentor.

Chapter 56

A ilsa landed on top of Maalik, breathing hard. Gris was dead. Nicnevan had killed him all those weeks ago; she'd watched it with her own eyes. She'd even buried him in the soft soil of Ephraim. How could he be walking around now? *You must have hallucinated*, she told herself firmly. The alternative was impossible.

"Ailsa?" a shout to her left caught her attention and then she was being tackled, pulled tight into someone's arms. She took a deep breath, recognising the person's smell and let herself be hugged. "I thought something bad had happened to you."

"Cameron," she whispered, feeling the tears welling in her eyes. She blinked them away, pulling back to get a look at him. Even in the semi-dark, she could tell he was pale. His scars stood out on his face and his cheeks were sunken, but his smile was bright as he looked down at her. "We made it."

"And this is—" Cameron stopped, taking in the demon sitting beside them. Ailsa imagined what her brother saw, trying to remember her first impression of Maalik. It had been dark then too, in a clearing in the forest. A crack of lightning had revealed his strange features: the fully black eyes, the golden antlers. Ailsa had screamed when she saw him. But Cameron recovered quickly, holding his hand out for him to take. "You must be the famous Maalik," he said. "I'm Ailsa's brother, Cameron."

"It's nice to finally meet you," said the demon, shaking his hand.

"Cameron, are Angus and the king here?" she asked. "We need to find them immediately."

"Everyone is here," he said with a grin. "I travelled down with Angus and Harris. Iona just got here today, three hours ago. And you'll have to meet Eilidh too—" He stopped himself. "Well, actually, there are a few surprises in store for you."

"Do they have anything to do with the Four Treasures," she asked, letting him pull her to her feet. "Because we've got some surprises too."

"You found it?" Cameron led them through the tents, skirting past groups of soldiers at campfires. Some played flutes and whistles and Ailsa wondered if they were the source of the music she'd heard earlier. "You found the Spear of Truth?"

"Not just that." She reached back to grab Maalik's hand. Cameron tracked the movement but didn't comment, leading them to a large tent flying the Eilanmòrian flag. The flaps were pulled back to allow light inside, but from their angle of approach, Ailsa couldn't see inside.

"Everyone's in Duncan's tent," he said, rounding the corner. Then, he called out, "Look who I found."

Ailsa pulled Maalik forward until she saw the people standing under the canvas, illuminated by the glow of torchlight. They sat around a single table, maps and parchment spread out between them. She caught sight of Harris first, his red hair hard to ignore. But as he stood from the table, she stopped. He wore a dark patch over his eye, held to his face by orange ribbons, and his face was scarred. *What happened?*

Then her eyes flicked to the man beside him. Angus's face lit up as she approached. At least he looked well, the same as he'd been when she last saw him. A blonde woman sat to his left, radiant in the soft light. Something about her was familiar but Ailsa couldn't place it. *Who is she?* She had to be important to be seated next to the king. Duncan was leaning over the table, looking tired but happy to see her. Ailsa was about to open her mouth in greeting when another man, older than her friends, leapt up and drew his sword.

"Stay back!" he shouted. He threw an arm out, across a red-haired woman sitting beside him.

"Iona?" said Ailsa, bewildered. Maalik's hand, still in hers, squeezed like a vice. She turned to glance at him, finding him staring at the stranger with a look of pure terror on his face. "What—"

Iona put her hand on the man's arm. "Alasdair, who is that?"

But the stranger did not lower his sword. "That," he said, his voice a growl of rage. "Is the angel who killed me."

Chapter 57

A ilsa forgot how to breathe.

It seemed like the whole room did too as they watched the scene unfolding around them. No one moved an inch for a long, drawn-out moment. Not until she felt Maalik shrinking back from her, from the accusing stares. Then, Ailsa sidestepped in front of him, shielding her demon with her body on instinct. Whatever was going on, Maalik didn't deserve to have a sword pointed at him.

Duncan recovered first. "Someone explain. Now."

"Alasdair?" Iona gave the man a shake, looking between him and Maalik in confusion.

But when Ailsa heard the stranger's name again, something clicked. Wasn't that the name of Angus's grandfather? She thought back to the portraits under the castle. The stranger could have been any Eilanmòrian man, with his light brown hair and pale skin, but it was his eyes that were striking. One was blue and the other brown. "King Alasdair?" But he was dead. "How?"

"I found him after Struanmuir was attacked." Iona bit her lip. "Alasdair, you must be thinking of someone else. Maalik isn't an angel."

The man's lip curled. "Not anymore. He was turned into a demon as punishment for killing me. And my daughter. I saw it happen."

If this man truly was the late king, then he was speaking the truth. Maalik had recounted to her many times the day his life changed, of the deep regret he still held. He tried to tug out of her grip, but she held fast, looking over her shoulder to see the guilt on his face. *Oh Maalik. You didn't mean to.* He was the best person she knew; every day since then, he'd devoted his life to helping others. Now, for this man to show up and undo all the progress he'd made in the last few weeks was unbearable. So, Ailsa made her decision, planting her feet firmly and raising her chin. "He was tricked by Dolor."

Iona dropped her hands. "You knew?" Her expression morphed from confusion to shock to hatred. "When?" she asked, voice low and dangerous. "When did you find out?"

"Maalik told me when I was tied to him," Ailsa told the room. "When I was sacrificed to a demon by those damn villagers, and he saved me instead."

"You knew I had been in love with Alasdair." Iona spat the words at her. "Why didn't you tell me? Why didn't you tell his grandson?" She clutched at her hair. "We were in his cabin."

"Maalik—"

Iona cut across her. "—is a murderer!"

"—is sorry." Ailsa sighed. *This is a mess.* "I know that doesn't sound like a lot, but every moment since that day he's been trying to make amends. Instead of allowing himself to become a demon in nature as well as body, he's been helping people. He's here to help us."

Iona shook her head. "I can't fight with him. Not after this."

"Well, you'll have to," Ailsa snapped. She could feel Maalik shaking behind her. "There aren't any other fire fae around. Not even other demons."

"What do you mean?" asked Angus.

Ailsa didn't take her eyes off Iona and Alasdair. "I destroyed their nest."

Harris barked out a laugh. At least someone was finding the situation funny. "You destroyed Hell?"

"They had Maalik's soul," she said as a way of explanation. *Because I have walked in and out of Hell for this man, and I'd do it one hundred times over.* They should know where she stood.

"So, he has a soul again?" Alasdair gave a mirthless snort. "Didn't stop him from killing me or mine last time. I want him gone from this camp and the people I love, before he hurts them too."

Duncan's face shuttered and Ailsa waited for the same command to leave his lips. But instead, he turned to his grandfather and said, "If we are to believe Ailsa in this, then he can't leave. We need Maalik to help us defeat the Edaxi." He looked to the demon behind Ailsa. "You're here to help, are you not?"

"Duncan, this is madness." Alasdair lowered his sword a fraction. "He—"

"—while I appreciate your guidance," said Duncan, cutting him off. "I am king. A king who is readying for the battle of our nation's soul. Maalik stays. That is my decision."

Alasdair took Iona's hand. "Fine, but I want at least the length of this camp between us and him." Without another word, he pulled Iona out of the tent, giving Ailsa and Maalik a wide berth. Neither looked back at them as they left.

Gods, this is terrible.

I for one am enjoying the drama, said Ishbel.

"There's one other thing I must say," said Ailsa. "There were people gathering up on the hill when we came through. I think they're dead." She thought of Gris and blanched. Maybe it really was him. "They tried to attack us."

"I'll get MacKenzie," said Duncan. "Thank you for warning us." He rose from the table, giving Ailsa a tight-lipped smile as he strode out and left in the opposite direction of his grandfather.

Ailsa didn't move from her stance in front of Maalik, looking around the tent from Duncan to Angus, Harris, Cameron and the mystery woman. "Aren't you going with them?"

"I don't know. Should we?" said Angus, directing his question at Maalik.

The demon's voice came out thin. "I never said I wasn't a monster."

Ailsa rounded on him, taking his face in her hands. "You are not one mistake made twenty years ago." To Angus, she said, "Dolor tricked Maalik into killing your grandfather and your aunt. He thought he was saving the world."

"So, you're here to try again?" asked Angus.

"I'm here to try to help," Maalik whispered. "But I understand if you want me to leave."

The prince came closer, holding his hands up. "Like Ailsa says, we've got no other choice. But I trust her, and she trusts you. I'll arrange a tent for you both. You should lie low."

Ailsa nodded, a lump in her throat. "Thank you, Angus."

"We all make bad decisions," said the prince. "It's what you do about them afterwards that makes you worthy or not."

Chapter 58

Maalik felt like he was moving through treacle as Ailsa led him through the maze of canvas to a tent of their own. He barely registered that it wasn't far from the king's war pavilion, in the opposite direction to where Alasdair had gone, and that none of Ailsa's friends had followed them. He hardly saw the pale beige fabric or the woven straw mat, haunted instead by the face of the man he'd murdered. Ailsa made him sit down on the floor and he immediately pulled his knees to his chest.

"Are you alright?" she asked, hovering beside him.

"No," he whimpered. "I'm sorry, Ailsa. I just—"

"Stop. Come here," she said, wrapping him in a hug. "I know we're trying to keep you demonic but—"

"I certainly don't feel angelic right now." He sniffed. "I just need you."

"You have me."

"I don't deserve you." *I'm a monster.*

She poked him in the side. "I've spent weeks trying to prove you wrong. Don't let this undo all of my hard work."

He shook his head against her neck. "I'd almost forgotten. With you and the witches and saving the world, I'd almost forgotten that I'm worse than scum—"

"You aren't."

"I killed someone."

Ailsa leaned back, her cool eyes raking over his face. "So have I. Come on, we've been through this. Mine is the only opinion that matters, right? And I think you're a hero."

Gods, she was incredible. And he didn't want to let her down. "I'll try to live up to that," he whispered.

A smile spread across her face, and it was like the clouds parting to reveal the sun. He suddenly realised his lips were mere inches away from hers; if Maalik leaned forward, he could taste them again. It was a constant hunger but, in that moment, there was something else compelling him. Gratitude that she'd stuck with him? Awe that she was with him in the first place?

He wanted to sink into her, to let her make him feel cherished. His resolve was seconds away from slipping when they heard someone outside their tent.

"Hello? I would knock but there are no walls."

Ailsa groaned, as if she'd been thinking the same as him. Now he took in her red cheeks, her darkening eyes. "Come in," she said, breathily.

The flap was pulled back to reveal Angus, balancing a tray stacked with dishes. "I didn't know what you'd like so I brought you a bit of everything."

He squeezed inside, followed by Cameron and then, to Maalik's surprise, a red-headed selkie that must have been Harris. Ailsa scooted away from Maalik, putting a proprietary distance between them. Maalik watched the selkie's face for signs of fear or even hesitation, but there were none. He waited until Angus had placed the tray down in front of them and then flopped down, right beside Maalik.

"Harris," he said, holding out a hand. "I'm sure Ailsa's told you about me, but I'm not all bad."

Maalik looked at the offered hand with surprise before placing his soot-stained palm in Harris's. "Nice to meet you," he said.

"You know," said the selkie, with a sly grin. "Aside from

the, you know, whole demon thing, you're handsome. I can see why Ailsa likes you—"

"Harris," she warned.

The selkie just shrugged, withdrawing his hand. "Am I not allowed to appreciate these things?" He rolled his eye. "I'm sure she likes you for more than your looks," he said, as if that's what she was taking offence at.

"Anyway, if Harris is quite done with his flirting," said Angus, grabbing a piece of bread. "There's a lot you've missed."

Ailsa hummed. "I'd say. Your grandfather? Struanmuir?" Maalik saw her eyes flick to Harris's patch. "Start there and we'll see where we get."

"Iona showed up this afternoon with Alasdair in tow." Angus snagged a strawberry and popped it into his mouth. "It just feels weird calling him anything else. Grandpa? Pops? She said Struanmuir was on fire when she arrived but all the selkies were missing. Seems like they've gone into hiding. Iona followed the Avalognians who did it and found Alasdair. That's about as much as we know."

Ailsa nodded. "What else have we missed?"

"The blonde woman in the tent?" said Cameron. "That was Eilidh. Nicnevan's daughter."

Ailsa seemed lost for words. "You found her?" Maalik asked for her.

"She had the Sword of Light. Then there was a battle in Ephraim and Irené was captured by Chao, the God of Chaos."

"That's when I lost my eye. A bit of divine wrath," Harris said. His mask slipped for a second, devastation plain on his face, before he covered it up again with determination. "But I'm going to get her back."

"And Nicnevan?" said Ailsa, quietly.

"Dead," Angus confirmed. "She died saving me."

Ailsa had told Maalik everything that had happened

before they'd met and in those in-between weeks, but he was sure he wasn't getting a full grasp of the gravity of all this. "So then that woman—Eilidh—is the Faerie Queen?"

"She doesn't want to be, but she is helping us, since she's an earth fae." Angus ran a hand through his hair. "She's also my sister."

Ailsa blinked beside him, taking all of this in. He brushed his pinky against hers, hoping the touch would ground her. "I'm glad you found her," Maalik said sincerely.

"What about you?" asked Ailsa's brother.

Again, she didn't seem ready to answer. "We found the Spear of Truth."

"Was it with the witches like the book said?"

Ailsa could only nod, turning her gaze to Maalik as the words dried on her tongue. *I can't*, she said with her eyes.

"Ailsa is one of them." He threaded their fingers together. "A witch."

It was at that moment that Cameron seemed to notice his sister's face was missing something. In the drama before, they all must have overlooked it. He leaned forward, tilting her chin up. "Your birthmark—"

"It disappears when changelings look upon their birth mother," Ailsa said. "But I was looking at a whole hall of people."

"When Eilidh saw Nicnevan, her whole appearance changed." He turned her face, brushing his thumb over her cheek. "Her hair colour, her eye colour, her nose. But you look the same, apart from the missing mark. Do you have any idea who your birth mother is?" Cameron asked, sitting back.

Ailsa averted her eyes. "I have some idea, but it doesn't matter now. They could all be dead. We escaped when Dolor and Timor attacked." She looked between her three friends. "They had the Stone of Destiny." She reached into her shirt, pulling the rock out to let it swing in front of her neck. "But not anymore."

"Oh, my gods," breathed Angus. "You got it back."

Maalik chanced a grin. "And the Spear of Truth too."

Harris whistled. "Good going, MacAra. That means—we have the stone, the cauldron, the sword and the spear."

Angus beamed. "And four fae to use them."

"We could actually win this," said Harris, tackling the prince.

Ailsa's answering smile was strained. "If we can all work together."

Maalik's heart, flying high for a moment, came crashing down. That was the problem, though, wasn't it? They were going to have to work as a team. But somewhere across the camp, one of the integral members was sequestered with a man he'd murdered, once upon a time.

"Tomorrow, we'll get everyone together," said Angus, as if he'd read Maalik's thoughts. He stacked together the empty plates and stood. "You all better have a good sleep tonight because tomorrow we're starting some very last-minute training. Nothing gets rid of frustration and solves problems like some good old-fashioned exercise."

I really hope he's right, thought Maalik as he watched the three men leave. Because if he wasn't, he dreaded to think what revenge King Alasdair might be tempted to in a training ring full of swords.

Chapter 59

The next morning, Ailsa woke with a headache, which she hoped didn't signal the day to come. She'd meant to stay up with Maalik, but the events from the day and night before caught up with her and she soon succumbed to sleep. When she blinked her eyes open though, Maalik was snoring quietly beside her on his stomach, one arm thrown over her hips. She took the opportunity to watch him as his back moved up and down with his breathing. With his eyelashes fanning across his cheeks and his lips pouted, he looked angelic. *One day soon,* Ailsa promised, *I'll get to see that for real.*

Soon the sun's rays made the interior of the canvas too hot, and Ailsa had to shake him awake, handing him a canteen of water Angus had left the night before.

"Ready for this?" he asked groggily.

Ailsa hummed her assent. As long as King Alasdair kept his opinions to himself, they'd be fine.

They got ready quickly after that, slipping out their tent and through the pavilions to a spot in the shadow of the abandoned castle. Its silhouette was a jagged outline against the sun, destroyed by years of sea winds. She found her friends there, in the daisy-speckled grass. Her attention immediately went to Iona, who stood alone and to the side. When Ailsa and Maalik approached, she stiffened.

Great, thought Ailsa. She really had hoped that only Alasdair would be a problem.

"Alright," shouted Angus, addressing them all. He'd

stripped down to his vest and a pair of loose trousers and Ailsa wondered if she was overdressed in her shirt and jacket. "Let's get you all warmed up and then we'll try some basic techniques."

It turned out that Ailsa was right. They'd only been going for half an hour and already she was sweating. She pulled off her outer layers, tossing them on the grass. *At least with Angus putting us through our paces, Iona's too busy to say anything.* She watched Maalik out the corner of her eye, noting the way his muscles shifted and how his breathing was steady.

"Show off," she muttered.

He sent a wink her way but kept his head ducked, trying not to attract attention.

Harris flopped down on the ground, throwing his arms and legs out like a starfish. "I'm done," he gasped. "I'm more of a sneaker than a fighter, you know?" Then he rolled onto his front and pulled himself across the grass like some sort of worm.

Angus rolled his eyes. "Right. Are you doing alright, Cam?"

"I'm fine," he said, following through with another lunge.

Angus looked as dubious as Ailsa was. Cameron was struggling, she could see it in the way his limbs shook, but he was also incredibly stubborn.

"Alright, let's pair up. Grab a practice sword and show me what we're working with."

Iona immediately grabbed Eilidh's wrist and pulled her further away, while Angus gave her brother a nod and went to collect their weapons. Which left Ailsa and Maalik to square off against each other.

"I'll go easy on you," she said, aiming to distract him from the accusatory looks she knew he'd been receiving all morning.

Maalik snorted, tossing her a sword from the container. "You realise I used to be a warrior, right?"

She took a practice swing, trying to remember everything Angus had taught her when they were searching for the Stone of Destiny. "And now you're a healer who reads too much. Try to keep up, old man." Then she lunged for him.

Maalik was better than she'd expected, actually. Ailsa knew her sword skills weren't good, but she tried to make up for it with her speed, thrusting and parrying as fast as she could. Maalik, on the other hand, met every blow with practised calm. He hardly moved his feet, but Ailsa couldn't get close and soon she was winded. Then, with one well-placed leg, Maalik had her toppling over, rolling as she hit the ground.

He held his sword tip to her chest. "Does this mean I win?"

She glowered up at him, feeling impressed despite herself. "I'll get you next time."

Maalik smirked, helping her up.

"Okay, everyone back together," Angus ordered.

They all trudged dutifully into place. Ailsa made sure to keep herself, Cameron and Eilidh as a barrier between Maalik and Alasdair but didn't dare look over at Iona. Instead, Ailsa kept her eyes on Angus as he paced up and down their line, correcting their posture as they held their wooden weapons.

"You need to learn to work as a team," he said. "And if you're struggling with that, just remember that you're all fighting against a cabal of gods who wants to wipe you and every other fae out of existence and enslave humanity." He sent a pointed look to Iona.

"They definitely seem like the bad guys," said Cameron, swaying slightly where he stood.

"Now, some of you are better with the swords than others," Angus continued, "so I'd like to try you out with some other weapons, see what you're most comfortable with."

"Does everyone really need to learn how to use swords and daggers if we have the Four Treasures?" called Harris, watching them from where he sat, his back against the tree.

"And what if they don't have the treasures?" asked Angus. "How will they fight then?"

Ailsa unhooked the axe from her belt and tested its weight for a moment before pulling it over her shoulder and throwing it in Harris's direction. It spun through the air, over and over, until it embedded itself in the tree trunk with a thunk.

"Hey, you could have hit me," yelped Harris.

Ailsa rolled her eyes. "I have good aim."

Angus nodded. "Right, let's get you some more throwing axes then. But you also need to learn to throw a spear."

"Maalik should be able to teach her that," said Iona, loudly. "That's how he killed your grandfather, after all."

Ailsa watched Maalik visibly shrink into himself. Her blood boiled. "He made a mistake and he apologised," she snarled back down the line. "He can't go back to fix it and Alasdair is alive now, what else do you want?"

Iona threw her sword down. "I want to find someone else to fight with."

Ailsa rounded on her. "There isn't anyone else. Would you rather the Edaxi win?"

"Of course not," she gritted out.

"Then get over it."

Iona turned to Eilidh and Angus. "Doesn't this bother you?" She pointed a finger at Maalik. "He killed your grandfather. And your aunt."

Cameron shifted uncomfortably. "He isn't evil."

"Iona." Maalik stepped forward so that Ailsa was no longer blocking him and held his hands up. "I truly am sorry. Dolor tricked me; I thought I was saving thousands of people by stopping the war." He shook his head, looking miserable. "I know it doesn't undo anything; I have spent the last twenty years paying for my reckless actions. There hasn't been a day that's gone by that I haven't relived those moments and wished I could have changed them."

Iona's lip curled. "I think I'm done here." Then she stormed from the clearing, heading back to camp with her back straight.

Harris whistled. "Sorry about my sister. She always was—passionate, when it came to Alasdair."

Angus ran his hands through his hair. "Well, she'd better get over it."

"If she doesn't want to fight anymore, can we find another water fae?" Ailsa asked. It didn't really feel like a solution, but the situation looked hopeless.

"Can't Harris help?" asked Maalik.

Ailsa shook her head. "He's a water fae but he doesn't have magic like Iona does. We'd have to find someone else."

"Which is impossible," said Angus. "No one can get through."

Ailsa frowned. "What do you mean?"

"You didn't hear?" Angus's eyes flicked up to the forest, high on the hill above them. "The dead you saw on your way here? There are more of them, blocking the way out."

"We're trapped?" Maalik asked.

"Essentially." Angus bent to collect Iona's sword. "Duncan has some soldiers up there, watching the situation, but as long as no one gets too close, they don't move. It's not all bad," he assured them. "We have the Stone of Destiny and there's still a battle to win. So, we carry on as normal." Angus looked out to the ships on the horizon. "Speaking of which, we'd better get back to it. Then, tomorrow, we'll get the Four Treasures out and see what you can do."

Ailsa bit her lip and got back into position. From where

she stood, she could see both the Mirandelli ships and the forest, teeming with the dead. She shivered, wondering how much of a brave face Angus was putting on things. *We're surrounded.* She wasn't a strategist, but even she could tell that this was a bad place to be.

Chapter 60

This is a mess, thought Alasdair, wrapping an arm around Iona's waist. This morning, she'd insisted on going to Angus's training, but she wasn't gone long, stalking into their tent and declaring she'd given up. Too bad then, that Duncan had demanded they attend the nightly meeting. Alasdair couldn't even look at the far end of the tent, where he knew the demon watched him with those huge, fathomless eyes. It was as if his fears had been brought to life in one person. And somehow Iona was supposed to work with him.

Something fierce inside him wanted to spirit her away, put as much distance as possible between the woman he loved and his murderer. But her friends needed Iona. And it looked like his grandchildren needed him.

"The scouts have reported back. There are even more dead up on the hill," Duncan told them, hands on his hips. "And it's not just them. They've been joined by the sick and the dying too."

"Just like at Ephraim," said Harris.

Alasdair's youngest grandchild blanched. "Are they ours? Or Mirandelle's?"

"Some of our soldiers saw people they recognised. But I imagine there are strangers there too," said Duncan, shifting in his seat. "They mean to frighten us before the battle has even started. How am I supposed to ask our people to fight their friends and family?"

"They're just waiting, though, aren't they?" Harris asked.

Alasdair gritted his teeth. "Until we fight Mirandelle's

army. Then we'll be attacked from all sides."

"If we can stop the Edaxi before that, though…" said Eilidh, trailing off.

"So, this is your plan?" Alasdair flicked his gaze between her and Iona and finally to the girl with the demon. Ailsa. He'd seen her around Dunrigh Castle in recent months, always keeping to the corners, like she was doing now. "Our army is a distraction while you four try to stop literal gods?"

"My army," said Duncan. "And Iona, Eilidh, Ailsa and Maalik won't fail. They just need time." He waved his hands at the map in front of him, turning his attention to his generals. "The biggest threat remains Mirandelle's soldiers. They're smart and ruthless. As soon as they land on the beaches, we must be ready for them. At the same time, we must expect an attack from behind. Angus?"

The prince stepped forward; his mouth set in a stubborn line.

"I need you to get your crew through any gap that opens. Steal a boat if you have to, just get them to that platform."

"Can't we sneak out before then?" asked Harris. "We'd have the element of surprise."

"That's gone," Duncan said sharply. "After you and Eilidh were almost caught, they'll be watching for you."

Harris had the grace to look sheepish.

"If it wasn't for us sneaking out, we'd never have known what was on that platform," muttered Eilidh.

Duncan narrowed his eyes. "Then we should use the information wisely and prepare. Angus, how has training been going?"

Angus rolled his eyes. "Not well."

"See that it does." But Duncan wasn't looking at his brother. He stared straight at Alasdair, raising his chin in displeasure.

"Can we talk about this alone?" Alasdair growled.

Duncan nodded and the room cleared. Iona turned to go, giving Alasdair a warning look. *Behave yourself,* she was saying.

Alasdair pushed his annoyance down, breathing slowly. "I'm not including Iona when I say: weren't there older, more powerful fae you could have chosen for this?"

"For some of them, I'm sure there were," said Duncan. "But these are the people my brother trusts. They are also all older than me. And I'm still the rightful King of Eilanmòr."

"You don't need to remind me how young you are, I know. I watched you grow up." *I really thought you'd be smarter than this too.*

"You weren't there, though, were you?"

"And who is to blame for that? The demon you've aligned yourself with." Alasdair said bitterly. A small part of him knew that he was being unreasonable, argumentative. It wasn't like him. But having to see his murderer walking around had his hackles raised.

Duncan tapped his knuckles on the map. "We don't have any other options. Ailsa and Angus have assured me that Maalik is not a threat. You need to let this go—"

"I can't. That's literally why I am here and not a mindless body amongst that horde. If, gods forbid, someone did that to you, you'd be the same."

"Everything I do, I do it to help my family and my country," said Duncan evenly. "I'd hope I would find peace in that, when the time comes. You've been given a second chance. Stop holding on to hate and live. It is well known that you were separated from Iona by duty. You don't have that duty now." Duncan's words were gentle, but Alasdair heard his other meaning. *You are not king anymore.*

"Fine," Alasdair said, blowing out a breath. He was right. Hadn't he just been telling Iona he was glad he got a second chance, without the responsibilities of power? He knew all too well the difficult position Duncan was in. "Be careful."

Alasdair knew he didn't have control. What had he expected? *For Duncan to come to you for advice.* Well, he was his own man, his own king. And he was doing what he could to protect Eilanmòr, which was his responsibility. It was with that thought that he left the tent, heading back to his own with purpose.

"Don't fight," Alasdair said as soon as he was inside. "Let someone else do it."

Iona was already in her borrowed nightdress, her copper hair cascading down her back. She looked like a princess in a faerie story, ready to be rescued. And, though Alasdair knew she could do that herself, he desperately wished she would let him. "I can't," she said, shaking her head.

He kneeled down beside her, cupping the back of her neck. "Then I'm sticking with you. When Mirandelle attacks. Duncan doesn't need me anyway."

"He does," Iona said sadly. "But as a grandfather, not as a ruler." She held his arm, running her thumb over his skin. "This means you'll be fighting with Maalik too."

If the demon really was the only option, he'd have to deal with it. "I will tolerate his presence until we win. And I won't run him through with my sword, even if that's what he deserves."

"I hate this," said Iona. "Ailsa is my friend, but I don't see how that can continue when she's sided with him."

"I'm sorry." He leaned his forehead against hers. "Not just for that. I feel like I've become a bit of an ogre these last two days. This isn't how I expected this to go."

Iona pressed a kiss to his temple and scooted back on the bedrolls, beckoning him with her. "Let's get some sleep," she said. "We've got a long day of not taking revenge tomorrow."

But, when Alasdair tried to fall asleep that night, all he could see was a spear; not aimed at his chest, but at Iona's.

Chapter 61

Ailsa approached the training grounds more warily than the day before. Her anxiety only increased when she saw King Alasdair had joined them. *At least Iona came back.* Yesterday, she hadn't been sure if the selkie was quitting for good.

"Did you bring them?" asked Angus.

Ailsa rooted around in her bag, pulling out the spear and the stone as everyone crowded closer. Everyone except for Iona and Alasdair, that is. *Well, she already has the cauldron.*

Eilidh approached, holding out her palm reverently. "I suppose that one is mine."

"And that's Maalik's," Ailsa said, eyeing the red and orange gemstone sword in Eilidh's hand. She waited expectantly as the faerie woman passed the weapon over.

"Careful," she said, "it gets hot."

As soon as Maalik wrapped his hand around the hilt, Ailsa saw what she meant. Flames erupted up the blade and she jumped back, watching in horror as the skin on Maalik's forearm cracked.

"It's alright," he said, before she could protest. "It doesn't hurt." The molten core of him glowed along with the sword. "It feels good, actually." He turned it over and the flames danced in his liquid black eyes.

"This is yours then." Ailsa shakily handed over the Stone of Destiny, not taking her eyes off Maalik. But when Eilidh took the stone, she let out a gasp.

"I see what you mean," she said, grinning. "Like it was meant for you, right?" She held the stone to her chest, closing her eyes. In a blink, she was standing on the other side of Angus.

"It'll take ten minutes for it to charge—" Ailsa started to say. But with another blink, Eilidh appeared behind Harris, tackling him to the grass with a laugh. There was no shimmering portal, not like when she'd used it. Well, at least Eilidh wouldn't have to wait between uses. *I suppose that's what happens when a fae with the proper magic uses it.*

"It's fun," Eilidh said as Harris pushed her off him. "You should try it, Angus."

His answering smile was tight lipped. "Remember the prophecy? *A warnyn, mortals handle thaim not.*"

That couldn't be right, though, could it? Hadn't Angus used the stone when they were leaving the Isle of Faodail, when they first found the stone? *There must be some catch,* Ailsa decided. *Those crusty poems always had hidden meanings.*

"Alright," he said. "Now we have to decide how best to use them. Eilidh, you've already worked out the stone and Iona has a handle on the cauldron."

In answer, Iona took something tiny from her pocket and held it out in her cupped hands. The cauldron got bigger and bigger, growing from the size of a thimble to a cup, to a bowl.

"How does the sword work?" asked Maalik.

Angus gestured to a rotted piece of wood, an old fence post lodged in the ground. "Try swiping at it." When Maalik started to walk closer, Angus stopped him. "No, from here."

Maalik glanced around, making sure everyone was out of the way, and then swung the sword downwards in an arc. Ailsa saw the moment the weapon's magic touched the wood, slicing it in a clean line. It hung there for a moment and then the two pieces fell to the side.

"Useful," said Ailsa, holding the spear loosely in her hands. "My turn. I'll warn you all, this is still a work in progress." But when she threw the silver and sapphire spear this time, she knew what to expect. She concentrated, watching it turn when she told it to, until it had flown a lap around their group and was heading back towards her.

Don't bottle it, whispered Ishbel.

The point raced for her but this time she didn't jump out of the way. She held out a hand, willing it to return. *Please,* she thought at it. The spear tilted slightly, and Ailsa thought for a split second that it would turn to Maalik beside her. But it only sailed towards her right, enough so that she could catch it, plucking it from the air with a smile.

Harris gave a whoop and both he and Cameron clapped from where they sat on the ground.

"Excellent," said Angus. "But now the work begins. You'll need to learn how to use the weapons together and how to involve your natural magic too. Get into the positions I showed you yesterday. Ailsa, you're up first."

Ailsa rolled her neck, taking her place. As she'd done all those times before, she reached up to the sky, feeling the familiar zing of energy filling her body.

Show them what you can do, said Ishbel.

Having them all watching her like this was so similar to a few days ago in Findias. Except, this time when the lightning sizzled across her fingers, there were no terrified whispers. She was, mostly, among friends here, on this grassy hill. These people would be relying on her powers all too soon. She let all the magic flow through her body and up to the heavens, grinning when she pulled the first bolt down, hitting the ground in front of her with a bang. Thunder filled the clearing a second later and Ailsa stepped back to see her handiwork; the soil cracked and scorched in radiating patterns, the same as those on her skin after she used her powers.

To her surprise, it was King Alasdair who spoke first. "That was impressive," he said in awe, as if he'd forgotten to be angry.

With a wave of her hands, the clouds cleared again. She flopped down beside Cameron. "Eilidh, what can you do?"

And so, Eilanmòr's champions showed off their magic. First, Eilidh burst into a flock of robins, flitting through the air before changing again into a cloud of bees. Iona pulled water from the sea down below, sending it splashing against her brother, plastering his red hair against his face.

Then it was Maalik's turn. He squared up to a boulder, embedded in the dirt, as his skin split. "I'll try not to let it hit anyone," he said, before flexing his muscles. Ailsa watched as his skin glowed, just like it had when they met Dolor in the woods, when the goddess broke Ailsa's back. She shivered at the memory. The earth shook as he got brighter and brighter. Then with a boom, a blast of magic shot out of him and towards the rock. Ailsa blinked against the light and when her eyes focussed again, the boulder was in red hot pieces, scattered across the grass. Maalik breathed heavily, sucking the power back into himself until he was no longer glowing.

"That was," Harris murmured, "really cool."

Maalik cringed. "I don't really like doing it. But do you think it'll be helpful?"

"Oh, I'm sure we'll find some use for you," Angus said, his eyebrows climbing into his hair. "You'll need to keep practising, however. It took you a while to get going—" He trailed off as his gaze caught on something in the direction of the camp. Ailsa turned to find a young man running up the hill towards them.

"Prince Angus," he huffed when he reached them. "You're to come quick. We've had word from our allies."

Angus and Ailsa exchanged a look before they set off, their friends in tow. Their training would have to wait, this was potentially very good news. Or very bad news. *Please be the former*, Ailsa thought as she took Maalik's hand in hers. Gods knew they needed it.

Chapter 62

Angus could see Duncan's panic bubbling under the surface, though he was making a valiant effort at pretending he was calm. His brother gripped a sheet of paper in his hands as he waited for his advisors and commanders to file through the tent flap. The space was packed, forcing people to sit shoulder against shoulder. Angus was pressed against Cameron, feeling the warmth of his body through his clothes. As if sensing Angus's trepidation, Cameron reached out and squeezed Angus's knee. On Angus's other side, Eilidh and Harris hovered, looking unsure.

"It's not good," said General MacKenzie, eyeing the crowd. "The letter came in from Akrosia this morning: the few ships they had are destroyed."

"How?" General Fraser demanded, his lip losing its signature curl.

"Merlo?" MacKenzie suggested. "Raiders? Who can say? Whoever it was burned them."

"So, who does that leave?" asked one of the majors.

Duncan cleared his throat. "We haven't heard from Edessa or Visenya. There wasn't much point in sending a word to Kemet, but I tried anyway. Nothing."

"They've abandoned us," said General Fraser and the whole room erupted into whispers.

"That doesn't make sense—"

"We're allies, and they've got to know they'll be next after Eilanmòr. They have just as many fae there—"

"But they don't have Ephraim. If the faerie court falls—"

"It already fell. Queen Nicnevan is dead."

"Doesn't she have an heir?" someone piped up, the room quieting again.

Duncan's eyes flicked to Eilidh for a moment. "Ephraim and the fae are in our lands so they have our protection," he said firmly. "In terms of our allies, we have to assume they aren't coming."

"The Nymph will come," said Harris.

Duncan didn't look convinced. "I hope so. But that's only one boat. We need to be prepared to do this alone."

A woman wearing a chain mail shirt and mud-caked trousers leaned forward. "With all due respect, Your Highness, I'm not sure this is a war we can win by ourselves."

The muttering started up again. *This isn't good,* thought Angus. They're losing control and hope. But where could they go? They were surrounded, with the dead at their backs and Mirandelle at their fronts.

"Maybe I can help," said Eilidh, raising her voice. "Harris has a theory that fae have some innate loyalty to me. If I can somehow call them to fight, unite them, it might be the advantage we need."

General Fraser snorted. "How are you going to do that?"

Angus fought the urge to snap at him. She didn't owe him an explanation but now everyone was waiting to hear what she was going to say. "Are you sure about this?" he muttered in her ear.

Eilidh nodded. "It's time to stop hiding from who I am."

"Are we missing something?" General MacKenzie asked, folding his arms.

Angus exchanged a look with Duncan, the two brothers readying themselves.

"I'm Nicnevan's heir." Eilidh stopped at that, biting her lip as the whole room fell into silence.

"And our sister," Duncan added.

There was a beat as all the soldiers processed that. Angus looked at General Fraser, feeling smug to see him speechless.

Eilidh hurried to explain herself. "Since Nicnevan died, fae have been finding me to, I don't know, pay their respects? I know it sounds crazy, but they can tell who I am. I'm going to try to put out a call, see if anyone responds. This is their war too."

"You expect us to fight alongside the fae?" General Fraser spluttered.

Harris let out a laugh. "You already are."

Duncan turned to their sister. "Thank you, Eilidh. We will take any help we can get. Let me know if you need anything." Then he addressed the crowd. "Eilidh is our half-sister, and I expect her to be treated with as much respect as any other member of the royal family." He paused to look every single person in the eye. "Things look bleak right now, but there is always hope. I have called a meeting with King Merlo to broker peace. If that fails, which I think it will, we'll launch our attack in two days. Our allies may find us before then, but if they don't, we still have a powerful weapon." He nodded at Eilidh and Angus. "Or rather, four powerful weapons. If we can stop the Edaxi, I believe we can stop the war before it really begins.

"Eilanmòr is small, but she isn't weak. Back in my grandfather's time, we beat the Mirandellis back. Since then, we've guarded our coast from the Avalognians. Look around those beside you." He paused. "These are the people you've laughed with, trained with, fought with. It doesn't matter your rank, on that battlefield we're all equals, defending our country from evil. We're not invaders; we haven't chosen this battle. But we will not stand back and let our enemy hurt our fellow Eilanmòrians." He stood, scraping his chair back. "Tonight, we celebrate with each other and tomorrow we prepare."

There were nods amongst the crowd and then the soldiers filed out when the king dismissed him, buoyed up, even in the face of bad news. *Duncan knows how to give a speech,* Angus thought. But he didn't miss the way his brother's face fell when he thought no one was looking.

Angus knew what that look meant. They were in deep trouble. And for all Duncan's talk of hope, he didn't believe his own words.

Chapter 63

Ailsa stood with her back straight as they watched the mass of frigates and galleons part. The mutinous waves crashed against their sides, but the ships refused to slow, not until a gap appeared and a single, compact craft came sailing through.

"It's a sloop," Maalik said, pressing his arm into hers. "Built for speed rather than attack."

Ailsa gave a hum in response, letting him talk.

"You can tell because it's got a single mast. And see that flag with the bird? That's the golden eagle of the royal family. The Mirandelli national animal is actually... what?"

"Sorry, I didn't mean to laugh," said Ailsa, fighting a grin. "You just talk a lot when you're nervous."

"Oh really?" He bumped his shoulder against hers. "What other quirks have you noticed?"

"You clench your jaw when you're annoyed." She flicked her gaze to him. "Look, you're doing it now."

"Very funny," he said dryly.

Ailsa watched him for a moment, noting the way he chewed his lip. "What have you got to be nervous about? King Merlo isn't coming to see *us*."

"It's not him. It's who else is going to be there. I really don't think I should go down with you."

She grabbed his hand and gave it a squeeze. "Eilanmòr is relying on you. Duncan wants you there." He'd specifically asked for Ailsa, Maalik, Iona and Eilidh. *Eilanmòr's champions.*

"But his grandfather doesn't."

"We're all on the same side. Alasdair just needs to keep his mouth shut." Ailsa stuck her tongue out to the air.

It was enough to make him laugh, at least. "My fierce protector," he said fondly. "Just stick close, okay?"

"Always."

***

By the time they'd found their way down the hill, the little ship was sailing into the bay, cutting across the sea as if it was as smooth as glass. It didn't slow, not until the bow was aimed at the sand, the friction bringing it to a halt.

Someone had erected a canvas on the beach, and Ailsa spotted her companions, already standing to attention underneath. The only person seated was Duncan, looking every inch the king in his armour and golden crown. His chair, however, was far from regal: one of the low-backed, wooden, folding seats Ailsa had seen around the camp. Five matching ones were arranged across from him, at the far end of the tent, empty and waiting.

Ailsa pulled Maalik to the edge of the gathering, as far away from Alasdair and Iona as she could manage. Just because they were there didn't mean they had to make it difficult. Not when they were united against a different enemy. She hoped that her friends felt the same.

Angus stood at Duncan's side with Cameron shadowing him. From the front, Ailsa supposed her brother would look like any other royal guard, but she didn't miss that Cameron kept one hand on Angus's back. Whether it was for protection or for comfort, she didn't know, but it made her smile all the same.

On the other side, next to Iona, Harris leaned against one of the poles with his arms crossed over his chest. He was whispering something to a magpie perched on his shoulder. In fact, now that Ailsa had noticed, there were a lot of magpies around. Some were flying up above the scene while others were resting on the canvas.

"How does the rhyme go?" Ailsa whispered, indicating the birds. "One for sorrow, two for mirth—"

"I count forty-one," said Maalik.

Ailsa squinted up at them. "What does that mean?"

"Probably that a certain faerie princess is doing her best to hide."

"Those are Eilidh," she realised.

"I just know I've never seen that many magpies in one place before." Maalik stepped closer. "I think they're getting off the boat."

Sure enough a couple of scrawny lads threw themselves over the sides of the ship into the shallow water and began hefting the hull further into the sand. None of Ailsa's companions made a noise as they watched their progress. When the ship was secured, a flood of servants piled out, carrying a sedan chair between them. Eventually, a man was handed down to the chair holders, his feet never touching the water.

Ailsa couldn't help comparing Mirandelle's king to her own. She knew Merlo was older; it was under his rule that they'd attacked Eilanmòr all those years ago, after all. But she hadn't expected him to look this sickly. It was clear that he'd been a stout man once, but he looked like he'd lost the weight quickly so that his skin was too big for him. Like Duncan, he wore some armour, but it was ill-fitting even if it was polished to a gleam. There was a pallor below his tan, like his body was fighting the cold. *Perhaps he's not used to the Eilanmòrian weather*, Ailsa thought.

The servants marched the sedan through the waves and up onto the beach and Ailsa was able to see who was behind the king. Her stomach dropped. It had only been weeks since she'd last seen Captain Scarsi in the ballroom of Dunrigh Castle, but much about him had changed. He no longer wore the bright blue and green velvets he'd favoured before. He was dressed in burgundy pantaloons and a golden breastplate. Instead of a helmet he wore a wide brimmed hat upon his head, with a single feather pointing to the sky. Scarsi didn't bother with a chair, choosing to splash down onto the sandbar and make his way to their canopy himself.

"He looks like fun," Maalik muttered. "Did you know gold is one of the softest metals?"

Ailsa's lip curled. "Does that mean I'd have no trouble sticking my axe in his chest?"

"Probably not the best time."

"On the battlefield then."

He shook his head, chuckling. "Such bloodlust."

"It's why you love me." As soon as the words left her mouth, she felt a thrill of anxiety. Was she even allowed to say things like that?

But she needn't have worried. Maalik dropped a kiss to her hair and whispered in her ear, "One of the reasons."

"Are you two done?" muttered Cameron.

You're one to talk, Ailsa thought. He could hardly keep his hands off Angus.

It wasn't long before the royal sedan halted and was lowered to the ground. The servants helped King Merlo up and it looked like he needed the aid. He was trying to hide it, but he leaned heavily on their hands, sneering all the while like he was disgusted by them or himself. Scarsi sidestepped his king, revulsion flickering on his face for a moment before he pulled on a look of arrogance instead.

"Your Highness," Scarsi said, bowing a fraction. "Thank you for your hospitality. General Scarsi, at your service."

"I know who you are," said Duncan. "Though the last I'd heard, you were a colonel."

Scarsi shrugged. "When you're in favour, promotions are readily given."

King Merlo shrugged off his servants and entered their pavilion, nodding once before sinking into a seat stiffly. "McFeidh."

"De Santis." Duncan folded his hands over his lap. "I'm sure you know of most of my friends and family here. You remember my brother, Angus? My grandfather?"

"Grandfather?" Merlo scanned the crowd of people. Ailsa knew the exact moment he spotted Alasdair because his face drained of colour and he half-leapt from his seat. "Alasdair?"

From where she'd positioned herself and Maalik, Ailsa couldn't see the late king's face, but she heard every drop of disdain in his voice when he answered with a curt. "Merlo."

"But how?" Merlo spluttered. "You faked your death all those years ago?"

"No, I was dead," said Alasdair. "You're lucky I decided to haunt Dunrigh rather than you, you old git. Time hasn't smiled kindly upon you, friend."

Merlo straightened. "Then how?"

"Ask him," said Angus, pointing a finger at Scarsi. "Your General had his men dig up our graves when he attacked Dunrigh."

"Is this true?" Merlo asked but Scarsi silenced him with the flick of a hand.

"My king and I are servants of the gods," he said. "We do not question their orders."

"Is that why you called this meeting?" asked Duncan.

Merlo began to speak but Scarsi cut him off again. "We are here to offer you a deal. Surrender and there will be no human blood spilt."

"Just fae blood?" Duncan guessed.

Scarsi sniffed. "Your highness, you are the King of Eilanmòr, not the Fae King. They may live in your land, but they do not answer to you. For too long have your ancestors fought for control, for safety for your people. Let us purge your country of the threat."

"The only threat I see here is you."

The soldier gestured around their group. "You are surrounded by them. Blinded to their evil."

Duncan raised a brow. "Is this the sort of nonsense you told my cousin?"

"Ah, how is Lady Moira?" Scarsi's smile was cruel. "In a prison cell? Or is she locked in her room? A cage is still a cage, even if it is covered in lace and silk."

Duncan's eyes twitched, as if he was trying his best not to roll them. "You may as well state your terms."

"You would remain king, but Eilanmòr would answer to Mirandelle."

Alasdair snorted. "You think you'll be an emperor, Merlo? Do you truly believe that's how this will end? I suppose we'll have to send you taxes, live under your law?"

Merlo puffed himself up. "Would it really be so bad? Mirandelle is the wealthiest country on the continent."

"You've presented your deal, get on with the threat," said Duncan, steadily. "What will you do if we refuse?"

"It's not what we'll do so much as what the gods will do. If you do not surrender, our armies will battle, but you know it is not about us. It's about them." Scarsi swept his gaze around the group, his eyes lingering on Iona, then Eilidh and then on Maalik and Ailsa. "Ah, Miss MacAra, I have heard much about you since we parted ways. You're no longer a changeling."

She tilted her head. "But you're still an ass."

He directed his next question back to Duncan. "Is this really the best you could do? You think that, because you have the

Four Treasures, your win is guaranteed?" When they looked at him in stunned silence, he cackled. "Yes, we know all about them. Myself and my comrades will take great pleasure in restoring the weapons to their rightful owners. I have seen what manner of monsters the gods will use against you. By the time they are done, you will beg them to take your little toys."

In the midst of Scarsi's little speech, one word stuck out to Ailsa. It seemed Angus was on the same page as her. "These monsters," he said, "do you mean you have fae working for you? How did you manage that?"

Don't they know you hate them?

"Some know that they are abominations. Others have been persuaded." He turned to Harris and smiled. "Take your princess, for example. She put up a good fight, at first. It took at least a week to break her. Your name was one of the last words she forgot."

It took less than a heartbeat for Harris to process those words. Then he was throwing himself forward, hands clenched into claws. Before he could leap at Scarsi, however, Alasdair had his arms around the selkie's chest, holding him back.

A shame, Ailsa thought.

"You'd better hope you don't meet me on the battlefield," Harris spat. "I will take great pleasure in ripping your eyes out. Trust me, it hurts."

Duncan raised a hand, signalling for Alasdair to pull Harris away. "If that is all, then this meeting is over. There is not a single thing you could say to make me betray my people, even those who are fae."

"No?" Scarsi's eyes narrowed. "What about your wife and son?"

Duncan stood, almost knocking his chair back. "Talk fast, Scarsi, before I forget the rules of diplomacy and gut you where you stand."

"Mirandelle has no part in anything, but I heard the

Avalognians had their own mission from my masters. They invaded Visenya yesterday."

"Impossible," said Iona. "The Avalognians have been attacking Eilanmòr's coast."

Scarsi shrugged. "It's amazing what one can achieve with some divine intervention. Imagine it, a whole navy of Avalognian raiders, working together. This is the sort of peace that can be achieved."

Duncan was suddenly breathing hard, no longer the cool, collected king he'd been moments before. "You talk of peace and invasion in the same breath."

"I am merely saying you have a choice: one or the other. Surrender and the Avalognians will be called off. There will be peace in Ossiana. But continue and you will face the wrath of the gods. And with Visenya invaded," Scarsi clicked his fingers, "there goes one of your allies. How many do you have left? How many have come to your aid?"

"We've heard enough. You can leave."

"Meet you on the battlefield." Scarsi sketched a bow and turned, signalling to the servants to head back to the boat. Ailsa loosed a breath, glad to see the back of him.

King Merlo stood next, and the sedan approached again. His reddened eyes darted between the chair and Duncan, back and forward. And then he did something completely unexpected. He sank to his knees, right there on the grass.

"Don't let them take me back," he whispered, looking over his shoulder at where Scarsi was still striding for the boat.

Duncan stared at the other king for a long moment. Then he did something Ailsa did not expect. "You can seek refuge with us here," he offered. "Say the word and—"

"My King!" shouted Scarsi. He turned to his fellow soldiers. "Collect King Merlo and bring him back on the boat. Now."

Merlo didn't put up a fight as he was pushed into the sedan, lip trembling. He didn't look back, curling up on himself as he was lifted and walked to the rowboat.

What was that about? Ailsa wondered as she watched them push him inside.

Think twice before you deal with the gods, said Ishbel.

Duncan was silent for a long moment, watching the sloop grow smaller and smaller. "It looks like this is it," he muttered. He straightened, bearing the weight of his crown once again. "Eat, sleep, spend time together. This war may last weeks, or even months, but it's all about tomorrow now. You'd better be ready." And with that he stalked off, followed by his guards and advisors.

Silence followed, like Duncan had taken all sound with him. But Ailsa imagined they all had the same question floating around in their minds: *are we ready?*

Ailsa bit the inside of her cheek, glancing at Iona. The selkie's shoulders were hunched and her mouth was pressed into a firm line. How were they ever going to fight together if Iona wouldn't even look at her and Maalik?

It was Eilidh who filled the silence, touching her fingers to the stone around her neck. "Angus is right; we need to put the past behind us and move on. So," she said, turning to her brother, "what's your plan?"

Angus ran a hand through his hair. "Duncan and the army will fight the Mirandelli and their allies; don't worry about them. Our job is to find the Edaxi and keep the treasures until we can destroy them. Stick close and if anyone tries to steal them, we'll take them down. Cam, you're with Ailsa. Alasdair, you're with Iona and Harris, I need you to look after Eilidh." He smiled at the demon beside her. "I'll stick with Maalik."

Ailsa felt a surge of warmth towards the prince. "Thank you," she murmured.

Angus nodded. "We'll provide back up," he said, taking

Cameron's hand. "We are a team. We look after each other. Understood?"

"Understood," they echoed back, some louder than others.

"You heard Duncan. I want to see you all eating, drinking and being merry for the next twelve hours." And with that, he took off, tugging Cameron along behind him.

"I'm glad their tent is far away from ours," muttered Ailsa.

"Mine is right next door," groaned Eilidh. She hooked her arm through Harris's. "Unless you want to have a sleepover, oh mighty warrior?"

Harris grinned. "I would never turn down my queen."

"Your queen requires you to grab an obscene amount of food from the mess tent first. If this is my last night, I'm eating as much as I want."

Ailsa watched them drift off, aware that Iona and Alasdair stood frozen a little way to her left. No one spoke for a long moment, until Iona cleared her throat.

"When we wake up tomorrow, we're allies, and we'll continue to be until the war is over. But then I think it's best if we never see each other again." With that, she turned and left, Alasdair rubbing a soothing hand down her back as he followed.

Ailsa let out a breath. "Probably for the best. I'm itching to hit her and that feeling will only grow over time if she keeps acting like a cow."

"I hate that this has ruined your friendship," said Maalik.

"She ruined our friendship by holding on to this grudge. He's alive now, isn't he?"

"I know I'd feel the same if someone hurt you." He took her face in his soot-stained hands. "Come on, I don't want to waste the rest of the evening on this." And though his eyes were as black and unfathomable as always, Ailsa thought they held a promise.

Chapter 64

The sun hadn't yet set, when Ailsa pushed Maalik towards their tent. She'd tried to eat but her stomach churned like the sea ahead, so most of the foot had ended up shoved onto the plate of the soldier beside her. She had tried to be subtle, but she knew Maalik had noticed. Still, he didn't argue when she announced she was finished, following her dutifully as she weaved back through the canvas village.

Ailsa hadn't seen any of her friends since their meeting, even though they'd sat in the mess tent for at least an hour. Eilidh and Harris had clearly grabbed their food and left before Ailsa and Maalik had arrived. Iona and Alasdair were no doubt avoiding them. And Cam and Angus… They'd be spending as much time as possible together. She wasn't sure if she was happy for them or mildly nauseated. She'd witnessed far too many heated glances between her brother and the prince. Had heard far too many murmured professions of love.

She turned to Maalik, watching as he shook out their blankets, and realised those were not the only emotions she was feeling. Bubbling under the surface was pure jealousy.

"I only got to let it out for one night," she whispered.

Maalik stopped. "Let what out?"

"My feelings," she said as she lowered herself to the pallet, pulling her knees into her chest. "For you."

He reached out to touch her elbow. "I'm sorry—"

"Did you know," she cut him off, "I haven't cried since I was twelve."

"Never?"

"I made a pact with myself; it was self-preservation. I've been shutting people out ever since." She raised her eyes to his. "I don't want to do that anymore."

The devastation was plain on his face. "Just a few more days."

"And if we don't get that? If we lose?"

"I can't, Ailsa."

She flinched back. "Then I can't stay here. I'll do something I'll regret—"

But just as she tried to stand, he grabbed her wrist, pulling her to him. Between one breath and the next, Maalik's lips were on hers. His mouth wasn't gentle, but his hands were as he lowered her to the blankets, covering her body with his own. Ailsa fisted his collar like it was the only thing keeping her from floating away and he groaned low, the noise sending goosebumps across her skin.

Maalik swept a hand down her side, all the way to her knee, before hitching her leg over his hip. She touched him mindlessly, fingers skating across the buttons on his shirt, but he seemed to take this as a direction, grabbing the fabric and ripping it so he could shrug off the barrier.

Gods. Ailsa's brain stuttered as she felt his bare chest under her palms. He was so warm, almost scorching.

"Tell me," he whispered, when they broke apart. He trailed open mouthed kisses down her neck, letting her collect the words.

Ailsa shuddered. *This is it. Maybe the last time I get to say it.* "I love you." Then she opened her eyes.

The white and grey feathers sprouted from his shoulders like a cloak, fanning out overhead. His wings weren't fully formed yet, but they pulsed with each ragged breath.

Ailsa reached up to touch one, marvelling at the softness.

She wanted to hate them; the wings were part of the reason they couldn't be together. But they were also part of Maalik. "Beautiful."

He dropped his head to her sternum. "That's as far as I can go," Maalik said through gritted teeth. Ailsa watched as the wings contracted, shrinking down and down until they were encased in metal once again.

"I understand," she croaked.

Maalik drew back, running a finger across her cheek, where her birthmark used to be. "I love you and, I swear, that won't be our last chance. The next time you say it, I won't hold myself back. I'm going to believe everything you've ever told me, and I'll stop pushing it all down. You have that power. To change me."

"I think that's better than a bit of lightning."

"Hold on to my heart, okay? Keep it safe."

Ailsa nodded. There were many words she wanted to say but none could pass her lips. Not until it was over. She cast around for something else to say, something safe, when she felt his muscles lock above her.

"There's someone outside the tent," he said, rolling over onto the bed.

Ailsa felt the cold immediately, as if a bucket of water had been poured over her body. "Who?"

"Ailsa?" a voice called. The tent flap was pulled aside, revealing Eilidh's flushed face. "Sorry if I interrupted something," she said with a wince as she took in Maalik's bare chest. "Angus sent me to find you. Something's wrong with Cameron."

Chapter 65

Ailsa spared one alarmed look at Maalik before she was up and following Eilidh through the tents. She was vaguely aware of Maalik jogging behind her, but she didn't turn round as Eilidh led them to the canvas beside the king's.

"In here," said Eilidh.

Ailsa took a deep breath and plunged into the dark interior. There were more people inside the tent than Ailsa had expected but as her vision adjusted, she barely stopped to glance their way before her eyes found Cameron, writhing on the floor. His back was bowed, and an artery pulsed in his neck as he gritted his teeth. Angus was above him, pushing back his hair.

"He's been like this for half an hour at least," he said, the panic turning his voice thin and cracked. "I didn't call anyone at first because they've been happening so often. But it just kept going."

"I tried to find a medic," panted Harris from the door. "No luck."

Ailsa crouched down on the other side of Cameron's twitching body, across from Angus. "Maalik, do you think—"

"Of course." He rolled the sleeves of his new shirt up and addressed the gaggle of strangers gawking at her brother. "Why are you here?"

"We heard the prince's shouts," said a young man with a breastplate half on. "We brought water."

Maalik folded his arms across his chest. "Good. More of

that. Leave it by the door and then form a ring around the tent. No one is to come in until I say. One of you should keep looking for a medic. I need some valerian, the root in particular. Boil it into a tea and leave it outside the tent. Harris? Could you watch for it?"

"Sure." Harris bit his lip, lifting the tent flap to let the soldiers file out. Ailsa swore she heard him mutter something that sounded a lot like '*that was hot*', before following after them.

Any other time she'd agree. She certainly felt a rush of gratitude as the demon knelt down beside Cameron with concentration furrowing his brows.

"May I?" he asked Angus.

The prince nodded woodenly, and Maalik brought his hand up to Cameron's forehead. "Would you hold the candle so I can take a closer look at him?"

Angus did what he was told, hands shaking. Maalik felt across Cameron's body with sure hands then inspected his mouth and lifted his eyelids. "How long have the seizures been happening?"

"Over a month," said Ailsa. "But they're not seizures, they're visions. The first one was at the ceilidh. He saw the bomb going off before it happened."

Maalik hummed. "And you said they never last this long?" he asked Angus.

"They usually only go on for a minute or so." The prince blinked. "Are you a healer?"

"I try to be," Maalik replied. "Have they been getting longer or was this one out of the blue?"

"Yeah, it's never happened before."

"How long ago was his last?"

"It was just before you arrived—three days?" Angus raised his wide, blue eyes to Maalik, and Ailsa was suddenly reminded that he was younger than all of them. "Can you do anything?"

Maalik lifted Cameron's wrist, feeling his pulse. "We have to wait." But her brother was already relaxing and letting out a groan. "Look, he's coming round now," said Maalik.

"Cam?" Angus leaned forward, sounding relieved. "Are you alright?"

But Ailsa knew something was wrong. Not just in the way her brother looked: pale and sickly. Cameron's gaze flicked around the room like he was searching for danger. Pain lanced across his features, whether from the aftershocks of his vision or from what he'd seen, Ailsa didn't know. She bit her lip, catching Maalik's eye in a silent question. *Is he going to be alright?*

But when he finally spoke, Ailsa felt a chill all the way down to her bones.

"Everyone..." said Cameron, his breath still heaving, "They're all going to die."

Chapter 66

There was something feral living under Angus's skin that he'd never felt before. Not until he watched Cameron as he was interrogated, recounting the details of his vision between hiccupping gasps. He'd had to do it as soon as he'd resurfaced, then again when General MacKenzie heard what happened. Now, Duncan was kneeling in front of Cameron, demanding he relive it for a third time.

Get out, Angus wanted to scream. This rage wasn't like him, but seeing Cam twisted in the sheets, a sheen of sweat coating his too pale skin, he had the urge to throw something.

Cameron didn't deserve this. He should have been resting. He shouldn't have to say it again.

"I saw everyone, one by one, lying at my feet." Cameron squeezed Angus's hand, like he needed to borrow his strength. "There was so much blood. And you—the bodies opened their eyes, but they were blank." He cut off with a low whine.

"He needs to rest," Maalik cut in, wiping a wet cloth along Cameron's brow. Angus felt a rush of gratitude towards the demon.

"Just a few more questions," Duncan commanded.

Ailsa clicked her tongue from where she was huddled in the corner, and it seemed to chastise Angus's brother.

In a softer tone, he said, "I know you've been through a lot, but this might save lives."

Angus still wanted to hit him.

"I need you to break it down," Duncan continued. "Where were we?"

"I... I don't remember? It was like I was in a black room." Cameron closed his eyes and Angus knew he was imagining it all once more. "But at the same time, I could see ships burning on the sea. And the Nymph sunk to the bottom."

Angus exchanged a look with Ailsa. Was that why they hadn't heard from the Edessans?

Duncan frowned. "Does that seem like your normal visions?"

Cameron scrunched his nose in confusion. "They've been different lately. More like dreams."

Duncan hummed, standing in the cramped space. "We need to carry on as planned," he said. "I know you've been right in the past, Cameron, but it won't help to believe this one now."

Angus spun round to face his brother. "That's it? He's told you what he saw and you're not going to believe him? What was even the point of this then? Cam's been up for hours answering your questions!"

"I can't ask my soldiers, my friends, my family, to fight tomorrow if I think they're going to die. And what is the alternative? Give up? Allow Eilanmòr to become enslaved? Watch you all die anyway when the Edaxi have the Four Treasures? So, I'm going to choose to believe we have a chance." Duncan wiped his palm over his face. "I'm sorry about all of this. We won't disturb you again." He turned to go, stopping just before ducking out of the doorway and looking Angus in the eye. "I love you. You know that?"

Angus gritted his teeth together. "I love you too, but I also kind of hate you right now."

Duncan sighed. "Noted." Then he was gone.

There was a beat of silence in the room, until Angus felt a hand on his shoulder. "We should go too," said Ailsa.

Maalik dropped the cloth into the water bowl and addressed

Cameron. "It's been a long night. When you're ready, drink the valerian tea. I've mixed a little nightshade root in there too; it'll knock you out for a few hours of dreamless sleep." Angus couldn't be sure with the demon's strange, black eyes but it seemed like Maalik gave him a meaningful look.

Angus nodded.

"Rest well," said Ailsa as she dropped a kiss to Cameron's head. Then both she and Maalik were gone, leaving them alone once again.

"Angus," Cameron croaked. "I'm so sorry—"

"No," Angus said, pushing back a strand of his hair. "You have nothing to be sorry about."

Cameron's chin quivered. "I hate being like this. I hate seeing those things."

"You heard Duncan, maybe it won't happen—"

"It happened for me." Cameron reached up to cup the back of Angus's neck. "I saw you die. I saw Ailsa die. I hope it won't happen, but I've already lived through it once. Do you know what that's like?"

For the blink of an eye Angus imagined it, seeing his friends dead before him. But as if he was pulling on a nerve, his mind shied away from the images. It was too painful. "I'm here," he said. "We'll survive and you can replace those memories with new ones. Why don't you drink the tea and go to sleep for a bit?"

Cameron inhaled deeply, his breath hiccupping a little as he did so. "Okay. You'll stay though?"

"I'll be here." Angus dropped a chaste kiss to Cameron's lips. "It's my turn to protect you."

It didn't take long, once Cameron had drained his mug, for him to fall asleep but Angus was still wide awake. He busied himself tucking the blankets in and quietly tidying the small space. Angus's feet dragged as he moved around, blowing out the extra lanterns that had been left behind. When all were extinguished, there was only a single candle to light the tent, burned down almost to the dish it was stuck to. It was the candle he'd started with, hours ago. Angus hadn't meant to use it for long; he'd only lit it when he couldn't find something in the dim interior. Then Cameron had let out a gasp and whatever he'd been looking for had been forgotten.

Angus watched Cameron's face, vulnerable in slumber. *He's safe,* Angus reminded himself. Cameron's lips were parted as he breathed slowly and the tight lines around his eyes were smoothed out. Sandy eyelashes fanned across his cheeks. Freckles dotted the bridge of his nose. When had he got those? Angus drank in his features, desperate to replace the image of Cameron, terrified and in pain, from before.

"You're going to hate me for this," he whispered. Then he was up and out of the tent.

He'd witnessed a few of Cameron's visions and each had come true. Still, Duncan was right. They had to stay and fight. Which meant that tomorrow could very well be his last. Their last. He couldn't save the people he loved. Except for one.

Angus drew himself up to full height as he stalked towards the group of soldiers, sitting round a campfire. *You'll be saving them too*, he reminded himself. "I need volunteers."

The soldiers stopped their chatting and Angus got a good look at them all as the flames flickered over their faces. At least two of them were younger than he was: a gawky teen boy and waif of a girl. He narrowed his gaze at them and jutted out his chin. "You'll do. I need you to help me get the man sleeping in my tent into a wagon and then I need you to ride back to the river. Further, if you can make it."

"But the dead," said the girl. "We're surrounded."

"I'll send my friend Laire with you. She's the unicorn. She'll help you get through."

The boy rose from his seat. "We'll miss the fight."

Good, thought Angus. "This is an important mission from your prince, do you understand?"

Without another word, the youths were moving. Angus thought he caught looks of jealousy from the older soldiers before he turned. *They know what's coming then.*

Cameron slept soundly as he was lifted into the wagon, lined with blankets and pillows. Angus just hoped he'd stay unconscious until he was far away. Guilt sat slimy and gnawing in Angus's gut as he stared down at his love. "You're too sick to fight," he explained to the air. "If there's even a chance that the vision is true, I can't have you here."

Laire nosed at Angus's neck, having waited patiently by his side since he'd woken her. "He's safe with me," she assured him. "The other two, though. Were they intended as a travel snack?"

"Behave yourself," said Angus, rubbing her chestnut fur. "Please look after him. And don't let him come back when he wakes up." *You're towing precious cargo. I trust you.*

"I'm in your debt," said Laire, her voice echoing in his mind. "But I liked calling you a friend."

Angus fought back the tears, taking a long moment to look over Cameron and the unicorn. Before he could talk himself out of it, he uttered a single word. "Go." Then he watched Laire lead the wagon into the night, waiting until he could no longer see them to crumple to the grassy ground.

Chapter 67

Ailsa hadn't slept. Not a single second.

When she and Maalik had returned to their tent the night before, they'd tried their best, slipping under their blankets immediately. But every time Ailsa closed her eyes, she saw her brother's sweat-soaked face as he snarled in pain and anguish. So, she'd kept her eyes open, trained on the demon beside her as the rise and fall of his chest slowed and his face smoothed out. The image was something to hold on to, something to cherish.

When Ailsa first met Maalik, he barely slept. Now, even though she felt desperate to speak to him, she was glad he could have peace for a few snatched hours.

She'd lain there for a while until she needed to move. Careful not to break his sleep, Ailsa had crept outside and found a patch of grass to sit on to watch the sky lighten with the dawn.

"A red sunrise," she said, trying to blink away the gritty feeling in her eyes. "Isn't that bad luck?"

The sky was red when Rocbarra sank, replied Ishbel. *Perhaps it's a good omen.*

"I don't suppose you could just ask the Goddess of the Sea to help you sink it again?"

When gods aren't actively trying to kill you, they're fairly hard to find. Maybe she'll hear the commotion.

Ailsa frowned at the sky again. "I don't think I want to take any chances." She reached out with her magic, a thrill tingling through her as she pulled the clouds together, playing with the electricity she felt there. It felt good to give it an out, to channel it towards something. Soon the horizon was dark grey, but she held the lightning back so as not to wake everyone in the camp.

You're almost as good as I was, said Ishbel.

"Shame I didn't have more practice then."

You'll get there eventually.

"I'm not really sure about that. As far as I know, Cameron's visions have never been wrong before."

She could practically feel Ishbel shrug. *Being dead isn't that bad. You'll just need to find some clueless girl to possess.*

Ailsa laughed at the dark joke. "I'm glad you picked me." But she bit her lip as the sky grew ever brighter and suddenly the joke wasn't so funny. All at once, with enough force to take her breath away, her mortality was a visceral thing. *This could,* she realised, *be my last day alive. My last day with my friends, with Maalik. My last day watching the sunrise, my last day smelling the rain.* She clutched at the grass under her fingertips, feeling the earth scrape into her nails, and let out a shuddering gasp.

I'm sorry, Ishbel said quietly.

And what was worse: if she fell, the Edaxi could take her broken and vacant shell and animate it— have it hurt the people she cared about.

"If…" Ailsa wheezed, "…if I die and they try to take my body, could you possess it, like Alasdair did with his? I don't want to be used."

You won't. I swear it.

Thunder boomed overhead, lightning slipping out as she reeled from her thoughts. Ailsa knew it was loud enough to wake the camp. Soon they'd be up, preparing for battle.

You could run, whispered Ishbel. *You and Maalik could leave.*

"I can't. They need me."

Well then, how do you want to do this? Frightened stiff? Weeping, as you face your end? Or are you going to fight? Kicking and snarling and taking chunks of them with you? Because I've seen the core of you; you're a fighter. You get that from me.

"It's a choice," Ailsa corrected her, stealing her spine. "And I choose it today."

Good girl.

Chapter 68

The camp was a flurry of activity. Soldiers darted about, ransacking the tents for every last weapon and piece of armour. Gone was the relative calm they'd enjoyed the last few days, replaced with a palpable fervour. This was after all, what they'd been waiting for. It was an honour to fight for one's country.

Honour? Ishbel scoffed. *That's just what generals tell their men, so they'll fight.*

"Just as well," Ailsa muttered as she and Maalik fought through the crowds. "Or we'd be even more outnumbered." The call had gone out half an hour before: the Mirandellis were on their way and there were hundreds of them.

That's not your concern, Ishbel reminded her. *Find the others and get down to that beach.*

Ailsa nodded, quickening her steps. How much time did they have before the Mirandelli boats landed? Already, the Eilanmòrian army was congregating on the sand while Duncan and his officers organised their rows. She'd watched the king charge down from the door of their tent, riding a white stallion and wearing his crown around his helmet. Duncan had looked regal, but Ailsa couldn't help but wonder if the horse was a bad idea. Wouldn't he be easier to pick out from the crowd?

Ishbel hummed. *Easier for his soldiers too. He must be visible, to give them courage.*

"I hope it does." Ailsa looked over her shoulder at the sea

below, where at least a hundred small boats neared the shore.

"Hurry," said Maalik, pushing her along.

They found Angus first, passing out daggers from a trunk to any soldiers he saw. Ailsa and Maalik slipped in beside him, helping until there was only one left.

"Thanks," he said, slipping the last knife into his belt. "Come with me; the others are at Eilidh's tent."

It was easier moving through the crowds with a prince in tow. Ailsa ran alongside Angus until they reached the right spot

Eilidh, Harris, Iona and Alasdair were waiting for them, dressed in chainmail and breastplates, just like her and Maalik. But someone was missing.

"Angus, where is Cameron?" She wouldn't normally have worried, except just last night he'd been curled up in agony. When she saw Angus's face, she knew she was right to fret. "Where is he?"

The prince avoided her eyes. "I sent him away."

"When?" Ailsa breathed.

"Last night. He was too sick, Ailsa. He'd have died—"

She cut him off, throwing her arms around him. "Thank you," she said into his neck. "You might have saved his life." She pulled back. "You know he's going to be pissed at you, right?"

Angus gave her a watery smile. "It's a price I'm willing to pay." He wiped his eyes, turning to the group. "Are you all ready?"

"Wait," said Harris, pointing at the treeline. "I think we're in trouble."

With a sick feeling, Ailsa turned to see a single figure amble out of the forest on the hill above them. They moved as if in a trance, dragging their feet over the soft grass. Then, one by one, others followed, appearing from between the trees.

The dead formed a wave, picking up speed as they barrelled down the hill towards camp. *Now we really are surrounded.* "We need to warn Duncan," she croaked, her throat suddenly dry. She tried not to focus on them as they came closer, afraid to see a familiar face.

"We will," said Eilidh. "But first, let me see if I can even the playing field." She stepped forward, holding out her arms. As Ailsa watched, something in her shifted. Eilidh's golden hair picked up in the breeze, revealing her delicately pointed ears. She closed her eyes as she pulled on a mask of serenity and breathed deeply, in and out. Ahead, the first of the dead reached the tents, ploughing into the canvas without a care, tearing the fabric with their bare hands.

"Eilidh?" Angus warned as they got closer.

"Hush," said Harris reverently. "The queen is calling her subjects."

The trees swayed, as if something enormous was pushing them out of the way.

"I don't believe it," said Alasdair.

From the forest, dozens of horses came crashing through. Except, they weren't ordinary ponies; they had weeds for hair and sharp teeth. *Kelpies.* They caught up with the dead, biting down on their clothes and tossing them out of the way, while behind them more creatures appeared. Cows with flowers woven into their shaggy fur. Spindly limbed humanoids with shell necklaces. Fiends from horror stories told around the fire and beasts from fairy tales. They all emerged from the forest as one, the Seelie and the Unseelie working together, for their queen.

Eilidh raised her hand as they raced towards the camp. "For Eilanmòr!" she shouted.

Her words were met with snarls and growls as they spread out through the tents, ripping through the canvas in a blur of horns and feathers and fur. And when they met the dead, there were no screams or shouts—only the sounds of crunching bones. The fae swept in, ripping apart their enemies, getting closer and closer.

"You did it," Ailsa breathed.

A young man appeared, his lifeless eyes fixed on them as he ran, heedless of the chaos behind. Angus and Alasdair drew their swords but before the man made it through the line of tents, a hulk of black tackled him, sending him sprawling to the ground. A faerie dog, the size of a pony, landed on the dead man's chest, its hackles raised. It howled, baring its teeth to the world before it sunk them into the corpse's neck, spraying blood over the soil.

Ailsa shivered, averting her eyes as she unwillingly imagined the feel of the faerie dog's teeth against her own throat.

"We'd better move before they mistake us for food," said Maalik, tugging on her sleeve.

"Let's go," Ailsa said as she was pulled away. It was better to keep their distance, even if Eilidh was with them. The fae were not tame. She turned her back on the carnage as her friends fell into step with her, heading for the next battle. "For Eilanmòr."

Chapter 69

From their position behind the lines of soldiers, Ailsa couldn't hear the speech Duncan was giving to his men. It didn't matter, though. She heard the answering shouts, felt the shift in the air as the army prepared themselves. Duncan raised his sword above his head and the crowd cheered.

Ailsa gripped the spear in her hand and checked over her other weapons. Two throwing axes, including the one Gris had given her all those years ago, hung from her belt, along with a knife. Ailsa felt her neck prickling as she thought about her former mentor, somewhere behind them. The fae that had come at Eilidh's call, still battled with the shambling army of the dead and dying, keeping them away from the Eilanmòrians' backs. The thought of his body being further damaged and desecrated made her cringe, but she still hoped he'd already been downed, at peace once more, somewhere amongst the tents.

She watched as the archers ahead took their places, focussing on the waves, where the Mirandelli boats drew closer and closer.

"Wait for it," Angus said.

Ailsa half expected the vessels to slow, to allow the occupants to alight, like Merlo's had done the day before. But the first boat barrelled straight into the sand bar, the hull scraping along the rocky shallows until it could go no further. The Mirandelli soldiers jumped from their crafts, splashing overboard. Then another boat joined them, and another.

Distantly, shouts went up and the first set of arrows shot into the air, raining down on their enemies. A few hit their marks, their bodies falling face first into the sea, but others raised their small shields, fending off the onslaught.

And now we fight.

At the blare of a trumpet, the first wave of Eilanmòrians raced forward, swords and spears raised. Those on horseback reached the enemy first, bowling soldiers over where they stood. Then, the two sets of foot soldiers met in a headlong collision, and the beach turned to chaos.

Angus's jaw flexed. "This is good. While the Mirandellis are still fighting through the water, we have the advantage." Because, while their enemy had the greater numbers, Eilanmòr had the right position.

More and more boats landed, spewing forth Mirandelli soldiers, while the next lines of Eilanmòrians ran off down the beach to meet them. There were so many people, Ailsa couldn't tell who was on their side in the madness.

"It's almost our turn. Skirt past the armies. Steal a boat. Get to the platform." Angus turned to look between them. "Are you ready?"

"You should cover Ailsa," said Maalik, quickly. "With Cameron gone, she'll be on her own."

Ailsa shook her head. "I don't need anyone. I'll stick close, I promise."

Angus watched her for a long moment, weighing up the decision. *Getting ready to fight me on this, more like.*

But then his eyes flicked above her head, and he froze. *Oh no,* thought Ailsa, following his stare. *What now?*

A dark mass flew through the air, above the forest. It still looked far away but it was moving fast, gaining ground every second.

"Eilidh, please tell me," murmured Harris, "that those are some of yours."

The Faerie Queen gulped. "I don't think so."

Ailsa watched with growing horror as the shadow grew closer, reminding her of another dark shape she'd encountered in an ancient forest. The Brollachan was a formless evil, ready to steal the bodies of its victims. But she'd defeated that monster, hadn't she? She thought of the other creatures she'd faced: kelpies and bog monsters and ceasg. All likely fighting the dead at Eilidh's command. And if there were so many of *them*, why wouldn't there be more Brollachan?

Ailsa's hand went to her axe. The Brollochan may have come at Eilidh's call, but there was no way even the Faerie Queen could control something so wicked. If it really was a Brollochan, it currently posed more danger than the attacking Mirandellis.

Angus apparently had the same thought, snapping them into action. "Forget about the battle. Ready yourselves."

Ailsa unlocked her muscles and reached out with her magic, storing up a charge. Beside her, she felt her friends harness their powers and raise their weapons.

The shape was almost above the camp now but as Ailsa watched, it split into two, and then four. Soon, there were at least ten objects, flying through the air towards them. *Ten Brollochan? Or something else?* The lightning crackled around Ailsa's wrist, but she held it back, waiting until the very last minute to unleash it upwards.

Stop, Ishbel hissed in her ear.

Now that they were closer, Ailsa saw that the shapes were actually people. But that was impossible, wasn't it? She saw no wings; how could they fly? That's when she spotted them. Between the figures' legs, each had a stick of wood. No, not a stick. *A broom.*

"Lower your weapons," Ailsa said, her voice wavering in relief. "It's the witches."

Chapter 70

Ailsa knew—whether she lived until she was a hundred or just until the end of the day—she would never see a more heart-warming sight than the one before her now. The witches drew closer on their brooms, looking beaten and battered but very much alive. Leading the pack, no doubt used to flying, was Zephyr. He hovered over the ground but didn't touch down, removing the broom from between his legs and floating in mid-air, like he always did. Ailsa rushed forward to meet him, Maalik close on her heels.

The young witch grinned tiredly as they reached him. "Found you," he managed to say, before Ailsa threw herself at him, enveloping him in a hug.

"How are you here?" Ailsa asked when she pulled back.

But he didn't have time to reply. More witches appeared behind him, this time landing at a run. First, Vega, then Keyne and Rain. Her friends looked dirty, with tattered clothing. *What happened to them?* Ailsa wondered.

"I can't believe this," she said thickly. "You came to help us?"

Vega dropped her broom and wrapped her arms around Ailsa's middle. She was so small, Ailsa could tuck Vega's head under her chin. "We've been flying for two days," she said. "We didn't know if we'd get here in time."

"And Findias?" Maalik breathed.

Keyne shook their head. "Destroyed."

"We managed to get most people out," said Vega. "But some weren't so lucky."

Gods. How had the Edaxi managed to get past their defences? "Who?" Ailsa asked.

"Sefarina, for one." Rain stepped forward, narrowing her eyes. "She stayed behind while we ran. Some others you may not know."

Ailsa stilled, taking this in. One of their leaders had been killed, probably in the worst way, knowing the Edaxi. "Nasima?" She choked a little on the next name. "Aster?"

But Rain merely pointed behind her. The silver-eyed priestess landed gracefully, surrounded by five other witches Ailsa thought she recognised. There was a young woman with bright pink hair, like a cloud around her head, that Ailsa was sure she'd spoken to at one of the Rites. It already felt so long ago. But when Aster met her gaze, everything she'd said to Ishbel came flooding back. *She could very well be my daughter.* Well, now that the priestess was before her, she could imagine a resemblance. The furrowed brow and sharp lines were all Rain, but then there was her hair and eyes, the exact same shades as Ailsa's.

"I tried to leave her behind," muttered Rain as Aster drew closer.

The priestess drew herself up when she reached them, surveying the battle ahead, which was still raging. "It seems you were right." She inclined her head. "We've come to fight. If you'll have us."

"Of course," said Ailsa, glancing over her shoulder. There really wasn't time for a proper reunion. "Are you ready?"

"Almost." Aster pulled some small containers from her pockets. "All this time we've been wearing war paint, but we've been sitting in our castle, safe and sound. Or so we thought. I only have limited colours," she said. "But I think we can make do."

The witches passed the paint around, smearing it on their faces in crude patterns, so unlike the beautiful designs they'd worn in Findias. They didn't linger, decorating their faces quickly and efficiently. Rain brushed her signature red across her brow, the dye staining her fingers. Keyne drew a sun on Zephyr's cheek while he painted a moon on Keyne's. When they were done, Aster nodded, about to slip the pots back into her robes.

"Wait," said Ailsa. Since she arrived in Findias, all those weeks ago, she'd felt like a part of her was missing whenever she looked into the mirror. Her changeling mark had been a part of her, something she had been so used to seeing—and in a blink it had disappeared. But perhaps it was necessary; to lose a part of herself in exchange for her heritage. In exchange for friends, and possibly family, who would fly across the continent to fight at her side. "I want some." She dipped her fingers into a pot of dark blue and swiped it across her cheekbone, in a familiar shape. Then, with a final flourish, she sent a crackle of electricity across her cheek, revealing her pale skin underneath. Because Ailsa was not a moon or a star or a cloud or the sun. Ailsa was lightning.

"What do you think?" she asked, turning to Maalik.

He grinned. "You look like you."

"We'll meet you out there," said Aster, placing her broom between her legs again. "And once the battle is over, I'd like for us to talk."

Ailsa nodded, watching the witches take off and follow their priestess into the sky. Rain was the last, giving Ailsa a long look, as if she was committing her to memory.

"Wait," she said, grabbing the silver-haired witch by the arm. "I seem to be down a guard." Ailsa cleared her throat. "Fancy stepping in?"

It was odd, after so much scowling, to see a smile on Rain's face. But somehow it was infinitely more precious, because Ailsa had earned it.

Rain clasped her hand. "Let's give them hell."

Chapter 71

They dashed back to their group and Ailsa met their confused stares with a shrug. "Rain, I'm sure I told you all about my friends, Angus, Harris and Iona. That's Eilidh, Angus's sister." She hesitated a second before ploughing on. "And Alasdair, Angus's grandfather." She turned to her friends. "Everyone, this is Rain." *My sister,* she finished in her head. *Maybe.*

Harris narrowed his eye. "You look really familiar," he told the witch.

"Does that line usually work?" Rain asked. "Sorry, but I'm with someone."

Ailsa would have to unpick that later. "Shall we?"

"Watch each other's backs," Angus reminded them. "And don't split up. We're safer as a group."

Then they were off, hurrying towards the mayhem. By now, the soldiers' ranks had broken, with the fighting concentrated in clumps. Still, the mass of bodies seemed like an impenetrable wall, keeping them from the sea beyond, where the whitecaps were tinged red with blood. Overhead the witches flew, throwing their magic into the turmoil. Ailsa spotted Keyne, surrounding the people below them in their thick smoke. Another witch was targeting someone below him, sucking the soldier's body up high in a column of air, before dropping them violently to the sand. But there weren't just witches in the sky. Some of Eilidh's fae friends flew past, seemingly grown bored of the dead behind them. Black birds the size of cows, with webbed feet grabbed enemy fighters while flocks of brownies circled their heads, confusing them long enough for Eilanmòrian soldiers to stab them. It would have been a hopeful sight, if not for the longships sailing towards them.

"Raiders!" shouted Ailsa over the noise. "We have to get to a boat quick, before they land."

They ran closer to the fighting until it was impossible to avoid it anymore. Angus and Alasdair drew their swords while Harris pulled out his knives as they threw themselves at the first Mirandellis in their path.

"Can you help them?" Ailsa asked Rain.

The witch pulled a small, curved blade from behind her back. "With pleasure."

Ailsa threw her hand up, dragging the distant clouds across the sky until they were overhead, grey and ready. "Alright, let's do this." Around her, she was aware of her friends' power building. Maalik's skin fissured while Eilidh's form shifted between human and beast. Iona clenched her fist, pulling the moisture from between the grains of sand. But they weren't there to fight. They held onto their magic, waiting, as they ran after Angus, Harris, Rain and Alasdair, avoiding the battling soldiers.

They were halfway to the water, when Ailsa felt a jolt go through her body. She stumbled on the sand but managed not to fall over. *Shake it off. Keep going,* she told herself. But pain stabbed through her again. She gritted her teeth, noticing that her throat was suddenly raw, like she'd swallowed glass. She blinked against the light, finding it brighter than moments before. And when Ailsa raised a hand to shade her eyes, she saw it. Her skin had turned a mottled black and purple, bruised in places she knew she hadn't been injured.

"Do you see this?" she asked those beside her. But when

she looked up, she was met with a frightening sight. Eilidh and Iona's eyes were rimmed red, as if they hadn't slept in days. Her friends' faces were screwed up, like they were experiencing the same pain she was. Catching sight of Rain, Angus and Harris, she saw they were similarly affected. Only Maalik and Alasdair appeared unchanged, continuing to fight their way forward.

With dawning realisation, Ailsa looked around them, searching for their allies. Every single Eilanmòrian she saw had the same bruises blossoming on their skin, the same reddened eyes. Some screamed in pain, doubling over, only to be stabbed by the Mirandellis they were fighting. Their enemies seemed immune to the strange affliction.

We're sick, Ailsa realised. She thought back to King Connall when she'd seen him on his deathbed months ago, covered in black lesions. And she understood. *This is what the Edaxi do to their enemies. It's a plague.*

"Keep going," she shouted. They didn't have the luxury of curling up on the sand like she wanted. It had taken weeks to kill King Connall, they still had time.

Maalik whipped his head around in confusion, which immediately turned to shock and concern when he saw her. "Ailsa, what's happening—"

"The same thing that's happening to everyone else. Except you and Alasdair." She fought against another wave of pain. "It doesn't change anything. We need to find a boat."

He nodded, not arguing with her. Fighting their way through was admittedly easier now, with their enemies easily forcing the sick Eilanmòrians back. Angus pointed to a gap in the bodies, and Ailsa spotted the waves crashing on the shore. They pushed through as a group, racing for the boats.

As they cleared the crowds, four figures stepped into their path. Ailsa and her friends skidded to a halt. She stored up her lightning, ready to strike down the obstacle, but when she took a proper look at the people, her heart stopped for a long moment as her world tilted. "No," she whispered. "That's not possible."

Princess Irené of Edessa, captain of the Nympho del Mar, stood with her feet in the lapping sea. Except, she didn't look like herself, not really. Her facial features were there but she was no longer made of flesh and bone. Irené was made completely of glass-like ice. She stared blankly at them, as if she didn't recognise her former companions.

Next to her was another familiar face. Back when Ailsa was first trapped in Hell and forced to stand trial, there was only one demon willing to help her. But when she went there a second time, Maalik's friend, Calix, was nowhere to be found. Now she knew why. Calix's face wore the same blank look as Irené. His hands were wreathed in flames, though his skin did not burn.

Ailsa had started to put the pieces together. *Fire and ice. But ice is just water...* She moved her gaze to the next person: a young boy, much too young to be on a battlefield. Below his elbows, his skin was grey and hard, like rock.

Rock is earth. Which just leaves...

The last woman was not empty like the others. Her grin was wicked, with sharpened teeth. A skull mask was pushed back onto her forehead and Ailsa immediately recognised her.

Ailsa's hand flew to her cheek, but not the one with the warpaint. On the other side, a single scar cut across her cheekbone; a reminder of when she'd been powerless under her captor's knife. "Brenna," she gasped.

The woman smirked. "You said you'd remember me."

"I said I'll remember that I'm strong," Ailsa corrected her, "and how it felt to kill you. I didn't manage that, but it looks like I'll have another chance."

"Big words," said Brenna. She darted forward a step, so fast that Ailsa almost missed it. Air swirled around her legs, picking the sand up to make a small whirlwind around her. "You know, when the Edaxi offered to help me tap into my latent power, I almost refused. But when they told me who I'd be fighting, I knew it would be worth the pain. I'm going to enjoy stealing that spear from your corpse."

"She's a Valkyrie," Maalik said in a hushed voice. "They're meant to escort the souls of the dead through the winds to the afterlife."

Winds. Air.

Ailsa didn't reply. Her worst fears had been confirmed. All this time, they'd been collecting the Four Treasures and the fae to use them, it had almost been too easy. Now she understood why. The Edaxi had known they'd bring the weapons to them. And they'd created champions of their own.

Chapter 72

*E*ilidh fought against the churning in her gut as she stared across the sands. She could sense them: four fae, with elemental powers. She didn't know any of them, but from Ailsa's words, Eilidh could guess she had some history with the Avalognian woman, at least. And when Harris saw who stood in the shallows…

"Irené!" His cry was broken. He lurched forward as if he couldn't believe what he was seeing. Angus grabbed his shirt, in case he made a run for her. Already, Harris was straining at the fabric, his chest heaving.

"This was the Edaxi's plan all along," said Ailsa. "To have their own fae fight us and retrieve the Four Treasures."

"We're not giving them up without a fight," said Maalik darkly. "Even if I have to kill a friend."

Eilidh followed his gaze to the other demon. He had black eyes, just like Maalik, but a pair of golden horns curled around his head where Maalik's antlers were. Maalik's mouth was set in a grim line, like he knew the man across from him and had already resigned himself to battle.

Had they chosen these people on purpose? Ailsa and Maalik knew their counterparts and Irené was Iona's friend. Her gaze drifted to the last figure. Was she supposed to fight him? He was just a wee boy. "They knew who would get under our skin," she realised. "This can't be a coincidence."

"So, what now?" asked Alasdair.

"We fight." Ailsa raised the spear. "We don't let them get

the treasures. And when they've been defeated, we continue with the plan."

"No one hurts Irené," Harris growled.

"I won't," Iona assured him with a hand on his shoulder. "We just need to get past her."

Eilidh saw the defiance bubbling up in him, knew he was seconds away from running for the princess. "Harris, look at me."

He turned to her reluctantly, the pain on his face nothing to do with the sickness weakening them.

"I need you to cover me. Can you do that?" She injected every last bit of authority into her voice, hoping it was enough. "Iona will deal with Irené and when we kill the Edaxi, she'll be saved. Your queen requires your help." It was a dirty trick, she knew. But if it was going to save his life, she'd happily play that card.

He stared at her for a long moment, fighting some internal battle, before finally nodding.

"Are you still muttering?" the woman jeered. "Or are you ready to hand over the weapons?"

Maalik's sword went up in flames. "Ready when you are."

Eilidh palmed her knife and reached up to cup the stone at her neck. "Meet you at the boats."

Chapter 73

Ailsa stalked forward, deliberately not looking anywhere but at Brenna. *You need to focus. Your friends will be fine.* She really hoped that was true.

The four fae split up, as if they knew who their targets were. *They're after the Four Treasures, that's why.* Ailsa gripped the spear tighter, uneasy. No one else had to throw their weapon at their enemy. How was she going to keep it out of Brenna's hands?

"The last time I saw you, you were on a sinking ship," Ailsa said as she advanced. She was sure she didn't need to remind the Avalognian that she'd been the one to sink it. Thunder boomed overhead, waiting for her command. Ailsa's hair stood on end at the electricity in the air. This was when she felt the most alive, unleashing herself on the world.

Brenna looked unimpressed. "I was scared of you back then. But now that my own magic has been unlocked, you are just a scared little girl, playing at being a hero. When the Edaxi told me who I'd be facing, I expected to be impressed." She snorted. "You're all barely out of the nursery."

Ailsa opened her mouth to answer, but in a blink, Brenna was gone. She spun around, looking for the woman until she felt a touch against her neck, soft as a moth's wing.

"I'm going to enjoy killing you," Brenna whispered, somehow right at Ailsa's ear.

Ailsa pulled a dagger from her belt, slashing through the air. But the raider was already gone, laughing as she darted back a few hundred feet, faster than humanly possible. That was the point though; she wasn't human anymore.

Distantly, Ailsa was aware of her friends engaging with their counterparts while those without the treasures watched their backs as the battle raged on behind them. Ailsa kept her eyes on Brenna, intent to catch her slightest movement.

How am I going to hit her if she's so fast?

You have lightning and a mythical weapon, Ishbel said. *Use them.*

Ailsa pulled her arm back and threw the spear towards her enemy. It sailed through the air, straight to her target, but Brenna just reappeared right in front of Ailsa, dagger poised and ready to strike her in the heart. Ailsa met her blade with her own, gritting her teeth as she deflected, but she lost sight and control of the spear.

Brenna smirked, disappearing again, and Ailsa was seized with panic. Was the fight over so soon? Had she already lost? But then her gaze snagged on Rain, knee deep in the surf, holding the spear in her hands.

"No!" Ailsa shouted. Because Brenna was around somewhere, ready with her knife. Sure enough, the Avalognian popped up out of nowhere, lunging for Rain. But the silver-haired witch was quicker, throwing the spear to Ailsa with one hand and bringing her sickle down with the other.

"Looks like we're playing a game of keep-away," shouted Rain. She spun, aiming to kick Brenna's feet out from under her.

Brenna darted away out of harm's reach. "Let's see how long before I can gut you both," she whispered into the wind, vanishing from view once again.

Chapter 74

Iona caught flashes of movement out of the corner of her eye but couldn't tear her gaze away from the woman in front of her. She was aware that her comrades had already engaged in battle, but her own feet were rooted to the spot.

Irené's skin was like glass, hard and crystalline; Iona could see right through her, to the ships and the ocean behind. It should have been impossible for her to move, but the ice didn't break or chip when she took a step. She raised her arm, holding her hand out, and waited.

She wants the cauldron. Or, rather, the Edaxi did. Who knew what they'd done to Irené to make her this way. Iona hadn't even known the pirate captain was part fae until after the battle for Ephraim. Harris had told Iona later that Irené's mother was a xana: a water sprite who dwelled under the sea. But xana came from the tropical waters of Edessa; why had Irené's magic manifested as ice?

The princess had to be in there somewhere. "Irené?" Iona bit the inside of her cheek. "Do you remember me?" When she didn't answer, Iona shuffled forward, her toes sinking into the wet silt.

"I don't like this," said Alasdair from behind her. "I know she was your friend, but you have to assume she's our enemy, if the Edaxi sent her. Remember that we have a job to do."

"Harris will never forgive me if I don't try." Iona turned to look for her brother, standing behind Eilidh as she approached the little boy. But he wasn't looking at their opponent. He stared out to the horizon with a slowly forming grin. It was a look of hope. Iona followed his stare, her heart stopping when she saw it: something golden had emerged from the water, pushing a wave in front of it. Reinforcements had arrived.

"It's the Nymph! They made it." The boat headed for the shore, further down the beach from them, where the fighting was strongest. As it surfaced, the two massive fish-eye windows came into view. It darted from the deep sea into the shallows, not slowing until it reached the sand bar. Iona watched as the top hatch was thrown open and the crew flooded the upper deck. "Look," she said to Irené, who had drifted closer. "Your ship."

Irené tilted her head, the movement of the ice catching the light.

Yes, thought Iona. *She heard me.*

But Irené didn't turn in the Nymph's direction. Her attention fixed on Iona as she bolted forward.

Iona's joy turned to lead in her stomach. She flung out her magic, finding the water and pulling it up out of the sea like she'd done at the Avalognians' camp. *Come on,* she pleaded, holding the water there. *Let her snap out of it.*

Two hundred feet. One hundred feet. Fifty feet. Irené sprinted towards her, arms out. And then, just when Iona's nerve was starting to fail, Irené's arms and shoulders shifted, erupting into piercing sharp icicles.

"Now!" Alasdair shouted from behind. With a cry, Iona pulled the wall of water up and over Irené's body, knocking her to the sand. Iona blinked against the spray but when she opened her eyes, she watched with horror as Irené froze the sand around her.

Then, with a flick of her hand, the princess sent shards of ice out, spearing straight for Iona's heart.

Chapter 75

Angus hovered at Maalik's back, facing the battle raging on the beach. Their soldiers were sick, but they were still putting up a fight. Angus thought he glimpsed Duncan's white charger at one point, but in the mass of bodies, it was hard to see.

Behind him, fire flashed hot and bright as Maalik tried to reason with the other demon.

"Calix, look at me. This isn't you. I need you to snap out of it."

But Maalik's opponent didn't heed his words. A second later, the flames roared, heat punching out from Calix's palm. An arm grasped Angus's stomach, shoving him to the sand before he could be singed.

Above him, Maalik breathed heavily. "Sorry. He doesn't know what he's doing."

"It's fine." Angus sat up. "I'm going to give you some space. Shout if you need me."

Then Maalik was up, stalking to his former friend as his skin fractured.

Angus stayed on the ground, assessing the fight around him. Ailsa and Rain threw the spear between them a little way away, blocking the Avalognian's knife whenever she appeared. She moved so fast, they barely had time to defend, let alone attack.

Eilidh was watching the little boy who stood swaying on the spot. Then, with a howl, he ran for her, swinging his stone arms at her head. At the last minute, Eilidh shifted, turning into a flock of magpies and flew behind him. Harris stood back, shouting something at her that was snatched by the wind.

Iona and Irené, meanwhile, were down the beach, too far away for Angus's liking. He watched as she brought a wall of seawater high into the air, crashing it down on the princess and sending her sprawling. But Irené stayed blank, freezing any water around her with a touch, sending it lancing for Iona. Alasdair dived in, blocking the shards of ice with his sword before it could reach her.

A shriek sounded and Angus whipped his head round, looking for the source. Ailsa's sleeve was torn, and blood coated the fabric, dripping onto the sand below. She'd managed to dodge the Avalognian, but not before she drew first blood. Things were looking dire with Eilidh too. With the boy unable to hit her, he turned on Harris, smashing a fist into the selkie's side. It looked like the blow barely connected but Harris was thrown, rolling and clutching his stomach with a teeth-baring grimace.

No one was gaining ground. *This isn't working,* Angus realised. The Edaxi had specifically chosen opponents who would unsettle his friends. Ailsa knew the Valkyrie and the demon was Maalik's friend. Angus imagined they chose the little boy because they knew Eilidh would find fighting him difficult. And they must have known Iona would hold back from attacking Irené. Aside from all that, their powers were evenly matched too. They'd be on the beach for hours at this rate and by then the battle could be over. "You need to switch!" he shouted at his friends. "Fighting earth and earth, or air and air, isn't going to work!"

Ailsa caught the spear again, nodding. "Eilidh, over here! Maalik, get the boy." She glanced down the beach, where Iona,

Irené and Alasdair were still fighting, too far away for them to hear anything Angus or Ailsa had said. Ailsa raced for the demon instead, pulling down her lightning as she went aiming straight for his chest.

Angus was about to throw himself back into the fight, when a frightened whinny pulled his attention towards the battle. Now he could see his brother, but the relief was short lived. He watched in slow motion as an arrow pierced the neck of Duncan's horse, sending bright red blood spraying from the wound over its white coat. The horse reared back as his brother held on for dear life, before falling to the side and disappearing from view amongst the soldiers.

"Duncan!" he screamed. His brother was down, somewhere amongst the rabble. He started forward; his careful planning abandoned. His friends would be fine; he had to save his king.

His shriek caught Ailsa and Maalik's attention.

"Go," shouted the demon, sending a blast at the boy and knocking him down. "I've got this."

Ailsa dived out of the way of the demon's fire. "Rain! Harris! Cover Angus!"

Then the grey-haired witch was at his elbow. "Come on," Rain said. "Let's go get your brother."

Angus couldn't care less how she knew. Distantly, he saw Harris shouting something to Eilidh, then running in his direction. But Angus couldn't wait for him. He threw himself into the brawl, sword swinging, with only one thought screeching through his mind: *find Duncan.*

Chapter 76

No matter what Iona did, Irené continued her attack. Iona sent another wave into the princess's face, but she kept coming closer and closer.

"Watch out," shouted Alasdair. They both dodged out of the way as another set of razor-sharp icicles flew at them. They rolled when they hit the ground, sending sand up into the air and covering their clothes.

"Irené!" Iona cried. "Listen to me, you don't want to hurt us."

But the princess was already lunging for them. Iona pulled the water out of the sand, sending it up between them as a barrier. Irené hit the spray, staggering back. Iona's relief was short lived though, when the water froze into a huge sheet and toppled towards her and Alasdair.

"Move!" They rolled again, just as the ice crashed down, sending jagged chips flying out to scrape at their skin.

Irené had not spoken in the time they'd been fighting but now, as she stood over them, illuminated for a moment by Ailsa's lightning flashing behind her, her words rang out.

"Give me the Cauldron of Life." Her voice was strange and echoing, as if she was speaking from far away or inside a cave. There was no recognition in her eyes, just the same blank stare.

What did they do to you?

"Come on." Alasdair tugged Iona up, dragging her into a run, in the opposite direction to their friends. "If we can lose her amongst the soldiers, maybe we can double back."

Iona looked over her shoulder as they sprinted. How were their comrades doing? Surely better than this. *At least they can fight back.* Her water had always been useful in a fight, but only if she meant to drown her opponent. But she couldn't kill Irené. Could she?

A scream tore down the beach and Alasdair's feet skidded, stopping them both. "Was that Angus?" They searched for Alasdair's grandson, finding him halfway up the shore, bolting into the clashing armies, with Ailsa's witch friend right behind him. "We need to go back."

But Irené was already upon them. The icicles on her shoulders grew longer and she reached back to snap one off, holding it aloft as she charged.

I have no choice, she realised. Iona reached out, pulling another wave high as Irené's ice dagger arced through the air. *Quick,* she urged herself. But she wasn't fast enough.

Alasdair threw himself in front of Iona, meeting Irené's blade with his own. The three of them were so close, almost on top of each other; every time Iona tried to move out of the way, Irené pounced at her. Alasdair blocked every slash, but Iona knew he was getting tired. Irené was practised, lethal, even in this vacant state.

Iona's wall of water was building, higher and higher. They just had to get far enough away for her to use it—to send it barrelling down Irené's throat. Tears flowed from Iona's eyes, preparing for the inevitable. *I'm sorry, Harris.*

But before she could bring the seawater down, Irené ducked, grabbing Alasdair's arm. Iona watched in mounting panic as the princess pulled Alasdair forward and spun him, so his back pressed against Irené's front. Then, without changing her expression, Irené took her ice knife and thrust it into Alasdair's side.

Iona's scream was wrenched from her throat. "*No!*"

Alasdair stared wide eyed at Iona, opening and closing his mouth in shock. Irené pulled the dagger out and immediately blood spurted from the wound, staining the sand below.

Not again! Iona's thoughts wailed. She couldn't lose him again.

Irené held the knife aloft, aiming for Alasdair's neck, where his arteries pumped. *If she stabs him there, he's dead.*

"Give me the Cauldron of Life and I'll let him go."

Iona sank to the ground, letting her wall of water drop. There was no way she'd be able to kill Irené in time. The wind whipped her hair across her face as the tears flowed. The decision was impossible: save the entire world or the love of her life. She thought of the promises she and Alasdair had made to each other. *He wanted to marry me.* She saw that dream slipping away with the tide, just like it had done before.

"Iona," he croaked. "Look at me." She met his mismatched eyes, glassy and red now. "I love you and I'll keep loving you for the rest of your life. Know that I'll always be with you."

Because, if given the choice, Alasdair would resist the peace of the afterlife again, just to watch her from afar. Torture, he'd called it, being a ghost. But he'd go through it again, for her.

I can't let him.

A memory resurfaced from weeks ago, of a prophecy told to them by a Bean-Nighe and everything clicked into place. *Family, friend, lover. One will die saving theirs. One will watch theirs die.* Iona took a shuddering breath. *One will betray the whole world to save them—*

"Fine," she whispered. "You can have it." She reached into her pocket, pulling the cauldron out. Then, with a sob, she hurled it through the air.

Irené shoved Alasdair forward and caught the treasure, her face never shifting from her vacant expression, even in triumph.

Iona dived for Alasdair's body, grabbing him before he could hit the ground. He blinked up at her. "You shouldn't have—"

"Shh," she said, pushing his hair back from his face. "I couldn't let her kill you." But she already knew she was too late. The last part of the prophecy rang through her like a death knell.

One will betray the whole world for them, yet it will be in vain.

Iona pressed her wet cheek to Alasdair's forehead and counted his breaths as he bled onto the sand. She barely registered the fighting anymore. Iona was in her own world of grief; the only other souls in it were the king in her arms and the princess splashing out to sea. She watched as Irené walked into the waves until she was waist deep in the surf.

The princess threw her arm out, sending her magic over the water. Ice formed impossibly over the surf, freezing the waves where they crested. Soon, the ocean was still and cold. And Iona felt her heart freeze with it.

Chapter 77

When Ailsa first met Calix, he'd shone brighter than any of the demons in Hell. Now he was a shadow of his former self, even as flames licked his skin. He wouldn't take his eyes off Maalik, fighting the little boy a few feet away, almost as if they'd been programmed to hit one target and one target only. It made it hard to grab his attention. On the other hand, it gave Ailsa a chance to strike first.

She could feel electricity coursing through her whole body, so it was easy to throw it out towards the demon. She aimed for his feet even though she knew a shock to his chest could easily kill him. He yelped and fell, mostly unhurt. If there was any chance of saving Maalik's friend, she'd take it.

Maalik seemed to have the same thought about the faerie child, blasting the sand around him instead of his young body. The boy threw himself at Maalik with his mighty arms, but her demon dodged out of the way easily.

Eilidh was not holding back with Brenna. The Valkyrie and the Faerie Queen did a strange dance, with Brenna racing between points so fast she was a blur and Eilidh teleporting ahead of her, slashing with her knife whenever she appeared.

Ailsa tore her eyes from the couple; she had to focus on her own opponent. Calix pushed himself up, his muscles bunching under his tattoos. He threw a fireball Ailsa's way, the flames singeing the hair on her arms as it narrowly missed her.

"Calix, I need you to stop." The lightning crept up her veins now, between the bruises, marking her in black patterns like it had done before. It was a sure sign that she was testing her limits. Ailsa tried throwing a wall of air up between them, but she'd never been as good as Sefarina was. It held for a moment before collapsing under Calix's heat. He sent another flame ball at her and she hit the ground, ducking out of the way.

Where are Rain, Harris and Angus? She scanned round as Calix advanced, sending a bolt of lightning at his feet again, knocking him over. She didn't see the prince, the selkie or her... whatever Rain was. When she couldn't find them through the hordes of battling soldiers, she looked down the beach instead, to where Iona had been.

But Iona was no longer on her feet. Ailsa saw a figure with Iona's bright red hair bending over something on the sand. And in the sea ahead of her, a crystalline woman pushed out into the waves.

Ailsa's breath caught. Was Iona injured?

She watched as Irené placed a hand into the water and waited. From where Ailsa was lying, it took her a moment to realise what the princess was doing. With a crack, Irené's magic spread out from the shore, stopping the waves in their tracks. *She's frozen the sea.*

Calix came for her again, launching more fire at her. This time, it came close enough to burn her, sending white hot pain up her leg. She shrieked, cursing, but leapt out of the way of more damage, throwing her power at him in retaliation. She aimed higher on his thigh and his body convulsed before dropping to the ground. *Sorry,* she thought. He appeared disorientated, like he didn't know how he'd ended up on the sand.

A little away, Maalik's snarl caught her attention. The boy's fist connected with his arm, making a sickening crunch. She watched Maalik hesitate, morality play across his face, before he seemed to make a decision. Holding up his other hand, palm out, he sent a blast at the young faerie. The explosion landed in front of the boy, sending him flying like a ragdoll. Ailsa watched for a beat, sure that Maalik's blow had been enough, but then he raised his head from the sand again, gaze fixed on Maalik.

Focus on your own problem, commanded Ishbel.

Ailsa turned her attention back to the other demon, expecting Calix to be where he'd fallen. But the sand was empty.

Where—

So fast she couldn't react, a hand closed around her throat and Calix lifted her into the air. Ailsa scrabbled against his grip, nails clawing against his knuckles. *Maalik!* She tried to shout, but only a muffled gasp got past her lips. Calix squeezed, crushing her windpipe in his huge palm, his black eyes showing no sign of recognition.

Use your magic! Ishbel shouted.

But she couldn't. *No air.*

Her vision blackened around the edges, but she held onto consciousness. Ailsa reached over her shoulder for the spear first, but her fingers couldn't close around the shaft. Her hand went to her belt next but as soon as she touched the handle of her axe, he was there, pulling it from her grip and throwing it to the sand.

Then her throat started to heat, and she forgot all about her weapons. *Too hot, too hot.* He watched her impassively as the fire under his skin built. Ailsa struggled in his grip, anticipating the burn, for his hand to blister and char her skin. Ailsa dug her nails into his knuckles, tearing at him in a desperate attempt to free herself as she blinked away tears.

Then suddenly the pressure and heat were gone as Calix let go. She landed, coughing and hacking onto the sand, rubbing at her neck as she looked up to see why he'd dropped her.

Maalik stood to his side, holding the flaming Sword of Light. The fire licked up and down the blade, but he paid it no mind as he watched Calix stumble, mouth gaping. The demon teetered then fell. And as he toppled, his body split into two halves, landing with a sickening, wet thud.

Ailsa looked away from the gore before her brain could really register it. Some things were too much, even for her. "You killed him," she croaked.

"He was going to kill you," he said thickly, devastation on his face.

She coughed again, feeling the truth in that statement. "Thank you," she said as she heaved herself up. *One obstacle down, two more to go.* She tried not to think about Irené and Iona and whatever had happened over there. Maybe she was mistaken. Maybe Iona had won.

Maalik nodded, turning back to the approaching figure of the young boy. He hesitated as the faerie stalked closer, the flames on his sword snuffing out. The boy brought his fist swinging round, aiming for Maalik's knees but the demon dodged out of the way at the last moment.

What is he waiting for? Said Ishbel.

He doesn't want to hurt a child.

He's going to have to.

A wicked laugh startled her from her thoughts and Ailsa whirled, only to be met with Brenna's grin, two feet away.

"Got you," said the Avalognian, pulling back her blade, aiming straight for Ailsa's heart.

Ailsa flinched back but just as Brenna went to throw her dagger, Eilidh appeared between them, shielding Ailsa with her arms out. Brenna jumped, the knife slipping out of her hands. With a growl of frustration, the Avalognian pulled another dagger from her belt, slashing at the Faerie Queen instead. But when the dagger's point should have made contact with Eilidh's gut, she burst into a swarm of bees.

Ailsa watched Brenna lock onto her through the cloud of insects. She stored up her power again, ready to strike but Brenna was quicker, she had the knife ready. The Avalognian ran at her, grabbing a handful of Ailsa's shirt and throwing them both to the ground, so Brenna's body covered her own. Just like it had when the woman sliced her cheek open.

"Let's see your demon try to save you now," she whispered into Ailsa's ear. "I'm going to bathe in your blood, lightning girl. And then I'll do the same to your friends." Brenna pressed the blade to her throat, right where Calix had held her, and tensed, ready to slice.

Ailsa could only gasp, looking up into the cruel face of the Avalognian, her pointed teeth revealed in a triumphant grin. She closed her eyes, waiting for the inevitable pain.

Just then a gold light flashed in front of her eyelids, and she snapped them open. The Valkyrie loosened her grip on Ailsa but not before she nicked some skin, sending liquid dribbling down her throat. Still, it was a price Ailsa was willing to pay for the sight above her.

Brenna sat back on Ailsa's legs, clutching at her stomach as Eilidh withdrew the knife she'd plunged through the Avalognian's back. Ailsa watched as Brenna swayed on her knees. Ailsa could almost sense the death creeping over her as she bled out through the gaping wound. And Ailsa realised she didn't have it in her to feel sorry.

"I will always remember you." Ailsa raised her chin, chest heaving, as she pulled her leg out from under the Avalognian and kneed her in the chest, sending her sprawling. Ailsa licked her lips, waiting and watching as the Valkyrie's body writhed. It didn't take long for her to still.

Eilidh stared down at Brenna's body, expression unreadable. "Two down."

"Three," shouted Maalik. The faerie boy's crumpled body lay sprawled across the sand a few feet away. This time he did not stir.

"Is he dead?" Ailsa asked, head pounding from the fight and the sickness plaguing her body.

"The explosion hit the side of his head." Maalik ran to him, checking his neck with careful fingers. "He'll be fine; just knocked out."

Hopefully he'll stay that way.

"What about Iona?" asked Eilidh.

Together, their gazes searched the beach. The sea was still frozen, but Irené had disappeared. Ailsa squinted down the sand, spotting a lone figure, red hair blowing in the wind, bending over something. No, not something. *Someone.*

"Alasdair," breathed Maalik.

But just as he said the late king's name, a slow clap rang out over their part of the beach, filling Ailsa with dread.

"You almost seem sorry," said a woman's voice. "What, did you want to kill him again?"

No. It can't be.

Dolor floated towards them gracefully over the frozen waves, grey and black against the white of the ice. She raised her hands and pain erupted through Ailsa, down every nerve and through every muscle. Ailsa curled in on herself, gritting her teeth so hard she thought she'd crack them. She was vaguely aware of her friends doing the same beside her.

No, no, no—

"Well done. You, mostly, beat our champions." Dolor was closer now, almost on top of them from the sound of her voice. She clicked her tongue, toeing Ailsa's leg with her shoe. "It seems you three truly are the strongest fae in the land. And look at that, you have three of the Four Treasures too." She caressed a hand down Ailsa's cheek, the sensation like needles. "You've all done such a good job; I believe you should be rewarded."

Screeching, soaring pain lanced through Ailsa, so intense that she couldn't think, couldn't breathe, around it. The last thing she heard before her body shut down, was Dolor's echoing laugh and Maalik and Eilidh's shrieks.

Chapter 78

arris dodged a faerie cow stampeding through the soldiers as he rushed to catch up with Angus. *If Eilidh doesn't need me, I should be at Iona's side. With Irené.* But it was too late for that. As soon as Ailsa had yelled for him and he'd seen Angus darting into the fray, he'd run after him without a thought. *Iona will be alright with Alasdair.*

Angus was just ahead, slashing through Mirandellis with his sword. He didn't pause to check if they were dead, continuing on as if hacking his way through a jungle.

The witch followed closely behind, swinging her sickle. *She's a good fighter*, Harris thought. When an enemy soldier raised his sword ready to strike her, she held out a hand and the weapon magically flew into her palm. With a flick, she drew it across his torso, blood blooming in the blade's wake. *She's a great fighter*, he amended.

When Harris reached them, he stayed close, sticking his daggers in anyone who tried to attack. Most people, however, were occupied by those they were already fighting. The Eilanmòr soldiers, despite their sickness and mottled skin, were not losing heart. And with the fae battling alongside them, the Mirandellis had found their match.

We're doing better than I expected, Harris thought with a frown. He didn't trust it.

"Over there!" called Rain, pointing to something white amongst the crowd.

Angus changed direction, heading where she pointed.

Please, let Duncan be alright.

But when they made it to the fallen horse, the king was nowhere to be found. The stallion's eyes had rolled back and there was froth around its mouth. *They punctured its lung.* But how had Duncan escaped?

The sky darkened ominously. All the lightning that had crackled overhead while Ailsa fought dissipated, while black clouds rolled in. Somehow, Harris knew they weren't Ailsa's doing.

"Something's wrong," he said, scanning the crowd.

Angus stood from where he'd been checking over the horse. When Harris looked out over the sea, his jaw dropped. The entire bay was frozen.

"When did that happen?"

As if on cue, a loud, child-like laugh echoed over the rabble. It caused fighters on both sides of the battle to pause, searching for the source.

Rain flexed her jaw. "I don't like this."

A low buzz hummed in the air, growing louder and louder. Harris covered his ears as his friends did the same. All around them, soldiers stopped fighting. Harris looked skyward again, watching as a particularly large cloud moved in their direction. *No, not a cloud*, he realised as it swooped down over the battle. *A swarm.*

The insects flew at them, flies and beetles landing on their bodies indiscriminately. No matter what they did to swat at them, the bugs kept coming. Harris shivered as they crawled over his skin. It was unpleasant, for sure, but nearby soldiers were screaming with fright. He tugged his eyepatch down over his mouth and nose. "Cover up. We still need to find Duncan."

As the crowd dispersed, running from the swarm, they saw him. Duncan was locked in battle with a dark-haired man, his sword clashing against the soldier's. The king gritted his teeth, throwing his opponent back with a grunt. Harris realised, with a jolt, that he knew him.

General Scarsi spat his blood onto the sand and rolled his shoulders as he eyed up his opponent. He shouted something at Duncan, but the words were lost in the chaos.

"We need to help him," said Angus, starting forward.

A sword came out of nowhere, slashing at Harris's stomach but he dodged at the last second, bringing his dagger up as a reflex into the attacker's armpit. The Mirandelli flinched away, pulled back into the crowd by another Eilanmòrian soldier.

"Stay together," Harris yelled as Rain defended another attack. They were no good to Duncan dead.

Angus nodded; his eyes fixed on where his brother still fought the General.

Then suddenly, as if Harris's ears had been covered, the clamour of battle died. *Have I lost my hearing?* But when he caught sight of Angus and Rain, he knew it wasn't just him. Something had sucked the sound away, even as the armies fought on.

Angus mouthed some words, pointing as if to say they couldn't waste any time, even if the noise was gone, but Rain placed a hand on his shoulder, jerking her chin ahead.

A little girl emerged from the mob, blocking their way. The soldiers around her kept their distance as she skipped forward, as if they too could feel the wrong-ness of her. Her auburn hair was pulled into two bunches at her side, but her smile was cruel. "Prince Angus." Her words cut through the silence. "I'm so glad we could finally play."

Rain pulled on Angus's armour, trying to drag him back and away from the girl, but the prince's gaze flicked to his brother, still locked with Scarsi.

"What is it that you fear, prince?" the girl hummed.

Harris, Angus and Rain were rooted to the spot, unable to move as she drifted closer. The flies buzzed silently around them, landing on their clothes and hair, but they couldn't bat them away. The girl eyed Angus. "Deep water," she decided. "Or being alone: losing everyone you love. And there are so many of them too." Then her attention moved to Rain. "That dark dungeon: the feel of the rats brushing against your skin, waiting to bite." Then she settled on Harris. "You replay that moment in your head, don't you? When the princess gave herself up for you. Would you like to see her now?"

Harris couldn't catch his breath as shadows twisted around the girl. The deity. Because this had to be Timor, Goddess of Fear.

Angus shook himself from Rain's grip and darted forward towards his brother. Harris was sure Timor would stop him but, to his surprise, she stepped to the side, clapping her hands in delight. But Angus only made it a couple of steps forward when Duncan's eyes snapped to his and the king faltered.

Harris watched with horror as Duncan's mouth formed his brother's name, just as Scarsi thrust his sword into the king's stomach. Harris didn't need to hear to know the sound coming from Angus as he stumbled was a scream.

Duncan's attention was ripped from his brother to the man across from him. In great, echoing silence, the king stared at Scarsi in disbelief. The General's smile was wicked as he said something to the king. And then he withdrew his sword from Duncan's gut. Scarsi turned with a knowing grin and held his blade out towards them, ready for their attack, as the king slumped to the ground and was still.

Angus dropped to his knees on the sand, clutching his sword uselessly, the fight gone from him. Harris gritted his teeth, throwing himself down next to Angus to pull him close, feeling Rain do the same on his other side. Angus's body shook with heaving, soundless gasps. Only Timor's laugh punctuated the silence.

"Oh dear, big brother is dead," she sang.

And as she said it, Harris knew it was true. *Come on, Angus,* he thought as tears pricked his eye. *We can't give up.*

But the prince couldn't move, his lips pulled back from his teeth in a noiseless sob. Harris held him, trying to keep the pieces of his friend together.

"I should probably leave the three of you here to die with the rest of them. But your terror is just too tempting," Timor said, moving closer.

She lifted her hands, spinning round in a circle, and the noises of battle slammed back into life. Now, Harris could hear as Angus keened in anguish, the noise slicing at his heart. *Bring back the silence,* he thought desperately.

"Time to wake up, everyone," said Timor.

Harris caught a movement out of the corner of his eye, and he turned, looking for the threat. *The corpses,* he realised, bile rising up his throat. *They're moving.*

As one, the fallen soldiers around them blinked their eyes open at Timor's command. They pushed themselves up like puppets on a string. Ready to battle again.

"And now," said the little goddess, "the world will burn."

Chapter 79

Ailsa's sleep was sticky, holding her under, as if her subconscious refused to let her wake. *Stay, stay, stay,* it said. *Bad things wait for you above.*

Maalik. It was hard to remember, but wasn't he in trouble? There were others too, weren't there? People who were relying on her.

There will be pain. She could feel it, whispering through her body, even now.

I have to, she decided, clawing her way towards the light. With every inch, the ache burned more fiercely. Ailsa steeled herself, pushing the rest of the way. She surfaced with a moan, blinking awake. Her body throbbed, every nerve ending protesting against the torture it had been through. But that wasn't the worst of it. Now that she was conscious, she remembered what had happened and what they'd lost.

"Another one is awake," drawled Dolor above her.

Ailsa peered through stinging eyes. She was lying on her side, cheek pressed into slick wood. A foot away, Maalik was in a similar position, facing her. He looked like he'd been awake longer, listening to whatever was going on around them. When he noticed Ailsa was awake, he winced in regret.

"That just leaves the soldier," said a little girl.

A man snorted. "He won't be waking up any time soon. Let's get on with it."

Something grabbed Ailsa's hair and she shrieked as she was hauled upright, her body protesting.

"It's alright," Dolor whispered in her ear in a mocking tone. "All your friends are here."

Ailsa felt her stomach drop as she realised the goddess was right. As she realised *where* they were.

It was the platform Harris had told them about. They sat on a huge wooden scaffold, hammered together hastily. But it was no longer floating on the sea. With the wind whipping past them, Ailsa could tell they were suspended high in the air, hanging over the ocean. On the platform, only three people stood tall and unhurt. Three deities. *The Edaxi.* Beside the sneering form of Dolor and the eagerly bouncing Timor, was a skeletal man dressed in armour far too large for him. Chao, the God of Chaos, had his long fingers steepled in front of the maniacal grin spread across his face. And at their feet…

A whine bubbled past Ailsa's lips. Angus, Harris and Rain lay before the girl, beaten and bruised. They must have been captured, just like her, Maalik, and Eilidh, who moaned beside her. She strained her eyes against the strong wind flowing around them, expecting to see Iona and Alasdair. Instead, she spotted Irené's crystalline body, sitting upright but curled in on herself. And at her side—

"*Cameron?*"

Hadn't Angus sent him away with Laire the night before? Now her brother lay crumpled on the deck, head lolling to the side. *He's the soldier Dolor was talking about.*

"The unicorn put up quite the fight, as did the two youths you sent with him. She cried over their fallen bodies, cursing me as I stole him." Chao chuckled to himself, delighted by his story.

Is Laire dead? An image of the noble unicorn defending her brother against the gods came unbidden into her mind.

On the other side of the platform, a man in a burgundy uniform, with a close-cropped beard, crouched down.

Chester Scarsi shifted, revealing another person, sprawled with their arms and legs out. Scarsi kept his eyes on the gods as he absently wiped his knife on the hulking body of the Mirandelli king. Merlo had sworn allegiance to the wrong people and had paid for it with his life.

"I want to play," Chao said, pulling Ailsa's attention back to the Edaxi. He bent down over Cameron and brushed a hand through his hair. "This one's mind has been so much fun these last few weeks. Imagine what mischief I'll have now he's finally here."

Angus groaned, pushing himself up. "Don't touch him."

The man cackled. "I've been touching him, all this time. Ever since his vision of Ephraim. Where do you think all those dreams of chaos and sorrow have come from?" He trailed a finger down Cameron's cheek. "We couldn't have your seer learning what we actually had planned, could we?"

Ailsa gulped. All this time, Cameron had been having awful visions of their deaths, and the gods had been planting them in his head.

"Enough, Chao," said Dolor. "Desper must speak to them first. Then we will have our entertainment."

A black shadow passed between the groups, hissing as it went. Even the other gods shrunk back from it. It floated over the wood until it came to Scarsi and the corpse of King Merlo.

"Such a good soldier," the shadow said as it hovered above Scarsi. "You fought bravely, Chester. Not many can say they took the life of two kings."

Two kings?

The General bowed his head. "I live to serve you."

The shadow paused. "And if we require your death instead?"

Scarsi's head snapped up, his mouth opening in shock and protest. But before he could get a sound past his lips, Dolor raised her hand and held it out in his direction. Immediately, Scarsi clutched at his chest, blinking rapidly as the goddess squeezed her fingers tighter. Ailsa knew, somehow, that Dolor had his heart, even from across the platform.

Scarsi tore at his clothes, desperately trying to remove her claws. "Why?" he croaked out.

She shrugged. "You've been very useful, but my brother needs a body." Then, with a smile, she squeezed her fingers together in a tight fist, leaving no room for his heart. Scarsi collapsed, blood dripping from his eyes and his nose.

"Pop, pop, pop," laughed Timor, clapping her hands.

"Beautifully done," said the shadow, inching closer to Scarsi's body.

Oh gods.

Ailsa watched in mounting horror as the shadow hovered over the General's corpse, then started sinking into it, disappearing, as if it was passing through his skin. Ailsa already knew what would happen next.

It's going to possess him.

Sure enough, Scarsi's finger twitched and then he sat up. But, while it was Scarsi's body, it was another being who regarded them through cruel eyes.

"That feels good," said Desper, climbing to his feet. He wandered closer, studying them all. "Welcome. I'm sure you're all wondering why you're not similarly dead yet."

Ailsa avoided looking at Maalik. If she did, she knew she'd succumb to her fear.

"We sent four soldiers onto that beach and only one came back. Did you think you'd won, when you killed them?" He clicked his tongue. "We were merely testing a theory. Eilanmòr thought they had the four strongest fae to wield the Four Treasures. It turns out they were mostly right." Desper grinned and four objects appeared in front of him. The stone, the cauldron, the sword and the spear. "We have the Four Treasures and four incredibly powerful fae to wield them. We could have looked for them ourselves, but wasn't it so much easier to have you bring them to us?" He chuckled, his gaze shifting to Harris. "I did hope your sister might join us, but she gave up the stone to our princess much too easily. Shame. Having those of Eilanmòrian heritage would have made the victory all the sweeter. I did enjoy your little rhyme."

Desper approached Ailsa's group, bending down on his haunches to look at them. "*'Treasure o' yird, the Destiny Stone, Transports the bearer tae whaur it is known'*. And to have the rightful Fae Queen to wield it too? Exquisite." He tilted his head. "*'Treasure o' water, Cauldron o' Life, Reverses conditions o' magik an strife,'*. Handy. Well, Princess Irené will have to use that."

"And Maalik." Desper nodded at the demon. "Did you know Dolor had her eye on you for a while? A warrior angel with just the right level of naivety to push towards the dark. *'Treasure o' fire, the Sword o' Licht, Cleaves through rivals, bringer o' micht.'* I can't think of a fire fae more suited to handling it."

"*'Treasure o' air, the Spear o' Truth, Niver misses, bites lik a tooth,'*." He licked his lips. "Our dear Ailsa. Your Avalognian friend told us how you ripped apart her boat. There was no doubt in my mind what you were then: a witch descended from Ishbel Lauchair's own bloodline. As soon as your spirit guide heard the spear was in Findias, I've no doubt she jumped at the chance to have her weapon back. Just think, if she'd never pushed you to go up there, we may have lost the spear." He snapped his fingers, standing up. "In fact, I would like to thank her myself."

There was a pressure growing in Ailsa's head. "What are you doing?" Claws sank into the back of her mind, scratching along its walls and dragging a whimper from Ailsa's throat.

"There's someone squatting in your brain," said Desper. "I want her out."

Ailsa felt like she was being cleaved in two. A wail rang inside her head, and she couldn't tell if it belonged to her. Then, slowly, a woman appeared, kneeling before her. She was older than in her portrait, with more grey streaking through her black hair. She brushed a hand over Ailsa's cheek, her skin wispy and insubstantial.

"Ishbel?" Ailsa whispered.

It was strange, hearing that familiar voice outside of her head. "*Shh, everything will be okay.*" But Ailsa could see the grief on her face. Desper had done what the witches could not: separated them.

"You've heard the stories, have you not, little witch? Of the island lost under the waves?" He pointed to Ishbel. "They say she destroyed it, but she was only trying to save the world. Her fellow priestess opened the wrong portal, allowing my siblings and I to break through. Imagine what else could have followed us, if it had only had the chance."

Ailsa reached for her magic, to lash out at the gods, but without Ishbel, there was another emptiness inside her. Her powers were gone.

Across the platform, Angus looked confused. "Ailsa isn't a priestess."

"No, she's not." Desper smiled. "But her spirit guide was. You can't see her though, can you? Only her descendants can." He drifted over to Rain who stared defiantly up at him. "How does it feel, to know Ishbel chose your sister over you?"

Ailsa looked to Ishbel, waiting for her to deny it. But the spirit nodded, confirming it now that she was incorporeal. Rain was Ailsa's sister. And they were both going to die.

"*Handlit apart, fierce i' the hour, Held close tae hand,*

maisterfull power'," Desper continued. "I have all four fae and all Four Treasures. And every one of you is going to help us. Below this platform, the sunken island of Rocbarra sits on the seafloor. You will all help us raise it, and the portals along with it. Merlo already sacrificed hundreds of fae to our cause—enough to pull the island out of the ocean, with the help of the Four Treasures."

Ailsa's mind was reeling but she still managed to spit out a curse. "We'll never help you."

"You will if you'd like to see each other alive after this. Don't overestimate your worth to me." Desper's mask of serenity slipped. "Using you would be poetic, but I could easily replace you, just like I replaced Iona. So, you will submit to us; wield these weapons. And then, if you're still alive by the end, we'll let you go."

"You're a terrible liar," said Maalik.

Desper shrugged. "Perhaps, but the alternative is that I kill you right now. It would be easy. Take King Merlo, for example." He gestured to the king's corpse behind him. "Timor caught him sneaking out last night. He didn't follow our command and look at him. Dispensable. Useless. Totally at our mercy. Your mortal lives are so fleeting, all it takes is one push and—"

Merlo's body slid off the platform. Ailsa expected to hear a splash, but there was no sound except the howling of the wind. *We must be really high up.*

Desper marched back over to Ailsa, Maalik and Eilidh. "Now, who could be next? Merlo was just a warning, but I'm sure you care more about *these* people?" He grabbed Ailsa's chin, making her look at her friends. "How about the selkie? Or perhaps the prince?"

Angus set his jaw. "I'm not afraid to die for the people I love."

Chao crowed. "That sounds like volunteering to me."

Desper's gaze went to the God of Chaos, and the body at his feet. "Or maybe Ailsa's brother would be a better substitute? You're willing to die, prince, but are you willing to sacrifice your lover?" He pointed at Cameron. "Chao, have Irené bring me the seer."

"No!" shouted Angus.

Ailsa tried to wrench out of Desper's grip as Irené uncurled herself, reaching for Cameron's unconscious body. "Stop!"

"The soldier is first, then we'll kill the other witch next," said Desper with a smile. "We only need one." He dropped Ailsa's chin but before she could get up, a wave of pain wracked her body, keeping her down. Desper backed up until he was at the edge of the platform and waited.

This couldn't be happening. She was about to lose her brother and her sister in one fell swoop.

Ishbel ran her ghostly hand down her back as the pain subsided slightly. "Ailsa, do you remember the rest of the poem?"

"Ishbel," she gasped as Irené hooked her hands under Cameron's arms, "you have to help him!"

But the spirit didn't move. "Do you remember?"

Ailsa shook her head, tears threatening to spill. "Something about killing any humans that touch them?"

"Yes, but then the last line," Ishbel prodded. "It said '*Cept Sovereign's bluid, whose talent forgot.*'" And then Ishbel turned to Angus's struggling form. "*Except sovereign's blood—*"

Ailsa hadn't learned to read as a child, but she never thought of herself as dumb. While others sat around, hashing out strategies and poring over texts, Ailsa saw opportunities, almost as if her mind was clearer. So, when Ishbel repeated the words back to her, she saw their true meaning and the path ahead. As far as she could see, there were two problems. One was getting the Four Treasures into the right hands. And the other was stopping Desper from hurting her brother.

Ishbel nodded like she could see Ailsa's plan forming. "Be brave," she said, her voice full of sorrow.

There was only one thing left to do. She turned to Maalik and brushed her fingers against his. Pain still lanced through her body, but she pushed it to the back of her mind as she studied his face. He had his teeth set in a grimace but when he met her gaze, something other than fear passed over his features. Ailsa took a moment to map him out, to memorise him. Then, with her heart breaking, she spoke her last words to him.

"Maalik, I love you."

Then Ailsa was on her feet, despite the agony ripping through her. "Rain!" she called as Irené dragged Cameron closer to Desper. "Angus needs to hold all Four Treasures!" She hoped that was enough, that her sister would know what to do.

She thought she heard Maalik's cry, but she paid him no mind, focussing all her attention on the god in Scarsi's body. *If he has a human body, can he die?* Ailsa wondered. *I guess I'm about to find out.*

Ailsa launched herself forward, boots slipping over the slick wood, so fast that the Edaxi couldn't react in time. She felt Dolor's power nipping at her heels, threatening to send her tumbling, but she pushed on, pumping her arms. Desper's attention went from Irené to something over Ailsa's shoulder and she hoped that meant Rain had listened. She couldn't stop to look, not as she got closer and closer to the god. He turned back to her at the last second, raising his arms but it was too late. Ailsa launched herself at Desper, saving her brother the only way she knew how. She sank her nails into the collar of his uniform and used her momentum to push them both backwards.

Right over the edge of the platform.

Chapter 80

"Maalik, I love you," Ailsa told him, her eyes glittering with unshed tears. Was it only last night that she'd last said it? When he'd told her to keep the words until the battle was over and they were free?

Maalik watched in mounting panic and comprehension as Ailsa pushed herself up, shouting to her friend. "Rain! Angus needs to hold all Four Treasures!" The scene unfolded before him, as if in slow motion.

Ailsa raced towards Desper while Rain raised her hands. He stared, mesmerised, as the weapons shook and then flew off the floor, heading straight for the witch.

"Angus, you have to catch them!" shouted Rain.

The Four Treasures hurtled towards the prince, who stood, arms spread. Maalik couldn't tear his gaze away as the treasures collided with Angus, sending out a blinding flash. When his vision returned, the prince was not holding four weapons—but one. He lifted the great sword in the air, the blade glowing bright. A beam of light erupted from the tip and Angus brought it down, aiming for Chao first.

The words from the prophecy came back to Maalik. *'Handlit apart, fierce i' the hour, held close tae hand, maisterfull power.' That's it. That's how to defeat the Edaxi.* Ailsa had worked it out.

Maalik didn't wait to see what happened next. Angus had the gods' attention so Maalik could finally get up and away from Dolor's influence. He turned back to look for Ailsa, to see what she'd do next. But her steps weren't slowing as she rushed at Desper. Maalik watched as she tackled him, her arms circling his borrowed body, and flung them both over the side of the platform to the frozen sea below.

Ailsa!

Maalik was aware he was yelling but he had no control over the words. His mind reeled, her name ringing over and over in his head. *Ailsa. Ailsa. Ailsa.* She was gone. Yes, the battle would be won, but at what cost? How was he supposed to keep on living without her?

I won't, he decided, rising up. *I cannot.*

The next time you say it, I won't hold myself back, he'd told her. *You have the power to change me.* That was still true, even if she'd thrown herself off the edge of the world. Ailsa would hold power over him even when they were nothing but stardust. He was devoted. Body and soul. Maalik battled the despair that threatened to engulf him and fought it with every good memory he had shared with Ailsa. He ran full pelt to the end of the platform, allowing every fibre of his being to believe everything she'd ever said. And, in faith, when he threw himself off, he did so with wings bursting from his back, as the gods shrieked in agony behind him.

Chapter 81

Angus trusted Ailsa, but he froze in fear as the treasures flew through the air. *If we were right about the prophecy... If she's wrong...* His gaze caught on Cameron—lying crumpled and unconscious on the timber floor. *Please let this work.* He'd already lost his brother; he couldn't lose Cam too.

Rain stood behind him, calling the Four Treasures to her with her magic. But they were not intended for her. Angus raised his hands, ready to pluck them out of the air. He needn't have worried. Somehow the objects knew their path. And when they reached him, they collided in a blinding flash.

Angus blinked, clearing his vision as he stared down at the weapon in his hands. Not a stone or a cauldron or a spear. This was a great sword, massive compared to the Sword of Light. The blade looked like it was made from dark, liquid metal, rippling in Angus's hands. From the tip, a beam of starlight burst forth, and Angus knew what to do.

Use me, it whispered. *Wield me and defeat your enemies.*

So, he brought it down, aiming first for the God of Chaos. Because it had been Chao who had infiltrated Cameron's mind. Who had tortured him with those images of death and destruction.

As soon as the ray hit the god, he shrieked, bursting into flames of pure white. Chao screamed as his body broke apart, piece by piece, until it disintegrated, floating off into the sky with the wind.

Angus registered Maalik heading for the platform's edge

and throwing himself off, wings unfurling, but he didn't let himself worry. He had a job to do. He turned his attention to the little goddess.

"Wait!" she shouted, no longer singing, no longer laughing. An emotion crept over her face, one that Angus was sure she'd inspired but never worn: fear.

He brandished the weapon, pointing the beam of light at Timor. The starshine caught her in the back as she tried to run from it, and she let out a scream of pure terror. In moments, she too erupted like a small sun exploding, leaving behind only dust.

Dolor growled, launching herself forward, hand outstretched. Angus felt her power reaching for him as she tried to cause him pain, as she tried to break him. But the sword worked its magic, shielding him from the onslaught.

Her lips pulled back from her teeth as she tried again and again. "I'm going to rip you apart!"

"No," said Angus, hefting the sword in his hands. "You're going to die. And I hope it's excruciating." Then, for the third time, he turned the beam towards a god. Dolor burst into flames as soon as the light hit her, her body melting to the floor in shrieks of pain that echoed in his ears even after the goddess was consumed.

Dolor was gone. Angus's arms shook from holding the great sword. But he felt no triumph as expected—only an overwhelming tiredness. His companions on the platform must have been similarly affected. No one made a noise as he lowered his weapon. *You have one more to go*, he realised. "Where's Desper?"

The question was met with a heavy silence until Eilidh spoke up. "Ailsa pushed him off. She went down with him."

The hanging platform began to shake, and Angus stumbled. "*You mean Ailsa is—*"

Rain grabbed his arm, a determined gleam in her eye. "Maalik went after her. Come on, we have to get off this thing before it collapses into the ocean."

Angus nodded woodenly, watching as his friends gathered. Harris lifted Irené's crystalline body into his arms, her skin fighting to turn back to brown where he touched her. Angus dropped down beside Cameron, watching his chest rise and fall, allowing the movement to ground him. He wouldn't allow himself to worry about Ailsa. To mourn her. No, first he had to get them to safety.

The edges of the wooden structure were already eroding, great chunks ripping off in the strong winds. The timber beams splintered and groaned, coming apart under their feet. Like a bird shot down, clinging to flight, it shuddered, threatening to send them all plunging down into the sea below. "Hold on to me," he said, raising the sword one more time. Because, if the Stone of Destiny was a part of it, the new weapon must have the same magic.

With his companions around him, Angus swept the blade around in a circle imagining the shore. The crashing surf. The soft sands. And in a final flash of pure energy, he carried them away from the structure, just as it fell back into the ocean to be buried under the waves.

Chapter 82

A ilsa hurtled *down, down, down,* through an opening in the frozen sea. Through some force, a colossal tunnel had been carved through the ice, all the way down to the sunken island at the ocean floor. As they fell, fissures cracked across the surface, sending huge chunks splintering off. Whatever power had been holding the passage open was gone. Ailsa hoped that meant Angus had succeeded.

Ailsa felt the moment Desper realised he was going to die. His arms scratched at her as they fell, trying to peel her off him, but then he stopped, squeezing her back instead.

"You made a mistake, witch," he hissed in her ear. "It is a long, long way down and I will use my last moments taking my revenge."

She kept her eyes closed against the salt spray and gritted her teeth. "Do your worst."

Images flashed behind her lids, as if Desper was sorting through them, seeing which one stuck. *The time she'd dislocated her shoulder. Cameron leaving her to play with some new friends. Her mother dying.*

"Ah yes, let's start there."

She was no longer falling. Ailsa saw herself sitting in a chair by the dwindling fire, listening to familiar rasping breaths.

"I was much younger when this happened," Ailsa told him, recognising the memory. "And my brother was there too."

"Ailsa?" her mother raised a thin hand off the blankets. "I need to tell you something."

Ailsa gritted her teeth. "My mother said that she loved me and that I had to fight." She whispered the words, more to herself than to Desper.

"I need to tell you something," her mother repeated. "You are not my daughter."

Ailsa rose from the chair and sat on the edge of the mattress. "You took me in when you could have turned me away."

Heather MacAra was as ghostly pale as Ailsa remembered her in her last moments. Her eyes were just as sunken and when she coughed a vein popped out of her neck like it had done those years ago. "What they say about you is true. You are a changeling."

Ailsa nodded sadly. "You knew that but still you loved me."

Her mother's face twisted into a scowl. "How can you be sure?"

"You loved me so fiercely I could never doubt it," she said with conviction. "And I love you too."

Frustration that was not her own coated the back of Ailsa's throat and the scene was pulled from underneath her. This time she was in the forest, the lanterns of Ephraim twinkling between the trees. Cameron kneeled before her, uncurling himself from where he'd lain when he'd been cursed.

"Ailsa?" he breathed.

"There were others there too," she called out, grounding herself.

"You truly are a monster," Cameron said. "You're just as bad as Nicnevan. All the fae are the same." His skin wrinkled and hardened and once again bark covered his arms and neck. "Look what you've done to me."

She cupped his chin. "You're safe back on the platform. Angus will look after you."

"What of me?" said a voice.

Ailsa turned, colliding with a pair of burning red eyes. But, as Gris walked out from the trees, the grey fur faded, leaving behind the body of a man.

"I believed in you, and I died for it."

Ailsa swallowed. *This isn't real,* she reminded herself. "You made a mistake and Nicnevan killed you."

"It should have been you," said Gris. "You should have died for me."

Her breath shuddered. "You taught me how to survive. You never would have wanted that."

He opened his shirt, revealing gaping and bloody wounds. "This is your fault."

"Nicnevan killed you, not me." Ailsa's face hardened. "And I cursed her for it."

Again, the scene changed. This time she was back in the ballroom of Findias, the moon full and bright through the windows overhead. The light filtered down, touching upon the slain bodies of the witches.

Vega's corpse was nearest, her throat red with blood. "You betrayed us," she said.

Ailsa let a whimper escape her lips. "You told me to take the spear. And you survived."

"Did I? Have you checked the battlefield?"

"If you hadn't led the Edaxi to Findias, we wouldn't have been fighting in the first place," said Keyne from beside her. "If you and your friends had left the Four Treasures alone, the Edaxi wouldn't have them now."

Ailsa took a deep breath. "The Edaxi don't have them, Angus does. If we hadn't found the Four Treasures, they'd have used someone else to get them."

This time, when the scene changed, she didn't recognise it. Was she in one of Duncan's tents? A bed sat in the corner and on the table was a pile of maps. A woman in armour stood to attention at the door. Her blonde hair was tied back in braids and her hand looked sure as she gripped the hilt of her sword.

"I don't know you," said Ailsa.

"No," said the woman. "But you know *of* me."

"This was the night," Alasdair said, materialising from the other end of the canvas. "If you've made peace with all your demons, you can face one of his."

Maalik appeared between the parted tent folds, clutching a spear in one hand. His eyes were still black, and the golden antlers remained upon his head, but now he also wore a pair of magnificent wings.

"No," Ailsa whispered. "I don't want to see this."

"Then we've found the right place," said Desper.

"Don't!" Ailsa screamed, too late. Maalik snapped his arm forward and the spear slid through the woman's gut, spraying her blood everywhere. She crumpled to the ground, holding her wound and moaning.

"I'm next," said Alasdair, stepping forward to die.

"It didn't happen like this. He was tricked." She watched the demon stalk closer to the king. "You are not him."

"I am and I always will be." He plunged the spear into Alasdair's chest.

Immediately, Maalik's wings were consumed by flames and the tent was filled with his agonised screams. Ailsa fell to the floor, curling in on herself and covering her ears. *Not real, not real.* She tasted Desper's satisfaction as Maalik writhed in pain.

"Let this be the scene where you stay for the rest of eternity."

"No," she croaked. "There is nothing you can show me that is worse than what would have happened if we were still on that platform." Ailsa raised a fist into the air searching for her magic. *You can do this*, she told herself. She looked for it, where it always had been, but found only air. *Come on.* It's not

Ishbel's. *It's mine.* Then, she felt it, a single spark, deep inside her. But it was enough. Ailsa concentrated, nurturing the flicker as she fell, until the familiar magic sang in her veins.

"And if this is to be my eternity," she said, gritting her teeth, "then it is yours too." The lightning inside her answered, crackling through every cell in her body. Now she could feel where Desper's fingers had sunk into her arms and where his mind was invading her own. She directed every zap of electricity, every ounce of anger, and unleashed it all upon him.

Their bodies convulsed together and Desper shrieked. *It's working.* Ailsa's vision blackened at the edges, but she held on until she felt the god give up, letting her go to plummet down alone. Ailsa's body, free from his grip, relaxed, falling like a ragdoll.

Any second now, I'll hit the ground. Then it would all be over. She'd made peace with it. Ailsa closed her eyes, picturing her friends' faces, and then Maalik's. She wanted it to be the last thing she saw before she died.

But then she felt something wrap around her and her eyes flew open again. Strong arms cupped around her back and knees as she blinked against the light, her vision filling with feathers.

And Ailsa finally, after all those years, allowed her tears to fall. Not in despair or regret, but in relief.

Chapter 83

"Maalik," Ailsa breathed as he slowed her descent.

He smiled down at her and she gasped. His golden antlers no longer poked out from his hair and his skin was smooth and uncracked. But those changes were not what made the tears fall faster. "Your eyes." How long had she wondered what colour they'd been, before he'd become a demon and they'd turned fully black? "They're amber."

He beat his wings, flying them upwards and away. The ice thawed and cracked, sending water surging to fill the hole in the ocean below. "Don't cry," he said. "You saved me."

Ailsa let out a wet laugh. "I think I'm supposed to say that." She swallowed around the lump in her throat, noticing her skin was no longer black with bruises, fire no longer licking under the surface. *I'm not sick anymore.* "Did Angus—"

"I think so, yes." He kissed her forehead. "We're going to be okay."

Ailsa tucked her head under his chin, letting the sobs wrack her body as he held her, flying them both to safety.

***

They soared up, watching the platform crumble, the pieces falling to the sea below. Their friends were nowhere to be seen, but scorches crossed the wood, radiating out from a single point. *Angus saved them,* Ailsa reminded herself.

"I wish I could have seen it."

Maalik hummed. "Me too. But watching you electrocute Desper had its own merit."

"Do you think he really died?" she asked as they glided over the wrecks of Mirandelli ships.

"I think Scarsi's body did." And that would have to do, for now.

Ailsa turned her gaze to the beach, where the crowds of soldiers had dispersed, no longer fighting. Eilanmòrian and Mirandelli warriors sat side by side on the sand, amongst their fallen comrades. The dead were at peace once more.

But it was the figures at the water's edge that had her attention. She counted them as they flew closer; eight in total, lying in the sand. One of them, a man with copper hair, pointed and let out a whoop.

"Ailsa!"

Maalik landed on the silt and let her go so she could launch herself up the beach, her eyes blurry from fresh tears. When she reached the red-headed man, she flung her arms around his neck, and he spun her around in a circle.

"You did it," Harris whispered to her. "You were right."

Then more hands were on her, holding her tight. Angus dropped kisses to her hair, making her laugh. Rain wiped her cheeks. Even Eilidh ran a comforting hand down her back. Ailsa let herself enjoy the impossible moment. They were alive.

"The Edaxi?" she asked, pulling back. She had to hear it from Angus.

His grin was haunted, but there all the same. "Dead. Blown apart. Though, we don't have Four Treasures anymore." He reached down, pulling a great sword from the sand, presenting it to her.

"And Cameron? Irené?"

Eilidh pointed up the beach, where four people lay on the

ground. Ailsa's brother was still unconscious, though some colour had returned to his face. Beside him, the princess was curled in on herself, as if she was trying to hold her body together. And far to their left...

Iona was huddled over a man, whispering words into his hair. King Alasdair's chest was barely moving and there was a deep wound in his stomach, the sand around him covered in his blood.

Ailsa's heart sank. They should have been celebrating but instead they were about to watch another one of them die. Iona will have to lose him all over again.

Trumpets sounded all around, and she looked up, searching for the source of the noise. Behind her, Maalik let out a huff of air.

"The angels," he said. "They've arrived to heal the injured."

Ailsa had heard of angels showing up on battlefields, ready to minimise the casualties, but watching them descend from the heavens was something else entirely. They spread out, clad in shining armour, flying for the corners of the beach where men and women lay dying.

"Does that mean," Ailsa asked slowly, turning to her own angel, "that you can heal people now, too?"

Maalik's grin spread across his face. "Let's find out." He strode over to Cameron first, waving a glowing hand over him.

Please, Ailsa thought. *Please work.*

Then Cameron was sitting up, coughing as he took in his surroundings. Angus ran to him, throwing his arms around his neck and landing them both back onto the sand.

"Cam!" he said, laughing. "You're okay."

"I feel..." He paused, as if taking in his body. "...much better. Even my headache's gone." He looked around at them all. "Did I miss it? The battle?"

Maalik didn't reply, raising his arms again, this time at the princess. Irené's skin shimmered, turning brown and fleshy once more.

Harris rushed to her, tugging off his shirt to cover her naked body. "There, you're alright."

She raised her head, focussing her eyes on him. "Harris? Chao... He..."

"It's alright," he repeated, pulling her to him. "He won't hurt you again."

Maalik stared down at her with a frown. "Her body is healed, but her mind isn't. She'll still have her powers and she'll need to learn to control them." Then he stepped away, heading for his next target.

Ailsa followed him as he drifted towards Iona and Alasdair, his hands glowing bright with healing magic. As soon as he came into view, Iona flinched.

"Don't hurt him," she sobbed.

Maalik's voice was gentle and calm. "I did that, once. Now I'm here to save him; if you'll let me."

The selkie hesitated. Alasdair's eyes were closed but his breathing was shallow. It wouldn't be long until he sighed his last.

"Do it," she said with a gulp. "I can't lose him."

Maalik stepped forward, raising his hands for the third time. The skin, where once it had been blackened with soot, lit up. He waved it over the king's fallen body, healing it.

But nothing happened.

"You cannot heal what is already dead," said a serene voice behind them. A man in armour stood a few feet away, watching the scene with vague interest. From his back, a pair of ivory wings sprouted. The angel regarded them. "It's good to see you restored, Maalik. Now you can join us in heaven, where you belong."

Ailsa's stomach sank as the angel's words settled within her. No, he couldn't leave. Not after everything they'd been through.

Maalik narrowed his eyes. "Vasilii. What do you mean? He's breathing. Alasdair is alive."

"The Edaxi reanimated his corpse. He's an abomination. The only reason he is breathing is the soul inside, holding on when he should let go."

So that was it then? Alasdair was going to die. Iona whimpered, smoothing the hair from her lover's face.

"This is the man I murdered," said Maalik, his face twisting. "Is there nothing I can do?"

Vasilii shrugged. "You can let him go."

"No," said Iona, rising to her knees but never letting Alasdair go. "You can't. I love him." As if that was enough.

Vasilii didn't look impressed. "Then you should count yourself lucky that you were able to spend more time with him."

Ailsa held back her growl. How could a being that was supposed to be so good, be indifferent to this? "You like bargains, don't you Vasilii? You took Maalik's soul in exchange for healing me. What would it take to save Alasdair?"

Vasilii flicked his gaze between them all, eventually landing on Maalik. He nodded, as if he'd made a decision. "I will heal your friend, but you must give me something in return. You must give up your immortality. You will no longer be an angel. You'll no longer be welcome in heaven."

Ailsa gasped in a breath. Could it be that easy? Could they save Alasdair and stay together?

Maalik turned, not to the late king, but to Ailsa. He brushed a hand over her tear-stained cheek, giving her a secret smile. Then he whispered the words that would seal his and her fate for the rest of their lives. "I accept."

Chapter 84

The streets of Dunrigh were filled with music and laughter once more. *It's a beautiful sight,* Ailsa thought as she looked out to the crowds. Children ran across the streets, trailing ribbons behind them. Old friends greeted each other, and families hugged, reunited against all odds. Still, it was bittersweet. Husbands, wives, and parents had been lost in the battle. And amongst them all, their king.

The king was long dead when they found him, surrounded by his fallen comrades. The angels could do nothing. Those who'd survived lingered on the beach long enough to give Duncan a proper funeral, burning his body so he would always be at peace.

The people of Dunrigh were still mourning their losses, all these weeks later. But this was a day of celebration, of looking forward.

Maalik wrapped an arm around her, breaking her from her thoughts. "Have I told you that you look stunning?"

"You're not bad yourself," she said, looking him over. His skin glowed in the sunshine, not from magic but from health and happiness. After his bargain, he was human once again. Well, almost human.

Maalik's wings tucked in tight. Somehow, he'd been allowed to keep them. *Perhaps Vasilii has a heart after all.*

"How much longer do you think they'll be?" he asked.

"Desperate to leave already? This is supposed to be a party."

The last coronation Ailsa had attended had been Duncan's;

they'd held it in the castle, behind the inner gates. But this time, the royal family wanted to involve their people too. It had been Angus's idea.

"Look," squealed Vega, tugging on Rain with one hand while she clutched a growling cat-sìth in the other. Hoolie did not seem pleased to find herself in an excited crowd; likely desperate to jump through space and time back to Zephyr. "There they are."

Two adults emerged from the gate, crowns atop their heads. Between them, a little girl held the woman's wrist and in the man's arms, a baby boy looked out into the crowds and waved his pudgy hand.

When Angus had returned to Dunrigh, Duncan's advisors called on him to state his claim to the throne. But Angus's first thought, when he found his brother, was of his nephew. Douglas was only three months old and already he'd lost his father. He was not about to be cast out from his home too. Angus agreed to take up the mantle of regent, until the boy was old enough.

The woman beside him grinned, lifting the little girl up too. The Faerie Queen had already been crowned in Ephraim, but Eilidh had agreed to join her brother, to share the celebration with him. Maggie giggled, pressing a kiss to her mother's cheek. One day, when the girl was ready, she too would be offered a throne. In the meantime, both siblings would watch over Eilanmòr, protecting it from danger, just like they'd protected it from the Edaxi.

Behind them, dressed in black, Queen Vashkha followed them. Her smile was sad, but she watched her son with pride as Angus presented him to the crowd, knowing he was in safe hands.

Angus handed Douglas back to his mother, kissing her on the cheek. Then he looked behind him, beckoning someone through the gate. Cameron peered around the wall sheepishly, dressed in a great kilt made of the royal tartan. He'd dyed his hair purple again, to match. Behind him, a unicorn pushed her nose into his back, urging him on.

Ailsa's heart soared at seeing Laire alive and well. When they'd found her on the road back to Dunrigh she'd been clinging to life. But with Maalik's gentle and non-magical healing, she'd almost fully recovered from Chao's attack.

Ailsa let out a cheer as Angus threaded his fingers with her brother's and pulled him into a sweet kiss. The crowd went wild.

"You could have been up there," said Iona. She stood to Ailsa's left, wearing a seafoam dress much too fancy for the streets of Dunrigh.

"I prefer being anonymous nowadays." Alasdair tightened his grip on the selkie's waist. "This way I get to have you all to myself."

Ailsa was glad Iona and Alasdair had forgiven them, but they really were insufferable sometimes. Maybe that was why Harris was leaving them so soon. "When do you ship out?"

Harris adjusted his patch, keeping his one eye on the royal family. "Tomorrow. After the party. Irené wants to go back to Edessa, to heal. The Nymph is waiting at the coast."

It made sense. The whole world had opened up to them again. "Just don't stop anywhere near Mirandelle. I've heard they're having a civil war." With King Merlo dead, his children and grandchildren were squabbling over his throne. "I'm glad Eilanmòr is in safe hands at least."

"What about you, Ailsa?" Iona asked. "Are you staying? Or heading back to Monadh to help?"

She should return north, to rebuild the witch palace, like Keyne, Zephyr and Aster had done already. But Findias was not her home, even if her mother was there. She turned to

Rain, watching the gates, where Angus and his family waved. "What about you? Do you fancy a detour?"

Her sister smirked. "What did you have in mind?"

Ailsa looked up at Maalik, returning his warm smile. "Somewhere hot. I'm not the only one with missing family."

"Well, prepare for a couple of travelling companions," said Vega, stroking Hoolie's rippling fur.

Rain nodded. "You know you're never getting rid of us."

Tears welled in Ailsa's eyes again. Now that she'd let herself cry once, it seemed she couldn't stop herself. *I'm so lucky,* she thought.

But her smile faltered. There was only silence in her head; no one replied. Until—

You're such a sap. Ishbel stretched like a cat in her mind. *Maybe I should have attached myself to Rain instead.*

I'd fear for the world if that happened. She doesn't need you echoing her thoughts of violence.

Ishbel tsked. *You'd keep us in check.*

Ailsa hummed, letting herself be carried away in the joy of the day once again. Back when Harris and Iona had found her, scraping a living on her beach, she'd been so alone. Now here she was, surrounded by the people she loved most, with their lives stretching ahead of them, full of possibilities.

Ailsa MacAra reached up, pulling the clouds aside, and allowed the sun to shine down on them, echoing their triumph. Eilanmòr had been saved, against all the odds. And no matter where they went on the continent, Ailsa had a family to come back home to.

Changeling, they'd once called her. And, Ailsa supposed, they hadn't been wrong. She had changed.

She'd been marked by magic and made by it. She'd been to Hell and back—literally. She'd fought gods and demons and won.

But more than that, she found love. She smiled, gripping Maalik's hand, pulling him behind her along the path and into the sunshine.

The End

Acknowledgements

We've reached the end.

I tried to imagine how I'd feel when I got to this point, but I don't think it's really hit me yet. I thought I'd feel sad, but I think I'm just excited to finally share the last part of the story. The truth is, The Four Treasures isn't over for me. I know I can keep going back, in my imagination. Perhaps I'll write some epilogues* and hide them in places where people will find them...

I'll start off with thanking the incomparable Anne Glennie. Thank you for taking a chance on me. If it weren't for you, The Four Treasures would have stayed in my Google Drive, collecting digital dust.

On that note, thank you to everyone who works with Cranachan. To Iain Glennie who sends me my money every six months. To all of my fellow Clan Cranachan writers but especially Barbara Henderson, Lindsay Littleson, Joan Haig, Joseph Lamb and Annemarie Allan for letting me moan in our group chat and giving great advice.

To Kelly Macdonald and Merryn Glover: it started with you both and I'm eternally grateful.

To my best pals: Loli, Martin, Cara, Walsh, Calum, Kirstin, Eilidh, Carine, Rachel and Alan. We don't often see each other, but there's no one I'd rather grow old with.
To my D&D friends, Hannah, Lisa, Talia, Jon: you're all Nat 20s.

Special thanks to my internet friends, especially Caitlyn, Jackie, Eleanor, Abi and Connor. You are absolute rock stars.

Thank you so much to the readers who have stuck with the books these last four years. I hope you enjoyed the adventure along the way and the ending made it all worth it.

To my students, past and present: you'll never know the joy you bring me every day.

Thank you to my family, Dad, Linda, Mum, Dad, Rachel, Diane, Martin, Neil and Blair. I know I don't say it enough, but I love and appreciate you all.

More than with any other book, I'm proud of myself for finishing. It's been a really tough year. But I bloomin' well did it. So thanks to me I guess.

Ranger and Scout: you are really good dogs. The best actually. You deserve many biscuits.

But, ultimately, it all comes down to Vince. My love for you is as big as the universe. Bigger even. I'm surprised every day that my body can contain it. Maybe one day I'll explode into tiny pieces and then you'll have to clean me up. It would serve you right too. Love you.

*Scan the QR code to read an Ailsa & Maalik epilogue...

About the Author

Caroline Logan is a writer of Young Adult Fantasy. *The Spear of Truth* is the fourth and final book in The Four Treasures series.

Caroline is a high school biology teacher who lives in the Cairngorms National Park in Scotland, with her husband and her dogs, Ranger and Scout. Before moving there, she lived and worked in Spain, Tenerife, Sri Lanka and other places in Scotland. She graduated from the University of Glasgow with a bachelor's degree in Marine and Freshwater Biology.

In her spare time, she plays Dungeons and Dragons, watches Disneyworld videos, and tries to make a dent in her *To Be Read* book pile.

Instagram: @CaroLoganBooks
Twitter: @CaroLoganBooks
Web: carolinelogan.co.uk